A MAP OF HUMANITY

A Map of Humanity

FIFTY-ONE STORIES WITH SETTINGS AROUND THE WORLD

Steve Carr

Hear Our Voice LLC

Contents

PUBLICATION/ COPYRIGHT

A Hear Our Voice LLC Publication
January 2022

ISBN *979-8-9853098-0-5*

Cover design by David G. Harms

ACKNOWLEDGEMENTS

Thank you to the following publications for publishing some of the stories in this collection:

Indian Periodical. The Galway Review. Twist & Twain. The Communicator's League. Cultural Reverence. Impspried Magazine. Fictive Dream. Nthanda Review. Me First Magazine. Zimbell House Publishing. Ariel Chart. Writers Block. The Elixir Magazine. Necro Magazine. Blue Lake Review. Down in the Dirt. Tessllate Magazine. Rhetoric Askew. Brave Voices Magazine. The Andreaspearat. District Lit. Cerasus Magazine. The Great Void Books. Fear of Monkeys. Spillwords. Two Sisters Writing & Publishing. Breadcrumbs Magazine. ILA Magazine. The City Key. Parsec Ink. Academy of the Heart and Mind. Dead Mule School of Southern Literature. Blackbird Publishing. Foreign Literary Journal. Active Muse. Portland Metrozine. The J.J. Outre Review. Torch the Veil. Door is a Jar. Mental Papercuts. The Ethicist. Varnish Journal. Defuncted. Prismatica Magazine. Close To The Bone. Slippage Lit. Breaking Rules Publishing. Agapanthus Collective. Drunk Monkeys.

1

THE BAMBOO WIND CHIMES

Prisha arose from a tangle of sheets and placed her bare feet on the straw mat next to the bed. The early morning sunlight that streamed through the slats of the shutter that covered the bedroom window glinted from the gold ring she wore on the toe of her right foot. She slowly stood allowing her head and body adjust to the dizzying act of standing, an effect of a genetic inner-ear condition that only occasional acupuncture treatments provided brief relief from. She took her blue flower-print sari from the back of the chair and wrapped it around her body and then walked to the mirror. The bindi in the middle of her forehead had faded to a very pale red. She removed the cap from the jar of kumkum on the shelf beneath the mirror and dabbed her finger into the red paste and then applied it over top of the faded bindi. From the reflection in the mirror, the refreshed bindi stared back at her like a third eye. She slipped her bracelets onto her wrists and then turned to watch as Dev rolled onto his back, smacked his lips several times, but remained asleep.

"You could sleep through a typhoon," she mumbled.

She left the bedroom, quietly separating the beaded curtains that hung in the doorway and walked into the main room of the house where their new television sat on a stand between the old refrigerator and stove. Next to the stove water dripped from the faucet of the sink where a small stack of unwashed dishes soaked in murky water in a plastic tub. She filled a kettle with water, placed it on the stove and turned the burner on under it. Shor's cry from the courtyard made her turn, walk to the front door and throw it open.

The peacock was standing next to the wall of the well, its tail feathers fully fanned out and quivering. In the house next to hers where her mother-in-law lived the windows and front door were open. *The old woman is up*, she thought, but didn't see her mother-in-law on the front porch where she usually sat first thing every morning or see her anywhere in the courtyard. The other house, directly across from hers on the other side of the courtyard, rented to one of the school teachers, Mr. Patel, was shuttered and silent. The meager rent Mr. Patel paid to live there supplemented Dev's income as a sales clerk at the men's clothing store located in the village. Mr. Patel always awoke before sunrise and walked to the school while most everyone else was still asleep.

When Shor cried out again, the jarring musicality of its cry echoing in the courtyard, Prisha looked down and saw a box tied with red string sitting on the door mat. She bent down, picked it up, and turned it over in her hands several times, noting how light it was and the slight movement of objects inside. Affixed to the top of the box was a small square of pale pink paper on which was written, "For Prisha." She placed her ear against it and shook it and heard the rattle of wood. She untied the string and held the string between her teeth as she opened the box. With one hand she peeled back white tissue gift wrap unveiling a set of bamboo wind chimes. She looked over at Mr. Patel's house and then turned and carried the box into her house. She pushed the tissue back into place, stuffed the string into the box, and then hid the box under the sink behind the pots and pans.

#

Sitting at the table, water dripped from Dev's thick, wavy hair onto the collar of his shirt. He poked at the small stack of dosas on his plate with his fork while staring out the window above the sink at the cuckoos who were making a racket in the trees. His shoes and socks were in his lap.

Prisha ran more water into the plastic tub, filling it to the top, causing the suds to run over the edges. She turned off the tap and turned to see her husband seemingly lost in thought. "You're going to be late for work again," she chided him. "If you get fired what do we do then?"

"Mr. Reddy isn't going to fire me," he replied without looking at her. "I've worked for him for too long and I'm his best sales person."

"You should take nothing for granted," she replied as she turned back to the tub and splashed her fingers around in the lukewarm water. She glanced out the same window as her husband was and watched a female macaque with its infant grasping on to its mother's underside scamper along the five foot high whitewashed wall that surrounded the small compound where they lived. While the village was becoming overrun with the hoards of monkeys it was unusual to see a mother with its child alone this far out in the countryside. The macaque leapt from the wall onto a tree branch and then climbed down the tree trunk and out of sight. Prisha turned her head again, this time to see Dev using one of the cloth embroidered napkins she owned to dry his hair. "Dev!" she exclaimed loudly. "You're so childish. Use a towel to dry off and not one of the napkins your mum gave us."

He wadded the napkin and playfully threw it at her. It landed at her feet. "Did you take Mum her breakfast?"

She bent down, picked it up, and shook it out. "I went to look in on her twice but she must have walked to the village very early. Her house is open but she hasn't been there." She gazed admiringly at the embroidery of images of peacock feathers stitched into the napkin and then laid it across the drainer filled with freshly washed plates and cups. Imagining she could see the box hidden under the sink she stared down at the sink basin as if peering through the white enamel and steel into the pots and pans below. "Mr. Patel is a very smart man, isn't he?"

"Not so smart," Dev replied. "He teaches school but it is to me he pays rent and he walks to work while I ride a scooter."

"He didn't inherit a father's property as you did, dearest husband," she replied.

He pushed his plate of uneaten food back, propped his foot up on the table and slipped a sock over it.

"Dev!" Prisha shrieked.

#

Prisha stood on the porch and watched Dev ride out of the compound on his scooter through the open gate. She ignored the racket Shor was creating by chasing the chickens around the courtyard. Usually she would have grabbed the broom and ran after the aggressive peacock, but now her thoughts were on Mr. Patel. He had always been so shy around her that receiving the gift of the wind chimes without him even having the courage to sign his name to the tag on it filled her heart with deep affection for him. She glanced over at her mother-in-law's house, and with no sign that the woman had returned, Prisha ran into the house, grabbed the box from under the sink, and then returned to the porch. There she opened it, took out the bamboo wind chimes, and climbed onto a chair. She hung them from a hook in the middle of the porch ceiling placed there for hanging holiday decorations, stepped down from the chair and then stared at them admiringly. The honey-colored lacquer on the carefully carved stalks of bamboo gleamed in the morning light. The first soft breeze that made them tap gently against each other and produce a series of melodic wooden notes brought tears to her eyes. She rushed into the house, filled a cup with tea, and then rushed back out onto the porch, sat down in the chair and stared up at the chimes while sipping on the tea.

It was only a sudden piercing cry from Shor that brought her out of her reverie. She looked up in time to see her mother-in-law coming through the gate. The peacock was like a pet to the old woman and it ran to her, its tail feathers quivering. The woman shifted the bag she was carrying from one arm to the other and patted the peacock on the head. Without hesitating, Prisha climbed onto the chair and took down the chimes. She jumped down, crammed them into the box, and then hurried into the house and returned the box to its hiding place. When she came out of the house her mother-in-law was standing by the well, picking ants from the stone wall that encircled the well, and feeding them to Shor.

"Where have you been all morning, Saasu Ma?" she called out from the porch to her mother-law.

Nearing seventy-five and hunched over from osteoporosis, the old woman slowly raised her head and glanced at Prisha. Although her son had married Prisha, ten years before, she couldn't escape the feeling that her daughter-in-law was always up to no good. His first wife had run off with another man, leaving her son devastated and publicly embarrassed. Saasu Ma kept a close eye on his second wife, although Prisha had always been a kind and dutiful wife and daughter-in-law. She lifted the bag, showing it to Prisha. "I went to pick some mangoes from Mr. Singh's grove."

Prisha walked across the courtyard, stopping a few feet from where her mother-in-law and Shor stood. "You should be careful, Saasu Ma, Mr. Singh doesn't like others picking mangoes from his trees. Dev could buy them for you from Mr. Singh and save you all the trouble."

"I love my son, but he hasn't the amount of intelligence that Saraswati gave to Shor to make the kind of deal I made with Mr. Singh. He let me have an entire bag of fresh mangoes for only three of my embroidered napkins. "

Prisha glanced down the well that had gone unused since plumbing had been installed in all three houses. The air that circulated inside it, rubbing against the stone walls, sounded eerily like the wind chimes. "Come into my house and I'll make you some tea and breakfast."

"You're too good to me," the old woman said.

#

Mr. Patel limped through the gate and stopped for a moment and rubbed his right leg, left weak and always aching since he was stricken with polio as a teenager. Standing near the well, Shor shrieked upon seeing the teacher. The two had nothing but animosity for one another.

Shor learned early not to physically attack Mr. Patel when he tried to bite the man's leg and was whacked on the head with the teacher's briefcase. From that point on they maintained a safe distance but Shor never ceased to let his displeasure with seeing Mr. Patel go unnoticed.

Hearing the commotion, Prisha ran out of her house with the freshly ironed embroidered napkin in her hand. Seeing Mr. Patel she stopped on the porch, smoothed the wrinkles in her sari and then stepped from the porch into the courtyard dirt. The macaque she had seen earlier that morning was sitting on the wall preening its infant's fur.

"Good day, dear Mr. Patel," Prisha called out to the teacher.

Mr. Patel pushed his wire rim glasses up to the bridge of his nose and squinted at Prisha who was blanketed in harsh white sunlight. "Good day to you too, Misses," he replied. "It's very hot today, isn't it?"

"Yes it is. I've just made you some iced tea thinking your walk back from school would make you hot and thirsty."

"You made it for me?" he replied, unable to hide his puzzlement. She had never made him tea before other than on nights when he played cards with her and Dev.

"Yes, please do come and sit on the porch and I'll bring it out to you." She turned and ran into the house.

He walked to her porch, sat on a chair, and placed his briefcase on his lap. He watched as the macaque with her infant cradled in one arm climbed down the wall, scurried across the courtyard, grabbing a chicken's egg left abandoned in the dirt, and scampered up another wall with the egg held in its teeth. It sat down, broke the egg open and poured the contents into its mouth.

Prisha came out of her house holding two glasses of tea filled with large ice cubes. She handed him a glass and then leaned against one of the porch posts as she drank her tea, watching him take sips of his. "You're nothing like my husband," she said after a few moments of silence. "You even drink your tea like a man with refined qualities."

"Dev seems very nice," he replied.

"Yes, he's nice. He never beats me or speaks harshly to me, but he never gives me gifts."

He took a large gulp of his drink. "I'm sorry to hear that. A wife should receive gifts from her husband."

"Do you like teaching?" she asked after a moment of quiet.

"Standing on my leg most of the day is difficult."

"You need a wife to massage it every night to ease the discomfort."

His cheeks turned red. He looked across the courtyard at his house. "Perhaps some day I'll marry, when I can afford to."

She drank the last of her tea. "I think any woman would be happy being your wife," she said. "It's the little things that a man does for her that makes all the difference."

He stood up and handed her his glass. "You should teach classes on how a woman should be treated."

"I wouldn't need a classroom to do that," she replied with a nervous giggle.

He blushed again and then stepped off of the porch. "Your husband will be home soon. We will have to have another evening of playing Satte Pe Satta sometime soon."

"I'll mention it to him," she said.

She watched as he walked to his house, practically dragging his lame leg along. Shor stood by the well and shrieked at him as he passed by.

#

As soon as Dev fell into a deep sleep, Prisha got out of bed, waited for the dizziness to pass and then put on the sari she had worn that evening She glanced at her bindi in the mirror before leaving the bedroom noting the brightness of the red kumkum. She took the box containing the wind chimes from behind the pots and pans, tucked it under arm, and then went out the front door. The courtyard was aglow with the iridescent light cast by a full moon. There were no lights showing from either of the other two houses. The windows and door at her mother-in-law's house were closed. Standing on the porch she took the chimes from the box, dropping one of the red strings that held the box together, unable to catch it before a breeze carried it off. She held the chimes, shook them slightly, and smiled as their music played softly.

"Only a man who loves a woman gives her such a gift," she murmured.

She put the chimes back in the box, placed it on a chair, and then crossed the courtyard. Resting by the well, Shor stood and spread his feathers as she passed. She opened the front door to Mr. Patel's house and went in, closing the door behind her.

#

At sunrise, Prisha left Mr. Patel's house, crossed the courtyard, seeing the macaque sitting on the wall with her infant, watching her. On her porch she gathered up the box in her arms just as her mother-in-law stepped out onto the porch of her house. "Good morning, Prisha. You're up very early this morning."

At first startled by her mother-in-law's sudden appearance, she quickly collected her wits. "Good morning, Saasu Ma. I was about to hang these wind chimes so that I could hear their music in the morning breeze."

Her mother-in-law left her porch and walked to the edge of Prisha's porch. "Yesterday you didn't mention getting them. I was afraid you didn't like my gift."

"Your gift?

"Yes, I sold a few of my embroidered napkins and bought the wind chimes for you for being such a good wife to my son."

"Your gift?" Prisha repeated, stuttering.

"I thought you would know that from the red embroidery string I used to bind the box with."

Prisha suddenly felt dizzier than she had ever felt before.

The End

2

THE ISLAND OF WOMEN

Sitting beside Rita's bed Cecilia takes a red bead from the bowl of beads on the stand next to the wicker rocking chair she is rocking back and forth in and guides the thin piece of leather through the hole in the bead. Deformed by years of crippling rheumatoid arthritis, that her misshapen fingers and hands can string the beads at all surprises me. Making the strings of beads and selling them at a shop in the El Centro and another shop in Cancun to tourists is how she makes what little extra she can to survive. She refuses money or any financial assistance from me even though I have been married to her daughter Rita for thirty years.

As she slides one bead after another onto the string of beads she is making she doesn't look up at me or talk to me. She hates me for marrying her only daughter and taking her to America so many years ago and now for bringing her back to this island to spend her final days.

Cecilia can speak English, but when she does speak to me, which isn't often, she speaks only in Spanish which is not my native language. I have difficulty understanding when it is spoken quickly, something Cecilia knows and exploits as a way of showing her disdain for me. But for now Cecilia is silent, threading the leather through the beads. I want to tell Cecilia that I am sorry; sorry that her daughter has been brought back to die on this island, but I have already told her it was Rita's wish to return here to her place of birth.

There is a warm, fragrant sea breeze coming in through the open window that pushes the white lace curtains inward into the room. They flutter, the sound of it like the whisperings of children heard from afar. Through the open window I can see but not hear the gentle waves washing slowly over the huge rocks along the nearby shore; a shore-line of thin strips of private beaches and rocky crags below a line of homes owned by mostly American expats and seasonal residents. I can also see the outline of Cancun's shore miles away across the stretch of bright turquoise Caribbean waters separating it from this island, Isla Mujeres. I have rented this house for the final weeks of Rita's life, and aside from Cecilia, and Amelia who assists in caring for Rita and occasionally cooks for us, no one comes here.

Looking at Rita asleep on the snow-white linens dressed in her favorite baby blue night gown, she looks much younger than her age. Her body has become small, thin and frail. The few strands of gray hair among the black stand out almost as a cosmetic fashion statement, not as a sign of her age. Her face is free of wrinkles and Amelia has put some light pink lipstick on her lips; this done before Cecilia's arrival this morning, not for Rita's benefit, but for mine.

"She always want to look pretty for you," Amelia said in broken English as she applied the lipstick while I sat by the bed holding Rita's hand.

"*Gracias, Amelia,*" I said, "*Muchas gracias.*"

"The time is near, yes?" she asked.

"Yes it is," I told her. "*Si,*" I added, uncertain what to say next.

Now, standing at the window, looking at my dying wife, at the head of her anger-filled mother looking down at the beads she is stringing on the leather strip, I feel the need to escape. "I'm going for a walk," I say.

#

Above me and to the east, thick white clouds fill the horizon of dark blue sky. It is September, the time of year for battering storms and ferocious hurricanes. I haven't listened to the radio and Amelia said nothing about an incoming storm. Even if she had known, Cecilia wouldn't have said anything even if a hurricane was about to blow me out to sea. I adjust the white ball cap on my balding head and walk the road headed toward the southern tip of the island. In the open air the breeze is much stronger and warmer then felt through the window in the bedroom where Rita lay. The ever-present aromas of fish, salt water and the scents from the palm trees and ferns that surround the nearby swampy lagoon assault my sense of smell. They are rich and exotic smells, like walking into a tropical hothouse. What few insects there are buzz briefly around my head, then are carried away by the breeze. Within a few yards of one another large green iguanas sit in the middle of the road bathing in the sunlight, then scurry into the lush grass along the road as I near them. At the roadside entrance to El Garrafon Park I walk along a line of parked taxis and mopeds.

"Ride, *Senor*?" A driver asks lazily from inside his taxi.

"*No, gracias,*" I say, walking faster.

From the road I can see the tourist-filled water along a small stretch of the park at the bottom of a hill. Brought there by ferries to scuba dive and see the bright colored coral on the seabed, a hundred or so tourists are standing in the water, each wearing goggles, bobbing their heads in and out of the water like strange sea birds to view the coral and whatever aquatic life they can see around their feet. I had once did this same thing with Rita, but that was years ago and long before hordes of tourists were brought to the island by ferry from Cancun. In those days, Rita and I didn't just stand in the water near the shore, but swam and scuba dived as far out and as deep as we could. She had swam here, seeing the coral and the sea life from the time she was just a toddler.

When the tourists came en masse she no longer wanted to swim at this part of the island. During our visit five years previously, we found a private alcove with a very small sandy beach on the eastern side of the island, a place she knew also from her childhood, nearer to the southernmost part of the island, Punta Sur. There in the water a few feet out I was dashed against the rocks by a very rough wave and climbed out of the water, scratched and bruised, and found Rita sitting on her towel, her head in her hands.

"Are you okay?" I asked her.

"Just another headache," she said, looking up and seeing my injured side. "I told you the undertow and waves were rough here. You could have drowned."

Going past the park and entering Punta Sur I am glad to put those things out of my mind; the early days of her illness as well as the tourists here now. Only a few of the tourists are walking among the paths that wind their way all the way to the narrow rocky tip of the island. I take one of the paths stopping only to look at the recently carved statues placed along the way, including one of Ixchel, the Mayan Goddess of Childbirth and Medicine. The statue's black painted eyes do little to ease my concern for Rita. Standing on the very tip of Punta Sur looking from high up out over the vast bright blue waters I know the days of simply being concerned about her are over.

On the way back to the house a small light brown mongrel with a stomach bloated from starving or disease or carrying a litter follows close behind me. There are small packs of these dogs, abandoned yet harmless, that roam the island being fed and kept barely alive by well-meaning tourists. This one gets no nearer then a few feet from me and stands cautiously outside the door watching me as I close the door. Inside the house it is very quiet.

"You have been out walking," Amelia says with the mixed inflection of it being a statement and question at the same time as she comes out of Rita's room with an arm full of linens.

"Yes I have. How is my wife?" I take off my ball cap and toss it onto the sofa.

"She is sleeping. Cecilia has gone home until tomorrow."

I want to say "good" but only nod.

"Your wife's mother she not understand why you are here," Amelia says in a hushed tone as if she will be overheard.

"This is where Rita wanted to be," I say. "She wants to die here."

"Her mother only interested in her daughter living here. To live is what makes difference to her, not the dying." Amelia looks over her shoulder, at the closed door to Rita's room. "Rita and I played together when young girls." Then Amelia smiles broadly. "That mother not agree with any man ever, so you are in good company."

"Thank you for that," I say, heading into my wife's room. "I think there is a storm coming, Amelia. You can go home. I can take care of my wife."

"*Si*," Amelia says. "A storm is coming."

#

Inoperable seemed at the time like a word a person used when talking about a car they couldn't get to run, not the inability to remove the tumor from Rita's brain. After all the tests, the scans, the MRIs, the countless neurological exams, it was the final word every doctor, surgeon and brain specialist used: inoperable. Rita took the news much calmer than I did, thanking them all for giving her some light at the end of the tunnel, even if it wasn't light at all. She saw the prognosis of eventual death as the eventual ending of the medicated headaches and nausea, periods of confusion and increasing lack of coordination. Three weeks before, when coming to Isla Mujeres, she needed my help and the help of a flight attendant to make it down the plane's aisle and into her seat. She said very little the entire flight from Virginia, but stared out the window almost the entire time.

"Home again at last," she said as Cancun and Isla Mujeres came into view as the plane began its descent.

I took her hand in mine. "Are you sorry you left the island?"

"No, because the island never left me," she said.

Those first days upon our return went by fast, too fast, and Rita wanted to see as much of the island as possible. At only about 5 miles from one end to the other and much less than that from the east side to the west, in the past we had easily walked it from end to end. This time we didn't venture far beyond the ubiquitous taxis to return us quickly home when she became quickly exhausted or was confused about where we were or what we were doing. The throngs of tourists in the narrow streets in the El Centro shopping district overwhelmed her and led to our quickly retreating to a bar along the waterfront just to find an escape until I could get a taxi to take us home.

The first visit with her mother also didn't go well. When we arrived by taxi Cecilia was standing in the open door of her small house on a side street leaving El Centro heading south as if she were guarding it from would-be robbers. Although she took her daughter in her arms and hugged her tightly, she said nothing to me. Sitting in her small living room I realized that nothing had changed or even been moved since our previous visit five years before. She and Rita spoke to each other in rapid-fire Spanish, little of it that I understood, while I looked at all the photographs on the walls of her and Rita. I was reminded once again that there were none of me, or of me and Rita, or of Rita's father.

Within a week Rita suffered a seizure and became confined to her bed. Most of the time when she was awake she knew where she was and what was happening around her, but she slept a lot, as if preparing for eternal sleep by taking frequent naps. On several occasions she awoke very confused and in a state of panic until either I or Amelia or Cecilia could calm her by gently rubbing her hand and talking to her in gentle, reassuring, soothing tones. More than once during the night as I lay beside her she would awake, grab my hand and ask, "Am I on my island?"

#

On this night with only a single lamp on, nearing midnight the room is full of shadows. With the curtains tied against the frame of the window I can feel the strong warm winds of the storm as it crosses the island on its way to the entirety of the Yucatan. Rain falls in vertical sheets. It is a storm, but not a hurricane, but the lamp light flickers on and off occasionally. Standing at the window in the darkness it's almost impossible to see where the beach along this house and the waters of the Caribbean begin. In the distance I can barely make out the lights from homes and hotels along the shore in Cancun.

"I want to go home," Rita says to me from behind me. I turn and see her trying to sit up. "I want to go home," she repeats.

I go to the side of her bed and try to gently urge her back against the pillow. "You're home sweetheart. I brought you home."

She is looking straight at me, her face half illuminated in the light of the lamp, the other half hidden in shadow. In her look there is an awareness. She knows what she is saying and as if suddenly punched in the stomach I now know it also. "Are you sure?" I ask her.

She covers my hand with hers and squeezes it gently. "Yes, my love, I'm sure."

Ending her life for her had not crossed my mind until this moment. This room, this house, was not her home. Isla Mujeres, the Island of Women, was. I had brought her back to it, but it was not enough. I slide my arm around her back and slip my other arm under her knees and lift her from the bed. She's so light. It's as if the life that was leaving her was carrying with it her weight. I carry her out into the hall and to the back door and then out onto the small wooden deck overlooking a small flight of stairs and beyond that the beach and the sea. At the bottom of the stairs I see in the darkness the dog from earlier that day, its eyes gleaming like shiny marbles from its small head.

The force of the rain even in the first couple of steps drenches us. Rita's long hair hangs like dark dripping moss from a dying tree. Before the final step I hear a creaking of wood beneath my shoe, then the wood gives out and my right foot and leg up to my calf goes through it almost throwing me off balance completely. Holding tightly onto Rita I squirm to pull my foot and leg up through the hole. It is the feeling of the dog's sharp teeth sinking into my flesh just above my sock that propels me out of the hole and sends me lurching forward with Rita in my arms. We land in the soft sand as the rain batters us. I feel the place on my leg where I was bitten and feel the thickness of blood. The dog is nowhere to be seen. I pick Rita up and carry her to the water and pause only momentarily until walking into the waves with her.

"Thank you," she says to me as I lay her body on the water where she floats for several minutes before disappearing beneath the surface.

The End

3

SING ME A RIVER

Pa had worn that old gray coat until it was almost nothing but a rag that hung on his big frame. It smelled of rancid venison, catfish and gasoline but Pa didn't mind any. He wore it almost everywhere and year 'round. He would have worn it at church on Sunday morning but that was where Ma put her foot down. Pa wasn't much into giving in to what other people wanted and didn't give a whit what people thought of him, but when it came to Ma, he deferred to her good judgment and wishes.

I was going on fifteen when we moved to a small piece of farmland near the banks of the Ohio River. Even before Ma unpacked the dishes, Pa had put on his coat and gotten his fishing pole from the back of the truck.

"You wanna come along?" he asked me.

"Can't, Pa," I said. "I have a piece to learn."

I untied the blanket wrapped around the piano to protect it during the move and sat down on the bench and watched him through the window as he headed off through a field of dead brown stalks of corn going toward the river. It was late fall and the trees had shed most of their leaves. Everything looked gray, as if nature was dying right in front of my eyes. Pa's coat served as camouflage and he was soon lost from view shortly after entering the woods that separated the farm from the river.

#

Cold air seeped into my bedroom through some of the small spaces between the boards in the wall and from around the window frame. The wallpaper was old and buckled or peeling and did nothing to keep the chill out. Ma had put some masking tape around the window and hung wool curtains but it didn't really help. I sat in my bed with the comforter my grandma had given me pulled around me and by lamp-light looked at sheet music and tried to memorize the notes. The wind whistled through the walls providing notes of its own.

"You awake in there, son?" Pa asked.

"Yeah, Pa. Just studying my music. Come on in."

Pa opened the creaking door and stuck his head in before coming all the way in. "You going to be okay here?"

"Sure, Pa. It's a bit chilly but I'll get used to it," I said. "You missed supper. How was the fishing?"

"Didn't catch a damn thing," he said.

He came in and moved the curtain aside and looked at the window. "Your Ma did a good job with the tape." He stared out the window for a moment then put the curtain back into place. "If you go down to the river be careful. I found a trap buried under some brush."

"What kind of trap?" I asked.

"For small game. Just big enough to injure you if you don't look out," he said.

"Okay Pa, I'll be careful."

Before leaving he stopped in the doorway. "I heard you singing all the way down to the river. You've been given a gift, son. Don't squander it."

"I won't, Pa."

During the night I lay in bed under the comforter and listened to the hooting of an owl as the wind whistled through the walls. I tried to attach musical notes to the sounds and fell asleep imagining I was listening to a song.

#

Ma was standing at the stove stirring a large pot of venison stew when Pa came in from outside through the back door. He sat down at the table across from me. The aromas of outdoors, wet earth and damp air, wafted toward me along with the scents of his coat. He put his feet up on another chair. The soles were covered in dry mud.

"That stew smells good, Gracie," he said.

"It's still got about thirty minutes to go," Ma said. "Where have you been?"

"I went down to the river," he said. "Watching up close all that water flowing by is a powerful experience."

Ma put the lid on the pot and sat down at the table. "Aren't you going to practice today?" she said to me.

"I had the music room all to myself during lunch time at school," I said. "I was able to play and sing for about an hour."

"You making friends there?" Pa asked.

"Not yet," I said.

"It's a new school. It'll take a little time," Pa said. "You been down to the river yet?"

"Not yet."

#

The dead stalks of corn crunched beneath my boots. The air was full of ice crystals, as if the sky wanted to snow but couldn't quite work it out. I had a wool cap pulled down over my head and a scarf wrapped around my neck and was wearing a heavy coat. Entering the woods I kept my eyes on the ground ahead of me, keeping a lookout for traps. I barely noticed the trees around me. I heard the river even before I saw it. The sound of it filled my ears. I was on dry earth but felt like I had been swallowed by a swiftly moving current. I lifted my eyes and gazed in wonder at the gray slate of moving water stretched out in front of me. The surface of the river was no more than a foot below the bank that I was standing on.

I looked down the bank a ways and there was Pa. His hands were in the pockets of his coat and he was facing the river. He looked like a statue or that he was a frozen. There was something private going on between him and the river. I felt like an intruder, and so I turned and went back the same way I had come.

#

Sleet and rain whipped the stained glass windows of the small church. I sat between Ma and Pa. Ma had her Bible open and in her lap. The pages of it were yellowed with age and the corners were creased or bent. I was to begin the morning services by singing a solo and I had the hymnal open and was going through the notes in my head. Pa was squirming as he always did in the suit he wore to church.

The church organist nodded at me and I went up to the pulpit and lay the hymnal on it and for the next four minutes nothing existed in the world for me but singing.

When I sat down Pa whispered in my ear. "That was real good son."

"Thanks Pa," I whispered back.

#

At dusk I stood on the porch and watched a flock of geese fly in v formation across the cloud filled gray sky. Darkness had already made one tree indistinguishable from the next along the boundary line of the woods. The fields had been turned into a marsh. The loneliness of the landscape bore into my bones

Pa came out of the house and stood next to me. "It's a beautiful sight, isn't it son?"

"Yes Pa."

"You still need to go down to the river," he said.

I said nothing.

Water dripped from the gutter and splashed in the puddle that had formed around the house like a moat.

#

Ma was in the kitchen when I got home from school. She was chopping celery and humming the same song I had sung at church.

"How was school?" she asked as I took a piece of the celery and bit into it.

"It was okay," I said.

The kitchen was the warmest room in the house. It was where Ma spent most of her time even when she wasn't cooking.

"Dinner will be ready soon. Can you go get your father?" she said.

"Where is he?" I asked.

"I saw him wandering across the field going toward that river," she said. The way she said "that river" was the same way she talked about other things she held in derision. That broken down car of ours. That high priced meat at the store.

I went out the front door and by the time I was half way across the field my boots were covered in mud. The storm had shaken off most of the leaves that had been clinging on. The bare branches were locked in combat above my head. Before reaching the river bank I found a trap with a dead squirrel caught in it. The teeth of the trap were clasped on its hind leg.

The river was swollen. A couple inches more and it would be flowing over the bank. I watched as a dead tree was carried along on the swift current. Pa was nowhere along the bank. I walked along it for a ways until I found his coat neatly folded and lying on a bed of wet leaves at the river's edge.

I sang at the church service for Pa. I sang about a river. I never sang again.

The End

4

THE CITRUS THIEF

Rain fell on the tin roof sending metallic pings inside the garage where Rosa lived with her four year old son, Manuel. She sat on a plastic lawn chair and peeled a navel orange with her teeth, sucking on the exposed juicy pulp as she tore away each section of peeling. Juice dribbled down her chin and dripped onto her floral patterned cotton shift. The juice of the orange was sweet and Rosa closed her eyes in delight savoring the flavor.

She shuffled the right foot back and forth on the floor. Her left foot she barely moved at all, it being turned outward at the ankle, a deformity since birth. She could walk, but preferred to sit, especially when in the garage, a one room shack she rented from Mr. Travers who owned the trailer park where the garage was located.

There was one lamp that lit the entire room. It was late at night and the lamp was on. Manuel was sound asleep on the twin bed he shared with his mother under a quilt that Rosa had sewn together. Other than the sound of the rain hitting the tin roof, there was silence.

#

Rosa was from Magdalena de Kino in Sonora, Mexico. Though work was plentiful in Magdalena de Kino, she couldn't find or keep a job because of her foot and crossed into the United States illegally through Nogales, Arizona with her husband, Elias, who also couldn't find work in Mexico.

"We will have more opportunity in America," he had told her.

She was pregnant with Manuel and they had enough money to get to Florida by bus where Elias planned to pick oranges. Elias disappeared shortly after Manuel was born in the emergency room at the local hospital and Rosa had not heard from him since.

#

Rosa wondered what effect the rainfall would have on the local citrus groves. Oranges and grapefruit shaken from the trees by the rain or wind would not lie on the ground for long, being picked up by the migrant fruit pickers as soon as the rain stopped, or sometimes even as the rain fell.

When she first went to find work picking fruit as soon as the manager or owner of the groves saw her foot they wouldn't hire her.

"A woman with a lame foot isn't what we're looking for," they would say.

Rain was sliding down the pane of window glass and glistened in the lamp light. Rosa stood up dropping the orange peels that had fallen into her lap onto the floor and went to the bed and pulled the quilt up over Manuel's thin shoulders and slipped her feet into her sandals. At the door she put on the poncho and a straw hat she had brought from Mexico, grabbed a burlap sack from a hook on the wall, then grabbed the handle of a rusty Radio Flyer wagon, then looked around the room and saw that everything was as it always was, then opened the door and went out into the rain pulling the wagon.

Stopping at the trailer where Mr. Travers lived, she knocked on the door and waited under the small awning momentarily shielded from the rain. When he opened the door he was in a terrycloth bathrobe and wearing knee high white sports socks.

"Rosa, what is it?" he said.

"I'm so sorry to bother you, Mr. Travers, but I have to go out and I wondered if you could keep an eye out on the garage since Manuel is alone?" She asked. "He's asleep," she added quickly.

"Yes I can do that, but Rosa you need to find a regular babysitter," he said.

"I will try Mr. Travers, but they will not do it for free. It's why I am going out again tonight. The more fruit I sell the better I can take care of Manuel."

"I understand," he said. "I'll look after Manuel again tonight, but this is the last time."

"I understand also," Rosa said as she turned and walked down the dirt road pulling the wagon behind her. The wagon had a shaky rear left wheel that squeaked with every turn. Other than the sound of the wheel squeaking and bumping along on the road and rain hitting its metal, it was eerily quiet. The cloud cover hid the stars and moon and in the darkness Rosa had difficulty seeing the fences and signs that let her know she had reached the citrus groves she usually got the oranges and grapefruits from; oranges on the right side of the road, grapefruit on the left.

It was the large no trespassing sign with the bullet holes in it that was nailed on a post alongside the fence separating the road from the orange groves that let her know she had arrived where she intended to be. She pulled the wagon up to the fence and let the handle drop onto the ground, then took off the poncho and threw it over the barbed wire, then climbed over the fence, pulling her deformed foot over last, and in the darkness searched the ground under the trees nearest the fence for any fallen oranges. With her straw hat drooping over head and her clothes soaked from the rain, she filled the burlap bag with about a hundred oranges before carrying the bag back to the wagon and reaching over the fence and dropping the bag into the wagon. She had already calculated that she could make about fifty dollars from the oranges, a portion of which would pay for someone to watch Manuel while she was selling the fruit, and another portion set aside to pay Mr. Travers the two hundred dollars in rent that she paid monthly. The earnings from the grapefruits would be added to that of the earnings from the oranges. She crawled back over the fence, pulled her poncho from the wire and was crossing the road when the beam of a flashlight shone in her face.

"It's that woman with the weird foot," a man's voice said.

"What are you doing here?" Another man, the one with the flashlight asked.

"Getting some fruit," Rosa said, feeling less afraid then she should. The mens voices had the accents of men from her native country and she considered speaking to them in Spanish, but decided against it. "I sell the fruit to take care of my child," she said.

"Where is your man?" The man not holding the flashlight asked.

Rosa hesitated before answering. "I don't know," she said at last.

"You could get shot out here stealing this fruit," the man with the flashlight said. "The guards who patrol these groves carry guns and shoot trespassers."

"They wouldn't shoot a woman," Rosa said.

"They shoot anyone," he said. "Besides when you steal from the owner of this land you are stealing from us. This is where we come to get fruit."

"There is plenty for everyone," Rosa said defiantly.

The man not holding the flashlight whispered into the ear of the other one, then said to Rosa, "You can continue to steal from here but you will have to give us half of everything you pick up."

"I need the money from the fruit I steal and sell to take care of my child," Rosa said.

"You can always earn money spreading your legs for the migrant workers," he said.

Rosa spat in his direction. "*Vete a la mierda, cabrón.*"

The two men laughed.

"You have a vulgar mouth for a woman out alone on a night like this one," the man without a flashlight said.

Flashing the beam of light back and forth across Rosa's face, the one with the flashlight said, "Take what you have in the bag but go home now and don't come back to this place or we will shoot you ourselves."

He directed the light to the handle of a pistol sticking up from the waist band of his pants.

Wordlessly, Rosa turned and pulled her wagon with the bag of oranges home. When she reached the garage she opened the door and was startled to see Mr. Travers sitting in the plastic chair with Manuel asleep on his lap.

"I heard him crying and came over to see what was wrong," Mr. Travers said. "He was crying for you."

"I am here now," she said pulling the wagon into the garage and throwing the straw hat onto a small table. She lifted Manuel from Mr. Travers' lap and carried him to the bed and laid him down on the quilt and kissed him on the forehead.

"It doesn't look like you did very well" Mr. Travers said, looking at the wagon with just the sack in it.

"I will do better tomorrow night," Rosa said.

"Remember what I said, Rosa," Mr. Travers said as he went to the door. "I'm not going to watch Manuel again. The boy needs his mother or father or another woman to look after him, not an old widower like me." He went out the door, closing it behind him.

Rosa removed the wet poncho and her wet shoes and clothes and hung them on nails on the wall of the garage, then put on the only store bought robe she owned, one that Elias had gotten for her on their honeymoon, and laid down next to Manuel, draping her arm over his frail body, and went to sleep.

#

By noon the sun had turned the rain from the night before into thick humidity that was like being in a hothouse. Rosa sat on a fruit crate on the sidewalk in the shade of the large bank building, the oranges neatly stacked into a pyramid inside the wagon. Manuel was sitting on the concrete tethered to her by a thin rope that she had tied around her waist and his. Sweat ran in rivulets down her back and between her cleavage, soaking the thin cotton material of her dress. She fanned her face with her straw hat as passersby hurriedly passed her, few looking at her or the oranges. She had given Manuel one of the oranges and he was rolling it back and forth on the sidewalk like a ball. She knew this spot, and was waiting for lunch time when bank employees would be coming out. The ankle of her deformed foot ached as it had from birth, and the last two Tylenol she had and taken that morning did not dull the aching. She repositioned it several times but nothing helped. She was rubbing her ankle when a security guard, Paul, from the bank came out of the building and walked up to her.

"Good morning, Rosa," he said. "It sure is a hot one today," he said, taking his hat off and running his hand over his graying black curly hair.

"Good morning, Paul," Rosa said. "Yes, it's very hot. I have some juicy oranges here that might cool you off if you would care to buy one."

Paul shuffled about nervously, "that's why I'm out here, Rosa. You can't sell your fruit out in front of this building anymore. The management has gotten too many complaints."

"I have been selling oranges and grapefruits from this spot for two years and no one has complained before," Rosa said.

"I know, Rosa and believe me I'm sorry, but it's the climate of things right now," he said.

"The climate of things? I do not understand," Rosa said.

"The political climate. Illegal immigration and all that," Paul said self-consciously in almost a whisper. "The management doesn't want to be seen as supporting what you do."

Rosa stood up, reaching down and pulling Manuel to his feet. "They do not support me," Rosa said. "I support myself." She handed Paul an orange. "You have been very kind to me, Paul. I will not make trouble for you any more." She picked up the handle of the wagon and with it and Manuel in tow she slowly walked home, her foot aching more with every step.

#

At nightfall she put Manuel in the wagon and left the garage and pulled him up the road leading to the groves where she always went. The moon was full and the night sky was crowded with winking white stars. Near the trespassing sign she pulled the wagon into the grass and sat down on the edge of the wagon next to Manuel softly singing the lullaby "ma cochi pitentzin" to him as she lay him down in the wagon and covered him with the burlap sack and sat running her fingers through his hair and over his cheeks. When two men appeared at the end of the road and coming her way she knew it was the same two she had met the night before. The one was still carrying a flashlight and waving it about. She stood up and went out into the middle of the road.

"What are you doing back here?" The one without the flashlight asked as they stopped a few feet in front of her, the other one waving the light across her face.

Before she could answer a shot rang out and the man with the flashlight fell to his knees. Rosa was at first too stunned to react.

"Run," the other man said as he began to sprint down the road leaving his friend on his knees, bleeding in the dirt. Then another shot rang out and the man who was running fell face first onto the road.

Rosa ran to the wagon and scooped Manuel up wrapped in the burlap sack and with him in her arms ran the same direction as the man lying on the road, dragging her foot behind her.

"Stop, thief," a man's voice yelled at her from down the road.

Rosa turned, "I am not stealing," Rosa shouted. "This is my son," she said holding her son up in the sack to be seen.

There was another shot. Rosa felt Manuel's blood trickle from the bag onto her fingers. She collapsed to her knees in the dirt and laid him on the road. She quickly pulled the burlap from his face, lifted his shirt and saw the entry point of the bullet in the middle of his chest. He was not breathing. As the man came up to her and carrying a rifle and a badge pinned on his shirt, she looked up at him.

"He was the fruit of my womb, not the fruit of your trees," she said, "and now you have stolen him from me."

The End

5

THE FAR AWAY HILLS

The house for the missionary and his wife stands on the edge of the village, its white paint turned gray from age and neglect. A veranda encircles the house so a walk around the entirety of it permits a view in every direction. The tattered bamboo chairs and mahogany tea tables on the veranda were flown in by helicopters forty years before, as was the lumber and nails to build the house, glass for the windows, and the inside furnishings. There are shutters on the windows but many of the slats are broken. There is a door on each side of the house that leads to the veranda, and a set of stairs, also on each side, that leads to the ground. There is space around the house for a flower garden, but it has gone untended for months, so it can barely be distinguished from the ground beyond it. The dirt is the color of tea with cream. The doors leading to the veranda are closed and have been since the last missionary and his wife returned to England. To the villagers, when there are no missionaries living in the house, it's as if the house doesn't exist.

Fifty yards beyond the other end of the village a clearing has been cut out of the jungle and is where the helicopter lands once a month that brings cloth to be made into clothing, food not found in the jungle near the village or grown in the gardens, medicine, tools, and transports people in and out. It's almost 150 miles to the nearest city. There are no roads that connect the village to other villages, or to the city. Beyond the village there is only jungle. For the remainder of the month that the landing for the helicopter isn't in use, the boys of the village use it as a football field.

Clarice has her face to the helicopter window hoping to see something other than the canopy of trees that hide the jungle beneath it. The inside of the helicopter is full of noise: the whirling of the blades, the clatter of the wooden boxes in the cargo hold knocking against each other, the three male villagers in the nearby seats who are returning from the city, yelling in Swahili, in order to hear one another over the din.

"We're about to clear the hills and then the village isn't that far off," John says loudly into Clarice's ear.

His breath is hot on her cheek and has the unpleasant scent of the spicy coffee he had to drink in the airport lounge just before they took off. Her left hand is in her lap and his hand is on hers, a sign of affection, but to her it feels like a weight to keep her in place; to keep her from clawing her way through the glass and leaping out the window. His shoulder is pressed against hers. He's a large man and doesn't realize the amount of space he takes up around him. Clarice bites into her lower lip as the helicopter flies above several hills that rise out of the jungle like ant hills. The treeline goes nearly to the top of them and then there is exposed earth, like a bald spot on top of a man's head. Clarice holds her breath for most of the time as the helicopter passes over the hills. She doesn't tell John that inexplicably she finds the hills terrifying.

"They're called The Fuvus," John tells her as he leans across her and plants his face next to hers at the window. "Fuvu is the Swahili word for skull."

There are four crew members on board the helicopter, the pilot, co-pilot, and two attendants who also assist with loading and unloading the cargo. Both attendants speak perfect English; almost too perfect, as if they purposely thought out every word and sentence before speaking them.

One of the attendants, Adroa, a tall, lanky man with a gold cap on his front upper tooth, gets out of the seat he has been sitting in for most of the flight and stands beside the seats that John and Clarice are sitting in. "We'll be landing in a few minutes," he says. "Make sure your seatbelt is secure." His voice booms.

Clarice turns from the window and looks at Adroa's eyes. They're almond shaped with thick curly lashes, almost feminine in appearance. He has high cheek bones and his nose is perfectly shaped. He's a man, but quite lovely. A smile crosses her face; a larger smile than she intended, and for a moment she's embarrassed by the intimacy of her own smile. She had talked with him in the boarding lounge for a few moments before they boarded the helicopter and liked they way he kept referring to her as madam. "Do you know what the weather will be like in Wingi?" she asks.

"It will be very hot in Wingi, madam," he answers. "It is always very hot in Wingi, even when it rains."

Adroa moves on to the villagers from where Clarice can hear them speaking in Swahili, and laughing. Adroa momentarily glances back at her, and her face turns red.

#

Stirred up by the helicopter's blades, a cloud of rust-colored dust hangs in the air as Clarice walks across the landing field toward the village. She has a firm grip on John's hand, the sweat in the palm of their hands gluing them together. The end of her long pony tail slaps against the middle of her back with every step she takes. In keeping with a missionary's wife she is dressed modestly. The hem of her long sleeve gray cotton dress is just below her knees. Her pumps are white and simple. The only thing extravagant about her is the zebra skin handbag she carries that she bought in a street market in Nairobi

Even before they enter the main street of the village, the villagers swarm around them, chattering excitedly in Swahili. The women of the village tug on Clarice's sleeve and run their hands down her pony tail. She looks from face to face, searching for someone near her age, a potential friend, but only feels the panic that has caught in her throat and chokes her.

"Hujambo," she says timidly to those she passes.

Saying hello is one of the few Swahili words she knows. Back in Indiana in the year leading up to leaving for Africa, John often scolded her for not learning the language. The hours she spent listening to language tapes were mostly spent daydreaming. She had waited until age thirty to marry. It was returning from Africa and establishing a home after John completed his dream of being a missionary she thought about while she was supposed to be learning Swahili. It rarely entered her mind what it would mean to spend a year living in the jungle being a missionary's wife.

Walking among the villagers, John is as friendly and talkative speaking Swahaili as he is when speaking to English-speaking parishioners at the Sunday church services. Peripherally, Clarice watches the sweat roll down the side of his face that he wipes away with the back of his hand. There are glimpses of him that that frightens her; his facial features seem distorted, as if his head is being cooked and has become swollen in the heat.

She can feel the need for a touch of makeup on her cheeks.

Huts built of tree branches, bamboo and palm leaves line each side of the dirt street. In front of some huts, large kettles of boiling liquid sit over small fires. The aroma of cooked meat wafts from the kettles. Those villagers not in the parade around the missionary and his wife stand in front of their huts waving as they hold onto the young children, most of whom are naked. The women in the village wear variations of brightly colored gomesi dresses. The men wear khaki shorts and t-shirts. No one wears shoes.

Approaching the house, Clarice tightens her grip on John's hand. The pictures she had seen of the house were taken years before, while the paint was white and gleamed in the sunlight. She can feel her heart thumping against her chest. At the base of the steps she bends over and vomits up the coke and sandwich she had back in the airport. Then she faints.

#

Clarice opens her eyes. She lays on the bare mattress and stares up at the slowly churning blades of the fan hanging from the ceiling. With each complete turn a chirping sound similar to a cricket is emitted from the fan. Namazzi applies another wet cloth across Clarice's forehead.

"Madam feel better now?" Namazzi asks. Her inflection is musical, but her words are hard to understand. Namazzi is elderly. Her advanced age shows in the wrinkles around her eyes and mouth. She wears a bright red gomesi that seems much too large for her frail frame. She has no teeth.

Clarice turns her head and looks out the open window and can only see the tops of the far away hills. "My husband?" she says.

Namazzi plumps the pillow under Clarice's head. "Bwana go to see church. Namazzi take care of you while he gone."

Clarice looks into Namazzi's eyes. They are deep wells, their expression hard to discern. "I thought the church burned down years ago."

"He look at burned church," Namazzi replied. She removes the wet rag and squeezes the water from it into a tin basin sitting on a stand next to the bed. "You rest now," she says as she picks up the basin. "Just call if need me." She carries the basin out of the room.

Clarice wipes the water from her forehead, sits up on the edge of the mattress, smooths back her hair, and adjusts the scrunchie around her pony tail. Scanning the room, she sees that the two wood crates containing their clothes and shoes, linens, blankets and comforters and other bedroom items, are sitting against one wall. A vanity dresser with an oval mirror and a stool is against another wall. A large dresser and an armoire stand by an open closet. The furniture is old, some are antiques, their wood badly in need of refinishing. There are nails in the walls and discolorations in the off-white paint where pictures once hung. An oil lamp and two candlesticks with new candles in them sit on top of the dresser. She rises from the bed and goes to the window. Standing on the veranda is a young man, shirtless, with his back to the window. He has his hand raised above his eyes and he's looking up at the hills. His black skin glistens with sweat. His slightest movement makes the muscles between his shoulders and down his torso ripple, like waves in a pond. Suddenly she is overcome with desire, and lets out an involuntary moan.

The young man turns around, and seeing Clarice staring at him, he smiles, displaying perfect teeth. "Hujambo, madam," he says with a slight bow of his head.

Unable to speak, Clarice steps away from the window and falls back against the armoire. She places her hand on her stomach and tries to control her breathing. It's several minutes before she looks out the window again. The young man is gone.

#

Namazzi and Hasnaa place the bowls of food on the table. Hasnaa is young and very pretty. Her yellow gomesi doesn't hide her advanced pregnancy. The two women go quietly from the kitchen to the dining room, the plodding of their bare feet on the wood floor the only sound they make.

Clarice scoops a spoonful of mashed sweet potatoes onto her plate. "Tell me about the church," she says.

John cuts into a piece of charred meat. "I wonder what this is," he mutters with amusement, and then looks at Clarice. "All that remains is the concrete slab that was the floor of the original church. A thatched roof shelter has been built on the concrete. They've been using it for the church and school."

Clarice takes some green leafy vegetable that she doesn't recognize from a bowl and places it on her plate. "Why didn't the previous missionaries rebuild the church?"

Smacking his lips as he chews on the meat, he answers, "They couldn't raise the money. It takes an incredible amount to have everything that's needed purchased and flown in."

"Do you have the money?" she asks as she stares at the food on her plate. The colors of the food are bright, dizzying. A wave of nausea rises in her stomach. She grasps the edge of the table to steady herself.

"No, but I can raise it," he says as he shovels a mound of sweet potato into his mouth.

Clarice releases her hand from the table and waves it about, aiming at every wall and furnishing in the room. "This house needs to be painted and new furniture needs to be bought. The windows need curtains and the floors need rugs. I don't understand why if there's a pump that brings water into the kitchen sink that you can't install a toilet in the bathroom. A missionary's wife shouldn't live in these conditions."

"But honey . . . ," he starts.

Clarice lifts her fork from the table and slings it across the room. "How dare you leave me alone with a strange woman within hours of our arrival here, while I was sick, just to go see a burned down church. I could have died."

The door to the kitchen swings open and Namazzi and Hasnaa walk into the dining room, followed by the young man who Clarice saw standing on the veranda. He has a shirt on, but it's unbuttoned to the middle of his chest. The three of them stand silently for a moment.

"This Akello," Namazzi says, pointing to the young man. "He Hasnaa's husband."

Clarice stares at Akello, at the way he stands with his legs parted, at the size of his muscular forearms. She wants him in the way she wanted John when they first married. Her jealousy of Hasnaa overwhelms her.

"I'm going to have a baby," she blurts out, still staring at Akello.

#

The mosquito netting around the bed flutters in the warm breeze blowing through the slats of the closed shutters. Pale moonlight, also, finds its way into the bedroom, streaking the floor and walls with white stripes. The fan is in need of being wound up and the blades move almost imperceptibly. A bright green chameleon crawls across the top of the vanity dresser, causing Clarice's bottles of perfume and lotions to rattle.

Clarice climbs out of bed, slips her feet into her slippers, and goes to the window. She pushes open the shutters, inhales the dry night air as if smoking a cigarette, and holds it in her lungs for several seconds before exhaling. Of any view from any window in the house, this is her favorite. The moonlight blanketing The Fuvus turns them into something magical; far away hills in a fairy tale. Heard from the jungle only thirty yards away, the cries of the chimpanzees, the screeching of the birds, and the hum of insects, takes on a melodic quality in the night. After twenty-nine days in Wingi she thinks of nothing else but returning home, but that is eleven months away.

When Akello arrives, and stands among the ferns at the edge of the jungle, he's washed in moonlight. Every night since their one night together, he stands there, waiting for her. They watch each other from afar. She looks at him dispassionately. Her longing for him was satiated right after they made love on a bed of vines on the jungle floor. She closes the shutters and returns to the bed, removes her slippers, and climbs in.

"Are you okay?" John asks as he lays his arm across her breasts.

For Clarice, it feels like a chain holding her in place, keeping her from struggling free.

He runs his hand over her abdomen. "When are you going to start showing?"

"Some women don't show for many months into their pregnancy," she replies. "I may be one of those women."

"You have no idea how blessed I feel," he says.

"Of course I do," she says. "I do too."

"Are you certain you'll be okay while I'm gone?" he asks.

"It'll only be a month," she answers. "Namazzi is here to look after me."

She rolls onto her side, facing away from John, and curls into a fetal position. "I left the list on the dining room table of the furnishings I want you to bring back so that you don't forget," she says. She stares at the shuttered window until she falls asleep.

#

Namazzi sits a cup of tea on the stand and speaks to Clarice through the netting. "Madam is not saying goodbye to the bwana?" she asks.

Clarice awakes and rubs the sleep from her eyes. "Good morning, Namazzi. What did you say?"

"The helicopter is leaving soon. Do you not wish to say goodbye to your husband?"

Clarice quickly gets out of bed. "Why didn't John wake me?" she mutters angrily. She sheds her night gown and yanks a dress out of the closet. Clarice knows that Namazzi is watching her. The old woman watches her intently any time they are together. Clarice slips the dress over her head, and locks eyes with Namazzi. "What?" she says brusquely.

"The bwana loves you very much," Namazzi answers.

"I know that," Clarice says. "What business is that of yours?"

"I'm old, but not blind," Namazzi replies. "Some day a baby will have to arrive."

Clarice sits on the vanity dresser stool and slides her feet into a pair of red pumps. "Of course," she says. She stands and looks at her reflection in the mirror, pulls her hair back into a pony tail, and secures it with a red scrunchie. She avoids Namazzi's eyes as she runs from the bedroom. Passing through the dining room she sees the list on the table, grabs it, and runs out of the house. With the helicopter in sight, she kicks up small clouds of dirt as she runs down the street. She pushes her way through a small crowd of villagers that stand between her and the landing field. John is standing near the helicopter, talking with Adroa.

Breathless, she runs up to her husband. "Don't I get a kiss goodbye?"

"I didn't want to wake you," he says. He puts his hands on her shoulders, pulls her to him, and kisses her, lightly.

Clarice can feel a shudder course through her body and hopes John doesn't sense it. She slowly pulls away from his grasp and holds out the list. "You almost forgot this," she says. "I just can't imagine living here much longer without the house being refurbished."

He takes the list and stares at it for a moment, and says one thing, although it's obvious from the hesitancy in his voice that he wants to say something else. "I wrote everything down in my note pad that's in my jacket."

The helicopter's engine begins to roar. In the noise, John says "I love you" before he climbs the ladder. Two villagers follow behind him. Left alone with Adroa, Clarice is unable to avert her eyes from the beauty of his. He looks at her in return, and she quickly turns away, suddenly feeling naked, exposed. She joins the rest of villagers at the edge of the field as Adroa gets into the helicopter and the blades begin to turn. Besides her stands Hasnaa holding her baby, and beside her stands Akello. As the helicopter rises into the air, Clarice and the villagers turn away to keep from having dirt blown in their faces. When the helicopter turns the direction it will be going, everyone but Clarice starts for the village.

She is watching the helicopter, smiling as she feels the first kicks of her baby. She looks toward the ring of fog that surrounds the top of the The Fuvus and sees the helicopter begin to spin out of control as it enters the fog. Moments later a fireball rises from the top of one of the hills. A sharp pain, worse than any pain she had ever felt before, grips her abdomen. She bends over and watches the blood running down her legs.

The End

6

THE LAST SAMPAN

The gentle waves of the Yellow River tapped against the sides of Wang Wei's sampan, producing shallow reverberations, like fingers drumming arrhythmically on the stretched animal skin of a tanguu drum. Along the docks that lined the river banks of Zhengzhou, the tiny white lights hanging from miles of cord draped from one pole to the next, from one dock to the next, gleamed brightly like fireflies. Beyond the docks the steady discordant hum of the city rose from its streets and factories even though it was well past midnight. Wang Wei's new bride, Ying Yue, lay on the bench at the front of the sampan, away from the cover of the bamboo roof at the middle of the boat, twirling the long braid of her hair with her index finger as she stared up at the starry sky. From inside Zhengzhou when she looked up at a night sky the brilliance of the stars was obscured by the brightness of the neon lights that glowed twenty-fours a day, but from the middle of the river the twinkle of each star was like looking closely at a candle's flickering flame. On her chest lay the new silk slippers that Wang Wei had given her as a wedding gift. They were studded with imitation rubies, sapphires and jade made of cut glass sewn onto the fabric in floral designs. They reminded her of the slippers her grandmother wore.

Although a good distance from the sampan, as a barge passed by, the sampan rocked back and forth on the rolling currents. Pitched from side to side, Ying Yue hurriedly grasped onto the sides of the bench and sat up, sending one of the slippers flying over the edge of the boat and into the water. It floated on the top of the water for a few moments like a dead fish before sinking beneath the waves. She snapped her head defiantly to one side, flipping her braid onto her back where it usually lay.

"What do I care about an old woman's shoe?" she muttered.

The river water that had splashed onto the floor of the sampan washed over her feet. She raised them, annoyed that she had nothing to dry them with and only one slipper to wear to go from the bench to where Wang Wei lay sleeping on a straw mat on a raised platform under the bamboo roof. Married only six days, she found his snoring to be one of his most annoying habits. As she considered how to get to the bed, the noises he was making sounded animalistic and uncouth. She looked up at the stars, sighed heavily, and then lowered her feet onto the floor. Holding the one slipper, she crossed to the bed, sat on the edge, and dried her feet on the edge of the cover that lay across Wang Wei's body. Lying on his back his huge stomach rose up beneath the cover like a steamed bun waiting to be broken open. She crawled onto the platform beside him and turned on her side, facing away from him. His breath always smelled of catfish; something else about him that annoyed her. Still gripping the slipper, she lay awake for some time thinking about the life she had left behind in Zhengzhou. She finally fell sound asleep while listening to Wang Wei's oldest son, Li Qiang, at the rear of the sampan whistling softly as he guided the oar from side to side in the gently flowing water.

#

The next night, Ying Yue sat on the bench pulling at a string that attached a sapphire colored fake jewel to the slipper she had carried around in her pocket since awaking that morning. She hadn't told Wang Wei what happened to the other slipper. She had seen his temper flare up during an encounter he had with a merchant on the docks and didn't want him taking out his anger on her, especially over something as insignificant as a slipper better suited to a much older foot. She glanced up at the star-filled sky and tried to isolate one star to look at it only, but looking at just one was impossible. She could see Wang Wei at the other end of the sampan talking to Li Qiang, but couldn't hear what they were saying. Noise and music from two slowly passing small, gayly lit party boats loaded with foreign passengers filled the night, blocking out all other sound. Li Qiang was the same age as she was and wearing the new shirt he had purchased in the city that afternoon, he looked like the boys she had gone out with before becoming betrothed to Wang Wei. A scream followed by an outburst of laughter from one of the boats drew her attention away from the father and son. When she returned her attention to the slipper, she saw that the sapphire-colored had fallen off.

She was busy searching the floor around the bench when Wang Wei suddenly appeared a few feet away. For such a large man, he moved about as silently as an apparition. She surreptitiously stuffed the slipper in her pocket.

"It's a beautiful night," he said as part question and part statement.

She glanced up at the sky trying to find the last star she had been looking at. "The skies look much different from inside the city," she said. "What have you and Li Qiang been talking about?"

"He's interested in a girl whose family I don't know," he said.

"Isn't it an old fashioned idea that you must know the girl's family?" she said. "You don't know mine."

"A father's duty to his son is much different and Li Qiang isn't accustomed to being around young women."

She stood up, balanced herself as the boat gently rocked back and forth, and started toward the living area under the bamboo roof. As much as she hated it, it was her duty as the wife to put away the cooking utensils and prepare the bed for the night.

As she passed him, he gently grasped her arm. "Will you accept my affection tonight?" he said.

"Not tonight," she said. She pulled her arm away, glanced up at the stars, and continued on.

#

Wispy clouds slowly passed across the starlit sky. Ying Yue was bent over the edge of the sampan, trailing her hand through the water as the boat slowly glided along. A large ship stacked with huge metal containers was a short distance ahead, pulling the sampan along in its wake. The ducks that she and Wang Wei had bought that day at a meat market on the docks swung from hooks on the end of chains at the entrance to the living area. The chains tinkled musically, like wind chimes. Wang Wei had been in a good mood, lavishing her with candies and other treats bought from vendors who had small stands set up on the piers. His mood quickly darkened for a few minutes when they stopped in front of a hair salon and she said she wanted to have her hair cut in a more modern style.

"Absolutely not," he shouted. Within minutes and beyond the salon, his mood returned to being jovial and affectionate.

It was twilight before they returned to the Sampan. As always, because Li Qiang's job was to steer the sampan during the night, he had spent the day sleeping. He was awoken by his father who wanted to use the platform he was sleeping on as a table to read the contracts and documents he had picked up at his lawyer's office. Li Qiang untied the boat from the pier and they set off for the nightly trip upriver. To alleviate the boredom that at times weighed on her like a boulder, Ying Yue retreated to the bench and spent the time observing the river and the sky, both seeming endless and vast.

She filled her hand with a palm full of water and splashed it on her face.

"Be careful, you could fall in," Li Qiang said from behind her.

Startled, she rose up and turned about. He was a few feet away and shirtless. Sweat glistened on his chest. She looked to the back of the boat and saw Wang Wei manning the oar, something he did during the day but rarely at night. Li Qiang had a wry smile on his face, as if he were holding a secret. Sometimes his handsome looks alarmed her; they made her heart beat faster than normal.

"Why is your father steering the sampan?" she said. "Are you ill?"

"My father said he was feeling restless and not yet ready for bed," he said. "I think his new wife leaves him frustrated."

Ying Yue's face reddened. "You shouldn't say such things to me," she said.

His smile broadened and then just as quickly evaporated. He looked up at the sky. "I see you often staring up at the heavens. What do you see up there?"

"The stars, mostly. The way they're arranged."

"Do you believe in astrology, that our fate is foretold in the stars?"

She turned around on the bench so that she was facing straight ahead, no longer looking at him. The immensity of the container ship was like seeing a mountain afloat on the river. "I believe in nothing," she said. "We live. We die. We are no different than the ducks hanging on the hooks."

He sat on the bench next to her, facing the opposite direction, watching his father at the back end of the boat. He slid his hand across the wood until his hand touched hers.

At his touch, she gasped, but left her hand where it was.

They sat that way for some time until Wang Wei called out that he was ready to sleep.

#

The next morning Ying Yue prepared eggs, rice and steamed dumplings for breakfast. While Wang Wei and Li Qiang ate, she rolled up the mat and covers she and her husband slept on, but left the platform in place for Li Qiang to prepare for his own sleep. She had hidden the slipper in the basket where she kept the covers but took it out and shoved it in her pocket intending to throw it in the river as soon as she could do it without being seen. The sampan was tied to a pier near the docks where Wang Wei would be meeting with the managers of his tea export business. It was the only sampan moored at the docks.

"Why do you not have a better boat in which to travel up and down the river, something with an engine, something more modern, or travel by train?" was one of the first questions she had asked Wang Wei after marrying him.

"Traveling on the river in the sampan reminds me that even the simplest things that need to be tended to requires some effort," he said. "It's why I'm successful and very wealthy."

She only thought of him as being cheap, but it was his wealth that drew her to him in the first place. They both understood that and accepted it, but it wasn't spoken of.

As soon as Wang Wei finished eating and left the sampan, and Li Qiang laid down to sleep, she sat on the bench with the intention of throwing the slipper away, but forgot all about it. Wang Wei hadn't questioned her why she wasn't wearing the slippers or why she was wearing the shoes she wore before they were married, so her anxiety about the slippers had melted away. She gave great consideration to the fact that Wang Wei was much older than she was and in poor physical shape so he would die long before she did, and leave her a very wealthy widow. The first thing she planned to do after his funeral was to buy as many pairs of shoes of all types as she wanted.

#

Although she hadn't seen Wang Wei's tea plantation that covered many acres on the outskirts of Zhengzhou, she had been told about it in great detail by Wang Wei and Li Qiang. That night when she was told by a courier that Wang Wei would be spending the night at the plantation instead of returning to the sampan, she resented not being taken to the plantation also. She dreaded spending the night on the sampan since it would be tied to a pier instead of traveling up or down the river. She had very quickly become attuned to the routine of the boat being tied at a dock during the day and plying the river at night. The starry skies at night and the river traffic during the day each held her interest. When Li Qiang found out that his father would be gone all night he quickly retreated to the front of the boat, staying near the oar. Ying Yue lay on the bench staring up at the sky, casting occasional glances at Li Qiang. They hadn't spoken since she felt his hand against hers. She was uncertain what the gesture meant, but it became fixed in her mind like a splinter just under the skin.

After midnight when the stars cluttered the sky, she prepared the bed, removed her shoes, and climbed under the cover. She pulled the slipper from her pocket and held it close to her chest, determined to toss it overboard when the right moment came along – uncertain what the right moment would be – but as much as she disliked it and had no use for it, blithely discarding it would mean she could no longer be so readily reminded how different she was from Wang Wei. It reminded her that she had married her father, or grandfather. She didn't want to be married to either of them. She rolled onto her side and gazed at Li Qiang who had removed his shirt and was bent over the edge of the boat, splashing water on his muscular chest. His wet skin glowed in the starlight. She fell asleep, awakened a short time later by Li Qiang.

"I love you," he whispered to her while kneeling beside her on the bed.

She didn't answer, not in words. She didn't love him any more than she loved Wang Wei, but she wanted him. She pushed aside the cover, and spread her arms, ready to accept his embrace and his kisses. She hadn't given herself to her husband and the thought that she would someday have to filled her with dread. In that moment, taking Li Qiang as a lover removed so many of her fears about remaining married to Wang Wei until he died. In opening her arms for Li Qiang, the slipper caught on the hem of her sleeve and was pitched into the river.

"The slipper!" she shrieked.

Frantically, she pushed Li Qiang away, pulled herself to the edge of the sampan, and stared out at the glassy swiftly moving currents. Not far from the boat the slipper bobbed up and down in the water.

"You must get that slipper," she screamed.

"It's just a slipper," he said, as he stood on the platform.

"Your father, Wang Wei, gave it to me, and he loves me, truly loves me," she said as her eyes welled with tears.

Li Qiang looked into her eyes, and without hesitation, jumped into the river. He never reached the slipper. The last thing that Ying Yue remembered seeing – when she dared to remember it afterward at all –

was seeing Li Qiang disappear beneath the surface of the river and not reappear, and how brightly the stars shone.

The End

7

MONARO GOES ON A WALKABOUT

Before the sun had risen, before the fog that formed hazy clouds that hung a few feet above the ground disappeared, the flies had already began to bite Monaro's skin. With his eyes shut, still clinging to the visions of the imaginary lands of his dreams that had filled his head while he slept, he listened for the imperceptible hum of the flies' wings. In his mind's eye the flies were as big as flying cassowarys and twice as ill-tempered. They looked at him through their bulbous emerald green eyes, awaiting the slap of his hand. When he tired of their biting, he opened his eyes and watched them escape the futile strike of his hand that missed them by inches. He turned his attention to the open window in his bedroom and gazed out at the morning darkness where kukaburras in the nearby grove of gum trees laughed as if greeting the slowly creeping sunrise with a party. There was a chill in the air. As Monaro sat up on the edge of his bed he kept his blanket wrapped around his bare shoulders. When his feet touched the floor he felt the scales of a slithering snake rub against the tips of toes. He quickly pulled his feet up and looked down at the floor where his worn, leather boots lay, their laces twisting and turning.

While his father, mother and four year-old brother slept, he went to the bathroom wearing the blanket like a cape, relieved his full bladder, and tossed cold water on his face. He stared into the mirror that hung above the sink, shifted his face so that it wasn't bisected by a crack in the glass that extended from the left upper corner to the lower right corner like a hairline scar. Turning sixteen that day, he didn't feel older, and his eyes that stared back at him from his reflection were the same eyes he had shut before going to sleep the night before. The glass undulated. Ripples crossed back and forth on its surface like a a thin layer of skin being brushed across from underneath by an invisible hand. He touched the mirror, gently, fearing his fingers would break through the glassy membrane. He looked away, at a mouse that scurried across the floor, and when he looked back at his reflection, the glass was as it should be. He brushed his teeth, ignoring how they grew like the canines of a dingo and then retracted. He then returned to his bedroom with the blanket over his head, thinking of it as the magic kangaroo skin he wore in his dreams.

The first light of morning shone through the window, the sun's rays revealing specks of floating dust and amoeba-like creatures that swam on the current of air that noticeably warmed with every minute that passed. He tossed the blanket on the bed and waited until it had crawled into place, spreading across the sheets and over his pillow, before he removed his pajama bottoms and slipped on a pair of shorts. It took him several minutes more to decide which shirt he would wear on this day that he would begin his walkabout. He would have one pair of shorts and one shirt to wear, and his boots, preferring them over sandals should he need to squash a deadly tarantula. He sat on the edge of his bed and put them on.

Before leaving his room he cast a wish-spell on it to keep it just as he left it.

#

Monaro watched as an ant crawled across the table, pushing it with the end of his finger. The ant looked up, bared its fangs and growled. Monaro quickly pulled his finger away and watched as the ant turned into a peregrine falcon and flew out the kitchen window. He poured honey onto a slice of bread and stuffed it into his mouth as his mother filled his rucksack with wild rosella shortbread biscuits. His father sat at the kitchen table sharpening the blade of a knife on a whetstone, the scraping sound resonating under the corrugated tin roof. His brother hopped about the kitchen, changing into a wombat and then a wallaby, and then back to a little boy with a cloth doll his mother had made him. It hung from his mouth by it's rag arm. Monaro wiped honey from his lips with the back of his hand, stood and cocked his head and listened for the trumpeting of the witchdoctor's didgeridoo and sighed loudly when he heard nothing but the sound of his own breathing leaving his lungs like gusts of wind.

"Who is it you listen for so impatiently?" his father asked.

Monaro remained silent about the witchdoctor. The witchdoctor had appeared in his dreams for weeks and cautioned him to not to speak of his existence. "I'm anxious to begin," he said.

His mother handed him his rucksack and kissed him on the cheek. His father gave him the knife and patted him soundly on the back. His little brother turned into a silvereye and flew around the room, chirping merrily. Monaro left the kitchen, walked through the small house to the front door and stood at the screen door for several minutes before stepping out into the reddish dirt. The empty cups and paper plates smeared with the remnants of grilled fish, and other bits of debris left over from the ceremonies and celebration held the night before by his family and friends, rolled about in the dirt, turned into ulysses butterflies, rose into the air and were carried away by the hot wind. He inhaled the succulently- sweet scent of cowslip orchids that grew wild around the house. His mother tended them like a gardener, softly kissing each new yellow and red bloom, inviting the bees to drink the nectar of the flowers.

He slid the knife under his belt and placed the rucksack on his back. He could feel the Dreamtime calling to him, like an itch in the marrow in his bones. He walked fifteen feet from the house before he saw the witchdoctor standing in a patch of scrubgrass at the side of the dirt road.

"I was worried you wouldn't come," Monaro said to him.

The witchdoctor, thin as a reed, wearing only a cloth that covered his genitals, and barefoot, raised his didgeridoo, put his vibrating pursed lips to it, and created the sounds of a flock of brolga screeching raspily as he did several dance steps, kicking up the dirt, forming clouds around his ankles. Then he vanished, leaving behind wisps of smoke that turned to rainbows.

Monaro began his walkabout.

#

A week later, chewing on a biscuit, Monaro stood on the edge of a plain where boulders shaped like human heads dotted the landscape. The biscuit changed to water and he gulped it down, relishing the sensation of the cool liquid soothing his parched throat. When eyes on the boulders opened and looked at him, he glanced up at the sun that seemed to fill the entire sky and regretted that he wasn't wearing a hat. He looked back at the boulders whose eyes had closed and turned to the witchdoctor who stood beside him whispering into the ear of a yellow spotted gecko he held in the palm of his hand.

"I'm sorry to interrupt you, Witchdoctor, but are these my ancestors?" he asked, pointing at the boulders, "or just the sun playing tricks on me."

The witchdoctor lowered the gecko to the ground where it instantly grew ten foot tall. "Everything is your ancestors," he said. His voice was like an echo from deep within a cave. "Your life and all that is in it, and everything and everyone that came before you springs from the Dreamtime."

Monaro contemplatively ran his fingers through his curly black hair, but pulled his hand away when the curls began to wrap around his fingers like the web of a redback spider. He looked out at the boulders again. Their eyes were still closed but they displayed inscrutable grins. "I know of the Dreamtime as all of my people do," he said, "but I can't explain it."

"The Dreamtime explains itself," the witchdoctor said. He patted the gecko, turning it back to its normal size.

#

Days later, early in the morning while the weather was cooler, Monaro followed the trail of a red fox that he had tracked with no real purpose, but was driven by the fox's scent. He trotted at a slow and steady pace through the scrubland, exhaling breaths filled with images of ancient, mountainous landscapes.

Following close behind, the witchdoctor chided Monaro. "Don't squander the purpose of your walkabout," he said.

Monaro stopped and scanned the horizon. Castlle-like sandstone formations baked in the rays of the slowly rising sun. He bent down, scooped up a handful of dirt, and tossed it into the air. The wind carried it to the horizon where it dropped to the earth and quickly grew into a hill.

"What should I learn from that?" he asked.

The witchdoctor lifted his didgeridoo to his lips, but before vocalizing into it, he asked, "What would you like to learn?"

Monaro looked up and watched two eagles dance a pas de deux in the sky. "If everything was created in the Dreamtime, what came before the Dreamtime?"

The fox stuck its head out from behind a lone acacia tree that stood surrounded by barren soil. It then stepped out into the open and turned into a young woman with long red hair that stuck out from her head like the vines of the outback sunrise plant. Her naked body glistened with beads of perspiration where fish swam inside each one and sunlight sparkled on their surfaces.

Mesmerized, Monaro called out to her. "Who are you?"

The witchdoctor made his didgeridoo disappear and then turned himself into a frilled-neck lizard.

"I'm Julunggul," the young woman said. "I've come to see that your initiation is complete."

"Initiation into what?" Monaro asked.

"Manhood," Julunggul replied. "Your witchdoctor may lead you the wrong direction."

The witchdoctor – the lizard – expanded his frill, raised his tail above his body and opened his mouth in an aggressive manner. "Be wary of the cunning fox," he hissed.

"I'm making my own path. The witchdoctor is along only as my teacher and spirit guide, " Monaro told her.

She raised her hands, pointed her ringed fingers at him and blinded him with rays of sunlight she cast from her fingertips. "We shall see what we shall see," she cooed like a dove, and then turned back into a fox. She then ran for the cover afforded by the tall grass in a nearby meadow.

In that instant Monaro changed into a fox also and chased after her.

#

Four days later Monaro awoke on the bank of a billabong that sat in the midst of a grove of tall callitris trees. He stretched, enjoying the softness of the moss beneath his bare flesh. Daydreams of when he was a much younger boy and sat on the riverbank beside his father and listened to stories passed down through his family for unknown numbers of generations floated through his mind like drifting clouds. The stories of when the white man first appeared, bringing with them disease and their strange ways, with no interest in the Dreamtime, had frightened him. Hearing a splash in the billabong, he sat up and saw the witchdoctor coming across the water, standing on the back of a crocodile. Monaro brushed red fox hairs from his skin and stood up.

At the bank, the witchdoctor stepped off the crocodile and threw Monaro's rucksack, clothes and boots onto the moss where Monaro stood as the crocodile turned and sank beneath the surface. "Did you learn anything from the she-fox I couldn't have taught you?" he asked.

Monaro smiled broadly. "Many things," he answered with a chuckle. "Some things about manhood can't be taught by a witchdoctor." He put on his clothes and boots and took a biscuit from the rucksack and put it in his mouth. When he bit into it his mouth filled with the pulp of the quandong fruit. He secured his father's knife in his belt, put the rucksack on his back, and faced the direction of the setting sun. "Does the Dreamtime lie in that direction?" he asked.

"It lies in all directions, but in no direction at all," the witchdoctor answered.

"There are a few hours left for walking in the coolness of twilight and the birth of moonlight," Monaro said as he began walking.

The witchdoctor raised the didgeridoo to his lips and made the sound of dingoes offering their staccato barks to the coming night. Fireflies gathered around his feet, preparing to light the way before the onset of darkness as he began to follow behind Monaro.

#

A week later, during the hottest time of the day, Monaro sat in the shade of a she-oak tree and scraped a piece of the bark with his knife, digging away the resin, and placing it on his tongue and swishing it around in his mouth before swallowing. The cones that clung to the tree's branches sang a yiri, a song about the Dreamtime, their almost syllabic vocalizing describing the rock formations that were nearby and had always been there since the dawn of the Dreamtime. Monaro had been taught a similar yiri by his grandfather so he hummed along as he fed on the tree's pulp.

The witchdoctor sat on a large rock a few yards away, luring several emu to him with seeds that jumped about in the palm of his hand. "These emu are your ancestors," he said to Monaro.

Monaro gazed thoughtfully at the emu. "How can that be, they are still living things?"

"Death of the body, the passing of your ancestors, is not the death of their spirits. The spirit of all things is renewed over and over as it has always been since the Dreamtime."

"When I die will my spirit come back to live in an emu?"

"Why ask about your spirit being renewed as an emu? The spirit of a rock is just as worthy," the witchdoctor said.

Monaro glanced at the rock formations and tried to imagine being part of them, being a rock, but thoughts of remaining still for so long made him feel uneasy. He tossed aside the piece of bark and slipped the knife into his belt. He leaned back against the tree and thought about home. He had never been away from it for more than a few days and he missed his family terribly. His parents had waited until he was almost beyond the age for a boy to go a walkabout, waiting until they too were prepared for him to be away for the time it would take to complete his journey. He closed his eyes and sedated by the heat, quickly drifted off to sleep.

He dreamt he was wearing the magic kangaroo skin while floating above a desert of bright red sand. Apparitions rose out of the sand, their hands reaching out to him, their mouths open wide, revealing a darkness like looking into the bottom of a well. The witchdoctor suddenly appeared, his didgeridoo to his lips, creating the sound of swarming bees as he drove the ghosts back into the ground. Monaro awoke drenched in sweat. Nothing in his body hurt, but he didn't feel well.

The witchdoctor stood over him, blocking the sun. "Your father is very ill and you must go to him right away," the witchdoctor said.

"How can I do that?" Monaro replied. "I've walked many miles away from home and getting back will take many days."

The witchdoctor laid his hand on Monaro's feverish forehead. "Form a picture in your mind of your father," he said.

Monaro closed his eyes. He thought of his father, a short, stout man with a hearty laugh and eyes that sparkled when he talked. Monaro pictured his father sitting on the river bank gutting trout with the knife he had given him. His father loved to fish.

#

"Remember, Monaro, no two fish are exactly the same, there are differences in the scales in every fish that ever swam in any water, and that is true going all the way back to the Dreamtime," his father said.

Clasping his father's hand, Monaro watched a water spider that lay on its back using its long legs to juggle air bubbles sent to the river's surface by fish resting on the bottom. "You're not well, Baba. Now is not the time for fishing," he said.

Using his free hand his father raised his spear above his head and aimed it at a shadow swimming just below the surface of the sunlit water. "It's always time for fishing," he said. He threw the spear and as the line that connected his father's wrist to the spear unfurled it turned into a branch from a wattle tree crowded with the blooms of golden wattles.

"But I've returned home to help you get well," Monaro said.

"Nonsense," his father said as he pulled in his spear. "You must complete your walkabout." A shadow in the shape of a fish dangled on the end of the spear.

"I worry you will not be here when I return, Baba," Monaro said.

His father pulled his hand free of his son's hand and lay the spear on the ground where the shadow thrashed about on a bed of spongy moss. "Remember what the witchdoctor has been teaching you," he said. "If my body is not here when you return look for my spirit in the rocks, plants or animals that you see for the rest of your days."

"Yes, Baba," Monaro replied. "How did you know about the witchdoctor?"

"We all have a witchdoctor with us when we need one."

#

Monaro worried that the kangaroos feeding in the meadow of lush grass that stood alongside a billabong would catch scent of the magic kangaroo skin that he wore in his dreams. Kangaroos could be very dangerous and kill a man with a single kick from their powerful legs. Many of those he was watching were does that had a joey standing nearby, which made the does even more aggressive than usual. When he was five he had been cornered in the front yard of their house by a large buck. His mother ran out of the house holding a pan of boiling water that she threw on it. Scalded, it ran off and never returned. It was that night that he had the first dream where he wore the kangaroo skin. His fear of them – albeit a sensible one – remained with him.

The witchdoctor was standing a few feet behind him. "You must go through them or around them, those are your only choices," he said as he shifted his didgeridoo from one shoulder to the other.

"Can't you make some sound that will frighten them off?"

"I wasn't given the gift of my magic to be used for scaring kangaroo."

A yellow-striped dragonfly appeared in front of Monaro's face and hovered there, staring at him intently through its large red eyes that resembled Christmas ornaments. Monaro waved his hand at it, causing the dragonfly to sink its razor-sharp teeth into one of his fingers. Monaro let out a yelp. The dragonfly flew off, with Monaro's blood dripping from its mouth.

"What's wrong now?" the witchdoctor asked.

"A dragonfly just . . ." he started and then looked at his finger which had no marks on it. "Never mind." He took his rucksack from his back, opened it, and fished around in the bottom for the last of the biscuits. He pulled one out and was about to take a bite of it when an idea struck him. He took out the last biscuits, returned the rucksack to his back, and then strode confidently through the kangaroos handing out pieces of biscuit to any advancing kangaroo. When he got to the other side of the meadow he turned to see the witchdoctor still standing where he had been, his mouth agape.

"I can always count on Mam," Monaro said before he turned and strode off toward an open plain.

#

A streak of lightning zigzagged across the night sky, slicing it in two. Monaro thought about the bathroom mirror and put his hand to his face. It didn't feel any different than how it felt before he began his walkabout. Sitting against a boulder, his back warmed by the heat stored in it from a day in the sun, unsuccessfully he tried to count on his fingers the number of days, or weeks, he had been away from home. "I've lost track of the days and nights I've been on my walkabout," he said to the witchdoctor who was sitting close to the campfire built in a pit in the dirt and intently watching the flames lick at a fish cooking on a spit built over the fire.

"Knowing the number of days and nights you have been away won't get you back home any sooner," the witchdoctor said.

Thunder rolled across the landscape. Monaro's head was filled with questions about the Dreamtime that he thought he should be able to answer, but there was still so much still unanswered. "Why does a man only go on one walkabout in his lifetime," he asked.

"Life for any man is nothing but a never-ending walkabout," the witchdoctor answered. "The first one is about teaching you how to think about the Dreamtime." He poked at the fish with a long twig.

Monaro leaned his head back against the rock. "Right now all I can think about is my father."

The witchdoctor removed the fish from the fire and placed it on a flat stone. He pulled a piece of it from the spit and handed it to Monaro. "To answer your question, you're only two days away from your home."

#

Before sunrise, in the cool aftermath of a rainstorm, Monaro began a slow trot across the usually arid plain. As he had done for most of the walkabout, he had his boots hanging around his neck. They thumped gently against his chest.

"Shoes should only be worn if you have no use for the soil from which all things spring and to which all things return, as it has been since the Dreamtime," the witchdoctor told him. "Do you understand?"

"Yes, I understand," Monaro replied. He didn't tell the witchdoctor that he preferred going barefoot because his boots caused blisters on his ankles, not because being barefoot gave him a better understanding of the Dreamtime.

The ground beneath his bare feet was wet but hard, as if incapable of being turned into mud. He looked at the land that stretched out in front of him and cast a wish-spell on it, hoping he didn't step on any thorns or into a hole. The loop that the witchdoctor had taken him on had half-circled this piece of remote landscape, but now they cut across it in order for Monaro to return home sooner. The witchdoctor followed behind, floating over the ground, his feet never touching the earth. It was sunrise before Monaro stopped and stood on the bank of the river opposite the bank from where his father liked to fish. He waded into the river and then swam across to the other side. When he came out of the water he saw that the witchdoctor was still on the other bank.

The witchdoctor raised his didgeridoo to his lips sending birdsong and then the sound of flapping wings into the air and across the river. Then he vanished.

Monaro ran the rest of the way home. His father was in bed and near death. His breathing was labored and shallow. Fish shadows swam on the blanket that covered him. Monaro knelt beside the bed and grasped his father's hand. "I'm home, Baba. Would you like me to tell you about the Dreamtime?" he asked, softly.

"Yes, my son," his father answered, "tell me everything you have learned."

"In the beginning there was the Dreamtime . . ."

The End

8

MADO KARA MIERU

Aika sat beneath the blossoming boughs of a cherry tree catching falling petals in the palms of her outstretched hands. Her lips trembled as she hummed a tune of her own creation. It was as light and lovely as the gentle breeze that kissed her cheeks, an expression of joy, a celebratory song of reaching her tenth birthday. The bright red kimono she wore was a birthday present sent to her by her sobo who lived in Fukushima, a city she heard her parents talk about, but had never been there herself. She imagined that any place where a kimono as beautiful as the one given to her by sobo could be bought must be a wonderful place to live, a magical place with Shinto shrines in the clouds and where streams filled with speckled amago flowed from the rocks. She had not seen her sobo in three years but remembered her mother's mother because of the pale pink powder she wore on her face and the long length of her silvery fingernails. She also remembered her sobo's hugs because they were warm and protective, like being on a futon and ensconced in woolen mōfu.

#

Kasumi found the blooming of the cherry trees slightly annoying. Although beautiful, they also reminded her of her boyfriend, Haruo. He talked endlessly of love, wrote notebooks filled with romantic poetry, and more than once said, "When the cherry trees blossom it is the season for the man to declare his love for the girl he wants to spend his life with." Yet, the trees had begun to bloom four days before and Haruo was nowhere to be found. Her calls and texts had gone unanswered and her *casual walks* at sunset on the opposite side of the street of his apartment building had gone without seeing light in the window of his apartment. She considered knocking on his door, but in her head her mother's voice warned, *that kind of behavior will only bring dishonor.* Kasumi had no problem with old fashioned ideas, but she hated feeling obligated to live by them. Her clothing, choice of movies, dancing, and how she decorated her apartment were all modern. No one in her circle of girlfriends even talked about dishonor.

Having passed by Haruo's apartment building, slowing her jogging down to a turtle's speed to hopefully catch him or his shadow in the window of his apartment, she sped on with renewed velocity and frustration, as a block from his building she entered Omoiyari Park. Here the cherry trees were well manicured and abundant. The pink petals from the blossoms floated in the air like large flakes of snow. The park was filled with their subtle, sweet fragrance.

It was only when she heard Aika's humming that she came to a stop. She glanced over at the little girl seated under a cherry tree and wondered why she hadn't heard that melody before. It was astonishingly simple yet captivating; a tune any serious pianist should know. She memorized it, and then ran on.

#

In her kitchen, Masako, stared out the window above her sink. The sight of the cherry trees in full bloom made her cry. Things of beauty always had that effect on her.

"You're too sensitive," her husband had told her on several occasions.

She didn't need to be told that. Growing up in a home where art, music, poetry and architecture were regarded with the same intensity as a profound religious experience caused her to be overly-emotional; she had been raised to wear her feelings on her sleeves.

From the living room, her student, Kasumi, was playing the Alla Turca from Mozart's Sonata No. 11 and doing a bad job of it. She had agreed to take her on as a student despite the fact that Kasumi didn't have the skill that most of her students had only because Kasumi's parents were paying her additional money to teach their daughter. Kasumi didn't know about it and Masako wouldn't have accepted their bribe, or Kasumi as as a student, had her husband not needed costly plastic surgery to remove the burn scars on his face that the public health insurance wouldn't cover. She had warned her husband the day he bought the fireworks that nothing good would come from it. Her husband knew nothing about her plans for the money.

She cringed when Kasumi hit another wrong key. She thought, *after playing piano for so many years, how is that even possible?*

The tea kettle whistled. She turned from the window, went to the stove and turned off the burner. She poured tea into two cups and placed them on a tray along with a small plate piled with a mound of mochi rice cakes. She picked up the tray and was about to go into the living room when she heard Kasumi stop playing the Mozart piece and begin playing a melody she had never heard before; a stunningly harmonic piece that was lilting, playful and yet profoundly rich musically. She went to the doorway between the kitchen and the living room and listened to what Kasumi was playing. Her young student's posture was perfect; something that was also usually problematic. Her fingers were dancing across the keys as if being guided by the hands of bunraku puppet masters.

She closed her eyes, focusing on the notes being played. Tears began to stream down her face.

#

Handed the basket of small branches clipped from a cherry tree, Chiyo, observed the delicacy of the petals of the blossoms, likening them to whispers, softly said words of affection.

"You were napping Chiyo-san and your friend, Masako, didn't want to disturb you but she left them for you," the nurse, Yui, said.

"The flowers are pretty enough to eat, like something that should be savored on the tongue, aren't they?"

"Yes, Chiyo-san."

Chiyo placed the basket in her lap, swiveled her wheelchair around and headed back down the hall to her room. The fragrance of the cherry blossoms filled her nostrils with the faint scents of rose, almond and vanilla. She passed by several other residents of the ydrdin who smiled at her, at the branches in the basket, at themselves for enjoying the moment. She pushed open the door of her room using her foot rests and wheeled in, immediately spotting where she would place the basket, on top of a stack of books that contained the works of her favorite poets, Matsuo Bashō, Ihara Saikaku and Kenji Miyazawa. "Visual poetry on written poetry," she murmured. She hoped that some day she too would be remembered for something as one remembers springtime for the blossoming of the cherry trees or for words written with a poet's flourish. It was then she saw a card inserted in the branches. She gently lifted it out and read it:

My dearest Chiyo-san, today I was presented with an amazing surprise and unintended gift of never heard before music. It was poetry for my soul.

Masako

# # #

Lightly falling rain on the blue, red and pink hydrangeas made them glow, adding spots of vibrant color to Aika's watercolor. The hydrangeas seemed to be a happy flower, their thick, bulbous blooms, like heads of fantastical creatures, all laughing in harmony. From her painting, they cheered her as she feared the Summer Festival would be canceled because of the rain. From through the window in her bedroom, she looked out at the colorful shrubs in her backyard as she dipped the paintbrush in the color pigment,then into a small dish of water, and then applied the mixture to the paper. It was attached to a small easel, a Christmas gift from her sobo. As she painted she sang a warabe uta she had learned in an earlier grade in school.

"Acorn is rolling, then he goes splash
Into the pond. Oh what to do?
Loach comes swimming, "Hi, how are you?
Let's play together, little acorn boy."

After a few more dabs and strokes of color she set the paint brush aside and picked up the blow dryer, switched it on and aimed it at the painting, hoping it would be dry and ready to be sold at the festival, if the festival opened at noon as scheduled.

#

Kasumi hadn't fully come to terms with what about Haruo made her the angriest: that he had moved to Kyoto to marry another girl without telling her beforehand, or that he chose to tell her in an email. Her only consolation was that her parents didn't berate her for mourning the loss of a guy who, as they had already told her, "Was unworthy of her." They attempted to fill the void left by Haruo's departure by arranging several dates with young men who they did feel were worthy who were from families they knew socially. Kakuji, the arranged date to the Summer Festival was studying to be an attorney which from the time they entered the city streets where the festival was being held was all he talked about, incessantly. Within twenty minutes of meeting him she learned how to drown him out by engaging the vendors at the various arts and crafts booths in meaningless banter. She had no real interest in any art, other than the art of playing the piano, although she was beginning to doubt if she had a future as a pianist. Her private teacher, Masako Sato, had become increasingly displeased with her playing, sometimes bordering on being insulting. Masako Sato was the most respected piano teacher in their prefecture, whose status made Kasumi often wonder why she had been taken on as her student. Kasumi knew her talent for playing the piano was limited, to say the least. It had started out as, and remained, her parent's ambition for her, not her own. She continued to play to please them, and to try to please Masako Sato. She attended university also, but hadn't yet found her place there either.

At a booth where watercolor paintings were being sold, she spotted one of hydrangeas that she thought was very pretty. She looked at it closely and saw the name Aika written in the lower right hand corner.

"Who is this artist?" she asked the woman behind the table sorting money.

"My daughter," the woman replied. "She has gone to buy some mizu ame. She has a sweet tooth. She'll be back soon."

"I would like to buy it now if that is okay?"

"Certainly."

Minutes later Kasumi walked away from the table with the painting rolled up and wrapped in tissue paper while her date followed behind, talking non-stop.

#

Moments after opening her door, Masako was handed a rolled paper covered in tissue paper by her least talented student, Kasumi. She liked the girl although she thought she was a bit scattered and a little immature.

"For me?" Masako said, blushing.

"I know you like beautiful things," Kasumi said. "Open it. I picked it up at the Summer Festival yesterday. Did you go?"

She began to unwrap the gift. "No, my husband and I spent the day seeing the hydrangea garden display in Omoiyari Park."

"I went to the festival with another date arranged by my parents," Kasumi said, heaving a loud sigh.

Every time Kasumi mentioned her parents, Masako felt guilty. She felt she should never have accepted the bargain with them in the first place, but she was getting closer to having the large amount she needed for her husband's surgery.

She tossed aside the tissue paper and unrolled the painting. She gasped, stared at it for several moments, and then began to weep from the beauty of seeing such a masterful work of art.

#

Sitting at the window of the dayroom, Chiyo looked out at the clusters of pale blue hydrangeas that grew out of the shrubs growing along the wooden fence of the back lawn. That shade of blue was her favorite color. The morning rain shower from the day before had left the hydrangeas looking healthier and plumper than they had looked for several weeks, as if the rain had quenched their thirst and left them satiated. She sipped on a cup of tea that Yui had just given her, gently advising her to drink it slowly.

"Chiyo-san is always in a hurry," the nurse said, stifling a giggle.

"I'm too close to death to slow down now," Chiyo replied. "My time not to hurry was when I was young."

"Chiyo-san will live forever," Yui replied.

Just as she knew that the season of the hydrangeas was relatively short, she knew her own time was growing short also, but what the nurse said was nice to hear nevertheless.

When the familiar hand of her friend, Masako, rested on her shoulder, she looked up at her and smiled.

"I've brought you a gift," Masako said as she unrolled the painting. "My worst student gave it to me, but I think you should have it to hang up in your room."

"Thank you, Masako, it's lovely," the old woman said as she gazed at the piece of art. She then leaned closer to it, and squinting, read Aika's name. "This Aika must have had years of training to produce such a work of art."

Standing nearby, Yui looked at the painting and smiled.

#

Aika danced kabuki-style through a meadow filled with chrysanthemums in Omoiyari Park. Her every movement conveyed an emotion beyond her years or experience. The way she bent her back, shifted her shoulders, bent her wrists, twisted her body, spun about, were all done in slow motion. Every movement of her head, skyward or toward the ground, were like the busts of Japanese sculptures. Her cheeks were flush with color.

The rose pink of her jacket sent to her by her sobo at the beginning of Autumn matched the color of the chrysanthemums. In the jacket pockets she carried different flavors of Kasugai gummy candy, each packet torn open at one end so that all she had to do was take one out and shake the candy directly into her mouth, which she did between every extended dance move; she was still a child after all. The strawberry gummy candy she was chewing stuck to her teeth and made her giggle as she tried to dislodge it with her tongue.

#

Jogging slowly on a path that bordered the meadow, Kasumi, stopped to watch the little girl, thinking she looked vaguely familiar, but couldn't place where she had seen her before. She thought, *how lithe, graceful, free of inhibitions, she is.* Dancing always made Kasumi uncomfortable, something she rarely did in a club when taken to one by a date. Haruo had once told her at a party where everyone was dancing that she danced like a startled flamingo which cemented her self-image as being clumsy with legs only fit for a bird. Despite trying not to, she thought about him a lot. She hoped he was as miserable as she was. Attempting to wipe him from her thoughts, she picked a chrysanthemum and inserted it into her hair behind her ear, watched Aika for a few minutes more, then jogged on.

#

With a chrysanthemum clenched between his teeth, Masako's husband curled his arm around her waist and guided her in a waltz around the kitchen. He was laughing joyously for no apparent reason.

He forgets his face is disfigured, she thought, dismayed and bewildered.

In the next room Kasumi was tinkling the keys, not working on the piano piece *Tre* by Kensuke Ushio that she had been assigned. When that stopped, and there was nothing but silence in the living room, Masako tried to pull away from her husband to go see what was wrong with Kasumi but he held her tight, kissing her softly on her neck.

Moments later Kasumi appeared in the kitchen doorway.

The husband and wife quickly separated. "What is it, Kasumi?" Masako asked, trying to hide her embarrassment. "Why have you stopped practicing?"

"I've made a decision Masako-san. I'm giving up playing the piano."

Thinking first of the money she still needed for her husband's plastic surgery, and then seeing the distressed look on Kasumi's face, she softly asked, with concern, "But why? You have put so many years into studying the piano."

"I'm going to have my ex-boyfriend's child."

Masako glanced down at the young woman's belly and noticed the slight bump and wondered how she hadn't noticed it before.

# # #

In the dayroom of the nursing facility where Chiyo lived, wearing her gray and white school uniform, Aika stood in front of the large glass doors that led out to the back lawn, now brightened by hundreds of daffodils that poked their yellow blossoms through a foot of snow. Flurries whirled about in the chilly breeze. Aika held to her lips the shakuhachi that had been passed down for several generations in her family. Her fingers ran up and down the holes in no specific order or pattern, the notes flying from the flute like chirping song birds that filled the hearts and minds of the home's residents who sat watching and listening with memories of warmer seasons.

Her mother, Yui, sat beside Chiyo, patting the old woman's hand in time to the shifting rhythms of the music Aika played.

"Your daughter's playing is magical, amazing,"Chiyo whispered to Yui.

"Thank you, Chiyo-san, Aika is a child with many gifts."

"How is it you never told me about her?" Chiyo asked.

"I would do nothing but brag, Chiyo-san," Yui answered, squeezing Chiyo's hand playfully.

"May I ask about her father, your husband?" Chiyo said, hesitantly and demurely.

"He died from cancer soon after Aika's birth. I have raised her on my own."

Chiyo turned her eyes to Aika. "I know someone who can further your daughter's musical talent if you'd allow me to make the introductions."

"That would be a blessing from Amaterasu-Ōmikami herselfm Chiyou-san. Thank you."

Aika raised the flute sending her music to the heavens.

#

In the hospital room, Kasumi lay in her bed, her baby cradled in her arms and drinking from her nipple. The vase of daffodils on the bedside stand lent the only color to the room. The card attached to them were from Masako, and signed, "With Love."

Her parents had kicked her out of their house as soon as she told them she was going to have Haruo's child. They continued to provide for her, including anything she needed to continue her studies at the university, but would have nothing to do with her beyond that.

She accepted it as her fate.

#

Masako had the bloom of a daffodil tucked into the bun in her hair, when her husband entered the living room and found her sitting at the piano, her fingers motionless on the keys. "Perhaps you should return to playing concerts," he said, coming up behind her and placing his hands affectionately on her shoulders."

She shook her head. "I've put all that behind me. My students . . .and Kasumi and her child . . .need me."

"You are now mother and grandmother all in one fell swoop," he said with a gentle laugh.

She turned on the stool and looked up at him. "Are you happy?"

"I'm with you. How could I not be?"

At that moment his scarred face was the most beautiful face in the world. Her eyes filled with tears.

#

Chiyo made a call to Masako. "I have a child I want you to meet. She has had no piano lessons yet, but I believe she may be a musical genius."

# # #

Alone for the first time on a train, going to visit her sobo, Aika saw the cherry trees through the window. They rained their petals down on the verdant spring grass. In her head she heard piano keys and scales.

\#

With her infant sound asleep, Kasumi looked through the nursery window to the garden she had planted in her apartment building court-yard surrounded by cherry trees. As a newly graduated horticulturalist it was her first accomplishment.

\#

Through the window of the kitchen, Masako looked out at the cherry tree blossoms. She felt better having returned to Kasumi's parents the extra money she had received from them.

\#

Chiyo placed her hand on the window pane and looked out at the cherry trees. Just before she took her last breath, she said, "That what you see through the window."

Mado kara mieru.

The End

9

FROZEN EARTH SONATA

This place, *this place,* where tall oak trees that border the fields shed the last rust-colored leaves of Autumn that blanket the earth shorn of hay, where the dry, dead leaves crackles under Gracie's footsteps, is soon to be the burial place of her beloved cat, Ginger. It is here, in *this place* where Gracie feels most detached from her home back in Ohio, disconnected from what defines her, as a member of a small community, as a school teacher just retired at age 67, that she wanders alone across a field, carrying the wooden pine box, built by her husband, Walt, that contains the body of Ginger.

Hanging tied to her belt is a small shovel. She hugs the box, the object she stubbornly refuses to think of as a coffin, close to her body. Though it's just imagined, and Gracie is well aware of it, she's giving warmth, her body heat, through the wood to her ginger-haired dead cat. Hours before, holding Ginger while allowing the vet to euthanize Ginger, was the hardest thing she ever had to do. Despite being told otherwise, and even after Ginger had become so ill from kidney disease in her last days that she could no longer stand, Gracie is convinced she murdered the one creature she vowed to never harm.

The air is crisp, full of moisture. It has brought a shiny, reddish blush to Gracie's cheeks, like buffed Red Delicious apples. She has stopped crying, sobbing, and wiped the tears from her face before leaving the cabin, but her tears, and her handkerchief, left her skin vulnerable to the elements. The leaves shaken from their tenuous grasp on the tree branches by the damp, steady breeze, flutter to the earth around her like wounded butterflies. Other than sounds she makes walking, it's silent. This is a place of quietude, only invaded intermittently by the barking of a dog from the nearest farm. The town in Ohio where Gracie spends most of her time – where she lives – with Walt, is also quiet, but not like this. There, in the town in Ohio, cars can be heard passing on the road in front of the house, and the shouts of children playing in the neighbor's yard frequently echo through the open windows. Gracie has often complained to Walt that it's too quiet here on this small farm where only hay is grown, that *this place* is like living in a cemetery. And now, in a bit of unintentional prophecy, she's looking for a place to bury Ginger.

Ahead, a single, small oak tree standing near the shallow manmade pond, replenished every spring with a small quantity of trout when its frozen water thaw, Walt lures the trout to their deaths with worms he digs from the ground and skewers on the hooks of his fishing pole. There beneath the tree's strong bows and beside its thick trunk is the place where Gracie decides Ginger should be laid to rest.

She sets the pine box on a pillow of leaves, unties the shovel from her belt, and uses it to brush aside leaves and twigs, revealing a nearly bald area of earth large enough in which to bury the box. She then begins to dig. In this place, *this place* that makes Gracie wish she were back home in Ohio with her friends and former students at her side, sharing this moment in laying Ginger to rest in a place there, perhaps in a spot where Ginger warmed her fur in the summer sun. She jabs the shovel in the ground, surprised that the ground is so hard even before winter has been officially declared. She thought it impossible that the ground would be frozen before the first frost of late Autumn had arrived, but the ground is so hard that it breaks her heart even more to think it was the place where she would place Ginger, an animal who had never experienced hardness or hardship during its sixteen years of life.

After some time, and sweating profusely, with the hole in the ground large enough for the box, she lifts it up and held in a tight embrace, kisses the lid, places it in the hole, and covers it with the dirt.

Carrying the shovel, with the breeze chillier, and the leaves on the ground and those that remained in the trees more agitated by the wind, and with her head bowed, she slowly walks back to the cabin and places the shovel against the door frame for Walt to clean. Inside, she throws two logs into the wood burning stove, stirs the bright red embers and ashes, and closes the door as flames ignite and swirl around the logs like multiple arms of a fiery creature. She removes her beige wool sweater, the one she knitted while attending Ladies knitting Club meetings in Ohio and hangs it on the coat rack, and then looks around the living room and over at the kitchen floor dreading collecting those things that belonged to Ginger.

Bereft, drained of emotion, as empty as the fish aquarium that still sits on a table in front of the window, its different colored pebbles still on the bottom like dull and faded jewels. Abandoned there by Walt who tired of transferring the fish back and forth between the cabin and their home in Ohio during their vacation jaunts to the farm. She takes her place on the sofa. Immediately the space beside her where Ginger always curled up beside

her, or stretched out, his front paws kneading the air, feels empty. So does her lap, where the cat's purrs would gently tremble through her skirt.

Then, Walt walks in, his heavy boots sending tremors throughout the room. He's a heavy man; everything about him his noisy, he carries loudness in his body. He fills every space he's in with that noise. Before retiring he worked in a concrete plant for forty years, running machinery and equipment that invaded Earth with its constant rumblings. He rumbles like a whirling concrete mixing drum.

He brings with him inside the cabin, the odors of the woods: tree bark, streams teeming with fish, wet earth. A dead beaver dangles from his meaty left hand.

"What did you do today?" he asks, his voice like sandpaper applied to the inner ear.

"I buried Ginger," she replies.

#

Snow flurries dance in the moonlit sky. It's beautiful to see, to witness, like watching a crime of wonderment being committed in front of her eyes, but Gracie only feels the cold that has filled the cabin, the space, *this space*, that is a prison from which she wishes to escape. She pulls tight around her shoulders the blue and pink knitted shawl the other ladies in the Ladies Knitting Club gave to her as a gift on the day she retired. The summer and fall since retiring sped by like a train heading through a dark tunnel. Nearby the burning logs put in the wood stove by Walt just before he lumbered off to bed crackles and snaps. She places her hand on the window and allows the condensation streak down from her palm print before removing it, staring at the wet lines that crisscross her palm, imagining they are tiny rivers that flow on in never-ending bad fortune.

Startled by a thump on the front door, she turns from the window, wipes her hand on her pale green nightgown, and stares at the door for several minutes, expecting it to open and seeing Ginger stride in, his fur and paws covered in dirt and frost. Turning to the closed bedroom door, the thought of waking Walt to see what made the thump sparks images of his confused, angry reactions when he's awoken from a deep sleep. Judging by his loud snoring, he was as buried in sleep as Ginger was buried in the hard ground. Tentatively approaching the door, the leather soles of her furry slippers sliding across the hardwood floor, she grabs Walt's industrial-sized long handled flashlight from the stand next to the door, and raising it as a weapon in readiness to hit an intruder on the head, she opens the door.

On the stoop just on the other side of the door, a large icicle that had broken free of the roof is stuck upright in the stoop, its pointed end buried deep into the wood, like an arrow shot into a target. She thinks, *Had anyone been under it they would most certainly have been killed.* A blast of cold air makes her look up, then she sees it, the thin layer of snow that carpets the landscape caught in the moonlight, sparkling like frozen teardrops that have fallen from the heavens. Her gasp is audible as she clutches her throat as if being strangled by the beauty of the scene. She steps back and grabs Walt's hunting jacket from the coat rack, puts it on, and swallowed by the large volume of heavy material that smells of hickory smoke, fish and dried deer blood, she pulls the door closed and walks away from the cabin, away from the safety of the space she never leaves after nightfall. There is light in this darkness. She slowly walks into it.

Quickly caught in a swirl of snowflakes, some attach to her face and instantly melt there, extinguished like candle flames snuffed out between two fingers. Gracie stands still, allowing the snow to bathe her in the damp cold and the moonlight to wash over her in iridescent warmth. Her breath forms small clouds with every exhalation as she surveys the surrounding landscape that is glazed with crystalline snow. Icicle earrings hang suspended from the branches of the trees that surround the farm, standing bare of leaves and seeming more rooted to the frozen earth than in warmer weather where they appear prepared to walk away in search of more fertile ground. Drawn to the tree where Ginger is buried, she walks on, the icy snow splintering beneath her slippers. There, she circles the tree trunk several times, kicking aside the drifting snow, unable to find the cat's last resting place. She thinks, *maybe the next thaw,* and walks away and heads toward the pond. Walt's large bootprints are still barely discernible just beneath the glistening coating of ice that marks his path to the pond. She knows he hadn't gone fishing that day and wonders aloud, muttering, "What reason did he have to go to the pond?"

Even before she gets to it, she can smell it. To her the pond has always had the scent of algae and the trout that live in it during warmer climates. By winter, Walt has fished most of them out. Those few left are trapped in the in the ice, frozen there like ice sculptures. She approaches it slowly and carefully; it's coated with snow, blurring the bank and the edge of the pond. There she sees Walt's bootprints go both directions, coming and going. *He was circling the pond,* she thinks. *But why? He knows there are no live fish left in it.* She turns and walks back to the cabin.

Inside she takes his coat off and hangs it on the coat rack. The fire inside the stove is still going strong. She opens the stove door and with her hands held near the burning logs, she rubs them, warming them. Walt's snoring rumbles through the cabin reminding her that she's not alone. This time, while he's asleep, is when he is the least silent; he tells her so little, giving little verbal indication of where he goes or what he does while they stay at the cabin. In *this space* she is mostly invisible to him. They don't talk about his fishing, or hunting, about his feelings, or about his thoughts about her, or her feelings, about anything. It's this last thing, her feelings, that she becomes most uncertain of. She wishes she had her friends from Ohio around to talk to them about her feelings, to validate them, to validate her.

#

The dirt road to the town nearest to the farm is muddy. Spring thaw has turned most of the earth to varying stages of liquification, from puddles to mud. Each time the tires get stuck, the mud acting like an adhesive that results in them spinning and bringing the movement forward to a halt, Walt slams his fist down on the steering wheel, cursing loudly. He gets out of the car, and in his boots he slogs through the mud to the back of the car and pushes the vehicle as Gracie gets behind the wheel and takes control of the pedals, stick shift and steering wheel. It's one of the few times during the time they've been away from Ohio he's allowed her to manage anything other than cooking and keeping the cabin clean. The last time after the car gets stuck just before reaching the paved road leading to town, he kicks off the mud that clung to his boots and returns to his place behind the wheel, and shoves Gracie back into her place in the passenger seat. She says nothing about the pain –

physical and emotional – being manhandled by him causes her. It's the kind of abuse that takes place nowhere else, only here, in *this here,* the here that wasn't Ohio. In Ohio she always feels safe.

The remainder of the ride into town she sits in stony silence and stares out the passenger-side window, musing how nothing ever changes here; houses never receive fresh coats of paint and the same clothes hang from the same clotheslines. She thought clotheslines were a thing of the past. Even everyone in her small town in Ohio had clothes dryers. Seeing so few people in their yards or on their front porch, makes her wonder, *What are they all hiding from?*

Entering the business area of town, Gracie turns her head to watch out the front window, aware that she and Walt haven't spoken to one another since he pushed her. Both sides of the street are lined with booths and stalls where pedestrians are walking from one to the next. Brightly colored ribbon is wrapped around the telephone wires and poles. The store awnings have all been withdrawn allowing the spring sunlight to shine on the sidewalks.

"Looks like there's some kind of street festival going on," she says.

"Yep."

"I'd like to get out and take a look at what they're selling at a few of the booths."

"Why?"

"Because I want to," she screams. *She screamed it.* Her voice filled the car, taking up the space previously filled by molecules. "Stop this car, now!" she screams. *Another scream.*

He slams on the brake, bringing the car to a screeching stop.

She opens her door and gets out, taking the air, and molecules, from the inside of the car with her and slams the door closed. If he immediately drove away or watched her walk away, she couldn't have said. She had disconnected from him in a way she rarely did.

The first thing she notices as she begins to walk along the line of booths and stalls isn't what is being sold, but the faces of the vendors or the other pedestrians. Their expressions are dour. There is no festivity in this festival. She doesn't recognize a single one of them. It's a market devoid of familiarity. She feels lost, adrift as a stranger in a small river of strangers, afloat amidst a gently flowing current of unfamiliarity. There's nothing to latch onto, nothing that defines her, or defines the location she is walking through. There is no here, here. She suddenly wants Walt to be nearby. She needs him to keep from drifting toward total obscurity.

When a Styrofoam cup is blown down the street by a moist breeze, she turns and watches it, thinking how much its color is that of snow. The thought sends a chill down her spine. Before she walks on, a female vendor with snow-white hair and lifeless blue eyes holds out a handmade apron patterned with toddlers chasing butterflies that is exactly like the other dozen stacked on the counter. "Something every grandmother should have," the female vendor says. Gracie gives fleeting thought to explaining why she and Walt never had children, but recalls it's something she has only shared with the women in the Ladies Knitting Club because they knew her and understood that Walt didn't want children. They knew Walt. They also *knew about Walt.* Sharing it anywhere else, especially here, *this here*, with women not in the knitting club diminished the importance of those women, and they were very important, especially when they seemed so very far away. "No, thank you," she replies and walks on.

At the end of the street a man selling snow cones holds one up and asks, "Want one? Only seventy-five cents."

She looks at the shaved ice in the white paper cone and wants to laugh at the absurdity of the moment, the absurdity of winter being offered in a cup. She wants to laugh, but doesn't.

Walt pulls up in the car and rolls down the window. "Time to go home," he says. "Back to Ohio."

The End

10

THE CLAY POT

The wind that swept across the Mongolian steppe carried with it sleet and snow flurries that melted as soon as it hit the grass that carpeted the rolling hills. The camels, horses and cattle that Nachin had crowded in the small corral not far from the ger shuffled about uneasily, not being used to defending themselves against such harsh weather or being penned in with one another. At the opened doorway of the ger, Nachin scanned the horizon, watching for sight of his older brother, Zhanzhin, to come riding over the hill on his horse. The fading light of twilight had darkened the landscape. The howls of a pack of wolves that had recently taken up residence in the distant hills echoed across the steppe.

"Come inside and shut the door. Zhanzhin may have stopped for the night at a neighbor's ger," his wife, Odsar, said from where she sat on their bed. She was holding on her lap their six year-old son, Erden. The boy was fidgeting, restless after being held to keep him from joining his father at the opened door where cold air rushed in.

"It's not like him to not be here in time for grandmother's birthday," Nachin replied. "He said in his last letter he would bring her something special from Ulaanbaatar."

Odsar looked over at the grandmother, Sarnai, who sat next to the stove, threading a piece of yarn through a tear in one of her blankets. The old woman's arthritic fingers trembled as she attempted to pull on the yarn.

"Your *emee* has forgotten that tomorrow is her birthday," Odsar said. "Please, Nachin, close the door. It is getting cold in here. Zhanzhin will get here when he gets here."

Nachin gave a last nervous glance toward the darkness creeping over the hills, sighed heavily, and then shut the door. He removed his gloves and boots and placed them on the straw mat with everyone else's boots and shoes beside the door .

Released from his mother's grasp, Erden, slid down from his mother's lap and ran to his father. "Did you put Altandöl in his bed?"

Nachin scooped the boy into his arms and lifted him. "Yes, son, your beloved pony is with his mother and they are both safe and warm with the rest of our animals."

The boy hugged his father's neck. "Thank you, *Aavaa*." He then quickly pulled back, suddenly impatient to be let back down. "Tomorrow I will ride Altandöl all the way to the city."

"Such a far distance my little, Erden?" Nachin said as he set the boy down and watched as he ran across the ger to his bed of blankets that lay on the floor and jumped onto it.

Before lying down, Erden kicked at the small mound of stuffed animals beside his bed, uncovering a monkey. He picked it up, and hugging it close to his chest, laid down. Making the gangly legs and arms of the monkey dance in the air for a moment and then saw his father raise the flap over the window on the door and peer out. "*Aavaa*, are the wolves going to eat Uncle Zhanzhin?" he said.

Odsar rose from the bed. "Of course not, Erden," she said. "The tough meat on your uncle's bones does not appeal to wolves." She put two pieces of damp wood in the stove and stood back as the fire snapped and popped.

Sarnai bit through the strand of yarn, breaking it in two, and tied the end. "I'll be seventy-four tomorrow," she said, giving Odsar a sideways withering glance.

#

At the break of dawn, Odsar wiggled her body away from Nachin's arms that encircled her and climbed from the bed, went to the stove, and threw in a few pieces of wood into the ashes. She lit the wood with a match and as flames rose from the wood she shut the oven door that closed with a metallic clang.

"Is that you, Zhanzhin?" Sarnai asked, rising up from her mat, staring bleary-eyed into the dim light inside the ger.

"It's just me, Sarnai. Zhanzhin hasn't arrived yet," Odsar said. "Sleep a little longer. If Zhanzhin arrives I'll be sure to waken you." She watched the old woman lie back down and then went to the door, raised the flap, and stared out at the mist that shrouded the hills and the yard that surrounded the ger. The animals in the corral were motionless, as if frozen in place. "Such strange weather," she mumbled under her breath. The freak blizzard that had killed most of their livestock two years before still weighed heavily on her mind. There was talk on the radio of the climate changing, but she had no idea what it meant.

She lowered the flap, turned, and scanned the ger, seeking out the gifts on the shelves that Zhanzhin had brought her each time he returned from the capital. The assortment of items he had given her – small statues, postcards, porcelain cups, colorful candles – didn't amount to much, but she treasured them. Her husband had no money to buy such frivolous things. She turned when she heard the patter of Erden's bare feet on the wood floor. The boy rushed to the tin pot kept in a corner not far from his bed, pushed down his britches and peed into it. Soon he would be old enough to venture out alone during the night and early morning to use the outhouse just like the adults did. When finished he ran to his mother and wrapped his arms around her legs.

"May I go out to see Altandöl?" he said.

She ran her fingers through his thick hair. "Not now," she said. "Later when it's warmer and after Zhanzhin has arrived. You can show your new pony to your uncle."

The boy's lower lip drooped. "Maybe Altandöl has forgotten me."

"That will never happen," she said. "Now go back to bed." She turned him about, affectionately patted his bottom and urged him toward the direction of his bed. When he settled onto his blanket, she filled the tea kettle with water and placed it on the stove. Minutes later she heard the beating of horse's hooves on the ground not far from the ger. She ran to the door, raised the flap and looked out the window. "Zhanzhin is here," she shouted excitedly.

#

Odsar, Nachin and Erden sat in a semi-circle on the floor, each with their eyes glued on the object wrapped in bright yellow tissue paper that Sarnai held in her lap. She was seated in one of the two chairs in the ger, next to Zhanzhin, who sat in the other chair. Her hands shook as she undid the bright red string that was tied around the wrapping. Her fingers trembled as she peeled away the layers of tissue paper. At last and with a great deal of emotion she held in her hands a clay pot that was painted bright red and decorated with images of the eight symbols of Buddhism in gold leaf and white paint. Tears flowed down the grandmother's cheeks as she held the pot up, showing it to each member of the family.

"I bought it at the finest gift shop in all of Ulaanbaatar," Zhanzhin said announced, his cheeks reddened with pride.

"It's the most beautiful pot I've ever seen," Nachin said. "You must be doing well."

"I now earn in a month mining what it used to take me a year to make with horses and cattle. Soon I'll have enough saved for a down payment on a truck. Come to Ulaanbaatar and I'll get you a job where I work."

Nachin glanced over at his wife who was staring at Sarnai's pot. He had never seen such a look of envy in her eyes. Before most of his livestock had been killed in the blizzard two years before he had hopes of one day bringing that look to her face. He returned his admiring gaze to his brother's beaming face. "I'll have to discuss it with my wife."

Sarnai leaned forward in her chair and held the pot in front of Erden's face. "Is it not beautiful?" she said.

The boy glanced toward the door. "It's not as beautiful as Altandöl," he said.

"You can't take a pony to the city," the old woman cackled as if the decision to move there had already been decided.

"Uncle Zhanzhin has a horse," the boy protested.

"Zhanzhin is a great man and you are just a boy who still plays with stuffed animals," she said. "No boys in the city have a pony."

Erden began to cry. "I'm not leaving Altandöl," he blubbered.

Odsar put her arm around her son's shoulders. "Of course you can't leave something you love," she said as she stared at the pot.

#

There was a chilly bite in the air, but no precipitation. A gentle breeze blew across the hills carrying with it the fragrance of grass and damp earth. Nachin had kept Altandöl and the mare in the corral but let the other animals out to return to where they usually grazed on the steppe not far from the ger. He left for Ulaanbaatar with his brother the day before to have a look around the city and to talk to Zhanzhin's supervisor about getting a mining job. Odsar stood at the wood railing that enclosed the corral and watched Erden lead Altandöl around the enclosure by a rope tied around the pony's neck. She and Nachin had chosen not to tell the boy that they might sell the animals and the land and move to the city. The pony seemed as attached to Erden as Erden was attached to it. Even without the rope, the pony followed the boy. Odsar had heard that some people in the city had dogs that were kept inside as pets. The thought of it made her shudder.

"Come see where I now have my new pot," Sarnai called out from the open door of the ger.

The hairs on the back of Odsar's neck stood on end. The old woman had moved the pot to different places within the ger ever since receiving it three days before. Each time she invited Odsar to see the pot in its new location, always receiving the same icy response from Odsar. Odsar was convinced that Sarnai did it to aggravate her, but had held her tongue. When Sarnai went back into the ger, Odsar spat on the ground. "Let Altandöl go now, Erden," she said to her son, her voice tinged with impatience. "I have other things to do."

The boy removed the rope from the pony's neck, hung it on the railing, and crawled through the rails. He took his mother's hand. "Don't worry *Eeej ee*, maybe *Aavaa* will bring back a pot like that for you."

"Your father will never bring me a pot as fine as that one," she said. With the boy's hand firmly grasped in hers, Odsar marched to the ger, flung open the door, and saw that what Sarnai had done with the pot was more than she even feared. On the shelf where her statues and post cards had set, the pot was the only thing on it.

Sitting by the stove, Sarnai looked up from the plate of dumplings that rested in her lap and smiled. "Do you like what I've done?" she asked in a syrupy tone.

#

Odsar stood at the edge of the yard and watched as Zhanzhin's truck bumped up and down on the road as it drew closer. Nachin had been away for three weeks, sending poorly written letters that detailed what he did at work during the day operating a machine that dug rock out of the ground and in the evening going about Ulaanbaatar with his brother searching for a place to relocate their ger and looking for a truck for Zhanzhin to buy. She had written back only once, telling him that the wolves had killed one of the cows and that Erden had begun riding Altandöl. "He hopes to turn the pony into a racing horse," she wrote. She hadn't told Erden that they were moving to Ulaanbaatar. She started to write in her letter how his grandmother was making her crazy with the pot, but scratched it out.

Sarnai was standing in the doorway of the ger holding onto Erden's collar, holding him back with one hand to keep him from running into the path of the oncoming truck. She held the pot in the crux of her free arm.

As soon as the truck came to a stop a few yards from where Odsar stood, the passenger door opened, Nachin jumped out, ran to his wife, and embraced her in a tight hug. "I have something to tell Erden," he said cheerily. He looked past his wife, and seeing his son in the ger doorway, called out to him. The boy broke free of his grandmother's grip and ran to his father.

Nachin knelt down. "I have the most wonderful news, my son. We're moving to the city."

The boy glanced over at the corral where Altandöl stood at the railing, its head poking out through the rails. Erden's eyes welled with tears. "What about my pony?" he said.

"That's the best part," Nachin said. "There is a place to keep the pony and its mother on the land where our ger will be relocated."

The boy's face exploded in an expression of joy. He threw his arms around his father's neck and smothered the man's cheeks with kisses.

It was then that Zhanzhin stepped out of the truck and carrying an object wrapped in the same yellow tissue paper that Sarnai's pot had been wrapped in, he walked up to Odsar and handed it to her.

#

As the truck slowly rambled along on the road, with the ger dismantled and in the back of the truck, and Altandöl and his mother being pulled along behind, Odsar and Sarnai sat in the back seat on either side of Erden, each holding identical pots in their laps. They hadn't spoken to one another, or to Zhanzhin, from the moment Odsar unwrapped her gift in Sarnai's presence. The scowls on their faces and their refusal to look at one another as the truck headed for the city told the remainder of the story of the clay pot.

The End

11

THE DIG DOWN BOYS

What did Sandima know about the origins from where the water flowed? Its movement was so slow that he barely noticed it other than that he stood in it up to his thighs for as many as ten hours a day, often returning to the same place after a year or so, as the mounds of mud and islands in rivers and streams were reshaped by natural erosion and floods. He knew there were trees on the banks that surrounded the water, and birds in the trees that filled the air with their cries and song, but the trees and birds had become so commonplace to him that they were taken for granted, like the air he breathed.

Sandima was sixteen; originally from Freetown, Sierra Leone, but he hadn't been in or near Freetown, or seen his parents and siblings since he was a boy of seven. Sandima would reply to anyone who asked, "What good is it to try to remember the ghosts that inhabited my past?"

How to search for diamonds amidst the mud, dirt and rocks he spread with his hands inside a large flat pan was all that he, or any of the Dig Down Boys, needed to remember.

Sandima had an advantage over the other Dig Down Boys. He had a lucky pan. None of the other boys made that claim about their pan. He found more diamonds in among the rock and stones in his pan after the mud was rinsed away than any of the Dig Down Boys.

"Some day, brother, you be a big boss because of that pan," the other Dig Down Boys told him.

On the day before his seventeenth birthday, Sandima stood in the water as he dug into the mound of mud, shoveling handfuls of it into his pan. He wasn't thinking about the mud, or what his hands were doing. The mud and digging into it was a symbiotic relationship, like that of the oxpecker and hippo. Finding the diamonds in the mounds and islands of the mud dredged up from the riverbed by the flowing river was his job. It had been his job for four years. His only job.

Before that he cleaned the huts where the bosses lived or washed their clothes or cooked their meat. He was like a wife, but not a wife, not in the sexual sense. They didn't hit or beat him unless he tried to run away, something he only tried twice. The vastness of the jungle, and the dangers that lurked within it, was more frightening than the bosses, so he returned to the camps each time on his own and accepted his punishment as a rite of passage. He learned to live with the reality that the day he was snatched from the street while on his way home from school was the beginning of a new life.

At his right, his friend Ibrahim used his fingers to pluck bits of shiny rock from his pan, flinging them into the water. "What might look like a diamond, isn't always a diamond," was a phrase the Dig Down Boys had learned was an axiom that could be applied to both digging and life. Ibrahim hummed as he worked. He hummed from the moment he carried his pan into the water in the morning until he walked out of the water at twilight.

At his left, Hassana, held his pan close to his face as he dug in the wet soil. His poor eyesight was tolerated by the bosses, but just barely. He worked twice as hard and faster than the other Dig Down Boys, never finding as many diamonds as Sandima, but enough to keep him around. Kidnapping and training a new Dig Down Boy was riskier and took more time than the bosses liked. Like Sandima and Ibrahim, Hassana earned his keep – the right to be fed, clothed and given a hut – and was able to put enough aside from his monthly pay to save for the day when he would be freed by the bosses and could seek life in a village, return to a city, or become a boss himself.

The three of them – Sandima, Ibrahim and Hassana – had heard of the horrors of working in the diamond mines, and were happy that they had spent most of their young lives feeling sunlight on their skin, rain on their backs and the light of day in their eyes. It mattered little to them that the diamonds they found would never make them rich. They weren't their diamonds anyway. What was found belonged to the company, with a few being given to the bosses.

Sandima stopped from digging in the mud long enough to glance from right to left, wondering what his friends had planned for his birthday. Hassana had arrived at the camp soon after Sandima, but as soon as Ibrahim had arrived the three of them became inseparable, like brothers. There were a half dozen other Dig Down Boys their age, and others had come and gone with regularity, but it was the three of them who had formed a lasting bond. He looked up and saw his boss, Boss Ousman, staring at him from the top of the mound, a scowl on his face, and quickly shoved his hands in the mud.

"Panther!" came the yell from another boss nearer to the trees on the border of the jungle.

In that instant as Sandima's boss turned to look toward the jungle, Sandima pulled a hand from the mud and dropped in his pan the largest diamond he had ever sifted out of the mud. Without thinking, he grabbed it and shoved it in his mouth. He spat out the mud that had adhered to the diamond just before Boss Ousman turned back and glanced down at him.

"Panther, Boss?" Sandima mumbled.

"Probably the one that has been hanging around the camp for a few days now," Boss Ousman said.

Sandima went on piling a mound of mud in his pan, rinsed away the mud, and began spreading the remaining rocks and stones around looking for diamonds. He rolled the one in his mouth around on his tongue, feeling the weight and shape of it; the edges were very uneven and sharp. This one would be worth a lot. More than any boss or the company that paid the bosses would ever expect. The diamond on Sandima's tongue would make him a very wealthy man. He had never given it thought before. To be wealthy. But he liked the taste of the idea.

#

"Tomorrow you of age to be on the path to being a boss, brother," Ibrahim said.

Sandima nodded thoughtfully. The heat from the campfire was almost too much. The flames on the logs were intense, reaching high into the air. Specks of fiery red ash were spat upward into the night sky. He took a large drink from the packet he grasped tightly in one hand. The alcohol in the liquid delivered an immediate punch. He rocked backward on the log. "I not become a boss," he said.

"Waaatttt!" Ibrahim and Hassana said in unison with equal surprise from the log they sat on. The fire separated them from their friend.

"You have enough money saved to do something else, brother?" Hassana said. Sandima was a blurry figure almost lost among the dancing shadows cast by the campfire. His eyesight was getting worse. One day he hoped he would be able to buy a pair of glasses. One day.

It was then that the cry of a panther echoed from the jungle beyond the ring of nine huts that made up the encampment. All three boys turned and looked the direction of the panther's cry. Several bosses ran out of their huts, waited for a moment, and not hearing anything more, went back inside. Other Dig Down Boys playing cards while crouching on a piece of cardboard not far away the campfire were momentarily silent and then broke into nervous laughter.

Sandima took another drink from his packet. The world was spinning. Happily. "I no need lots of money. I have lucky pan, remember, brothers?" he said.

"Sorry to say this after all this time seeing you with that pan, but a pan is just a pan," Ibrahim said. "Better to have plenty of money in your pockets like a boss. That is what luck is."

Sandima stood and waited for the ground beneath his feet to stop moving. "Wait and see. I will buy myself, and you my brothers, everything we have ever wanted and take us wherever we choose to go."

"You drunk," Hassana said. He and Ibrahim broke out into loud laughter.

Sandima walked away. His head was pounding, both from the inside and out. Why were some birds and the monkeys so loud at night? He started on the trail leading to where they had been digging for diamonds. He wanted to dip his body in the water. He needed time to think and in the coolness of the water was an ideal place to do that. He would be strip-searched by a boss and a Dig Down Boy, acting as guards, before going into and coming out of the water, but he didn't care. Packet alcohol did more than make the smile on his face feel permanent, it also acted as an anesthetic. Earlier it had made it possible to swallow the diamond, unseen, while sitting only a few feet from the others. At the water he removed his clothes as he was ordered to do by the boss standing guard.

"Why you take a bath so late at night, boy?" the boss said.

"To keep the panther from seeing me naked as a bushbuck, Boss," Sandima said. "I no want to be lure the panther with my flesh."

"Panther see you day or night," the boss said. "They see things we don't."

Still feeling the effects of the alcohol, Sandima staggered into the water, lowered his body until he was immersed up to his chest, and remained perfectly still. He hadn't given much thought to how it would feel having a diamond in his belly. As his stomach began to churn, it dawned on him that passing the jewel through the rest of his body and out of his anus could possibly be complicated. And painful.

\#

Sandima rose from the straw mat on which he slept. The diamond had moved from his stomach to his intestines. Doubled-over with pain, he walked to the door of his hut and looked out. Moonlight shone through the canopies atop the kapok trees that surrounded the encampment. Hazy smoke drifted from the extinguished campfire into the air, and then carried off by a balmy breeze. Behind him, on their mats, Ibrahim and Hassana slept soundly. His pan, and theirs, were hung on the walls of the hut. In the ambient light they looked like tribal masks, other-worldly and frightening. He left the hut in search of water to drink. He thought, *Maybe water would wash the diamond further down.* Near Boss Ousman's hut he found several jugs of water. He removed the cork from a jug and began to drink from it.

Boss Ousman came running out of the hut, a rifle in his hands. Seeing Sandima, he said, "Boy, I thought you were a wild animal."

Fighting the cramping in his bowels, Sandima straightened up. "Sorry, Boss, but I had a terrible thirst."

Boss Ousman walked over to Sandima and placed his hand on his shoulder. "I will give you your birthday present early," he said. "At daylight you begin training as a boss."

Sandima broke out into a sweat. "Thank you, Boss," he said between clenched teeth as he bent over. The pain in his gut went straight to his head.

"Are you okay, boy?" Boss Ousman said. "You look sick."

"I'm fine," Sandima said, and then he passed out.

#

Two days later Sandima woke up in a strange hut. The lower half of his naked body was covered with a piece of cloth. His lips were parched and his throat was as dry as withered fruit. His anus ached. He started to scratch his nose and realized his hands had been placed on his chest and were bound together by hemp. He looked down and saw that his ankles had also been tied together. His thoughts immediately went to the diamond he had ingested. *No one should swallow a diamond that jagged and size.* There was no doubt that it had come out. He then thought about death. How had he escaped it? From the diamond? From being found out stealing from the company? From stealing from Boss Ousman?

From outside the hut came the sounds of shouting, rifle shots, and running footsteps. The word "panther" was repeated loudly and clearly.

Sandima sat up. Dizziness blurred his sight for a moment, and then his vision cleared. There he saw in front of him, leaning against a wall, his pan. He sighed with relief. It was like finding an old friend who he feared he would never see again. It had lost its luckiness. But it was still a friend.

The door to the hut opened and Boss Ousman walked in, his hand gripping the thin, bare shoulder of a a small boy, leading him in. The boy was trembling, his eyes wide open, an expression of abject fear on his face. "So, Sandima you are awake from the fever already. Swallowing a dirty diamond that cut up your insides was not a wise decision. "

Sandima cleared his throat and ran his tongue over his lips, trying to bring moisture to them that didn't exist. "Why am I not dead, Boss Ousman?"

"When you shit out that diamond I think I strangle you with my own hands, but you have been a good and faithful Dig Down Boy all these years, so I keep you alive. For Now. But you will not be a boss and you have forfeited everything you have earned until now. I will not mention your attempted theft to the company."

The boy struggled to free himself from the pain of the boss' grip.

Boss Ousman tightened his grip on the boy even more. "This is Amadu who was to be yours, just as you have been mine, but now I must give him to someone else to serve and be trained by." He then shoved the boy onto the ground next to where Sandima lay. "Amadu has much fear, but potential as a Dig Down Boy."

Sandima exchanged glances with Amadu. Tears had welled up in the little boy's eyes.

"From you he can still learn," Boss Ousman said. "That stealing could cost him his life." Laughing sardonically, he turned and left the hut.

Sandima then asked Amadu the first question asked any new boy to be groomed as a Dig Down Boy. "Where do you come from?"

"Freetown," Amadu said.

"That is a far distance," Sandima said.

"Not so far," Amadu sniffled. "They drove and walked in circles before bringing me here to confuse me, but Amadu not easily confused."

"Tell me more," Sandima said.

It was nightfall by the time that Amadu and Sandima shared their stories. Both were from Freetown and both had been kidnapped while walking home. Amadu – like Sandima when he had been kidnapped – was seven years old.

"I prefer to die," Amadu said when Sandima finished telling of his life as a Dig Down Boy.

It was quiet and still outside the hut when Ibrahim and Hassana entered, signaling to Sandima to speak in whispers.

"What is your boss going to do to you, brother?" Ibrahim asked as he and Hassana knelt down beside him.

"He keep my savings. I back to day one as a Dig Down Boy." He glanced over at Amadu and then back at them. "This boy maybe know the way back to Freetown. It is too late for me to rejoin my family but he will need my help to get back to his."

"How would you do that, brother?" Hassana said.

"In doing what I ask, you too may lose your savings, if what you do is discovered " Sandima said.

"I can wait a while longer for eyeglasses," Hassana said. "Tell us."

"First, untie me," Sandima said.

#

In the middle of the night, as the rays of a waning moon shone through the spaces in the hut's hay and bamboo roof, the shouts of "panther" erupted from the opposite side of the encampment where Ibrahim and Hassana had hidden themselves in the bushes to be kept from being seen as the ones shouting. As bosses ran from their huts in haste and confusion, carrying their rifles, Sandima grabbed Amadu's hand, and his only possession, the pan, and ran from the hut and across the encampment, leading the boy into the jungle. They ran until Sandima thought they were a safe distance from the encampment. As they stopped to catch their breath, the guttural growl of the panther came from the nearby bushes. Just as it leapt out, Sandima raised his pan into the air, and with a single arch-like splice he severed the panther's head from its body with the edge of the pan.

"Still a lucky pan," Sandima said, grabbing the boy's hand again and running the direction of Freetown.

The End

12

THE ELEPHANT TRAIL

My white, linen shirt clings to my skin, glued there by sweat drained from by my body by the oppressive heat and humidity. Sitting on the front porch of the bungalow that stands alone on a plot of land carpeted with with common nut sledge, I swat away the large flies with a bamboo fan while sipping on tepid tea. The air is alive with the constant hum of insects and the chirping of the pied mynas whose nests fill the enormous banyan trees that encircle the village. Several young boys are kicking a ball to one another on the dirt road that passes in front of the bungalow, but is an offshoot of the main road that cuts through the village. The boys play silently, the only noises they make being the impact of their bare feet against the ball, or an occasional whoop of excitement, uttered by accident; they have been told not to disturb the new missionary and his wife.

The screen door opens and my wife, Leah, steps out of the bungalow onto the burlap welcome mat she bought in New Delhi before we caught the train that took us to the nearest village to this one, which is a hundred miles away. We came to this village by riding in a rickety, crowded bus, the only two white people aboard the bus. The dust blew in through the open windows covering our clothes with a thin layer of light brown powder and dirtying our faces. The word welcome is written in Hindi on the welcome mat.

"It'll be dark soon. Ananya is preparing dinner now," Leah says as she goes to the porch railing, leans against it, her body limp, her limbs dangling in a way that resembles a wilting plant, and watches as one of the boys picks up the ball and runs down the road. He's chased by the others, all disappearing beyond the banyan trees. She slaps at a flying insect from in front of her face and says, "We've been here a month and every day is the same."

"I warned you that you might find it boring," I tell her as I hold hold the cup of tea over the railing, and dump out the last of it. "Perhaps if you became more involved at the school . . ."

Leah quickly turns, as if shot through by a jolt of electricity, her eyes lit with fire. "Nothing I know would be of any use to the children of this village," she says with a mixture of venom and embarrassment. It's her way of reminding me, again, that she only has a high school education. "If only you had told me the truth about where we were coming to!" she exclaims, her voice crackling with rage. As if escaping a sinking ship she rushes to the screen door, but there she abruptly stops as if reminded that in all of India there's nowhere else for her to go, and gazes at me with the compassion fit for a man about to face a firing squad. "I'll come get you when dinner is ready," she says softly, and goes in.

#

The dining room is aglow from the flames of the lanterns that set on tables in each corner in the room. Faded, worn, tapestries with traditional depictions of the Hindu Gods Vishnu, Brahma, and Shiva hang on the walls. Their edges flutter, stirred by the breeze from the slowly rotating blades of the ceiling fan located above the table. On one wall there is a simple wooden cross. The window is closed, shutting out the invasion of insects that usually occurs every dusk. The loud, menacing growl of a tiger that roams the border of the village and has killed two of the villagers can't be kept out; it's a reminder that there are dangers that lurk about here unlike the dangers back in Minnesota.

Ananya pushes open the swinging door that separates the kitchen from the dining room and enters carrying a tray holding four bowls and a plate of naan. As she walks in she brings with her the scents of saffron, garam masala, curry, and cinnamon. She's wearing a bright yellow sari that wraps around her slender body in layers and drapes over her black hair. There's a vermilion dot in the middle of her forehead; she's a married woman. The silver bracelets on her wrists jingle as she places the tray on the table. Silently she scoops servings of rice, vegetable masala, and fish rubbed with spices on our plates, and puts slices of mango and naan on smaller dishes next to the plates.

"This looks delicious, Ananya," I say as I inhale the spices wafting from the masala.

She nods and smiles wanly, but doesn't look at me. Her eyes are the shape of almonds and her dark skin the texture of silk. In the month we've been here she has said less than a dozen words to me. We watch each other warily. Her glances are always furtive; my stares are direct.

She turns her gaze to Leah and after a moment of searching the inscrutable expression on my wife's face, she says, "I hope this is to your liking, *Mahodaya.*" She never calls my wife by her name, but instead uses the Hindi word for madam.

Leah blinks hard, as if suddenly awakened and stares down at the fish. "There wasn't any chicken?" she asks.

"You asked that I cook fish, *Mahodaya,*" Ananya replies, barely able to mask the hurt in her tone.

Leah looks at Ananya, smiles warmly, and gently places her hand on Ananya's arm. "Oh yes, forgive me Ananya, I forgot."

"Tell me, Ananya. Doesn't your husband mind that you cook for us every night?" I ask as I shovel a chunk of potato dripping with reddish-brown curry sauce into my mouth.

Ananya adjusts a bracelet on her wrist, averts her eyes from mine, and says, "My husband is working in New Delhi while I remain here to look after our parents." She repositions the cloth that covers her hair. "Will there be anything else?" She's looking at Leah when she asks this.

"Not for now," Leah and I say in unison.

For the remainder of the meal Ananya remains in the kitchen. Leah is quiet throughout the meal, studying her plate as if it were a getaway map. When we finish eating, Leah helps Ananya clear the table. Before leaving the dining room I hear the two of them in the kitchen whispering and giggling like school girls. There's a musicality to their merriment, like the warbling of song birds.

#

Seeing Leah through the mosquito netting around the bed is like looking at her through a gauzy mist. She's sitting on the stool to the vanity dresser and staring at her reflection in the mirror as she takes long, slow strokes with the brush through her blonde hair. The bedroom has the scent of jasmine, the fragrance of the perfume she sprays on her wrists before coming to bed.

"Ananya is very pretty, don't you think?" I ask.

"You're just now noticing?" Leah replies. She places the brush on the dresser, stands and removes her robe. She's wearing the pale blue nightgown she wore during our honeymoon the year before. Walking to her side of the bed she appears to float, like an apparition. She extinguishes the flame in the lantern by the bed and climbs in. I reach over to touch her, to caress her.

"Not tonight," she says.

I then notice in the ambient light two of Ananya's bracelets on Leah's wrist. "Did Ananya give those to you?" I say.

"Of course," Leah says. "She wants me to feel less lonely."

The cotton sheet that covers my body suddenly feels like a pile of rocks, pinning me to my place in the bed.

#

The school is a large one room structure built of cinder blocks brought here from New Delhi. It's unpainted and there is no glass in the four windows and no door. The thirty-one students share desks that have broken tops and wobbly seats. There's a crack down the center of the blackboard. I teach the upper grades in English, while Mehul teaches the younger grades in Hindi. Mehul is a bachelor and lives alone in a small shack behind the school. He's made it clear that he resents that I live in the finest house in the village that is paid for with foreign currency.

"Your brand of modern colonialism is no better than the old colonialism," he told me angrily the first day we met.

Other than to discuss students, he rarely talks to me.

I'm at the blackboard and writing verbs when I hear shouts and screaming coming from the center of the village. The students rush to the windows and climb on one another to see what is happening. "*Haathee*," they begin to yell with panicked excitement. I stand behind them and see villagers running toward the direction of the bungalow.

"What is it?" I say to Mehul who is standing in the doorway.

"Elephants are on their trail," he says. "They are extremely dangerous."

"Where's the trail?"

"It runs alongside where you're living."

I push him aside and run out of the school and down the road, shoving aside the villagers who have clogged the road to get a glimpse of the elephants. They've seen wild elephants before of course, but their fear of and fascination with them is palpable; they gawk, but stand ready to run. I've only seen elephants in zoos. I stop fifty yards from the bungalow and see that Leah is standing in the yard with Ananya, not ten yards away from an enormous bull elephant and a smaller, albeit still large, cow. The elephants have stopped and are rocking back and forth, waving their trunks, and flapping their ears. The bull's bellowing is deafening. There is no actual trail, but where they stand is the same path the elephants take whenever they enter the village.

Then the bull charges at the women.

Helplessly I watch as Ananya pushes Leah aside and out of the path of the charging elephant, and shouts as she waves her arms. With all the ferocity of a runaway train the elephant knocks her to the ground and then tramples on her. Their rampage done, the two elephants run into the brush beneath the banyan trees and disappear from sight.

I reach Leah as she begins to crawl to the broken body of Ananya. I take her in my arms and rock her as she wails.

"She was in love with me," Leah says, choking back a sob.

I want to respond, to explain that if Ananya had actually been in love with her, it was meaningless.

She looks into my eyes, possibly searching for my soul, and says, "I was in love with her too."

The End

13

FAR AND AWAY

The crystal drinking glasses on the table vibrated, forming ripples in the water. The ice cubes tinkled. The floor beneath Amanda's feet trembled. She looked up to see the bamboo blades of the ceiling fan pause momentarily, as if assessing the situation, before continuing to rotate. The chain hanging from the fan swung slightly. At the other end of the table, her husband, Clark, continued eating the last of the chicken adobo on his plate, seemingly oblivious to the tremor. Soy sauce dribbled down his chin that he dabbed away with a linen napkin while continuing to chew.

Princess came through the door that separated the kitchen from the dining room carrying a large silver tray, the one Amanda received as a wedding gift from her grandmother. Silently she picked up Amanda's plate still half-covered in adobo and placed it on the tray, and then circled the table picking up the empty bowls and finally Clark's plate. His was scraped clean.

"What's for desert tonight?" he asked her.

"Madam Amanda say no desert tonight," she answered with Filipino inflection while glancing sideways at Amanda.

Clark leaned back and patted his rotund stomach. "Perhaps that's for the best," he said with a chuckle.

As Princess started back to the kitchen, Amanda reached out and grasped her arm. "Did you feel the shaking just before you came out here?"

Princess glanced down at the gold bracelet on Amanda's wrist and then looked into Amanda's worried eyes. "Is just the hearts of Magayon and Pangarnon beating for each other," she said. She pulled her arm from Amanda's hand and went into the kitchen.

"You should just ignore the volcano like I do," Clark said.

"How can anyone ignore a volcano?"

He stood and picked up his Bible from where it had sat open by his place setting at the table and held it against his chest, over his heart. "I have to go to the village. Rosamie's husband may not make it through the night."

"Must you go to their house again?" she said. "You know how much I hate being in this house alone at night."

"It's my duty as the only missionary in this region," he said. "Princess will be here." He walked around the table and kissed Amanda on the forehead. "You could work on the painting you said you started last week. What's it of?"

"Nothing important," she muttered.

He turned and left the dining room. A few minutes later there was the sound of him going out the front door.

Princess came out of the kitchen. "Would Madam like me to follow Mister again?"

Amanda nodded. "I need to know for certain if my husband is having an affair with that Rosamie woman."

"Yes, Madam," Princess said. She held her hand out and smiled approvingly as Amanda removed the gold bracelet bracelet and placed it in her palm. She slipped the bracelet onto her wrist and left the house.

#

The Mayon Volcano was illuminated with the colors of twilight: purple, gold and blood red. The volcano rose up from the flat, verdant landscape that surrounded it as if placed there by accident by the hand of God. Its sides were covered in tracks of dried lava giving it the appearance of having been clawed by a giant. Amanda was seated at her easel on the patio outside of the bedroom. She looked back and forth from the painting in front of her where the volcano took up most of the canvas to the volcano that occupied most of the horizon. The volcano terrified her but she kept painting it, adding dabs of dark blue to the volcano's cone.

As she painted she tried to ignore the lights of the village that was much closer to the base of the volcano. Most everyone who lived there were farmers and their families, some who could trace their families living in that village for many generations. They chose to stay there despite the death and destruction visited on them by volcanic eruptions. The road leading to it was unpaved and bordered on both sides by fields of sugarcane. Other than the trucks that carried the cut stalks of sugarcane from the farms to the processing plant hundreds of miles away, the only wheeled vehicles that went in and out of the village were motorbikes, bicycles, and carts pulled by oxen. The house she lived in sat alone from any other house near the start of the road, a few hundred yards from the rarely traveled paved highway. When she didn't have the radio on, it was a place of utter silence.

She dropped the paintbrush into a jar of Turpenoid and wiped the paint from her fingers with a wet cloth. She stood up, draped a piece of linen over the painting, and went into the bedroom. The ceiling fan made a clicking sound with every turn of the blades. The ruffles of the canopy over the bed fluttered in the fan-generated breeze. The eyes in the oil painting she had painted of Clark stared at her from above the dresser, filled with the same mocking laughter he directed at her in real life. The painting was the only item in the bedroom that she hadn't brought with her from their home in Vermont. The painting of her husband was the first one she painted soon after they settled in.

Everything she and Clark owned, most of it purchased by her wealthy parents and given to them as wedding gifts, had been packed and shipped to the Philippines with only one teacup being broken along the way. But it was a very expensive teacup. Clark told her that they would live where they were living for only a year. That was two years ago. She tried to relax about living so near to a volcano, but it was far and away the most difficult part of living in what she considered was a very strange place. Although they were friendly, she had made no friends among the villagers and she thought of Princess only as a servant.

On the top of the dresser, beneath the painting of Clark, was her opened jewelry box. There were far fewer pieces in it than what she had brought with her. Princess did nothing without it costing something, especially when it came to snooping on Clark.

#

Amanda awoke with a start as her bed shook. She sat bolt upright when a porcelain figurine sitting on a corner table fell onto the floor and broke into pieces. As quickly as the shaking had started, it stopped. She glanced around the room. Hazy morning sunlight shone through the slats of the shutters on the door leading to the patio, forming patterns of horizontal bars across the floor and walls. Seeing that Clark wasn't on his side of the bed, it took her a moment to recall that she had awoken during the night and realized he hadn't returned from his visit to Rosamie's. As many times as he had gone into the village he had never stayed away the entire night. She pushed aside the mosquito netting, climbed out of bed, and opened the doors leading to the patio. Mixed in with the oppressive humidity was the slight scent of sulfur. Between the house and the volcano, the landscape was as it always was, but Amanda could have sworn that the fields of sugarcane had decreased in size, shortening the distance to the volcano.

She spun about on her heels when the bedroom door opened. It was Princess. She was holding a small tray with a teapot, saucer and cup on it.

"I bring Madam's morning tea," she said.

"Where's my husband?" Amanda asked.

"He stay the night at Rosamie's house," Princess replied as she walked into the room and placed the tray on a table. "He still there when I left the village when sun rise." She poured tea in a cup and carried the cup to Amanda. "Rosamie the prettiest woman in the village."

Amanda knocked the cup from Princess' hand, sending it crashing onto the bed, staining the white satin sheets with tea. "Yes, you've told me that dozens of times already." She went into the bathroom and slammed the door.

#

It was shortly past noon when Clark walked into the house. His face was red and coated with perspiration. His shirt was drenched with sweat. "My bicycle had a flat and I had to walk most of the way home," he muttered as he entered the dining room where Amanda was seated at the table, attempting to glue together the broken figurine.

Without looking up, she asked him, her voice icy, "Why were you gone all night?"

He wiped sweat from his forehead with the back of his meaty forearm. "Rosamie's husband died and I stayed with her for a while to make sure she would be okay, and then I spent the rest of the night sleeping at Ben Caputo's house."

"What about me? What if I wasn't okay?"

"Why wouldn't you be okay?"

She glanced at the open window and pointed at the volcano. "Do you even care that I, that both of us, could be killed by that volcano?"

"Don't be ridiculous," he said. "I'm going to take a long, cool bath." He turned and left the room.

Hearing something outside the bedroom door, Amanda rushed to it and flung it open. Princess was kneeling on the hallway floor.

"What are you doing there?" Amanda hissed.

Princess slowly stood up. In a hushed voice, she said, "Mister Clark not tell truth. He go to Rosamie's house but not come out."

#

Books fell from the shelves in Clark's study as the entire house shook. Amanda gripped onto the front of his desk to keep from being knocked to the floor. The rumbling of the tremor only lasted for several seconds, but the total silence in its aftermath frightened her even more. She glanced out the window and saw a thin plume of white smoke rising from the volcano's crater.

"I tell you, that volcano is going to erupt," she screamed at Clark who had turned his chair and was staring toward the village.

Without looking at her, he mumbled, "Maybe you're right." He stood up and faced her. "Get your things together and be prepared to evacuate."

"You mean our things," she said, repressing her hysteria.

"Your things. Nothing in this house has ever been ours. You've loved your china, antiques, and linens much more than you've ever loved me."

"That's not true," she fired back. "I've tried to make a home for us while you spend all of your time in the village."

"I'm a missionary," he replied. "The people of that village is why I'm here."

"And what about Rosamie?" she snapped. "Princess said . . . are you in love with her?"

He shook his head in disbelief. "I'm going to the village to make sure Rosamie and everyone else gets out okay." He stormed out of the room.

Sobbing, Amanda ran to the window and stood there until she saw Clark on her bicycle and heading toward the village.

#

At dusk, six military troop carriers – enough to carry the entire population of the village - passed the house and went down the dirt road. Amanda stood on the porch steps sipping on iced tea from a silver goblet, one of a set of eight given to her by her aunt. Six cardboard boxes packed with china and other household items, four suitcases, and a steamer trunk were stacked on the porch.

Princess came out of the house and pushed aside a suitcase with her foot before joining Amanda on the steps. "Trucks go in empty and come out empty."

"What do you mean?" Amanda asked.

"Village our home. We do not leave. Volcano not change that."

"What if it erupts?"

"What if sun not shine anymore?"

Amanda turned and studied the woman's face. In the two years since arriving in the Philippines she had looked at Princess countless times, but hadn't studied her face in the same way she studied objects for a still life painting. Princess' age was indeterminate, her skin free of wrinkles, her eyes bright and clear. It was only the graying at the roots along the hairline of her forehead that suggested she was no longer young. Amanda's eyes rested on the pearl earrings in Princess' ears. They were a one-year wedding anniversary gift that Clark had given to her just before they left the United States.

"You didn't lie about my husband being with Rosamie all night, did you?" Amanda asked her.

"Princess never lie," she answered. She walked down the steps, got onto her motorbike and headed for the village.

Amanda drank the rest of the tea and then opened a box and placed the goblet inside. She went into the house and walked from room to room hoping that if the volcano did erupt, her furniture and paintings would somehow survive.

#

In the middle of the night Amanda awoke to the rumbling of trucks speeding past her house and sat up on the sofa where she had fallen asleep. She got up and rushed out the front door just as the last truck came to a screeching stop in the road alongside the house. Immediately her attention was drawn to the fiery red glow being emitted from the volcano's crater. She turned when two men in military uniforms in the back of the truck shouted at her in perfect English.

"Are you the missionary's wife?" one yelled.

She looked at the dozen or so women and children seated in the back of the half-empty truck, all who she recognized, but knew only a few of their names. They were only a small fraction of the population of the village. Princess was seated near the tailgate. "Yes, I am. Where is my husband?"

"He stayed behind," the other soldier answered. "You coming or not?"

Amanda ran down the porch steps and to the truck. "Princess, tell me . . . is he?"

Princess looked up from the black lacquered jewelry box in her lap and held out her hand. "You have everything. Princess have nothing. What does Madam want to know?"

Amanda slid her wedding ring from her finger and placed it in the palm of Princess' hand. "Is my husband with Rosamie?"

Princess clasped her fingers around the ring. "Yes. He say he love Rosamie."

"Get in, lady," one of the soldier's yelled. "That volcano is going to blow at any time now."

"I'm not going," Amanda said and then turned and walked back to the house. Behind her the truck pulled away and sped off into the darkness. She stood on the porch for several minutes staring at the volcano. The air was thick with the smells of lava, sulfur and ozone, and hot, as if an electric heater had been left on for too long. She picked up the suitcase that had her painting supplies in them and went into the house.

Two hours later, while she was on the patio and seated at the easel she turned to see Clark rush into the bedroom.

"I had to make sure you got away," he said.

She glared at him. "Princess told me about you and Rosamie. You've been lying to me all along."

"It's Princess who has been lying just to get your jewelry."

Her cheeks reddened. "You know about that?"

"Of course I know. I know everything about you. That's why I love you and always will."

At that moment the volcano exploded. Its fire, exploding rocks and hot ash spread across the landscape at incredible speed, incinerating the village, and burying the fields of sugarcane with burning ash. Its destruction swallowed the missionary's house and its occupants in swirling clouds of gray and black.

The End

14

SWIMMING TO MONTEVIDEO

Swimming, my arms slice through the water, one arm, and then the next. Over and over. My fingers are held firmly together, and pointed, like the head of a spear. My shoulders swivel from side to side, twisting my torso. My muscles are like pulled taffy, pliable, twisting, elastic. A continuous flow of power – an electric current of physical, bodily, energy – courses through my legs. They are scissors cutting the water. My feet are fins, paddles, webbed-like, kicking and churning up the water, leaving a continuous splashed trail of bubbles in my wake. The water is cool. It slides over the smoothness of my flesh. I shed it like ever-changing layers of liquid skin.

At times I stop to play, to frolic. Beneath the surface I do somersaults, spins, twists and turns. I am a dolphin, an otter. I am buoyant; my body at times an inflatable toy suspended and submerged in liquid. I descend like a rock and ascend like a missile. I flap my arms, remaining in place like a jellyfish, like a hummingbird. The sounds of my underwater movements are muffled in my ears, at times the loud echoes of exploding bubbles, splashes and currents, and other times like that of the sound of butterflies landing on cotton balls.

In the absence of fish or other swimmers I swim alone. Being in water is sometimes a lonely place to be. At other times it is an escape into splendor.

I climb out of the pool, carrying the smell of chlorine with me, and stand on the cold tiles and remember Montevideo.

#

A balmy breeze drifts across the Rambla. A constant flow of pedestrians crowd the longest continuous sidewalk in the world that runs along the beach, the two separated by a low wall. This wall that I sit on. Beyond the brackish water of the Rio De La Plata lies the dark green water of the Atlantic Ocean, the river and sea divided by an act of nature; an estuary. The overhead sun is cooking my skin to caramel brown as rivulets of sweat run down my bare back. That same sunlight makes the water sparkle as if a million shards of floating glass were reflecting the sun's rays. What is spoken here is Spanish, and the words rise from the throng of passersby with no more meaning than the buzzing of insects. I know only a few words and phrases of that language.

Seagulls circle and swoop above the crowded beach, their screeches penetrating the din of voices from the people laying on towels and sitting under large multicolored umbrellas. I am a stranger among a thousand other strangers.

A cargo ship stacked with rust colored containers crosses the horizon.

A young woman in a striped red and white flowing skirt and wearing a broad rimmed straw hat sits down near me. "*Hola,*" she says when she catches me staring at her.

"Hello," I say.

"Are you from Uruguay?" she says in perfect English.

"No, I'm here on business."

"I'm not from here either," she says. "I'm here by myself."

"Me too."

"I wonder what are the statistical odds of two foreigners meeting so randomly on this wall like we have?" she says.

I smile, and turn to see that the cargo ship is no longer in sight. "My name is Donna," she says, reaching out her hand.

#

My wife, Janelle, is sick. The chemotherapy has drained her of energy and she's nauseous. She lays in bed, a spent version of her former self, like a discarded Barbie doll with a bald head and without one breast. I don't think it's her life as it was that she misses, it's her beauty.

"You smell like the pool," she says as I lean across the bed and kiss her on her ashen gray forehead. "Did you have a good swim?"

I'm instantly aware that my swimming reminds her that my body works in ways that hers no longer does. I pull back, conscious of the aroma of chlorine that wafts from my flesh.

"I'm sorry. I should have showered at the gym," I say.

She closes her eyes and for a brief moment I wonder if it's to shut me out or to hide her despair.

"Do you need the pain medication?" I ask.

Her eyes open and fix on my face. I can feel the tan on my skin.

"No," she says. "Tell me again about your time in Montevideo."

I sit on the edge of the bed. "There's not much more to tell you. I spent most of my free time in my apartment."

#

In Montevideo, sitting at the small writing table by the open living room window, the fragrance of sea water is like a subtle perfume. I purchased the table at an antique store nearby, the only piece of furniture that is mine in this furnished apartment. The wood is so polished I can see my reflection in it. The table top has an inlaid design of starfish and sea horses. My laptop is on the table, its screen glowing brightly. There's an email from Janelle.

It reads, "Urgent you call me as soon as you get this email."

Probably a hair or makeup emergency, I think.

Donna comes out of the bedroom. She's wearing beige shorts, a white blouse and sandals and has her straw hat in her hands. Her toenails are painted the same color green as the ocean.

"Let's take a walk on the Rambla while the sun is still up," she says.

I close the laptop, get up from the table and cross the room to where Donna is standing. Her perfume reminds me of honeysuckle. I take her in my arms and kiss her, passionately.

Pulling away from me, she says, "If I didn't know better I'd say you've fallen in love with me."

I've always thought some things were better left unsaid.

I take her hand and together we leave the apartment, take the elevator to the first floor and leave the building. Calle Juan Maria Perez is much like many of the other streets in the Pocitos area of Montevideo. It's lined with tall apartment buildings and leads to the Rambla, less than a block away.

#

"Do you want me to come home?" I say into the cellphone.

"You don't have to, not yet," Janelle says. "They are going to start the chemo right away but I'd like you here when they do the mastectomy." Her voice catches; she's holding back from crying.

"Why didn't you tell me sooner about the cancer?" I ask.

"I didn't want to spoil your time in Montevideo," she says.

I look out the window, at the white stars splattered across the night sky. I then look at Donna who is stretched out naked on the sofa like the woman in the painting, *La maja desnuda* by Goya.

"When it starts getting bad I'm not going to be one of those people," Janelle says.

"What people?"

"The people who bravely fight through their cancer treatment." she says. "When it comes down to it, I'm not a brave person."

#

With the silt stirred up around us in the Rio De La Plata, Donna and I swim around each other like circling sharks. She has her hair pulled back and tied into a pony tail which accentuates her high cheek bones. In the strong sunlight she bears a strong resemblance to Janelle. We're far out from the beach, further out than anyone else.

"I'll leave my wife," I say.

"Don't be silly," she says. "If you left your wife while she's sick I'd despise you for it."

"I can't leave you behind," I say. "I'm in love with you." It had to be said.

"For now, maybe you are, but some day I'll just be a woman you had an affair with in Montevideo."

#

Today, Janelle was told she would lose her battle with cancer.

My lungs ache, burn, as if stuffed with hot coals. My arms are heavy, weighed down by invisible rocks. My legs feel disjointed, broken. I've lost the rhythm of swimming. Unable to correctly coordinate the movement of my body through the water, each lap I swim feels like ten. I climb out of the pool and try to catch my breath.

Something is gone that I fear I'll never get back. The splendor of a swim.

The locker room is damp and hot. It has the vague scent of decaying plants. It's like the rain forest. At my locker I remove my trunks and wrap a white towel around my waist and walk to the shower. Under the steaming hot water I try to wash the smell of chlorine from my skin.

I try to scrub from my body the memory of Donna and Montevideo.

The End

15

THE SCARLET SARI

The juvenile macaques played in the remains of what once was the Hotel Lakshmi, where those who were nearly homeless lived, but was now but a shell, most of its interior and windows carried away. It is was now just a ruin, something from the past; a crumbling eyesore. When it was gone, every brick removed, a highrise apartment building would be built in its place. Living space in Mumbai was hard to come by, commerce usually taking precedent, but here the plan was to provide upscale housing for those that could afford it; built in Shivaji Naga, an area of the city occupied mostly by the poor. Ravaged by construction workers with jack hammers, what remained of the building was visited daily by engineers and architects who observed the destruction like pathologists at an autopsy, feverishly awaiting the day the foundation for the new building would be laid.

Mukesh was one of them, an architect. Although often told he had to wear a work helmet when around the crumbling building as it was being dismantled, he rarely did.

Then one day a macaques tossed a brick from the top of the structure, dropping it right on Mukesh's head. Knocked unconscious, his skull split open, he was rushed to the hospital.

Diya, his wife, age 23, younger than him by twenty years, arrived at the hospital thirty minutes later, called there by Mukesh's best friend, Dinesh, an engineer, who had been at the site also and witnessed the accident. He had explained the whole situation to her over the phone as she frantically dressed. Mukesh was in surgery when she walked into the waiting room outside the room where Mukesh's head was being sewn back together.

She sat down next to Dinesh, and wringing her hands, said, "Why wasn't he wearing his hat?"

"As you know, he and I grew up together. He has always tempted fate," Dinesh replied. "Marrying you is the only thing he did without the possible threat of the universe coming down on his head like the brick did."

Crying softly into a linen handkerchief embroidered with images of peacocks, she stared down at her feet that poked out from the hem of her sea green sari, thankful the toe ring on her left foot kept her from being carried away from this plane to the next by the sheer force of the emotions that stirred deep inside her. "But to let a monkey drop a brick on his head!" she said to Dinesh between bouts of sobbing. "It shows a total lack of forethought."

Dr. Acharya, a young, handsome surgeon, came out of the operating room an hour later, and standing, looking down at the seated Diya and Dinesh, told them that the surgery went fine, that Mukesh "would fully recover from his injury and the surgery." He turned his gaze to Diya. His dewy brown eyes stared into hers. He was transfixed by her beauty, that which he could see, and that which he couldn't, but was certain existed deep inside her. He remained there, silent and mesmerized, unable to still his pounding heart.

It was Dinesh who brought the doctor to his senses. "My friend has a good job but hospitals are very expensive and my friend doesn't have a lot of money. Can Mukesh be cared for at home?"

Stammering as he tore his transfixed gaze from Diya, Dr. Acharya, replied, "He should stay here for another two days and then he can go home after that as long as he has someone who can nurse him back to health."

"I can do that," Diya said. "I once thought of becoming a nurse and have read several books on that subject."

"While your husband is with us I will take it up personally to endeavor to teach you everything you will need to know."

"I will forever be in your debt," she replied, finding in his eyes, the refined shape of his nose, the fullness of his lips, and the gentleness of his voice, features she found alluring, but resisted their tug on her heart and soul. She loved Mukesh and only Mukesh.

#

The bandage encircled the entire top of Mukesh's head giving the appearance that the cap of a minaret had been placed there. Although he was a Hindu, he couldn't help to think that maybe there was some significance to taking on a Muslim structure as a temporary part of his anatomy. Like most thoughts he had since awaking from the surgery, he knew this needed more reflection. When Diya held up a mirror so that he could see for himself the way his mustache and beard was being trimmed by her, his eyes inevitably wandered to the bandage.

Dr. Acharya had taught Diya how to wrap his head, guiding her hands with his, although as Mukesh witnessed, it could have been done just by being told how. In the two weeks of being home, the surgeon had visited at least eight times, spending his time at Mukesh's bedside, mostly talking and laughing with Diya. Mukesh had no reference to go by to determine if this was normal behavior for a doctor, but in his new enlightenment he believed the problem lay in him and wasn't a problem unless he wanted it to be one. His enlightenment had sprung up beneath his bandage and leaked down to the tip of his new, and growing, beard.

Having finished re-bandaging his head, Diya looked at it, at him, with satisfaction. The color in his cheeks had mostly returned. "You're looking healthier," she told him.

"I feel healthier," he said. "Healthier inside and out."

"Healthier inside?"

"The brick falling on my head has raised my consciousness. I'm thinking more clearly."

She lifted the pan containing the used bandages from the stand beside his bed and turned to leave the room. She stopped momentarily to look at him, thinking indeed there was something different about him, about the way he spoke, as if he knew things others didn't. She found it annoying and hoped that once a bandage was no longer needed he would return to his old self – and cut off his beard. She left the room wondering if she should discuss the matter with Dr. Acharya.

#

Dinesh was in the room the morning that the bandage was removed for good from his friend's head. He stood near the door, watching anxiously as Dr. Acharya slowly uncovered the thick mop of hair that had grown on Mukesh's head in the two months since the brick had nearly ended Mukesh's life. Mukesh was seated in a chair with Diya at his side, holding his hand.

"I'm being reborn," Mukesh said with solemnity.

"It will be very good to have you back to work," Dinesh said. "The last bricks from that old hotel were carried off days ago and tons of soil and concrete have laid the foundation. It's now time for us architects and engineers to finish our work."

"What is architecture? What is engineering?" Mukesh replied. "Aren't the things we build or tear down meaningless artifacts of our need to seem useful?"

Befuddled Dinesh, replied, "People live and work in what we build or tear down."

"A person can live or work anywhere if they have discovered within themselves the inner truth of what it means to build or tear down. I don't plan to build or tear down anything beyond my consciousness."

The doctor pulled the last part of the bandage from Mukesh's head. Only a hairline scar that ran between Mukesh's parted hair remained as evidence that a very serious injury had occurred.

"Your husband owes your nursing and tender care to how well he has healed," Dr. Archarya said to Diya.

"What is healing?" Mukesh said. "Aren't we born healed and taught as we age to reject that healing?"

Diya yanked her hand away from his. "Stop that gibberish, Mukesh," she grumbled. "You're driving me insane."

"I am enlightened. Aware," he replied.

She turned to the doctor. "Do you not see what that monkey's brick has done to my poor husband. He believes he is now a guru. All day long he speaks in circles and riddles."

The doctor stroked his chin, thoughtfully. "The shock of sustaining a blow to his head may have unsettled his senses, but I'm certain that in time he'll return to normal."

"In the meantime we'll end up on the streets and starve to death," she replied, anxiously twisting her blue and white sari's pallu.

Dr. Archarya put his arm around her shoulders. "There, there, no one is going to allow you to end up on the streets or to starve."

#

Later that afternoon, Diya went to the dress shop where she went to buy the most expensive clothes that now hung in her closet, and bought a very costly scarlet sari. The color of it was so vibrant that it took a few moments for her eyes to adjust to looking at it when she tried it on. With it in a box and wrapped in tissue paper, she stopped at the beauty salon and had her hair washed, trimmed and styled. She bought a bottle of perfume, her husband's favorite scent, at a Bombay Perfumery Shop, and purchased a tikka embellished with a faux sapphire and a pair of affordably priced gold loop earrings at a jewelry store. When she arrived home in the back of a motorized rickshaw she gave the driver a hefty tip before going in her house. She had put a small dent in their savings, but figured it was worth it if it would help her husband recover from being enlightened.

She fixed the evening meal without allowing Mukesh to see her in her new scarlet sari until the moment she brought the food out of the kitchen and sat it on the table. He was seated at one end of the table, as always. She stood by her chair at the other end of the table, trying to act nonchalant as she posed in her new sari, tossing her long hair from one shoulder to the next.

"Aren't we going to eat?" he asked at last, paying little attention to her looks or what she was doing.

Annoyed, but deciding there was still time to arouse his desires before bedtime, she sat down and lifted the lid on the dish of lamb rogan josh, his favorite. A cloud of curry fragrance rose into the air. "Don't you see, dear husband. I've prepared a special meal for you."

He looked at the simmering food. "I don't eat meat of any kind," he said. "I'm a vegetarian."

"Since when?" she said, biting her tongue to keep from yelling at him.

"This morning," he replied. "An enlightened being would never eat something that has a soul. That could be an ancestor of mine or yours that you have fixed for our dinner."

She slammed the lid down on the lamb rogan josh, and jumped up. "Until you stop this foolishness I won't take this new sari off, ever. That will enlighten you to how bad an unwashed wife and sari can smell. She tossed her head back and stormed out of the room.

"What new sari?" he said to himself.

#

Alone in their bedroom Diya sat on the bed and began to sob. She missed her old husband, the one who didn't ponder aloud things that made her head ache. He hadn't said a romantic thing to her from the moment he awoke from the surgery, which wasn't like him. He was the only man she had ever sex with, and it had never been what she read it should be like in the magazines, books and on the internet, but she missed it nevertheless. He had always been gentle, kind, attentive and affectionate. The new Mukesh seemed only interested in expressing what he said were profound thoughts, and then he would go to great lengths talking about why no thought was profound, that all thoughts were recycled. She took off her new earrings and flung them across the room, kicked off her shoes, and then laid back on the bed and fell sound asleep.

She awoke the next morning and sat up. Her sari was crumpled and wrinkled and her hair disheveled. Seeing that Mukesh's side of the bed hadn't been slept in, she knew he must have slept in the hospital bed that he had been sleeping in while recovering in the spare bedroom. She got up and walked to her vanity dresser and stared at herself in the mirror. Her tikka hung clasped to a few hairs to the middle of her fore-head. Just beneath that her bindi was smudged above her left eyebrow. She removed the tikka and wiped away the bindi with some face cream and a tissue. Suddenly, her face felt naked and exposed. She quickly dabbed her finger into a jar of kumkum and dabbed it between her eyes. Then she put her finger into the kumkum again and dabbed that on the end of her nose. Five minutes later her entire face was freckled with kumkum. She quickly ran a brush through her hair, adjusted the sari, and left the room, barefoot.

Outside the room where Mukesh had slept, she heard Dinesh's voice. He was speaking loudly, emphatically. "Don't you even care that the foundation of the building is now ready to be built on?"

"We must ask ourselves, what is a foundation?" Mukesh replied. "If you peel away one foundation, isn't there another one underneath, so on and so . . ."

"Shut up!" Dinesh yelled.

Diya opened the door and went in. Both men stared at her.

Eyeing her up and down, Dinesh asked as politely as he could, "Diya, aren't you feeling well?"

She crossed her arms. "Perhaps you should ask my husband how I am feeling."

"When we put a flame to our skin, that creates the feeling of pain. There is no question of that," Mukesh said. "But my young wife has confused unmet expectations with feelings."

Her eyes ablaze, Diya glared at Makesh, saying nothing for several moments, rendering the room silent. "We shall see about that," she hissed, and back stiffened, head held high, turned and marched out of the room"

# # #

A month went by and true to her word, Diya never took the sari off and bathed only those body parts that extended beyond the scarlet cloth. She reduced the effect of inhaling her own stench by carrying around her new bottle of perfume and dabbing it under her nose whenever needed. Strangely, to Diya's way of thinking, the one person other than Mukesh who didn't seem to notice her odor, was Dr. Acharya. In fact it stimulated his ardor for her.

As always, on the premise of inquiring into Mukesh's health, the doctor arrived at their home carrying a bouquet of gardenias and orchids for Diya, which he handed at the front door. With great exuberance, he announced to a nonplussed Diya "This marks our fourth anniversary."

"Fourth anniversary?" she replied, nervously. "What do you mean?"

"Maybe not the fourth anniversary exactly, but nearly the time we have known one another, and dare I say, formed an attachment."

"I'm not atta . . ." she started.

He cut her off. "I understand. You're a married woman and you don't want to betray your husband, even if he is mentally unsound, but from the moment our eyes met, it was obvious we were meant for one another."

She looked down at the dirty, tattered hem of her sari. It had dragged on the floor so often that it resembled an old dust rag. That part of her sari was no longer scarlet, but had turned a dull, pinkish beige. She then looked up at him. "Don't you see what I'm wearing, how I look?"

"You have worn that scarlet sari for weeks to entice me, to allure me," he said. "It has worked. I'm enthralled by you. Every waking moment I think only of you."

"I'm another man's wife."

"You are the embodiment of the goddess Lakshmi."

"The goddess Lakshmi is the cause of me being in this state to begin with," she protested. "It was from the top of a Lakshmi namesake that my poor, confused husband was hit with that brick, thrown by a monkey, need I remind you."

He grabbed her and took her in his arms. "Remind me with your lips," he said, and then kissed her passionately while grasping at the folds of her sari.

She struggled free from his hold and then slapped him. "You are no better than my husband. He only sees what is the unseeable and you don't see the real me at all. Now get out and don't return. She shoved him back across the threshold, threw the flowers at him, and slammed the door.

Breathless and gasping for air she leaned back against the door. Tears began to flow down her cheeks. She then looked down to see that in the brief tussle with the doctor, her blouse had been torn just below her left breast. She then slowly made her way to the bathroom, where she removed her sari, blouse and petticoat, and then stepped into the shower and turned on the water.

An hour later, in a clean light blue sari with gold trim she walked into the bedroom where Mukesh slept, carrying the scarlet sari in her arms. He was staring out the window.

"I've come to tell you that I'm leaving you," she said.

He turned from the window and smiled, not at her, but a smile that originated from somewhere inside him. "We are all clouds at the mercy of the winds that blow us."

"I'm not a cloud," she said. She tossed the scarlet sari on his bed, turned and left.

At the front door she picked up her two suitcases and went out.

The End

16

AKIKI, THE MAGICIAN

Just past sunrise, as a thick halo of fog encircled the top of the Karisimbi volcano, Akiki stepped out of the thick vegetation of the jungle surrounding David Russell's hut. He stopped for a moment and glanced at the yard around the hut, cleared of trees, grass, nettles, and creeping vines, leaving a patch of nearly bald earth. There was nothing new to see, and as he sniffed the air, nothing new to smell, other than David's aroma, unusually faint for a human. He grunted softly and ambled a few yards closer to the hut and sat down in the dirt. After picking an army ant from his fur, he stuck it in his mouth and bit down on its crunchy body. The taste of the ant brought him a great deal of pleasure and calmed his nerves. He stretched out his large hands, briefly closed his eyes, and opened them to see four small bright red kowaii in his hands, two in each palm. He began to juggle the fruit, forming circles in the air that increased or decreased in circumference as he shifted his hands. His grunts and belches steadily rose in volume.

When the door to the hut opened and David appeared in the doorway, wrapped in a heavy blanket, Akiki blinked his eyes and the fruit vanished.

"You're here very early this morning," David said to the large silver-backed mountain gorilla.

Akiki lightly thumped his chest and then tapped his eye with his thick index finger.

"My camera?" David said. "Yes, I'll be taking pictures after I've had my morning tea and toast."

Akiki turned his large head and stared at the jungle, then turned back to David. He pulled his lips tight against his teeth, a sign of concern.

"Have the poachers been around again?" David asked.

Akiki shook his head, mimicking David and other humans who studied and photographed his group. David understood the gesture's meaning.

"I'll try to hurry," David said, then turned, went into his hut, and closed the door.

Two golden monkeys appeared in the branches of a tree at the edge of the yard. They chattered noisily to Akiki.

"I know, I know. David has been told," Akiki said in an accent that resembled David's midwestern US drawl. "Now, go away." He clapped his hands and the monkeys disappeared in a poof of mist. He clapped his hands again, then he too vanished.

#

An hour later David and Mukisa, one of the Mahinga National Park rangers, appeared at the entrance to the small clearing among a grove of bamboo trees where Akiki and his extended family – several females, infants and a few juvenile males – lolled about among the broken bamboo stalks and piles of leaves. The men stood perfectly still, awaiting to be noticed by Akiki who lay on his back with his newest infant, Namazzi playing on his huge stomach. His favorite female, Dembe, the mother of Namazzi, sat nearby, eating the pulp of a bamboo shoot.

Seeing David and Mukisa, Akiki exhaled a breath, clearing the air in front of his daughter's face of the butterflies dancing there like marionettes on strings. He sat up, gently lifted Namazzi, and handed the infant to Dembe. David put his camera to his eye and Akiki heard it click several times as he stood and pounded on his chest, producing a sound similar to beating on a hollow log. He made his way through the broken bamboo to the two men, who slowly dropped to their knees, their heads bowed in submission. Akiki grunted loudly, nodded east, then turned and led the way into the jungle.

Paths made by the gorillas and other animals wound through the trees and nettles like tributaries, made damp and occasionally muddy by the constant dripping of rainwater falling from the tree canopies. Akiki knew exactly where he was leading David and Mukisa; the poachers rarely ventured far from the paths. They left their scent on everything they touched and, try as they might to do it quietly, still made noise as they set their snares and traps.

The first snare Akiki led the men to had the broken body of a small bushbuck caught in its tangle of rope and tree branches.

Cutting the dead animal from the snare, Mukisa shook his head. "It's a never-ending battle against the poachers. They'd drive all the animals in the park to extinction if we let them."

David snapped several pictures of the snare and nearby snares and traps that hadn't been sprung. He lowered the camera and glanced at Akiki who stared in the direction of the settlements, beyond the park boundaries, at the base of the mountain.

"Don't ask me how, but I think Akiki knows the existence of his kind hangs on a very thin thread," David said to Mukisa.

Mukisa sliced through the rope of a snare, releasing the bent-over sapling it was attached to back into an upright position. "Too many of his own family have been caught in these traps or been carried off by poachers for him not to know what a danger man poses."

Surreptitiously, Akiki freed the bubble that he had been holding in his fist and watched it float away.

#

Sitting on a mound of bamboo with his group seated in the grass around him, Akiki reached inside an old ranger's hat he'd found in the jungle and pulled out a small golden monkey. He held the struggling monkey for several moments as the other gorillas watched with rapt attention, then covered the monkey with the hat, hesitated a moment, and pulled the hat away. The monkey was gone. The group pounded the ground with their fists, stomped their feet, grunting and barking with delight.

The report of a far-off gunshot caught Akiki's attention. He stood up, tossed the hat aside, and grunted nervously, then waved his hands, gesturing for the group to leave the clearing and return to relative safety among the vines and bamboo. As the group disbanded, he exchanged a kiss with Dembe and gently patted the top of Namazzi's head. His natural instincts reminded him time and again not to be so affectionate with his offspring, that it would make them soft, but he couldn't help himself. Watching as she carried their infant to safety, he made a bunch of wild celery appear in his hand and stuffed it into his mouth. He was chewing on the celery when David and Mukisa arrived at the entrance to the clearing and knelt down.

David held his camera to his eye and snapped several pictures of the gorilla as he st in the hazy rays of late afternoon sunlight, the silver hair on his back glistening.

Akiki thumped his chest and turned his head in the direction of the gunshot.

David nodded. "Yes, we heard it too, old boy," he said softly.

As rain began to fall, Akiki pulled a large leaf from a tree and followed his family into the thicket.

#

David awoke to pounding on the door to his hut. He sat up on his cot, rubbed the sleep from his eyes, and peered at his watch. It was a little before 4 AM. "Who's there?" he called out.

"It's me, Akiki," a deep voice from the other side of the door replied frantically.

"It's a bit early for practical jokes, Mukisa," David replied.

There was a brief silence, then came, "They've taken my Dembe and Namazzi."

David threw open the door and saw a naked man, about his height but much bulkier and muscular, his chest, arms and legs matted with thick black hair. He looked into the man's eyes and saw in them Akiki's unmistakable keen intelligence and gentleness. "But, how…?" His voice trailed off as he tried to comprehend what he was seeing.

"I need your help," Akiki said. "The poachers raided my group, killed two who were trying to defend them, and carried off Dembe, Namazzi, and another infant." He hung his head. "I was lured away from my group by sounds the poachers made in another part of the jungle. It was foolish of me to leave them unprotected."

David gathered his composure. "You can't be blamed. Let me get dressed and I'll get Mukisa and the other rangers."

"There's no time to get Mukisa," Akiki said. "The lives of my female and infant are at risk."

Twenty minutes later David and Akiki, who was now wearing one of the hut's curtains tied around his waist and a too-tight shirt of David's, followed the trail left by the poachers. They said nothing, their steps barely making a sound on the soft earth and broken vegetation, slowed by David's inability to keep up despite Akiki's difficulty adjusting to his human legs. When they broke out of the jungle at the border of a large swath of deforested land it was early morning and the settlement could be seen in the distance, bathed in dawn's gray light.

"I've lost Dembe and Namazzi's scents," Akiki said as he stared at the settlement, his lips pulled back in the same way they did when he was Akiki, the mountain gorilla.

"Don't give up hope, Akiki," David patted him on the back.

Akiki flinched. Being touched by a human was a new experience, and not one he liked, even if it was David whom he had grown to like and trust in the nine years they had known each other.

They continued on, following the well-trod path through the field of bulldozed earth and tree stumps. As they approached the settlement, the aromas of cooked food, garbage, and human waste grew stronger, forming a cloud of noxious odors hanging a few feet above the ground where it mixed with the early morning mist. Entering the first unpaved street of the settlement, Akiki abruptly stopped. The nearness of so many humans leaving their shacks and tents to begin their day filled him with fear and loathing. These were the beings who were wantonly killing the mountain gorillas.

David saw Akiki hesitate. "Now that we've come this far, we have to go on if we're going to find Dembe and Namazzi."

"Yes, we must go on." Akiki moved forward.

They made their way through the throng of settlement inhabitants until they reached the edge of a marketplace. Vendors had set up tables and stalls selling everything from woven baskets to bananas.

"There! Dembe's scent!" Akiki shouted, pointing to a stall where several men were gathered behind a table piled with burlap-wrapped objects. He rushed toward the stall, followed by an alarmed David, and grabbed one of the men by the shoulders, shaking him. "Where is my female and infant?" he screamed in the man's face. The other men pulled him from Akiki's grasp. David spotted a freshly bloodied bundle. He peeled back the cloth. In it lay two adult mountain gorilla hands.

"Akiki," he said, softly.

Akiki turned, saw the hands, and cried out, "Dembe!" He clapped his hands and vanished.

#

"Will Akiki understand when you tell him Namazzi was probably sold as a pet?" Mukisa asked David as the two neared the clearing where Akiki and his group could usually be found foraging for bamboo shoots.

"He understands much more than anyone can imagine," David replied.

Akiki and his group weren't in the clearing. The men spent several days trying to track them down without success; Akiki's family had disappeared in the jungle.

The End

17

THE ALBATROSS

Sunlight reflected off the Monument of the Discoveries. As Henry the Navigator looked out over the Tagus River, so did Peter Myles. He had a pair of binoculars to his eyes and watched as sailboats, cruise ships, barges and cargo ships, traveled the glassy, blue water. He then scanned the 25th of April Bridge that connected Lisbon to Almada, and watched as traffic hummed across it. A slow-moving train traversed its lower platform. He lowered the binoculars and realized that Lloyd was still talking to him.

Lloyd was always talking. He had a tourist guidebook in his hands and was flipping through the pages. "It would be nice to stay in a real hotel for a change, even a cheap one, but if we're going to spend another night in a hostel we should find one while it's still early."

Peter let the binoculars drop against his chest, held there by a strap around his neck. He adjusted the shoulder straps on his backpack and turned away from the river. The large square that separated the monument from the beginning of downtown Lisbon was packed with tourists. On one of the benches in the square sat a young man with a backpack at his feet. He had a map spread out across his lap and was studying it. Peter watched him for several minutes, and when no one else sat down next to the young man, Peter said to Lloyd, "I'm going to sit down for a few minutes."

Lloyd was still talking. "You like to sightsee. We could find a hostel in the Baxia aria. There are tunnels that we could explore dating back to the Romans near the hostel there. If we do, I'll need to buy a nasal inhaler at some pharmacy. Subways and tunnels play havoc with my sinuses. But you know that already, don't you? That subway ride you suggested we take in Porto nearly killed me."

Peter walked away.

Lloyd looked up from the guidebook. "Where are you going?"

"To sit down," Peter said over his shoulder.

While walking through a flock of pigeons, Peter put his binoculars in their case and snapped it shut. He politely fended off a woman dressed in black who wanted to read his palm for 10 Euros. He reached the bench where the young man was still looking at the map, and plopped down. The bench shook.

The man glanced over at him and smiled genially, and then turned his attention back to the map.

Peter took from his shirt pocket the blue handkerchief he had bought in Lucerne and wiped the sweat from his forehead. "Sure is hot today," he mumbled. He looked over, and getting no response from the man, he said it again, louder and clearer.

The man looked at him. "Did you say something?" he asked.

Peter wiped the sweat from his neck. "I was just commenting on how hot it is today."

"Yes, it is," the man said, with an added nod. He ran his finger along a red line on the map.

Peter tucked the handkerchief back into his pocket. "You're an American also, aren't you?" Peter said.

The man turned the map over. "Yes, I am. Where are you from?"

"Cincinnati," Peter said. "You?"

"Seattle."

Peter removed his backpack from his back and placed it at his feet. He leaned over and reached out his hand. "My name's Peter Yarbrough."

The man shook Peter's hand. "Jeff Longly," he said.

Peter scooted a few inches nearer to Jeff, pushing his backpack along with his feet. "Are you traveling alone?"

Jeff grasped the top strap on his backpack. "Well, uh, why do you ask?"

Peter chuckled. "Don't get me wrong. I'm not out to rob you or anything like that. I saw you sitting here all by yourself reading that map and I wondered if you were waiting on someone."

"There is no one," Jeff said. "I prefer to travel alone."

Peter pointed at Lloyd who was staring at him with an expression of impatience on his face. "I'm with him," he said. "Or I should say, he's with me. I started out traveling Europe on my own and then I ran into him."

Jeff glanced at Lloyd. "He looks like he'd be interesting to hang out with."

"I thought the same thing at first," Peter said. "His name is Lloyd Hudson. I met him in a faded restaurant in a small, rainy town on the main line between Brussels and Paris. There were mirrors on the walls all around the room. He was the only other customer in the restaurant and we struck up a conversation. He said that he had become separated from his traveling companion and had no way to contact him. We talked and shared a bottle of wine. He seemed perfectly okay. He said the mirrors were making him dizzy, so we left the restaurant and he's been with me ever since."

Jeff folded the map and tucked it into a pocket in his backpack. "You could have gone your separate ways if you had wanted to."

"It's not that easy," Peter said. "He's like gum that has gotten stuck on the bottom of my shoe."

The woman in black came up to Peter and said, "*Ter sua palma lida?*"

"No, I don't want my palm read," Peter said.

The woman walked away.

"Did you travel by train?" Jeff asked.

"Mostly, but we hiked the Camino de Santiago," Peter said. "All 500 miles." A chill went up his spine. "He complained the entire way that his feet hurt. I had to carry his backpack for more miles than I care to remember."

Lloyd closed the guidebook and walked toward where Peter was sitting.

Seeing Lloyd walking their way, Peter said to Jeff, "Oh good, you're going to get to meet him."

Jeff looked at his watch. "I really should be going."

Peter placed his hand on Jeff's arm. "Please, I need to hear him talk to someone else other than me, even if only for a few minutes."

Jeff lifted his backpack into his lap. "Okay, but just for a few minutes, and then I need to go find a hostel."

When Lloyd got to the bench, Peter shifted to the far edge, leaving a space between him and Jeff. He pushed his backpack in front of him. He introduced the two men.

Lloyd regarded Jeff warily, but right off said, "Your face is sunburned. You should always wear sunscreen. I carry it with me all the time. I have suncreen with a high SPF in my backpack if you'd like to use some."

"No, thank you," Jeff said.

"Have a seat," Peter said to Lloyd.

Lloyd took his backpack off, placed it on the ground, and sat down between Peter and Jeff.

"Have you seen all the sights in Lisbon?" Lloyd asked Jeff.

"No, I just arrived here this morning."

"Us too, but already we've seen almost this entire waterfront," Lloyd said. He pointed at the Belém Tower being admired by a hundred tourists. Its white tower was gleaming in the sunlight. "The guidebook says that's some kind of major tourist attraction, but I just don't find it that interesting." He opened his guidebook. "What guidebook do you use?"

"I just travel by maps with no real agenda in mind," Jeff said. "I like to feel like an explorer when I travel."

Lloyd shook his head and uttered, "Tsk, tsk, tsk."

"Lloyd has our entire route planned out according to his guidebook," Peter said. "From here we travel to Southern Portugal and then cross over to Spain. Isn't that right, Lloyd?"

"Poor Peter would still be staring at the crazy mirrors in a restaurant where we met if I hadn't rescued him." Lloyd said with a smug chuckle.

"Show Jeff the pictures you took inside that souvenier shop in Fátima," Peter said.

"Oh, the religious statues in the shop were a real hoot," Lloyd said. He fumbled around in his backpack and pulled out his iPhone, found the pictures, and stuck the iPhone in Jeff's face.

The woman in black came up to Peter with her hand held out. *"Ter sua palma lida? apenas 10 Euros."*

"You're persistent," he muttered, and then said to her, *"Sim."* He took 10 Euros out of his shorts pocket and handed it to the woman. He then held his palm out.

She studied his hand very carefully for several moments, and then said, *"Você deve fazer sua própria fortuna."* She stuffed the money into a skirt pocket and walked away.

"I must make my own fortune," Peter mumbled to himself. He looked over and saw Jeff nodding politely as Lloyd explained in great detail every picture he was showing.

Surrepititously, Peter picked up his backpack, stood up, and walked away.

The End

18

LUCIA ON THE BEACH

Lucia La Rosa came from a Sicilian family with a long, storied past. She lived alone in a house near the beach at the southernmost end of the island. She had inherited the house when she was only sixteen from a favorite aunt who died from a heart attack while seated at the dining room table. The table remained in the same place it stood with the six chairs seated around it just as they were when the aunt died six years before. A handmade light blue Sicilian burrato embroidered lace tablecloth passed down through generations of La Rosa women covered the table, held in place by a stone mask that lay in the center of the table. The mask was recovered from one of the island's ancient Roman ruins; its value incalculable. The shutters to the dining room were always kept open, allowing the breezes that carried the salt air from the Mediterranean Sea to blow in night and day, in fair and foul weather. Lucia's orange tabby cat, La Tigre, a mouser who had been the deceased aunt's cat and turned his nose up at man-made cat food, spent most of his time lounging in the chair next to the window, being shooed from it only when Lucia sat there to write poetry in one of her journals while staring out at the beach and ocean.

On the eve of her twenty-third birthday, as the sun set, Lucia stepped out of her house and onto the marble tiles of the portico of the house and watched as plumes of black smoke rose from the top of Mt. Etna. She shoved her long hair that had fallen over her ears back onto the top of her head and adjusted the gold hair comb studded with emerald chips, one of the many pieces of jewelry left to her by her aunt, so that it held her bundle of hair in place. The front of her house, where she stood, faced a road that ran between the villas that lined the beach or were perched on small hills on the opposite side of the road. The sweet, yet spicy scent of the ubiquitous white plumeria hung in the air. While gazing at the whitewashed stone villa on the other side of the road owned by an American couple that she had seen but never met lived in it during the winter months, she inhaled the fragrance of the flowers and wondered what it was like to live anywhere else but in Sicily.

The slight tremble beneath her bare feet that vibrated through her entire body brought her attention back to the volcano. All her life she had expected it to erupt. As the moments passed and it continued to exhale clouds of black smoke into the air and do nothing else other than make the ground shake a little, she turned and went back into her house. Her friends were throwing a Birthday party for her at Carladina's Restaurant that was located on the beach a few miles away. She thought it was time to preserve this moment, the time spent awaiting the moment when she would put on her new dress to go to the last Birthday party of hers she ever intended to attend, and write a poem about it in her journal. She pushed La Tigre from the chair, picked up her pen and journal, gazed out at the darkening sky and sea, and then began to write.

#

Like electrified ivy, miniature white lights were wrapped around the poles that held up the red and white awning of Carladina's Restaurant. Lucia walked under the awning just as a smattering of volcanic ash began to rain down from the night sky. Carrying a faded and slightly worn small bright blue clutch purse that her aunt carried for many years, she opened the door, walked in, and searched for her friends inside the small restaurant before seeing them sitting at a table under a large beach umbrella striped with the colors of the rainbow out on the back patio.

Accursio, the head waiter who never attempted to hide the crush he had on her said to her cheerfully in emphatic Italian as she walked past him, "*Buon compleanno.*"

"What's happy about it?" she replied before going through the doors out to the patio. There, her nine friends circled around the table, stood, raised their glasses of wine and began singing "Happy Birthday to You."

For the next hour as the group ate, drank, sang and chatted noisily and happily, Lucia stared out at the water and watched the white sails of a small boat gleaming in the ambient light of a star lit sky as it crossed the water not far from the shoreline. Unable to rouse herself from the ennui that had overtaken her, she kissed her friends on their cheeks, thanked them, and left her party early. She climbed onto her scooter and then remembered she had left the clutch purse at the table where she had been sitting. She went back inside, and after she and her friends searched the patio, and Accursio looked about the entire restaurant, she left the restaurant without it, with promises from Accursio that he would find it or if it wasn't found, "Throw himself into the volcano from shame."

#

She entered the house, kicked off her shoes, walked into the dining room and flicked on the lights. La Tigre was sitting on the chair with a dead mouse dangling from his teeth by its tail. The balmy ocean breeze ruffled the cat's fur and made the edges of the tablecloth that hung over the sides of the table flutter. She then went into the kitchen, put a tea kettle filled with water on the stove, and turned on the flame beneath it. While waiting for the water to boil she removed her dress and laid it over the back of a chair. In her bra and panties she opened the back door and realized that the sailboat she had seen while at the restaurant was the same one she now saw riding the waves not far from the beach behind her house. Seeing it puzzled and frightened her although she reasoned that it was merely coincidence that it had reappeared so near to where she lived. The floor beneath her feet trembled almost imperceptively from a tremor caused by Mt. Etna just as the kettle's whistle began to shriek. She closed the door, turned off the flame beneath the kettle, and filled a cup with the hot water and dropped a tea bag into the water.

Returning to the dining room she saw that the mouse no longer hung from La Tigre's mouth. She pushed the cat from the chair and sat down and sipped the tea while watching the sailboat appear and then resappear over and over as the waves around it rose and fell.

#

At age eight after her parents were lost in the Mediterranean waters in a boating accident, their bodies never recovered from the depths, the orphaned Lucia came to live with her aunt and uncle in the house where she now lived. It took her months to adjust to living with them and in a house where everything was old and were rarely moved from one spot to another. The pictures that hung on the walls had always hung in the same place. The pendulum that never swung from side to side as it was designed to do in the lower cabinet of the grandfather clock had never budged an inch. Uncle Marco, who had once been a hitman for the Sicilian mafia, sat in the overstuffed chair in the living room, slowly aging just like the radio he always listened to that he could only get one station on. It played American swing music from the 1940s. Aunt Gianna replaced only one thing, the hair that fell from her head after chemotherapy with a wig that was a few sizes too large and sat askew on her bald head.

Lucia spent most of the time on the beach, building sand castles and searching for seashells that she kept in old purses given to her by her aunt. She kept an eye on the ebb and flow of the tides, watching for her parents to wash ashore. While friends came and went, coming into her life and leaving it depending on her level of enthusiasm in being with them, which was as inconsistent as Mt. Etna's subdued eruptions. It was the volcano that anchored her to Sicily and the thing that filled her with constant terror.

"If it blows, it blows," her aunt would tell her.

"Won't it kill us all?" Lucia asked.

"Maybe yes, maybe no."

Her uncle died a few years before the death of her aunt. She forgot him soon afrer he died except for the time he spent in his chair. The memories of her aunt who never recoverd spiritually or emotionally from the cancer – it sapped her of any zest for life – were like apparitions that constantly hovered in her thoughts.

#

Early the next morning, Lucia opened the front door to her house to see a taxi pull up in front of the villa owned by the Americans. She watched as the taxi driver opened the trunk to his car, took out several large pieces of expensive-looking luggage, and carried each one up the long path to the villa while the couple stood by and watched. The couple were younger than Lucia remembered. She looked on with a mixture of surprise and envy as the taxi left and the husband took his wife in his arms and kissed her passionately. She wondered if they were always so loving together or just happy to have returned to Sicily. In her entire time with her aunt and uncle, she had never seen them do even as much as hug. As the couple turned and walked hand in hand to their villa, Lucia looked down at her feet. Lying on the marbled floor was the clutch purse she had left at the restuarant. On top of it was a brightly colored envelope with the words "Happy Birthday" written across it. She picked up the purse and the card and carried them into the house, closing the door behind her. In the dining room she tossed the unopened envevlope onto the table and then opened the purse expecting to find her identifcation and the money that had been in it. She looked inside it and then turned it upside down, spilling seashells into her hand. She quickly dropped them onto the floor as if they were pieces of volcanic ash that had burned her skin, stepped back and stared down at them. In that moment Mt. Etna rumbled loudly. La Tigre jumped down from the chair where he had been eating the remains of a mouse and ran under the table. Moments later when nothing else happened, Lucia went into the kitchen and fixed a cup of coffee. She then opened the back door and sipped on the coffee as she watched the sailboat glide across the calm waters of the Mediterranean.

A large number of the La Rosa extended family had attended Aunt Gianna's funeral. In the Catholic church Lucia sat in the front pew only a few feet away from her aunt's open casket. Before the priest quietened them, the women mourners, all dressed in black, cried and wailed loudly enough to rival the noise being created by a minor eruption of Mt. Etna. Lucia wore a floral print skirt and sandals, shocking the rest of the attendees who had paid no attention to her from the day her parents disappeared. The rumors spread by the La Rosa women that Lucia's mother and father had sailed off to enjoy a life of leisure in a foreign country got back to Lucia through her aunt who decried the gossip, but never refuted the claim. Sitting in the pew, the last words that her aunt said to her before she died echoed through her mind. "A woman's sexuality is like a volcano, ready to erupt at any time."

Once her aunt was buried, she returned alone to the house that had been left to her, shed her clothes and spent several hours sitting nude on the beach staring out at the sea. It was then that she decided she would end her life on her twenty-third birthday. It was an arbitrary number with no significance other than Aunt Gianna was twenty-two when she lost her virginity to Uncle Marco and secretely claimed to Lucia, "Life was a pile of stinking manure from that day on."

#

Lucia put La Tigre out on the portico and closed the front door and locked it. She then went from room to room to get one last glimpse at every piece of furniture and the painting and pictures on the walls that seemed frozen in another time, long past. In the dining room she tore open the envelope and despite feeling nothing, smiled at the picture of a balloons shaped like hearts on the front of the card and inside it a note from Accursio wishing her a Happy Birthday. She placed the card on the Roman mask and went into the kitchen. There she opened the back door, stripped off her clothes and walked out to the beach. Her footprints in the sand disappeared within seconds after she made them. At the edge of the water, as small waves of warm ocean water washed over her feet, Mt. Etna erupted.

The End

19

THE BELL RINGER

Brother Michael rang the bell a little after dawn, just as he did every morning. He liked ringing the bell. It gave him a sense of purpose. He had quit his studies in political science at an Ivy League school to become a monk, something that threw his parents into paroxysms of anguish and his friends into states of dismay and belief.

"Whatever will you do as a monk?" they asked, incredulous.

"Something simple. Something useful," he answered.

He loved monastic life. The daily routine, the comradeship of the monks, the quietude, suited his personality. The one thing he wanted was a new bell.

Even though he didn't own the bell, he wanted a new one anyway. He thought of the bell as his and he thought the Saint Bernardino of Sienna Monastery deserved a new one.

#

Inside the halls of the monastery, the dry, hot breezes of August carried the faint smells of yeast and baked bread. In the middle of the night, unlike during the day, the air seemed in constant motion, carrying with it sand collected from the surrounding Arizona desert. Installation of air conditioning was regarded as an unnecessary expense. Each of the abbots of the monastery, past and present, felt the monks of Saint Bernardino didn't suffer enough, so modernization was seldom considered practical, for both financial and spiritual reasons. Even during the night when the desert cooled somewhat, the windowless cells in which the monks slept remained particularly hot and uncomfortable, where small fans were permitted to be used, but only if the outside temperature was above 80 degrees Fahrenheit.

It was only 79 degrees Fahrenheit when Brother Mark, the abbot, rolled over onto his back on his cot, and drenched with sweat, suddenly died from a heart attack. When the morning bell was rung in the center courtyard calling the brothers to prayers, the abbot's absence was immediately noticed. Rigor mortis had turned Brother Mark's body stiff as cardboard, the expression of shock and agony, molded onto his facial features. He was 86 years of age and not expected to live much longer anyway, but the brothers who found him had the decency to act surprised.

By later that afternoon, Brother Mark's body was placed in a pine box, carried out to the monastery's crowded cemetery and buried with a cement marker that gave only his religious name, his birth name abandoned long ago, and the dates of his birth and death. All 48 of the monastery's monks attended his funeral and burial. Not a single tear was shed. The thinking and religious doctrine being that death offered greater rewards than life, after all, so why mourn the abbot's passing. There was no mention made that he wasn't well-liked, in fact, he was widely despised.

With the kitchen closed that afternoon to observe the abbot's passing, the 16 monks who returned to it to re-ignite the ovens in which the loaves of San Bernardino's bread were baked, grumbled only a little bit that the abbot's death and burial meant they would have to work later that night. They had a daily quota of loaves that had to be baked in readiness to be sent out to the stores, restaurants and bakeries the next day. The quota only changed if orders increased – or heaven forbid – decreased. The quota board was watched over and discussed with the same keen interest by the monks, that they regarded their own immortal souls. The only twenty-first century upgrades made to anything in the monastery was the installation of computer software programs that kept track of orders, shipping, and general accounting. The computers and their operators were overseen by Brother Joshua, who was among the sixteen monks allowed to attend community college classes, in his case to keep his computer training up to date. He was 71.

He was also one of the monks who entered Brother Mark's cell and found him dead. "I wonder how this will affect the sales figures for our bread?" he wondered aloud.

Overhearing Brother Joshua, his youngest friend in the monastery, Brother Simon, the monastery's chief baker, whispered to him, "You'd be a great abbot. You alone understand what the financial ramifications are of installing a new abbot who doesn't understand selling bread."

That gave Brother Joshua something else to think about as Brother Mark was lowered into the ground. The monks of the monastery would select a new abbot by secret ballots in a week's time. He knew without giving it much thought that he only needed 25 votes to be the next abbot.

He also knew he wasn't liked much more than Brother Mark had been.

#

During the evening meal which took place shortly after Brother Mark's burial, the monks were quiet and reverent, not that they felt anything but relief that their old abbot was dead, but they felt it their spiritual obligation to at least pretend to find the abbot's empty chair at the head of the table worthy of prayerful contemplation. There was a great deal of chatter but it was done in hushed tones and between spoonfuls of potato soup, slices of bread with bread and honey, and an orange.

Like all of the monks, Brother Michael had an assigned chair at the table. Where a monk sat depended on his length of time in the monastery beyond time spent as a novice, who were never counted in anything and couldn't vote. They were non-entities until they were fully initiated as a monk. Brother Michael sat in the middle of the long table, seat 24, across from Brother Jerome, a burly monk with the strength of a professional weight lifter. For all the years they had been in the monastery together, he didn't know Brother Jerome very well, but had one reason to like him; he had repeatedly pressed Brother Mark to no avail to buy a new bell as the bronze bell was an eyesore, no matter how much the bell ringer buffed a new shine out of it.

#

After Brother Mark had laid in his grave for about five hours, right after evening prayers, Brother Solomon, the only nurse in the monastery, was cornered in the back of the chapel by Brother Aaron and Brother Noah after the rest of the brothers had left to go wash and then go to their cells to pray and sleep.

"We think you should be the next abbot," Brother Aaron said, tightly gripping Brother Solomon's shoulder causing the accosted brother to wince. Pounding bread dough had given Brother Aaron inordinate hand strength. "We think you should put your name up to be the next abbot."

"Yes, you would be a shoe-in," Brother Noah said, wrapping his muscled arm around Brother Solomon's back and pulling him close to him. Brother Noah worked in the garden where countless hours of hoeing the earth and digging holes had the other brothers referring to his strength as being Samson-like.

"Me? Really?" Brother Solomon replied, surprised they thought so. Brother Solomon, the monastery's only nurse was also one of the most spiritually inclined and devout monks in the monastery.

"Do you think it would be the heavenly father's wish that I petition the brotherhood to make me the abbot?" he asked looking first at Brother Noah and then Brother Aaron.

"We can't speak for the heavenly father, but the younger brothers would be behind you," Brother Aaron said. "Why must all abbots be near death in age?"

Brother Solomon was 54, near the average age of all the brothers. "It's the strength of the younger and healthier brothers that keeps the monastery afloat," he said, whispering, fearing he was saying something that might bring disfavor down on him from the almighty above.

"Certainly," Brother Noah said.

"And we could finally get that gym built that we younger brothers have wanted for some time," Brother Aaron said.

"If it is God's will," Brother Solomon said. "But I always believed healing the sick was my vocation not being the abbot."

"Of course," Brother Noah said, "but God wouldn't have given some of us the physiques fitting Michelangelo's David if he didn't intend for us exercise them. And only a nurse heading this monastery will understand the need for better work out equipment."

The three brothers left the chapel, went to their individual cells, and got on their knees beside their cots and prayed for a running track to be built around the monastery.

#

Three day later, Brother Michael stood at the base of the bell tower and looked up at the bronze bell still surrounded by early morning haze. He had his hand on the rope that led to the bell, knowing by instinct and having been the bell ringer for 14 years when to begin tugging on it, thus awaking the brothers. He had suggested to the senior monks that he ring the bell in honor of the just deceased abbot as soon as everyone knew what happened, but they thought it an unnecessary ornamentation to an otherwise somber occasion. He didn't like Brother Mark either, and with some guilt thanked Christ for allowing the abbot's death to happen, but once he uttered those thanks, he thought ringing the bell might be looked upon favorably by the residents of heaven, which happen to also include the newly deceased abbot. It was a joke among the brothers that a departed soul had to be insane to hang around the monastery any longer than it had to.

He had heard murmurings in the showers among the few other monks who awoke at the same early time that he did about who should be the next abbot. Brother Luke's name was mentioned because he was an advocate for planned recreational trips away from the monastery, as was Brother Job's name mentioned because he supported a weekly movie night and including movie DVDs in the monastery's library. Other names that were mentioned were Brothers Solomon and Joshua.

The thought had entered Brother Michael's brain during the evening meal right after Brother Mark's death that Brother Jerome would be a fine abbot because then a new bell would be installed in the tower. But no one would vote for Brother Jerome to be the abbot.

Brother Jerome had no interest in the making of or sale of bread which was how the monastery was sustained and he was only the monastery's mechanic, whose sole purpose was to keep the bread delivery truck running.

#

"If only Brother Mark had left some clue as to who he wanted to succeed him, then selecting a new abbot would be much easier," Brother Joshua said as he bent over the financial ledger checking for the accuracy of the figures of the previous day's bread production numbers. The abbot's death may have had played a role in the overall increased production of loaves. Among the bakers, Brother Mark wasn't liked. He sampled too many of the loaves which meant the brothers in the kitchen sometimes missed their quotas.

"If he had given such a clue, you becoming the next abbot may not be as easy to accomplish as it will be," Brother Simon said looking over Brother Joshua's shoulder at the ledger as he tried to decipher the scribbled numbers.

Brother Joshua's head collided with Brother Simon's chest when he closed the ledger and sat back. "There is only two days before the vote takes place for the next abbot," he said. "There aren't enough brothers who would vote for me based on the gossip that goes around so how do you see it as being easy to accomplish?"

"We tell everyone that you just discovered Brother Mark had been embezzling funds, since he was the only monk who could write checks on the monastery's bank account, and that only you as the next abbot has the financial wisdom to repair the damage that was done."

Brother Joshua stood up and began pacing the small office where the two were located. It was one of the few rooms in the monastery that had a window. Always kept raised a few inches because Brother Joshua liked fresh air, even fresh air that was hot and smelled of rotting vegetation and decaying garbage piled nearby to make compost for the gardens. "Lying to the brothers doesn't seem right," he said. He went to the window and took a deep breath. "Besides, what possibly could Brother Mark have done with any money he would be accused of embezzling?"

"I'll have to give that some thought," Brother Simon said. "In the meantime I need to get back to the kitchen to make sure those lazy bakers are doing their jobs or the monastery won't produce a single load of bread."

#

Brother Michael leaned against the wall just below the window to the office where he had been listening to Brothers Joshua and Simon. He had in his hands the bucket, rags and polish he used to shine the bell every day. "A shiny bell is a godly bell," he liked to say to anyone who asked why he spent time shining such a badly shaped bell that produced such discordant ringing.

"You deserve a better bell to ring," some of the brothers told him.

He never mentioned that it was Brother Mark who kept the monastery from getting a new bell.

Overhearing the brothers in the finances office, he immediately began to wonder how he could use their scheming to his advantage to at least get Brother Jerome's name on the ballot.

#

Brothers Solomon, Aaron and Noah were hidden behind the garden shed. The sun beat down on the shed's tin, intensifying the heat the three men already felt. Beneath their tunics, sweat covered their toned bodies. A day of working in the garden in such hot weather had taken its toll on all three of them although none of them would admit it.

Brother Solomon, in particular, was feeling his age. His joints ached and the hot weather had drained him of any energy. He looked forward to doing nothing more than sitting in the coolness of the infirmary tending to sniffles and minor burns and cuts and bruises. There was something annoying about listening to the younger brothers plotting his bid to be the next abbot.

"But there are four brothers who want promises that a swimming pool will be put in," Brother Aaron said.

"We can't promise that,"Brother Solomon said. "We could throw pails of water on them," he said with a smirk.

"Four others want morning calisthenics instead of morning prayers," Brother Noah said.

Brother Solomon threw up his arms. "That's completely out of the question. I fear we're all going to hell before the vote even begins."

"We have to promise the younger monks something. We don't have a majority of the brothers on our sides yet," said Brother Aaron. "Maybe we're going about this all wrong."

"How so?" Brother Noah asked.

"Maybe instead concentrating on turning brothers to Brother Solomon, we should focus on turning them against anyone else."

Brother Solomon groaned loudly.

From the other side of the shed, Brother Michael smiled broadly as he turned to go back to the bell tower and await the call for the evening meal.

#

In the final day just before the ballot listing the monks who would be up for the role of abbot would be revealed, it was widely recognized that Brother Joshua of the finances office and Brother Solomon, the monastery's nurse, were the two monks certain be on the ballot. Anyone else who gave it a glimmer of thought or had a few supporters fell to the wayside, convinced that their spiritual life on Earth was destined to be involved in the mundane matters of keeping the monastery running.

In his quiet way, Brother Michael circulated among the brothers, letting it be known in very subtle terms that the lie being circulated that Brother Mark had been an embezzler was a falsehood perpetrated by the power-hungry Brother Joshua and his chief supporter Brother Simon. He made a cogent argument that it would have been impossible for Brother Mark to have had a mistress and a love-child he was sending money to, because Brother Mark was too mean and ugly to attract a woman, even if he had ever had a chance to meet one. The finances were fine, he assured the other monks.

"If Brother Solomon became the next abbot, there would be no other monk with the training as a nurse to run the infirmary and in general nurses were hard to come by." It was a simple, but effective argument.

On the eve of the election at the evening meal he stood at his place at the table and made an impassioned plea that the brotherhood choose an abbot who was modest, whose skills could be taught to another monk, and who served the monastery with spiritual devotion. "Someone like our humble mechanic, Brother Jerome."

"Me?" Brother Jerome, said with great surprise as he looked up from his plate of potatoes and vegetables.

#

On the morning of the election, Brother Michael rang the bell as he always did, attended morning prayers as he always did, and had breakfast in the same way he always had, seated in the same seat he had sat in for some time. Then to his horror he found out his was the sole name on the ballot. A disgraced Brother Joshua, when confronted about the lie about Brother Mark removed himself as a possible candidate. Brother Solomon also said he had no interest in being the abbot. "I would miss the smell of antiseptics too much," he said. Brother Jerome was never seriously considered by anyone. No one else wanted to fix the constantly failing delivery truck motor or fix its flat tires.

"Why me?" Brother Michael asked as one after another voted for him.

"You have the monastery's well-being as your sole concern," he was told.

He didn't tell them that getting a new bell was really his only concern. As abbot he could order one but he'd never be able to ring it.

God works in mysterious ways.

The End

20

THE NOTE

Boon-Mee's saffron robe reminds him who he is. He's a Theravada monk, a bhikku, aged 24, from a small village near Bangkok. The color of the cloth symbolizes simplicity and detachment from materialism. Boon-Mee finds the color pleasing. It reminds him of the color of the clouds in a sunset sky. It's the same color as the robe worn by the Buddhist monk, the bhikku, who walks in front of him, and the monks, the bhikkus, ahead of that, and the ones behind him. He has a dark gray woven bag hanging from his shoulder, just like the other monks. There are twelve monks in the line, from the most senior monk at the head to the novices at the rear. Boon-Mee is the seventh in line. He wears no shoes and leaves his footprints in the dirt as he quietly treads to the village, the same village the line of bhikkus travel to every morning. He holds his alms bowl in the folds of his robe, keeping it hidden. The bowl is never shown publicly unless alms are being placed in it. His bowl has a lid. He has meticulously washed and dried both bowl and lid. It's part of his daily activities, part of his discipline. Wearing the saffron robe, thoroughly cleaning the bowl and lid, and walking barefoot in the dirt on the way to the village, are all parts of who he is.

He enjoys life as a monk. Improving himself as a way of improving the world makes sense to him.

Up ahead he sees women and a few men of the village lined up along the side of the road in front of their homes with baskets of food, their alms, awaiting the monks. Boon-Mee tries to ignore the rumbling of his stomach. Every morning as he walks to the village to accept his alms, to perform the ritual of the bintabaht, his stomach begins to make noises. He fears that his noisy stomach will be heard by the other monks or by the women who give him their alms. The sounds his stomach makes in the morning bintabaht is worrisome and a daily cause for self reflection. He tries to accept it, to let it go, it's such a small thing, his gurgling stomach, but as he participates in the morning bintabaht it weighs heavily on his mind. He's told no one about it, especially the abbot of the monastery where Boon-Mee lives.

The line slows and at the bhikku at the head of the line is Kob Chai who recently turned age thirty-six. Keeping his head bowed, he takes his bowl from his robe, removes the lid, and holds out his bowl for a woman who then places in it a scoopful of sticky rice taken from a large pot and shoves sticks of incense into his bag. He doesn't look at her face and she avoids looking at his, although she smiles. As a layperson her joy comes from giving to a monk. She is one of the women who arrives early, just past sunrise, carrying with her a wood crate to sit on until the bhikku arrive. She kneels when she first sees them coming down the road and remains kneeling as she puts rice in the bowls each morning. Her alms never varies; it's always a scoopful of sticky rice. She is always the first layperson in the line to make a gift of her alms.

And so it goes in the same way for the next monk, and the next one, and the one after that, until Boon-Mee steps up to the woman. Her sudden giggle alarms him, but he doesn't react. He can't talk to her, ask her why she giggled. Was it the sound his stomach was making? So he goes from layperson to the next accepting their alms.

It isn't until the next to the last woman in line that he sees her hand drop a folded piece of paper – what looks to be a note – into his bowl along with a baggie filled with dragonfruit. He doesn't look at her face, but he knows the back of her hand. There's a mark on it, a birthmark, dark brown, in the shape of a butterfly.

He steps in front of the last layperson, accepts her alms of a baggie filled with cooked noodles while watching peripherally if the woman who gave him the folded paper does the same with the next bhikku. She doesn't. He resists looking at her face, only watching her hands as she places a similar baggie in the bhikku's bowl. As he walks on, concentrating on the unconditional love that Buddha imparts in the alms transaction is difficult. All he can think about is the note in his bowl that he covers with his lid and returns to beneath the folds of his robe.

He walks back to the monastery, quieting his mind, at peace with himself. He first washes his feet, puts on his sandals. A Buddhist monk must not wear a footwear that will cover his toes and heel. This makes slippers or sandals allowable. He then enters the dining room where he prepares to empty his bag and bowl onto large trays as the others do, where it will be divided up so that each monk receives an equal and comparable share. But before he turns his bowl over, he surreptitiously reaches his long, slender fingers in, formed into pincers, takes out the note, and transfers it to a fold in his robe.

Before eating the only meal of the day at 11 a.m., with his plate filled with small amounts of rice, fried fish, green beans, stir fried vegetables, noodles, with a dragonfruit, a banana and a stick of incense laying to the side, he and the other bhikkus place their hands in their laps, close their eyes, and chant the mantra Aum maṇi padme hūm (Praise to the Jewel in the Lotus).

#

Boon-Mee was sixteen when he decided to become a monk. He was an only child. After finishing school early, thought it was his time for his ordination in the Sangha, the monastic order. He had originally intended it to be for a short time, a year at the most, just like both his father had been a monk for two years before the age of twenty. His mother had entered a Sangha for seven months but was never given full ordination as a nun because unbeknownst to her, or anyone else until it was discovered, she was pregnant with Boon-Mee. Becoming a monk or nun, even for a short time, is a way to receive good karma and merit. All the time that Boon-Mee was growing up, his mother gave alms ever morning to the bhikkus from the nearby temple where they lived instead of in a monastery.

His parents taught him the 227 rules of the Pāṭimokkhais, the code of monastic discipline, long before he sought his ordination.

#

The almost daily routine of having his head shaved is the only time he is ever touched by anyone, except the few times he has needed to see the doctor or dentist. Kla Han who lives in the next room shaves Boon-Mee's head. Not having hair is a way of showing detachment from the need for material things. They say very little to one another as Kla Han runs the razor over Boon-Mee's shaving cream lathered scalp. Talking is seen as unnecessary. For a monk conversations need to be internal, not external. Boon-Mee wants to tell Kla Han about the note that is now hidden under his pillow, but admitting that he has the note would bring up many questions better suited to be addressed by the abbot.

He clears his throat. "Secrets are a form of deceit, are they not?" he says, almost in a whisper. He looks up to see Kla Han nod his head. He then says, "If you found something in your food that didn't belong there what would you do?"

"Not eat it," Kla Han responds.

Boon-Mee sighs.

Kla Han finishes shaving Boon-Mee's head and wipes away the remaining shaving cream with a towel.

They then reverse roles. Nothing more is said.

After Kla Han leaves, Boon-Mee sits on his bed and takes the folded paper from under his pillow. He can see through the paper the faint traces of ink. He turns it over and over in his hand, tempted to unfold and read it, but he knows that succumbing to temptation, any temptation, is disrespecting the teachings of Buddha and ignoring one of the 227 rules of the Pāṭimokkhais. As the patter of gentle rain on the awning above the small balcony outside his room reminds him he should be meditating, he shoves the note back under his pillow and goes out to the balcony, sits cross-legged on a block of wood, and closes his eyes. Moments later he finds all he can think about is the note. His eyes spring open.

He thought this kind of obsessive thinking about anything other than the teachings of Buddha was a thing of the past. He rises from where he's seated and goes back into his room. He lights a candle and then inserts the end of a stick of incense into the flame. As swirls of fragranced smoke fill the air he takes the note from under the pillow with the thought to set it afire. It's Buddha's teaching that eventually all things perish, decay, return to a state of nothingness, so why not the folded paper?

He holds it near the candle but can't will his hand to place the note near the flickering flame and set the note ablaze. With his shoulders trembling, his hand shaking, and tears streaming down his face, he returns the paper to its hiding place beneath his pillow.

#

Pichai is the abbot, the head bhikku of the monastery where Boon-Mee lives. It's Pichai's hand he hears knocking on his door to awaken him very early, before sunrise, like every morning. This morning, Boon-Mee has awoken before Pichai knocks. It's Pichai, and only Pichai, that Boon-Mee has spoken to when the need arises, mainly to answer difficult questions about the Buddha's teachings. Upon the rapping on the door by Pichai, Boon-Mee sits up, determined to talk to the abbot about the note. It's highly unusual that he jumps out of bed in such haste. He dons his robe and slips on his sandals. He wants to catch Pichai before he has walked too far away. Boon-Mee then reaches under his pillow to retrieve the note to show it to the abbot.

It's gone!

In a panic, Boon-Mee flings his pillow aside, and frantically searches the bed for the note, but doesn't find it. He looks under the bed. Not there!

Was Buddha testing me? Did the note ever exist at all? he wonders, trying to reach a level of calmness and inner peace.

He removes his robe, showers, and puts on a clean robe. Without putting on his sandals he goes out on the balcony and sits down and gazes out at the grove of banyan trees trying to put the note out of his mind once and for all, having decided it was an illusion, something he needed to wake up to the fact that reaching nirvana, the goal of the Buddhist path, was not going to be easy, nor should it be. There was only one wholly enlightened being, and that was Buddha.

He crosses his legs, closes his eyes, and quietly chants the Aum mani padme hūm.

The sun has risen, casting a luminescent light across the landscape, when he opens his eyes. The air is filled with the song of myna birds. The other sound he hears is the rumbling of his stomach.

One day I must ask Pichai what it is that my stomach is telling me, he thinks.

He rises from his seat and goes back into his room. It will soon be time to go on the bintabaht. He takes one last look at the bowl and lid, making certain of their cleanliness which he saw to the night before, and then he shakes out his bag and hangs it onto his shoulder. He then kicks off his sandals. That is when he sees it. The note is stuck on the bottom of his sandal. How it got there he has no idea, but he finds himself suddenly angry. Angry with Buddha.

He peels the note from his sandal and drops it in his bag. He leaves his room, leaves the monastery, and takes his place in the line of bhikku and novices standing at the beginning of the path leading to the village.

#

Up ahead the laypersons await the monks, their baskets and pots of food on the ground before them or in their arms. Boon-Mee's stomach gurgles and rumbles. A rainfall during the night has made the path muddy. The mud is cool and soothing as it coats his feet. As he walks, his bowl hidden in the folds of his robe, he's determined to show Buddha that he understands and follows the Noble Eightfold Path: right understanding, right thought, right speech, right action, right livelihood, right effort, right mindfulness and right concentration.

The line slows as Kob Chai steps up to the first layperson, takes his bowl from the folds of his robe and presents it to her. This happens again and again as the line moves forward, the monks silently accepting their alms. Boon-Mee reaches the first woman who puts a scoop of rice into his proffered bowl. This morning she doesn't giggle although his stomach is making noises as loud as the day before. Yesterday it was just a giggle, nothing more, no meaning attached to it, he decides. He goes from layperson to layperson accepting their alms. Finally reaching the woman, the hand with the butterfly birthmark, placing her alms of fried pork in his bowl, he lowers his hand into his bag and takes out the note. He looks her in the face, and hands it to her.

A monk handing anything to a layperson is such an extraordinary event that it catches the attention of a few other laypersons as well as the bhikku and novices following behind him.

Boon-Mee walks on, feeling free of the note at last.

#

Boon-Mee's expulsion from the monastery is done quickly. His robes are taken from him and he he's handed a pair of jeans and a t-shirt and given enough money to catch a bus home.

In the bus, watching the scenery pass by as he stares out the window, he knows his parents, his entire village, will feel the shame of having a defrocked monk returning back to their fold. But on his mind isn't so much that, or Buddha, but the note.

The End

21

THE TALE OF THE RED LANTERN

Jade-colored rain fell on Xitang, splashing into the waterways whose surfaces glistened like emeralds between the multicolored houses. Li Qiang, a young man of nineteen, sat on a wooden bench, his nose pressed to the glass of the window of his bedroom, watching Wang Lei, who sat underneath a large umbrella, paddle his sampan with a long oar slowly through the water. He adjusted the shawl embroidered with green and blue dragons around his shoulders, and sighed loudly.

Wang Yong, his brother, aged nine, looked up from the straw mat he was sitting on and cutting pieces of red paper into the shapes of rabbits, no two of them alike. "You do that a lot," he said.

"Do what?" Li Qiang asked turning from the window.

"Make those sounds," his brother said. "You sound like the radiator in my school room when steam is coming out of it."

"I'm so bored," Li Qiang said.

"Take Li Li out of her box or write a story," Wang Yong said. "Or you can help me cut out rabbits and dragons to put on the lanterns."

"I'm a man now," Li Qiang said. "I'm growing tired of doing those things."

"Then I can have Li Li?" Wang Yong asked excitedly.

"Of course not," Li Qiang snapped at his brother. "She'll always be mine to take care of, but I don't want to do it every minute of every hour."

Zhang Jing pushed aside the dark blue curtain hanging in the door to their bedroom and stuck her head in. "I have some black tea for you Li Qiang," she said. "May I come in?"

"You can come in Auntie," Li Qiang said, "but I'm as full of tea as the canal is full of water."

She walked into the room, holding a blue cup with gold designs of ginkgo trees on it with steam rising from the dark liquid. With every step the tiny bells on the tip of her shoes tinkled like raindrops falling on tin. "It has done your health good to drink it," she said. "It's good to see you getting your health back after such a long illness." She stepped over a small pile of Wang Yong's cut outs and handed the cup to Li Qiang.

He took the cup, sniffed it as he always did, turned up his nose, and then took a sip. "That it is hot is the only good thing I can say about it."

"You shouldn't be sitting so near the window," she said. "The cold draft isn't good for you." She wiggled her foot, producing music with the bells.

"I'm bored and want to watch the sampans," he said, taking another sip of the tea, forgetting that he didn't like it when the scent of honey suddenly wafted up from the cup.

"You should play with Li Li, or write one your stories," she said, and then walked out of the room, taking her music with her.

Li Qiang sighed loudly.

"See, just like the radiator in my classroom at school," Wang Yong said.

#

Li Qiang sat cross legged on his mat and held his left arm out straight and watched Li Li crawl up it, felt her go around the back of his neck, and then held his right arm out and watched her scurry down it into the palm of his open hand. "What a good little mouse you are," he said to it, bringing it near to his lips and blowing it a kiss. He scooped some cooked riced out of a small, green, porcelain dish with his finger-tips and held it to the mouse's mouth and smiled as she began to nibble on it.

"Li Li, is a very smart mouse, isn't she?" Wang Yong asked as he flipped through his pile of cut outs. The idea of balance and harmony had been instilled in him when he was quite young, so he wanted to make certain he had the same number of dragons and rabbits.

"The smartest I've ever seen," Li Qiang said. "But it's not her only quality. She's also very pretty."

Wang Yong leaned forward and peered closely at the fluffy white mouse, as if seeing her for the first time. "She just looks like a mouse to me," he said. "Mā doesn't like her very much."

"Mā is afraid of mice," Li Qiang said placing the mouse on a bed of shredded newspaper in a wooden box. "If Mā knew Li Li the way I do she would love her as I do."

At that moment their mother pushed back the curtain. She was holding a broom and dust pan. A loose strand of hair hung limply down the side of her face. "You boys need to roll up your mats so that I can sweep the floor in here. The entire house needs to be swept clean of ghosts and bad luck from the year before," she said. "Tonight Auntie is preparing long noodles as way to say goodbye to the year gone by and to begin the new year early. It would be nice if after we eat you could read one of your stories to us Li Qiang, if you're feeling up to it. But right now there's a lot of cleaning I have to do so put away those cut outs, Wang Yong, and that awful rat, Li Qiang, and do as I asked."

"Yes Mā," Wang Yong said picking up the dragons and rabbits from the floor.

"Li Li isn't a rat," Li Qiang said under his breath, closing the lid on Li Li's box.

#

Standing at the window after the rain had stopped, Li Qiang watched Wang Lei as he steered his sampan the opposite direction he had seen him going that morning. He had known Wang Lei from a distance his entire life and had watched Wang Lei's hair become gray and his beard grow long enough to touch his round stomach. Li Qiang tried to wave at him, but Wang Lei went by without seeing him. Li Qiang picked up his notebook and went into the dining room. The walls were covered with long red cloth and paper banners, each of them with the same words: "May you enjoy continuous good health."

"Is there nothing else to wish for?" Li Qiang asked as Auntie came into the room from the kitchen carrying a huge plate of steamed vegetables. The bells on her shoes rang a melodic tune.

"Since you're getting better we want it to continue to improve," she said putting the plate on the table. "I'm so glad you're going to read us one of your stories. It has been a long time. Your parents are so happy about it. Is it a new one?"

"Yes, it is," Li Qiang answered. "Is Bà home?"

"He's taking a nap before we eat," she said.

"Not any more," Li Qiang's father said as he came through the open doorway into the living room. He turned to Li Qiang. "You look almost entirely improved, son," he said, lovingly grasping Li Qiang's shoulder. Bà underestimated his own strength, as always, and made Li Qiang wince from the power of his big hand.

"I am, but everyone is making such a fuss about it I feel like crawling in the box with Li Li," Li Qiang said.

"Not before we have some of Zhang Jing's noodles," his father said with a laugh.

"Just remember not to cut them as you eat them," she said. "That way we ensure that the entire family will live long lives."

#

In the living room with his father, mother and aunt seated in soft chairs and Wang Yong stretched out on a mat on the floor, Li Qiang sat upright in a chair in the middle of them, opened his notebook, and flipped to the middle of the book.

"High up in the mountains there lived a hermit whose name no one knew and neither did they know where he came from. He lived inside a cave where he had built walls of bamboo and dragged in bales of hay to spread about as a floor. He built furniture from the branches of fallen ginkgo trees tied together with hemp. He lived near a village that had no doctors or anyone who knew about how to use herbs or natural remedies to cure ailments or how to do acupuncture. It was rumored that the hermit was wise about medical matters.

"When a fever broke out, striking many in the village, the elders of the village had no idea what to do and went about the streets wailing and weeping in despair, hoping the hermit would hear them. The hermit did hear the echoes of the elders cries and came out of the cave, captured a quail, tied a note to its feet with the instructions on how to cure fevers, and sent it to the village. As soon as the quail landed on the street, the elders killed it and ate it without reading the note. This happened several times as the hermit watched from the mountain. Finally the hermit gave up and stopped trying to help and returned to his cave. When many of the villagers died, an elder passing by the cave while looking for bamboo shoots went in and said to the hermit, 'have you no heart? What prevents you from coming down to see what is wrong?'

The hermit scratched the long hairs on his chin and said, 'I heard you and sent ways to return health to those who were sick but you kept killing the messenger.'"

#

At night as Li Qiang lay on his mat covered with a bright red cover embroidered with tigers, he let Li Li play in his hair and run across his face. "If only you were a real live girl," Li Qiang whispered to the mouse.

"Did you say something?" Wang Yong asked from his mat against the opposite wall.

"I wasn't talking to you, but now that I am, how am I ever going to find a wife by the end of this year as I planned since I am just now returning to good health?" Li Qiang said.

"Is it so important to you?" Wang Yong asked. Wang Yong had many interests, but girls wasn't one of them.

"Lately I think of nothing else," Li Qiang said. He placed Li Li in her box and rolled onto his side, facing away from his brother, and fell asleep.

#

"Wake up sleepy head," Li Qiang's father said to him as he prodded him gently with his big foot; a foot that was slightly larger than the other one. "Today we say goodbye to this past year and to your unfortunate illness."

Li Qiang rolled onto his back and rubbed the sleep from his eyes. "Good morning, Bà. I was dreaming I was on the sampan with Wang Lei and he was telling me the most fantastic tale."

"You must write it down before you forget it," his father said.

Li Qiang sat up and looked up at the large red lantern covered with rabbit and dragon cut outs hanging in front of the door. "Wang Yong has been busy already this morning," he said.

"He said you wanted some special luck so he put it together for you in the middle of the night," his father said.

"It will take more than a red lantern with cut outs glued to it to give me what I want," Li Qiang said.

His father went to the door, turned and said, "Write the story down that you dreamt about and then come have your last breakfast of this year."

"I will, but I need to feed Li Li first," Li Qiang said.

"All mice should be as lucky as Li Li is," his father said, exiting through the curtain that got momentarily tangled on his big foot.

#

After feeding and giving water to Li Li and writing the story down that he remembered from his dream, Li Qiang came out of his bedroom just as his mother was carrying a large vase of flowers into the living room. "Those are pretty, Mā," he said.

"To end the year with beautiful flowers is also a good way to begin the new one," she said, going into the living room. His mother had a saying for every occasion that had been passed down for generations.

Li Qiang followed her and stopped at the entrance to the living room. There were several red vases filled with large bouquets of flowers on the tables. In the middle of the room a table had been set up and on it were platters of oranges and tangerines with rinds that gleamed, a candy dish piled with dried sweet fruit, and several bowls of peanuts. Pictures of deceased ancestors, most with inscrutable expressions, hung on the wall with the corners of the frames draped with red silk. On every wall was a red banner with gold lettering wishing everyone a long life or reminders to be thankful for good health.

"Are many relatives and friends coming this evening Mā?" he asked as she rearranged one of the bouquets.

"I believe so," she said. "Auntie and I are making enough dumplings, bamboo shoots, nian gao and zung zi to feed a small army." Before she married, Mā had been a cook at a military base, so she knew what she was talking about. "We're hoping you will read one of your stories for entertainment."

"Yes, Mā."

#

Just before it was time to greet those who had gathered in the living room to say goodbye to the year that ended and in anticipation of the New Year's festivities to begin tomorrow, Li Qiang stood at the window and looked out at the glowing red lanterns hung on the outside of the houses up and down the canal. Their reflections wavered in the water's glassy surface. Wang Lei's sampan was moored on the dock along his house.

He took Li Li from her box and petted her and blew kisses into her face. "I owe my returned health in part to you my little Li Li." He placed a piece of steamed dumpling with red bean paste on it in her box and sat her down next to it and watched her begin to nibble on it before closing the lid. Before going through the curtain in the door he picked up his notebook, ran his hand across Wang Yong's rabbit cut outs on the lantern, said a wish, and then went out to join the family's friends and relatives.

Sitting in the chair in the middle of the crowded room, Li Qiang opened his notebook and began to read.

"Zhang Li, the most beautiful princess in all of China, was very ill and was being taken by sampan up the Yangtze River on a very long journey to see a healer said to be the most knowledgeable in all the land about her particular illness. He would have come to her but he was blind and didn't travel. The princess's companion and caretaker, Madam Li Xia, who had the face of a salamander, was an old woman who had been with her since she was an infant, but was more strict than was needed. She didn't allow Zhang Li to talk to the young handsome man named Wang Ping who was steering the sampan. Zhang Li spent most of the time lying on pillows under the protection of the sampan's straw roof, sheltered from the sun and rain.

"Wang Ping could see that the princess was very ill and was very concerned that he might not get her to the blind healer in time, so he never rested and rowed and steered the sampan day and night. His effort was not enough for Madam Xia and she would berate him for not making the sampan move faster and belittle him when he took time to eat or drink, which he seldom did anyway.

"Princess Zhang Li could see how much effort Wang Ping was putting into getting them to the destination as swiftly as he could, and when Madam Xia wasn't watching, the princess would toss him pieces of fruit that he could eat while he steered the sampan.

"Days and days passed and by virtue of getting plenty of rest and the calm of riding on the sampan, the princess' health greatly improved, but Wang Ping became very ill and was still steering the sampan, but near death, when they arrived where the blind healer lived.

"'Is there someone very ill aboard the sampan?' the healer asked, sensing an aura of bad health that hung over the sampan, before stepping aboard.

"'Yes, the princess has been very sick,' Madam Xia said, wringing her hands. 'You must tend to her at once.'

"The blind healer examined the state of the princess's health and said to Madam Xia, 'the princess has only a slight case of anemia from not getting enough sunlight, but other than that she is healthy. You have come a great distance for nothing,' he said. As he started to leave the sampan he tripped over the body of Wang Ping who had fainted on the floor of the sampan. 'Who is this who I have fallen on?' the healer asked, placing his hand on Wang Ping's fevered brow.

"'That is just the useless oarsmen,' Madam Xi said haughtily.

"'Please do whatever you can to make him well again,' the princess pleaded, coming out from under the covering of the sampan. I will work with you to make him well again,' the princess said, much to the horror and shock of Madam Xi.

"For ten days the healer and the princess tended Wang Ping, and gave him herbal medicine, food, plenty of fresh water, and allowed him to get plenty of sleep. Wang Ping recovered his health and just before he was about to take the princess back to the palace, the blind healer said to the princess, 'there is still a sick one among you who has not been healed and a lengthy stay with me might restore her health.'

"'Then it should be so,' the princess said.

As the sampan left the dock to return home with just Wang Ping and the princess, the only one who didn't understand why she was being left behind was Madam Xia."

#

As everyone was clapping and chattering about the wisdom of the story, Li Qiang saw a beautiful girl sitting next to Wang Lei. He knew he had to meet the girl and so he approached them.

"I'm glad to see you here, Wang Lei," he said. "I hope you're enjoying yourself."

"Very much so," Wang Lei replied, "Let me introduce you to this young lady who I just met who was standing on your doorstep as I was coming into your house. Her name is Li Li."

Surprised at her name, Li Qiang turned to the girl who was wiping away a bit of steamed dumpling with red bean paste from the corner of her mouth. "Someone who helped me get over being ill is also named Li Li," he said.

"She's lucky if she gets to hear such wonderful stories all the time as the one you just read," Li Li said.

"She says very little about my stories," Li Qiang said, "but I would enjoy reading more of them to you some time."

"It would be a great privilege," Li Li said.

Going back to his room with his notebook under his arm and practically floating on air with happiness, Li Qiang, rubbed the lantern one more time, and then sat the notebook on his mat, picked up Li Li's box, and opened it.

The mouse was gone.

The End

22

WALK AWAY

Baina's footprints are left in the crumbling dry earth. She leans to the left to balance the weight of her naked child that she carries on her right hip. Her pale green cotton wrap-around skirt that reaches to her calves, loosely fitting pink t-shirt, and face, are covered with a thin layer of white dust from the dirt stirred up by the hot winds. Her braids that hang down to the middle of her back are dyed brick red from a mixture of clay scooped up from the creek that runs alongside the village and berries plucked from the bushes that line the creek. The other women in the village keep their heads wrapped, hiding their hair, protecting their scalps from the harsh sunlight. She passes by us avoiding our glances; she has no interest in us and has had none since we arrived here.

Sitting on a folding canvas stool, Marcie gulps water from a plastic bottle as she watches Baina walk by. She lowers the bottle and wipes the excess water from her parched lips with the back of her hand. "She's really quite lovely," she says of Baina.

I thought that very thing the first time I saw Baina two days ago, but never said so. I watch as Baina raises her child higher on her hip. The glare of the sun prevents me from seeing her clearly as she gains distance from where we sit. "She doesn't seem to like us being here," I say.

"I'm not so crazy about us being here either," Marcie says.

The flies here are ubiquitous and their weight on my flesh when they land is noticeable, like pebbles falling on my skin. I swat at them with a stick laden with leaves, but it does little good. Smells, topsoil, and bits of debris, are quickly carried away by the wind, but the flies seem to hover effortlessly in the air.

Baina disappears inside her shack at the other end of the village. Marcie stands up, stretches, and then wipes away the dust that had accumulated on her sunburned cheeks. "I'm going to try to take a nap," she says. She kisses me on the cheek, a kiss as soft as a butterfly landing on cotton, and then opens the tent flaps and goes in.

A small herd of goats enter the village with Keb right behind them, guiding them with his staff. The goats have small bells around their necks that jingle metallically. Keb is over six and a half feet tall and very thin. His hair is gray and his skin has the texture and appearance of aged black leather. He wears a pair of shorts, but no shirt or shoes. He stops in front of our tent.

"Don't lose hope. Your jeep parts will arrive soon," he says in English heavily accented with Afrikaans.

"We're paying for our foolishness," I say. "We should never have left the highway."

His laugh comes from deep within his lungs. His grin spreads across his face, exposing his toothless gums. "Your luck is that your vehicle break down near our village."

"So true," I say. "Tell me, Keb, why is it that Baina dislikes us so much?"

Keb shakes his head and looks toward the direction of her hut. "She's not originally from this village and she has no friends here. Now that she has no husband, her baby is only thing she find pleasure in."

"What happened to her husband?"

"He walk into the bush country and not return."

#

The jeep sits on the side of the dirt road with its hood raised. In the moonlight and covered with dust it has the look of the carcass of a wild animal. The quiver tree that stands nearby is like a sentinel whose skinny trunk appears as if it can barely hold up its head of tangled branches. The calls of coucals from their nests in the nearby brush is like one-note hoots made through hollow tubes. The cracked earth beneath my boots crunches with every step. When night fell, so did the temperature, and the tepid sweat that soaked my shirt earlier is now chilly against my back and chest.

I open the trunk to the jeep and take out my leather suitcase, lay it on the ground, and open it. I take out a bottle of liquid body wash, a tube of toothpaste, a bag of hard mint candies, two new handkerchiefs I had bought at the airport in Johannesburg, a pair of socks, a packet of wet wipes, and a bottle of aspirin, and place the items on a towel. I return the suitcase to the trunk, and then lift the towel by its four corners, and holding the corners together with one hand, toss the bundle over my shoulder.

It's about two miles from the jeep to the village and the near-desert landscape bathed in moonlight is stark and seemingly endless. We had decided to leave the main highway to take a jaunt on the back roads, never expecting we would get lost, or that the jeep we rented would break down. It was Keb who came upon us while he was herding his goats and took us back to his village. Our traveling companion, Chris, and Naeem, a young man from the village, left on foot to the nearest town to get help. That was two days ago.

The village is quiet when I enter it except for the sounds of voices coming from inside the plywood and corrugated steel shacks. To avoid going by our tent I've entered the village from a different direction, and it takes me a few minutes to catch my bearings. The village isn't very large, but it fans out in circles and all of the shacks look the same. It's only when I see the tent at the other end of a village path do I realize I'm standing in front of my destination: Baina's shack.

I lay the bundle at her door and as soon as I turn to walk away I hear her door open.

"Why do you come to my home?" Baina asks bluntly, gruffly. Her baby is nursing on one of her nipples.

"I brought you some gifts," I say. I point to the bundle on the ground.

"Why?"

"I heard your husband was lost in the bush country."

She taps the bundle with her foot. "He not lost," she says and bends down, picks up the bundle, turns, and goes back into her shack.

#

In the middle of the night the air is hot and still. Marcie is on her side facing the open tent flaps. Her breathing is labored, as if gasping for a fresh breeze that never comes. Moonlight has set the inside of the tent aglow in the color of the tent's bright yellow nylon. The silhouette of a lizard slowly creeping along the outside top of the tent takes on different shapes with every movement it makes, like that of a black cloud drifting across the sky. My face is awash with perspiration that has pooled beneath my eyes and in my ears. The smell of mosquito repellent that Marcie doused the inside of the tent with is thick and acrid, but in the absence of mosquito netting, it seems to have worked. Without the mosquitoes buzzing in my ears or feasting on my skin it's easy to forget I'm in a rural part of South Africa, hundreds of miles from a city.

I climb over Marcie, careful not to wake her, and when outside of the tent I stand and stretch, my fingers grasping for one of the millions of stars that are clustered in the night sky. One of the many emaciated mongrel dogs that inhabit the village slinks out from behind a stack of empty oil barrels and stares at me warily for several moments before trotting off toward the open scrublands. When I turn my attention to the direction of Baina's shack I see her standing naked in the street not far from her doorway, bathed in moonlight. She tilts her head back, spreads her arms, and begins to slowly turn.

"What are you doing out there?" Marcie says to me from inside the tent.

I turn to see her pale face yellowed by the light inside the tent. "Getting some fresh air," I say.

When I turn to see Baina, she's gone.

#

Keb hands me a bowl of fresh goat milk. I slosh it around for a few moments before taking a drink. Although warm it's surprisingly refreshing and sweet. I drink the remainder and hand the bowl back to him.

"Where is Baina from?" I ask him.

He pulls on the rope tied to the goat that he milked. It's now struggling against the hold the rope has on it to return to the rest of the herd. Looking at me appraisingly, Keb replies, "Kenya."

With the heat of the day, the flies have returned.

"She said her husband isn't lost," I say and look up to see a sparrowhawk circling in the sky in a repeated tight orbit as if trapped there.

"Maybe not lost and just walk away," he replies. He unties the rope from around the goat's neck allowing the goat to join the other goats grazing among the sparse patches of grass.

#

With their skirts hiked up above their knees the village women kneel in the mud along the creek, splashing their laundry in the muddy water. Their children and a few dogs play among the bushes behind them. Kneeling on the bank of the creek apart from the others, is Baina, who has her infant strapped to her back. Her braids are coiled into a cone shape atop her head. While the other women chatter in Afrikaan interrupted with bursts of giggles as Marcie and I wade into the creek to bathe the stench of sweat from our bodies, Baina keeps her head down, silent and seeming withdrawn.

The water is tepid and is like stepping into thin soup; bits of mud and grass immediately adhere to my legs. The floor of the creek is smooth and slick beneath the soles of my bare feet. We wear shorts, t-shirts and ball caps. The cap that Marcie wears is the one I bought for her in Paris. There's an Eiffel Tower logo on it. Marcie is a few feet ahead of me. I watch her blonde pony tail sway back and forth as she balances herself with every step.

She lets out a yelp, and cries out, "I've been bitten," just before she falls back against me.

I catch her in my arms. "What do you mean you've been bitten?"

"A bite. On my ankle," she shouts, on the verge of hysteria.

I lift her up and carry her to the bank where Baina stands watching, waiting. I step out of the water and lay Marcie on the ground. The other women gather around as Baina wipes mud from Marcie's ankle, exposing two round puncture wounds a quarter of an inch apart.

Baina looks up at me, her eyes steely with calm. "Snake," she says. "Take her to my house."

Inside her shack I lay Marcie on a straw mat on the bare dirt floor. I take a quick glance around. There's a small fire pit dug in the dirt in the corner of the room and a candle stuck into the neck of a bottle sits on a wood crate along with a small mirror and hairbrush. The things I gave to her are laid out in a circle on the floor beneath the only window.

"Leave now," Baina tells me and opens the door.

"But, my wife . . ." I begin.

"Will be sick but not die," she says.

#

It's nighttime and after several hours sitting on a stump outside of Baina's shack and hearing Marcie puking, Baina opens her door. "She will sleep here tonight," she says. "In the morning bring us some fresh milk." She closes the door.

On the way to the tent I see Keb latching the gate to the pen for his goats. In the darkness of a moonless night he appears even thinner than he is; a skeleton covered with a hide of skin. My voice startles him when I call out to him. He whirls around, not seeing me at first.

"The chatter of the women of the village made me think you were a demon," he says with a nervous laugh.

"What chatter?"

"Baina is performing her dark magic on your wife," he answers. "Did I not tell you that many in the village believe Baina is a witch?"

"No, you didn't mention it."

He looks around, checking to make sure he isn't seen talking to me in the darkness, and then comes nearer to me. "Have you seen that her child never cries?"

I hadn't noticed it, but now that he brought it to my attention, I don't recall the infant uttering a sound. While I could recount every detail about Baina – her appearance, her speech – the child had been an almost invisible being, there but not there. I glance the direction of Baina's shack and quickly feel ashamed of myself for questioning for a moment if Baina was indeed a witch. "It's superstitious nonsense," I say.

"Maybe so, maybe not," he replies. "You Whites see the world differently than us born on African soil."

If possible, I could feel the color of my skin, the whiteness of it in comparison to his and compared to everyone in the village.

"In the morning I will need to buy some milk," I say and then turn and walk to the tent.

#

At the break of dawn, yelling coming from within the village awakens me. I pull on my pants, crawl out of the tent and look up the street toward Baina's shack. There's smoke rising from the shack's roof. I rush down to where Marcie is standing barefoot in the dirt. She looks stunned, unable to turn her head away from the flames that have engulfed the door and are eating through the walls. Many of the villagers are standing around, some shouting as they shake their fists at the growing inferno as if angry that the fire is an invader in the life of the village. Some of the men rush to and from the creek and toss buckets of water on the nearest shacks.

"What happened?" I say to Marcie, grasping her shoulders and staring into her blue eyes.

"Baina woke me up and told me to get out of the shack." she stammers. "She pushed me out just before it all went up in flames."

"What about Baina and her child?" I ask, glancing around and not seeing them.

"I don't know. I just don't know," she says as she falls against my chest, shaking and sobbing.

It's then that I notice that the things I had given Baina are on the ground where Marcie and I stand, encircling us.

#

In the hours after the fire I alone searched the ashes and burnt hull of Baina's shack looking for signs of Baina and her child, and find nothing. The villagers stood about watching me, speaking in whispered Afrikaan to one another, but stayed back from Baina's destroyed shack.

Chris and Naeem, who have returned just hours ago with a mechanic who has fixed the jeep, tell me they saw Baina walking toward the bush country with her child strapped to her back. They stopped their vehicle and called out to her, but she kept walking.

With the tent and sleeping bags folded and returned to the jeep, we stand around saying goodbye to Keb. "It's not the earthly Baina your friend and Naeem see," he says. "She has returned to looking for her husband in her spirit form."

As Marcie climbs into the jeep, she says, with nervous laughter, "No man is worth all that trouble."

The End

23

NOISE

The sound of the 5:10 train coming through town was comforting. In the morning darkness of her bedroom Mrs. Lilly sat up on the edge of her bed, pulled her robe that had been draped over her walker from the top crossbar and slipped her arms into the yellow cotton sleeves. She positioned her legs between those of the walker and placed her hands on the rubber hand grips and stood up, and then balanced herself as she turned with the walker toward her opened bedroom door. The hardwood floor was cool and smooth beneath her bare feet as she slowly made her way out into the long hallway that led to the den, bathroom and at a right turn to the kitchen and a small breakfast nook. By memory and years of experience she knew the width between one wall to the next without need for any light, the exact location of the doors, and where every painting was hanging along the way.

In the kitchen she turned on the light. It was spotless thanks to Estelle, who was as finicky about neatness as Mrs. Lilly, and had been her housekeeper and cook since the days when Mr. Lilly was still active as a physician at the local hospital, some twenty years ago. The temperature of the floor had become cooler, owing to the white marble tiles imported from Spain. Beneath a large window that looked out on a well tended back yard was a white porcelain sink. Over the window hung a pair of lace curtains imported from the Azores. Antique plates with scenes from Granada and Toledo, Spain hung on the few spaces available on the walls for such things.

Mrs. Lilly crossed the kitchen to a counter where sat a large cookie jar purchased at a shop in the old Jewish section of Lisbon. Balancing herself on the walker with one hand she removed the lid and set it aside on the counter. She bent over and inhaled the aroma of Estelle's homemade oatmeal cookies. She took out two and set them on the counter than replaced the lid. She put the cookies in a pocket in her robe and made her way to the small dining room and sat down at a mahogany table that was against a wall with a window facing the house next door. She took the cookies from her pocket and placed them on the table and then sat down at the table in a cushioned chair she had inherited from her grandmother, a Southern Belle from the pre civil war days. Staring out at the neighbor's house, with the light from the kitchen glowing softly into the breakfast nook, she nibbled on the cookies savoring the cinnamon and subtle seasoning of nutmeg as she waited for Estelle to arrive.

At exactly six o'clock, the time she always arrived, Mrs. Lilly heard Estelle open the front door, shut it, and make her way to the back of the house, turning on lights in the parlor and large dining room along the way.

"Good morning Miss Lilly," Estelle said as she entered the breakfast nook. "How are you feeling this morning?"

"Just fine, Estelle. My joints are a bit achy like always."

Estelle went into the kitchen and could be heard preparing breakfast as Mrs. Lilly finished the cookies. Soon, Mrs. Lilly was greeted with the smell of fresh coffee and the sound of eggs frying in the skillet. Estelle always hummed while she cooked and cleaned and while Mrs. Lilly found it sometimes annoying, she had taken to trying to figure out what tune was being hummed without ever asking Estelle what it was. Estelle brought breakfast in to the nook on a small silver tray; a gift from a friend long deceased, and placed the coffee and plate of hot food on the table in front of Mrs. Lilly.

"Those folks up yet?" Estelle asked, looking out the window.

"I don't believe so." Mrs. Lilly answered. "Thank heavens."

Estelle chuckled lightly and went back into the kitchen. Mrs. Lilly ate the eggs and toast and drank her coffee listening to Estelle cleaning up, and humming. Mrs. Lilly watched out the window for signs that her neighbors had indeed decided to start their day, which coincided with when the pleasantness of her own day always began to decline. To Mrs. Lilly her neighbors were a nuisance, loud and perpetually busy at one intrusively noisy task or another in their yard or on their house. Their four hyperactive children brought Mrs. Lilly's general sense of serenity to an abrupt end. This section of High Street was not known for such unbridled and unwelcome activity.

The Longs had moved in six months ago, him a new professor at the nearby all men's college, and her a housewife who seemed to have nothing to do all day while her older children were at school except expose her youngest children to the outdoor elements or knock on neighbors doors and impose herself upon them. Her name was Francine, a New Yorker with an accent that lacked any refinement. Soon after moving in she had attempted to insinuate herself into Mrs. Lilly's life by knocking on the door and having the effrontery to introduce herself, but Mrs. Lilly quickly put a stop to it declaring that she had a headache and wasn't accepting visitors. Francine had ignored the subtle invitation to leave and continued talking even as Mrs. Lilly closed the door in her face. Francine had not returned since then, but the entire Long brood made their presence known on a daily and almost hourly basis from sunrise to sunset.

It was Francine who was on Mrs. Lilly's mind when the front door of the Long house swung open and Mr. Long, Edward by name, bound out it in only a pair of pajamas, retrieved the morning newspaper from their front lawn and then ran back inside slamming the door shut. As always, Mrs. Lilly was aghast. In all her life she had never slammed a door.

"Its begun," she called out to Estelle.

Mrs. Lilly finished her breakfast having watched Edward Long and his two older children leave the house, he on his way to the college and the children on their way to school. They were a vociferous lot, sending shouts of parting pleasantries until the children had turned the corner and were out of sight and Edward Long had gotten into his eyesore of a vehicle and noisily driven off up High Street. Then the two youngest children were brought out to the front yard where Francine Long sat on the front stoop of their home and watched the children fight and claw their way through one skull crushingly noisy game after another.

Having had enough, Mrs. Lilly stood up, walked her way through the large dinning room, an elegant space highlighted by an English walnut table, low hanging crystal chandelier, and large English paintings of different breeds of dogs, hunters on horseback in pursuit of foxes, and pastoral scenes of shepherds with their flocks. She gripped the walker tightly as she made her way back to her bedroom where she changed into a green print dress and slipped into a pair of white patent leather pumps. With Estelle's assistance, Mrs. Lilly opened her front door and went out onto the front porch and sat in a wicker chair and glared at Francine and the children.

Mrs. Lilly spent the better part of that morning, as she did most mornings, providing eyes and ears as witness to the calamity she considered the Long family to be. Francine and the children would at intervals disappear into the house for varying lengths of time only to reappear seeming more energized to wreak havoc on the peace and tranquility of High Street. To add to it, the Longs seemed to have no limit of needs for one type of repairman or another who by use of hammers, leaf blowers, lawn mowers, drills and backhoes raised the noise decibels to ear achingly high levels. By noon that day, Mrs. Lilly was near apoplexy with outrage, and after being assisted back inside by Estelle, sat at the table in the kitchen nook and could barely eat her lunch of celery soup and a tuna salad sandwich.

"Something has to be done," she told Estelle.

Estelle nodded knowingly and went into the large dining room and began polishing the walnut table with great intensity while humming.

#

After Estelle had prepared her evening meal, cleaned up and departed, Mrs. Lilly sat in the chair at the desk in the den where her now deceased husband once spent hour upon hour pouring over medical journals and taking copious notes that he committed to memory. But it wasn't her husband she was thinking about, but how to rid herself and the neighborhood of the Long family.

It had occurred to her early in the afternoon that she could make calls to all the neighbors and solicit their cooperation in the matter, but after short consideration she decided the idea of using the telephone to call people who she rarely talked with in person to be a somewhat socially vulgar way to seek assistance. Over the years those who she had once entertained in her home had either died or moved elsewhere, leaving mostly strangers who for the most part only wanted peace and quiet and rarely sought out their neighbors. She was certain that they would agree with her that the Long family was an unwelcome addition to High Street, but seriously doubted that they would willingly join her in an effort to drive them out.

Sitting at the desk with the banker's lamp aglow as evening set in, she decided that she would have to use something more than her power of social persuasion to take care of the problem. The whole situation was new to her, never before finding anyone living so near to her to be so repugnant in their actions as to warrant such a carefully considered strategy as she hoped to employ to good effect. Her life had been mostly unencumbered by those who she found distasteful, having been raised in a proper affluent Southern home and marrying young to a doctor from Savannah who was as cultured and refined as she was. The occasional rudeness she experienced in public by complete strangers was not considered out of the ordinary for anyone of any class, but rudeness of such caliber living next door was intolerable. By 10 P.M., an hour past her customary bed time, she still was seated at the desk but had not solved the problem.

She went to bed and spent a restless night barely sleeping. Twice she got out of bed and went from room to room, the only sound being that of her walker on the hardwood floors. Even before the 5:10 train passed through town she was seated in the dark at the table in the breakfast nook and looking out at her neighbor's house. She nibbled on an oatmeal cookie, not enjoying it as she had the ones the day before, and found her thoughts drifting to the large oak tree in the Long's front yard. It had been a frequent recipient of care by tree trimmers since the Longs had arrived, and had been carefully pruned and had the top trimmed down several feet, but was unquestionably a majestic old tree.

"If only it would fall on their house," she pondered, imagining ways that such a thing might happen. By the time Estelle arrived Mrs. Lilly had not figured out how to bring the tree down on the roof of the Long's home, and decided that the plan was flawed anyway because roofs can be repaired and it would be too much wishful thinking that the tree would drive them permanently from their home, unless it fell directly on them while they slept, which seemed a far fetched notion.

"You look tired, Miss Lilly," Estelle told her as she placed a breakfast of fresh fruit, a lightly buttered toasted English muffin and a cup of coffee in front of her.

"I've been busy thinking," Mrs. Lilly said as Estelle returned to the kitchen and could be heard cleaning and humming.

The morning went as the one before it had, with Edward Long slamming his door after getting his morning paper and going back indoors, then later he and his children departing in different directions with their usual lack of decorum. Mrs. Lilly dressed and again was assisted by Estelle out to the front porch where she ruminated about how little she knew about how automobile brakes were interfered with to cause them to malfunction, or how poison could be put in a jar of tea and delivered to the Longs. She had no idea how one acquired poison, would not be able to take the tea to them herself, and she decided she would most likely be found out to be the guilty party if she carried out such a crime. Mrs. Lilly looked on as Francine and her two youngest children went in and out of the house throughout the day, imagining many forms of calamity that could befall them and thus forcing them to leave the neighborhood, none practical or within her ability to make happen.

She and Estelle said even less to one another that day than usual, which rarely went beyond very trivial matters anyway. Mrs. Lilly realized that the one person she counted on the most, she knew little about. She knew Estelle had a husband and two grown children, but that was the extent of it. Estelle came to work on time, did what was asked of her, and then went home each day promptly at six P.M.

That night a few hours after Estelle had gone home Mrs. Lilly wished that she wasn't alone. She wasn't feeling well at all.

The night passed with Mrs. Lilly being in such a state of agitation regarding the Longs and unable to lie down even for a few minutes that she paced from one end of her home to the other, her hands growing more cramped and fatigued as she gripped onto the walker. She stopped at the window in the breakfast nook many times looking out at the dark house next door, hoping the Longs were each dead in their beds, sent to the afterlife by some leaking toxic gas.

#

When Estelle arrived at her usual time she opened the door and found Mrs. Levy on the floor by the front door, her eyes wide open and her breathing so muted that at first Estelle thought her employer had died.

As the ambulance arrived and carried Mrs. Lilly out of the house on a gurney the last noise she heard was the slamming door at the Long house.

The End

24

TOMIKO TAKES THE TRAIN

Tomiko's joints ached, especially her knees. She gingerly raised the hem of her kimono and stared at them for several moments as if seeing them for the first time. Nothing seemed to ever make them feel better for very long. Acupuncture, hot baths, daily swims, herbal teas, massage, the small white pills her doctor gave her; all failed to ease her from the constant suffering. She lowered her skirt, took a sip of tea that had turned cool, almost cold, in a matter of minutes, and spit it back into the cup. When her canary, Ichika, began to sing loudly from its cage near the window, she looked up, suddenly worried that her beloved pet wouldn't be properly taken care of or be given enough attention while she was away. Her neighbor, Emica, who would be looking after the bird, was a kind woman, but nearing eighty years old. Emica had lapses in memory that often made Tomiko worry about her own state of mind. She was six years older than Emica.

She slowly stood, picked up the cup and saucer it had set on, and shuffling across the kitchen in a new pair of uwabaki – a Christmas gift from her great granddaughter who lived in San Francisco – carried them to the sink. Careful not to get the white gloves she was wearing from getting wet, she rinsed the cup and saucer off and put them in the drainer. Through the slightly raised window above the sink she watched a small group of young boys jostle one another as they went down the alleyway on their way to school. The boys made little noise, moving along silently like dancing Bunraku puppets. She closed the window, walked to Ichika's cage, pressed her face against the mesh screen and clicked her tongue against the back of the upper plate of her false teeth. The bird stopped singing, jumped from an upper dowel to a lower one, nearer to Tomiko's face, and pecked at the screen.

"You be a good girl for Emica," she said to the bird. "Your mama will be back in two days."

Ichika tilted her head, looking at Tomiko first with one eye, then the other.

Tomiko took a piece of rice cake from the pocket in her apron, opened the cage door, and placed it next to the overflowing cup of bird seed. She closed the door and smiled as the bird hopped to the cake and began pecking at it. She removed her apron, hung it on a hook by the door, and left the kitchen. In the living room she watered her overgrown money tree plant, then removed her uwabaki and changed into a pair of sandals. She slipped her arm through the handle of a small purse, pushed it up her forearm, and covered it with the sleeve and opened the front door. She then lifted the lid of a large woven basket sitting by the front door and peered in, then gently closed it. She picked up a small suit case and carried it and the basket out the door, shutting it behind her.

The taxi was already at the curb outside her building when she walked out. The driver, Itsuki, who she had known since he was a boy, forty years ago, got out, and approached her. "Today is the right morning for me to be here, Tomiko-san?" he said bowing slightly, a huge smile on his face.

"Yes it is, Itsuki," she said, handing him the suitcase.

"Where is it I am to take you, Tomiko-san?"

"Today I take the train back to the place of my birth as I do every year."

He looked about and seeing no one else, he said, "By yourself? Is that wise, Tomiko-san?"

"I have no choice," she said. "My family and friends are all busy this year."

#

At the curb of the Tokyo train station, Itsuki took the suitcase from the trunk of his taxi, and then helped Tomiko, who was holding onto the basket, out of the back seat.

"Please, Tomiko-san, wait a few days and I'll take the train with you," he pleaded with her as reluctantly handed her the suitcase.

"I must go now," she said. "Same time in August every year."

He bowed, slightly and with a worried expression on his face, said, "Yes, Tomiko-san. I understand. I will be here in two more days to greet you on your return."

"Thank you, Itsuki," she said as she turned and merged with a crowd going into the station.

Inside the station, Tomiko was momentarily disoriented by the din of voices and the hum of the train waiting at the passenger platform, ready to depart. A policeman stopped a few feet from her, eyed her and her basket, and then continued on.

"Let me help you," a young man wearing a cowboy hat, with brown hair that hung to his shoulders and a beard and handlebar mustache said as he took her by the elbow and led her to the open door of the train. He had a guitar hanging from his shoulder and backpack strapped to his back. He guided her to two seats that faced each other and helped her sit down in one and then he sat in the one facing her. "I'm Jimmy Rowe," he said. "Do you speak English?"

She stared down at his cowboy boots and then up at his friendly, smiling face. "Some," she said.

He put her suitcase and his backpack in the overhead compartment, and settled back into his seat with his guitar resting across his knees. "I'm from the U S," he said.

She nodded. "Yes, I thought so" she said knowingly. "I am Tomiko Higashi."

"It's a pleasure to meet you," he said.

"You must excuse me Jimmy Rowe, I do not want to seem unfriendly or unkind, but I am of an older generation and it is not our custom for women traveling alone to speak with strange men, especially foreigners."

He hesitated for a moment before saying, "I understand." As the train doors closed and it began to leave the station, he raised his guitar and held it against his chest, his fingers resting on the strings.

She opened the lid to the basket sitting in her lap and peered in. "How is my Heisuke feeling?" she said to the sleeping tabby cat curled up in a ball on a pillow. The cat's tail fluttered. It opened its eyes, squinting, and meowed softly. "Poor old Heisuke," she cooed as she reached in and petted its bright orange fur. The cat closed its eyes, and purring quietly, returned to sleep. She closed the lid and turned to watch the scenery as the train accelerated, quickly leaving the station behind.

#

Jimmy Rowe lightly strummed his guitar with his eyes closed while humming softly to himself.

"Excuse my contradiction in behavior," Tomiko said, reaching over and tapping his knee with her gloved hand, "but may I ask what music it is that you are playing that is so enjoyable to listen to?"

He opened his eyes. "It's called country music," he said. "I'm going to a music festival in Fukuoka to play there."

"You are famous singer, then?" she said.

He chuckled. "Not at all. I just wanted to see Japan."

"Why?"

"My great grandfather was a soldier and came here in WWII," he said. "He spoke of it often before he died."

She looked out the window, not at him. She tried to see the landscape, the city structures, the shiny train station as he might see them, but she couldn't through the tears that welled in her eyes.

"Fukuoka, Hakata Station, coming up," a woman's voice announced over the intercom.

"I change trains here," she said, her voice choking. She stood up the same time as he did. He retrieved his backpack from the overhead compartment and hung it on his back and handed her the suitcase. "I wish we could have gotten to know one another better," he said to her as he slung his guitar over his shoulder by its strap.

He started to take her elbow to help her down the aisle. She quickly pulled away. "Please, no, Jimmy Rowe," she said icily.

"Goodbye. I'm sorry if I offended you," he said as the train came to a stop. He walked on, not receiving a response.

#

While waiting on the passenger platform for the train that would take her to her destination, Tomiko bought a Styrofoam cup filled with noodles and some raw fish from a vendor whose stand was set up near the entry way into the station. She sat down on a bench and ate hurriedly since her train would arrive soon. She opened the basket lid and tried to encourage Heisuke to stand up and to eat the fish, but he would do neither. "Poor old Heisuke," she said soothingly to the cat as she massaged the top of its head. She stuffed the last noodles into her mouth with wooden chopsticks just as the train to Nagasaki arrived. She wrapped the fish in a napkin and placed it in the basket with Heisuke and tossed the cup and chopsticks into the trash bin. Carrying the basket and her suitcase she crowded into the train with the other passengers and too her surprise and delight found two empty seats by a window at the end of the car. She placed her suitcase at her feet and cradled the basket in her lap.

Within minutes a middle aged Japanese man in a business suit and carrying a briefcase approached her and pointed at the empty seat beside her. "May I?" he said.

She nodded, reluctantly, and scooted nearer to the window as he sat down.

"I am Eichi Saito," he said. "I have a software company in Nagasaki. Do you own a computer?"

She shook her head. "I am an old woman and have no use for one," she said bluntly. "Please, if I may ride to Nagasaki in silence I would be humbly grateful."

"Certainly," he said, politely bowing his head. He placed the briefcase in his lap, opened it and took out an eBook and began to read.

She turned her head to the window and rode to Nagasaki looking out at the scenery, withholding the urge to laugh when Eichi Saito took a handkerchief from his pocket and held it against his nose as the pungent aroma from the fish began to waft from the basket.

#

The sidewalk outside the station in Nagasaki was packed with people awaiting taxis or to be picked up by family members or friends. Tomiko slowly pushed her way through them, holding the basket cradled against her chest with one arm and carrying the suitcase with the other. She crossed the street and waited for a tram amidst another throng of new arrivals to the city. When it arrived she boarded it and was given a seat up front by a young woman who remained standing in front of her while holding onto a handrail.

"O-bāsan, where are you visiting from?" the young woman asked.

"Tokyo," Tomiko said.

"Is there no one in Nagasaki who could have picked you up at the station?"

Slightly disturbed by the young woman speaking to her in such a casual and inquisitive manner, Tomiko said flatly, "I had family here once, but they are no longer living, and I have no friends here."

"Nagasaki is always so crowded during the remembrance," the young woman said. "I hope you have pre-booked a place to stay."

"I stay at the same place I stay every year," Tomiko said. "It is a block away from the Peace Memorial Hall."

The young woman looked at Tomiko's gloved hands holding onto the basket. "I wish gloves were fashionable again for all women to wear," she said.

"Mine aren't for fashion."

#

The hotel room was very small, with a twin bed, small dresser, and sink. The restroom was down the hall. She set the basket on the bed and raised the lid. Heisuke was asleep, his chest barely rising and falling as he breathed. She laid the suitcase on the top of the dresser and then sat on the bed, took her purse from her arm and placed it next to her, and then removed her sandals and socks. Her white socks had gotten dirty during the trip as had her gloves. She then removed her gloves and laid one across each leg. She held her hands up, and gazed thoughtfully at the mass of scars on the back of each hand and at the deformity of her fingers that no surgeon had been able to repair. Her hands were a reminder of the miracle that she had survived the atomic blast with just those injuries while everyone and everything else she knew when she was age ten had been obliterated in the fire storm.

#

A little after midnight, April 6th, Heisuke died while sleeping at Tomiko's side.

Tomiko arose from the bed, dressed, and placed Heisuke in the basket. She quietly left the room and carried the basket down the stairs, past the desk clerk who was sound asleep in his chair, and out of the hotel. She walked to the Peace Memorial Hall and placed Heisuke at the base of the Peace Monument. She looked up at the large bronze statue of a seated man with one hand raised, pointing to the heavens, whispered a little prayer, and then turned and returned to her hotel room.

#

When she returned to Tokyo she met Itsuki outside of the train station as they had planned.

"How was your trip to Nagasaki, Tomiko-san?" he said.

Her voice choked as she replied, "I think it will be my last train trip."

"Yes, maybe that is for the best, Tomiko-san."

He put her suitcase in the trunk of his taxi but she held onto the empty basket as she got into the back seat. There she placed the basket in her lap and wrapped her arms tightly around it.

The End

25

NEEDLE IN A HAYSTACK

A hot wind blew across the highway, carrying sand and bits of grass that pelted Cristela's unprotected face. She lifted her four year-old daughter, Lilian, from the pavement and held her in her arms, adjusting the shawl that covered the girl, protecting her from the elements. Lilian gripped her mother's dust-covered sweatshirt and rested her head on her mother's shoulder. Using a trick she had learned after weeks of walking, Cristela flexed her back muscles and, without using her hands, shifted the heavy backpack, rolled tent, and bedroll she carried to relieve the pressure they were exerting on her spine. A semi-truck passed by her and the line of immigrants who walked along the edge of the highway showering them with dust. A cloud of dirt hung in the air for several moments before dissipating. Lilian began to cough.

Cristela looked into her daughter's coffee-colored eyes. "Are you okay?"

The girl nodded, and then coughed.

Cristela stepped into the dirt alongside the highway and took a plastic bottle of water from the waistband of her pants. She lowered Lilian into the dirt, unscrewed the cap on the bottle, and poured water into the girl's mouth.

As water dribbled down her chin, Lilian asked her mother, "Are we there yet?"

Cristela took a small drink of water, grimaced at the tepidity of it, and swallowed. "Not yet, *mi corazón,* but soon." She gazed up at the hazy sunlight that streamed through a layer of thick, gray clouds. Almost more than anything, she wished for rain. She lifted Lilian back into her arms and rejoined the line.

#

The scrubland along both sides of the highway stretched out for as far as Cristela could see. A coyote's bark resounded in the glow of the purplish twilight that spread across the landscape. Sitting on the mostly emptied backpack, she opened the flap to her green nylon tent and peered in at Lilian, who was asleep on a straw mat. The girl had her thumb in her mouth.

Yanira, who sat nearby on a piece of cardboard with her husband, Luis, took an apple from a bag and handed it out to Cristela. "You shouldn't worry so much about her," she said. "She will make it to the United States just fine."

"Will she?" Cristela said as she took the apple.

"If you stand on a large rock you can see the lights of a city," Luis said.

Cristela wiped the apple on her shirt, and then took a large bite from it. The tangy pulp sapped the moisture from her mouth. To the east night had fallen, and was quickly erasing the light from the sky. She ate the apple while watching Luis and Yanira lay out their bedrolls.

"Sleeping in the boxcars was much easier," Luis said as he sat on a colorful blanket.

Yanira sat down beside him. "That already seems so long ago," she said. She untied her gym shoes, took them off, and placed them in the dirt beside the blanket.

"The clacking of the train wheels frightened Lilian," Cristela said. She nibbled the last of the pulp from the core, and then tossed it into the dirt. "Maybe we should have paid to ride in the back of a truck the entire way."

"Never," Yanira responded without hesitation. "You heard the horrible stories. Our lives could have ended, locked in in the back of a truck and left to die in the desert. Our feet and backs ache, but at least we can breathe."

Cristela took off her left shoe and stared at the hole in the toe. "The first thing I'm going to buy when I earn the money is new shoes for me and Lillian." She placed it in front of the tent, and then did the same thing with her other shoe. Before she climbed into her tent she watched as Yanira laid down. Luis laid next to her and put his arm around her.

#

Two concrete, pale gold arches over the two lane highway, and a guard booth on both sides of the arches, was the entry point to the United States. A few cars and trucks idled in line on both sides of the border. A tall mesh fence topped with coiled barbed wire stretched out from the arches, forming a barrier between the southern and northern parts of the small town it divided. Cristela sat on a guardrail and watched, smiling, as Lilian chased a little bright green lizard that scurried in the dirt. The girl giggled each time the lizard escaped her grasp. The rest of their group stretched out along the highway, most of them also sitting on the guardrails. The other children were amusing themselves by playing games in the dirt. Lilian didn't know her very well, but she watched as Ana walked up and down the side of the highway rocking in her arms her nine-month-old crying infant, Oscar.

Yanira came from the front of the line and sat down next to Cristela. "We have to wait on the authorities before we can ask for asylum and be let in," she said.

Cristela nodded. "We knew that would happen. Will it be very long?"

"Luis talked to the guard, who said buses were waiting for us and they would be here soon."

The image of air conditioned buses with padded seats flashed through Cristela's mind. "We will enter the United States in luxury," she said.

Yanira put her arm around Cristela's shoulders and hugged her. "Haven't I told you from the moment we left our village that everything would be okay?"

Lilian came up behind Cristela and tugged on her mother's shirt. Cristela turned. Large tears were rolling down her daughter's cheeks. "What is it *mi corazón?*"

"I killed it," the little girl blubbered. She held out her hand, showing the end of the lizard's tail.

Cristela picked up her daughter, wiped away her tears, and kissed her cheeks. "You didn't kill it, *mi corazón*. It will grow a new tail."

#

Six large, solid gray buses were lined along the highway on the United States side of the arches. On the sides of each bus was a red, white and blue seal with an eagle behind a shield and, in large lettering, the U.S. Department of Homeland Security. Bars on the windows were half raised. Men and women in light brown uniforms, with holsters and guns strapped to their torsos, milled about outside each bus. The engines hummed like hornet nests in the late afternoon sun. The immigrants stood at the fence, most with their fingers grasping the mesh wire, and gawked at the buses and U.S. government officials.

Lilian held onto Cristela's leg as the two stood at the fence. Cristela ran her fingers through her daughter's long black hair. "We'll have a home soon," Cristela told the child, trying to sound more confident than she felt. She turned to Luis and Yanira, who stood next to her holding onto each other, and asked, "Why do they have guns?"

"We're very dangerous," Luis said gravely, followed by a nervous laugh. "They think we carried bombs with us all the way through Mexico."

"But they went through everyone's belongings before loading everything in that bus, so surely they know we have no bombs," Cristela said anxiously, not understanding Luis' attempt at humor.

"They carry guns to remind us who is in charge," Luis said.

Cristela took the bottled water from her waistband and shook the small amount of water that remained in it. "I've left a trail of plastic bottles all the way from home to here," she said earnestly. "If the *pandilleros* could follow the bottles, they could easily find me and kill me. They carry guns also." She unscrewed the cap and gave the water to Lilian.

Four of the men from the buses came to the arches. One held up a bullhorn. "Men, and boys over age seventeen, first," he announced.

A chorus of chatter erupted among the immigrants.

"Why you first?" Yanira asked Luis as she threw her arm around his sunburnt neck.

"As you always tell Cristela, there is nothing to worry about," he said. He kissed her, pulled her arm from his neck, and joined the males who shuffled to the archway.

Yanira grasped Cristela's arm and watched as Luis and the other men were directed to four buses. Yanira lost sight of Luis, and unable to determine what bus he was on, she joined the other women who were calling out for their husbands. At the top of her lungs she yelled, "Luis, *mi amor!*"

After the bus doors closed, the man with a bullhorn called for the women and children to board the last bus.

#

The buses stayed on the highway, taking the immigrants through the outskirts of the city. The bus carrying the women and children was the last in the line. As buildings and structures became more scarce and the buses entered a stretch of highway bordered on both sides by desert scrubland, Cristela stared out worriedly between the bars on the window, holding the sleeping Lilian in her lap. Yanira sat in the seat next to her. Re-finding her courage and positive attitude, she offered encouragement to the women seated nearby.

"Our men are only buses away," she told them. "We'll be reunited soon."

In the aisle seat behind Yanira, Ana softly hummed a lullaby to her infant.

One uniformed man stood at the front of the aisle and another at the rear. A young woman, also in a uniform, walked up and down the aisle, stopping at times to speak reassuringly in both Spanish and English to the immigrant women and their children. Her name tag on her breast pocket gave only her last name: Rogers. She had long red hair that she wore in a ponytail, and a smile that never seemed to evaporate from her face. As if to unconsciously remind herself that it was still there, her fingers frequently fluttered on the holster that held her gun.

"What a beautiful baby," she said, stopping at Ana's side for the fifth time since the buses had left the border entry.

"*Gracias*," Ana said, and then corrected herself. "Thank you."

"May I hold him?" Rogers asked.

Ana hesitated before handing Oscar to her. "He's my world," she said.

"I'm sure he is," Rogers said. She stood in the aisle and rocked Oscar in her arms. Moments later the baby opened his eyes and began to whimper. "I'm afraid I've awoken him," Rogers said, and handed him back to Ana. "Is his father on one of the buses?" she asked.

Ana shook her head. "His father is in prison." She kissed the baby on his forehead. "Where are we going?" she asked Rogers.

"Not far," Rogers said. "We'll be there soon."

Being seated by the window and blocked somewhat by Yanira, Cristela and Lilian had garnered little attention from Rogers. When Lilian stirred, and then looked up at her mother with tears in her eyes, Cristela glanced over the back of the seat to see Rogers standing in the aisle three rows back.

"What's wrong *mi corazón?*" Cristela said softly to her daughter.

"I want to go home to Beatriz," the girl whimpered.

"Beatriz now has a nice, new home with *Tia* Lupita," Cristela said affectionately. "I'll get you a new kitty when we get to our new home."

The buses began to take a winding turnoff from the highway. Craning her neck over the seat in front of her, Cristela tried to look through the front windshield to see where the buses were going, just as all the other women on the bus were doing.

#

The large metal gates slowly slid to the sides, opening the way to an area several football fields in size that was enclosed in a nine foot high chain link fence. A dozen other gray buses were parked at the far side of the enclosure. Jeeps and pickup trucks lined one side of the fence. A maze of fences enclosed a hundred different cage-like cells, each large enough for twenty men. Men and teenage boys sat on wood benches inside the cells, or paced back and forth like caged animals. Uniformed men and women carrying batons walked between the cells. In the middle of the enclosure stood a large block-type building that was once a large warehouse used for storing goods and merchandise brought from Mexico.

As the line of buses slowed along a long row of empty cells, the women and children in Cristela's bus clamored to watch out the windows along the left side of the bus, but quickly grew silent.

Only Yanira spoke up, calling out to Rogers, "What place is this?"

"It's for holding while we wait for word about your dispositions," Rogers said. "But you women and children will be housed inside the building."

The wheels on the bus screeched as it came to a stop behind the others. Uniformed men and women opened the doors to the empty cells, and directed the men into the them as they exited the buses. Through the open window, Cristela thought how similar the sound of the footsteps of those being led into the cages, was to stones rolling down a hillside. Yanira stood over her, watching for Luis. When he appeared and was guided into a cage by two uniformed men wielding batons, Yanira grabbed on the bars of the window and screamed out to him, "*Luis, te amo.*" The other women in the bus began to call out to their husbands, brothers and sons. Many of the younger children on the bus began to cry.

Lilian buried her face in her mother's chest.

Gently running her hand down the length of her daughter's hair, Cristela whispered, "It'll get better from here, *mi corazón.*"

#

Cristela held Lilian tightly in her arms as she scanned the inside of the warehouse. From inside, it seemed even larger than it appeared from the outside. The floors and walls were painted the same shade of light gray, the same color of the stones in the creek near the house where she had lived. Pale light streamed through a row of closed windows that ran along the walls just beneath the ceiling. Although the building was cool and air conditioned, it was also full of unpleasant odors. Flourescent lighting cast its harsh glow from fixtures in the ceiling. A maze of wire cages, like the ones outside, had been set up to house the women and their children. The din of echoing voices filled the warehouse.

Barely able to hear the questions that the uniformed woman behind the table was asking her, Cristela shrugged to many of them, and watched in silence as the woman filled out a form attached to a clipboard. After the woman said, "That's all," Cristela turned to Yanira who was standing behind her and shook her head, bewildered. She was led to a cage where Ana sat on a cot, her sleeping baby lying next to her. Five other women, none with children, were also in the cage. A uniformed woman shut and locked the cage door.

"What about my friend, Yanira?" Cristela asked the woman through the wire.

"This cell is full," the woman said, and walked away.

Cristela looked at the women sitting on their cots. They had haggard faces, thier naturally brown skin turned to the color of ash, drained of vitality. They were all young, most only hours or days from completing their trek from Mexico or Central America. They spoke in Spanish to one another, sometimes yelling to be heard.

Cristela sat on the cot next to Ana's. She had traveled nearly 2,000 miles in the same small group as Ana, yet hardly knew her. She sat Lilian beside her and gave the girl the comb she kept in her pocket and the locket she always wore around her neck to play with.

"Will they give us any food or water for our children?" Cristela asked Ana, concerned about her daughter.

"Yes, I asked the woman at the table if I could get baby food for Oscar and she said we would all get food and drinks very soon," Ana answered. She rubbed her left breast. "I've been producing less milk lately."

#

The next morning Cristela awoke to the sound of the cage door being unlocked. Lilian was asleep next to her, her small body pressed against her mother's. One man in uniform and three women in dark blue scrubs entered the cell. The man remained at the door, swinging his baton as the women went to Ana's cot and woke her up.

"We need to have your baby seen by a doctor," one of the women said.

Ana sat up. "I don't understand. My baby is fine."

"It's a precaution," the woman said. "We need to make sure your baby isn't carrying any diseases." She looked at a form on a clipboard. "Your baby girl is named Eileen, correct?"

Ana picked up the sleeping Oscar and held him close to her chest. "No, he's a boy. His name is Oscar."

The woman flipped through several sheets of paper. "Oh, of course. Here he is," she said. She tucked the clipboard under her arm. "We'll take good care of him."

One of the other women reached out for Oscar.

"I'll go with him to see the doctor," Ana said.

"That won't be allowed," the woman with the clipboard said. "You won't be away from your baby for very long."

Cristela sat up and watched, perplexed, as several toddlers were led by their hands by two women in scrubs down the aisle between the cages.

"You won't hurt him?" Ana asked, her voice breaking as she handed Oscar to the woman with the outstretched arms.

"Of course not," the woman said. She left the cell, Oscar cradled in her arms.

The remaining women turned to Cristela. The one with the clipboard said, "Your child will need to see a doctor also. She will only be away from you for a short time."

Cristela leaned over Lilian. "Wake up *mi corazón.*"

Lilian opened her eyes and gazed sleepily at her mother's face. "Are we going to go get Beatriz?" she asked.

"Not now," Cristela said. "You're going to see a doctor."

#

In a line of women, Cristela walked through the back door of the building and into an open area enclosed with a high fence. She shielded her eyes with her hand as they adjusted to the return to natural light. The aromas of bodies and stale air were replaced with the dry, earthy scent of the desert. Like everyone else, she had been told she would have thirty minutes to get some exercise. She looked around at the women who stood in groups of three and four, talking in hushed tones but barely moving, like dazed storefront mannequins. When she spotted Yanira standing by the fence at the other end of the enclosure she dashed across the lot and threw her arms around her friend.

"I'm so happy to see you," she said. "The past twenty-four hours have felt like days."

Yanira hugged Cristela, holding her tight for several moments. "Have you heard?" she asked.

"Heard what?"

"They're sending us back."

Cristela stepped back, feeling as if she had been punched in the stomach. "But we just got here and we're seeking asylum," she said. "How can they send us back without hearing our stories?"

"We'll be able to tell our stories, but it won't matter. The government has made the decision to not allow us to stay."

"It can't be true," Cristela said.

Yanira took a folded sheet of paper from her back pocket and handed it to Cristela. "This is from Luis. The men have sent notes to their wives telling us what I have just told you."

Cristela hurriedly unfolded the note and quickly read it. "But how do they know?" she asked, crumpling the note in her fist.

"They were told first. We are to be told later," Yanira replied.

Cristela threw the note at Yanira. It hit her friend in the chest, fell to the ground, and was blown across the lot by a hot breeze. "Why would they care about Lilian's health if they were going to send her – us – back? She's with a doctor at this very moment."

Yanira wrapped her arms around Cristela. "All the children have been taken. None have been returned."

Cristela broke away from Yanira's grasp and ran to the back door of the building just as it opened. Rogers came out with a clipboard in her hands.

"Where is my daughter?" she screamed.

Rogers stared at Cristela's face with a vacant expression. "What is your name?"

"I'm Cristela Flores. My daughter is Lilian."

Rogers scanned the forms on the clipboard. "Ah, here you are," she said, looking at a form. "There is nothing written here about you having a daughter."

# # #

A stream of muddy water ran down the middle of the dirt street as rain poured from dark, gray clouds. Cristela kept to the side of the street as she ran down it, trying to stay under the protection of roof overhangs. She clutched a small leather pouch to her chest. At the end of the street where a large puddle had formed, she stood at the door of a small shack, gathering her thoughts, before opening it. Inside, a single bulb hanging from the center of the shack cast a dim light on the eight men and women seated in a circle on folding chairs. The resounding pinging of the rain on the corrugated tin roof sounded like that of pebbles being tossed on it. The men and women in the circle turned their heads towards her, most offering only weak smiles.

"I'm sorry I'm late," Cristela said. She untied her wet scarf, hung it on a nail beside the door, and unzipped her nylon jacket. She took a chair that was leaning against a wall, unfolded it, and placed it between a man and a woman. She placed the satchel on her lap and looked around at the group. Their expressions were even more downcast than usual. "Did I miss something?" she asked.

"It's about Ana," a young woman wearing a black shaw said. "She hung herself last night."

The air left Cristela's lungs, and for a moment she thought she was going to faint. She wanted to scream, but bit into her lower lip, drawing blood from it. She bowed her head and crossed herself. Silently, the others did the same. When Cristela opened her eyes and raised her head the others were looking at her with grave, but expectant, expressions.

"Do you have any news about my Ernesto?" a man in ragged jeans seated across from her asked.

"What about my Ivania?" the woman seated next to her asked. She held in her hands a small bouquet of flowers held together with a bright green scrunchie with her daughters name sewn on it.

Cristela opened the satchel and pulled out a small stack of papers. "The lawyers here and in the United States are doing everything possible to find our children," she said, "but they say it's like finding a needle in a haystack."

The End

26

THE LEGIONNAIRE'S CONCUBINE

Everything was the same hue of brown as the sand in the desert. The clay brick streets and small, squat huts looked ancient, turned that way by the heat and sandstorms that swept across the barren landscape. In that desolate place there were no flowers, so the bright red of roses or purples of violets were seen only in the brightly colored kangas and scarves worn by the women. So too, the many bracelets they wore that jangled musically as they walked and the tinkling of the bells around the goats in the herds provided the only pleasant sounds. The songs sung by the merchants in the marketplace were dirge-like and weighed on my ears discordantly. There was an old woman who sat on a stool in front of her hut and sang from sunrise to sunset in a voice so raspy and wracked with age that it set my teeth on edge.

The only shirt I wore – a trade I made with the goat herder Abeeku for the shirt of my Legionnaire's uniform – had lost all but one of its buttons and in spots the material had worn through, on the verge of becoming holes. My faded blue trousers belonged to Asha's husband who had been gone for three years, having gone south to fight with a terrorist group in the jungles of a southern country. The rest of his clothes that he left in a burlap sack had all been sold or given away by Asha who hoped her husband would return one day, but she lived as if she knew he'd never return. As many times as the pants had been washed or saturated with my own sweat, the scent of her husband, Taj, still clung to them, or so I imagined I could still smell him. Asha told me his sweat smelled like spice. She spoke of Taj often, much more than I liked. Asha lived with me as my wife, but we knew we'd never marry. I hoped that when I got out of that hellhole I'd return home to my own wife who I hadn't been in contact with in six months, which was just before I deserted from the French Foreign Legion. The only way to communicate with anyone beyond the boundaries of the village was to give a letter to someone passing through and pay them to take it to a post office in a larger town and then hope they'd do it. I gave money and letters to merchants passing through, but there was no way to know if the letters were sent and no way to get a letter in return. Asha warned me that no one who could be trusted had passed through the village in a year. I could have traveled on foot with merchants to larger towns, but the distances were great and the journey arduous. I was willing to bide my time in the village.

I kept the boots I wore as a Legionnaire wrapped in a piece of cloth and hidden beneath the bed. Asha made the sandals I wore out of scraps of leather and hemp, but I preferred to go barefoot. Most of my body had already tanned to the color of caramel because of long hours training in the glare of harsh sunlight, but in the sandals my feet baked nearly the color of Asha's light ebony skin. The soles of my feet formed an armor of callous that protected them from the burning sand. It was only either the very young or very old who walked around the village without wearing sandals. I was twenty-six. The white turban I wore to protect my head from the sun covered my blonde hair, which Asha likened to something not finished, *usifaulu*, undone, as if it was in need of real color. The people of the village stopped staring at me as the stranger I was, and although I had no friends among them other than Abeeku and Asha, I was no longer spat on in the marketplace. Asha was well-liked in the village which may account for my not being turned in as the deserter I was to get a reward, or even worse, being murdered in my sleep.

Asha's hut was made of clay and thatch, and although small, it didn't feel cramped. The bed, made of straw that Asha changed frequently, was the largest item in the room. She had a very old steamer trunk given to her by Taj on their wedding day that she kept her clothes in and on top of that sat a small mirror. Just like all the other women in the village, Asha didn't wear makeup, but she liked to sit in front of the mirror and paint designs on her face using colorful paints she made from plants and vegetables. There was nothing in the hut that suggested I lived there. I arrived wearing my uniform and that was it. It was Asha who found me nearly dead from dehydration and sun stroke lying in the sand at the border of the village. I had crossed fifty miles of desert on one canteen of water and pure will to escape.

#

My wife's name was Janine. We had been married for six years, during four of which I was in the United States Marines with multiple tours of duty in war zones, and then I joined the Legion. She threatened to divorce me when she found out I was going to France to enlist as a Legionnaire and perhaps she did. She's an attractive, smart woman who never anticipated spending her marriage waiting for her husband to return home from the military, especially a foreign one. I received one letter from her that was terse and angry in the three months I was at Fort Monteaux. I didn't blame her, and still don't. In the last letter I sent her before I deserted in the dead of night I told her that I loved and missed her, which was true, but I should have told her before we got married that I never planned to stay in one place for very long. Asha knew my wife's name but nothing about her. I didn't show her the photograph of Janine that was in my wallet. In it, Janine is in her wedding dress.

My identification as a member of the Legion was also in my wallet. Perhaps I would have completed the four month training as a Legionnaire if I hadn't seen the writing on the wall. Despite being a former Marine, I was accused of being undisciplined and a trouble maker and was on the verge of being thrown out. Instead, I ran away before that could happen, which if I had been caught, could have landed me in prison for three years. Asha only knew that I was once a Legionnaire and then I stopped being one. She asked no questions. Like everyone in the village she had no love for the French Foreign Legion. Fort Monteaux was fifty miles away, but as the villagers liked to say, "Ina miguu kubwa." It has big feet.

It was stifling hot in the hut during the day, and although it was no cooler outside, while walking about the village, the sand-filled breezes removed the sweat that poured from my body. At Fort Monteaux we were forbidden to remove our shirts while outside unless we were doing physical training. I felt trapped in the uniform; like being in a suffocating straitjacket. Asha walked with me sometimes, staying close to my side, but never touching me, neither did I touch her. Her English was poor, but adequate, and she chattered on about the gossip she had heard from other women in the village. Sometimes we would wander through the marketplace, which was small but active, where merchants and villagers sat on rugs placed on the ground with their wares and foodstuffs around them. There were nothing electronic for sale since the village had no electricity and the fruit that was sold bordered on being rotten as it was all brought to the village from somewhere else. Yams, bolts of material and stacks of bracelets were ubiquitous. I didn't tell Asha I carried enough money in my wallet to possibly buy out the entire market. I bought her a bracelet once, but she gave it to the old woman who sat outside her hut and sang.

I didn't know Asha's exact age but the girls of the village married at age fourteen or fifteen if they were lucky enough to find a husband. It was Abeeku who told me that the engagement between Asha and Taj had been unusually long as he was from a distant village and the families squabbled over Asha's worth. Eventually, Asha's family was given three goats and several chickens for her. There was a maturity to how Asha carried herself, as if she understood the woes of the world and carried them on her rigidly held shoulders. She laughed and giggled like a schoolgirl, however, when she was talking about Taj. I rarely made her laugh.

There were two wells in the village, both dug by government agencies that showed up to inspect them every few years. At sunrise every morning Asha would take her pale to the well, fill it with water and return to the hut. We would both drink hollow gourds full of water and then she would pour a portion of the water into an earthen basin and set the pale aside. Then, using a rag, she would stand in front of the mirror and wash her body with the water in the basin. While I lay on the bed, she would then bathe me. During this, she hummed melodically the entire time.

It was when she returned from the well one morning that she told me three Legionnaires were in the village and asking questions about me. They had been looking for me for months and thought no man would be crazy enough to travel this far on foot, until I showed up nowhere else.

#

Four days passed and I remained in the hut the entire time. Through Asha I learned that the Legionnaires had set up a tent on the edge of the village and had been routinely circling the village in their jeep. The village chief had kept them from doing a hut-to-hut search. I had never discussed with Asha why I had left the Legionnaires, but several times since the arrival of the other Legionnaires, and now that it was out in the open, she called me *mtoji,* deserter, in the same tone she used when allowing her anger about Taj's desertion to show through. During the sweltering days I laid naked and inert on the bed, my body awash in my sweat while Asha came in and out of the hut, reporting back to me what the Legionnaires were doing, and tending to my needs. Unable to sleep at night, I looked out the small window at the star-speckled sky and listened to the cries of vultures that circled above the village.

In the morning when she bathed me, Asha no longer hummed.

On the night of the fourth day I told Asha that I was leaving, that I had to escape being caught by the Legionnaires. As she sat in front of her mirror and painted sun-like figures on her cheeks, I put on my clothes, and then unwrapped my boots and put them on. The boots felt foreign, unnatural, as if I could feel the gravity holding me bound to the earth.

"Kuja na mimi," I said. The thought of asking her to come with me had suddenly sprung to my mind and surprised me when I said it. In that moment I realized I loved her.

Without saying anything she opened her trunk and took out several kangas and scarves and tied them in a bundle. She blew out the wick of the oil lamp and we snuck from the hut and down the street. The village was quiet except for the tinkling of hollow, wooden chimes that hung in the doorway of a hut. We walked to the edge of the village, to the border of the desert, heading south. I felt the heat of Asha's body beside me and smelled the scent of the homemade lotion made from honey that she put under her arms and between her legs. Suddenly, she stopped.

She looked back at the village.

"What is it?" I asked.

"Taj," she said and then turned and walked back.

The End

27

A DEATH IN THE DINING CAR

Snow and sleet battered the windows of the observation car as the train slowed to a crawl along the ice-covered tracks. The men dressed in expensive tweed and sheep's-wool traveling attire smoked cigars, drank brandy from crystal snifters, and talked of the stock market and the current price of gold, while keeping a wary eye on the drifting snow that covered the desolate landscape. It had been miles and miles since a man-made structure had been seen, a weathered, slightly leaning barn, standing alone on a hill far in the distance. Some thought it was where cattle or other livestock were kept safe from the winter elements; others claimed it was deserted, a type of decaying symbol of an era long gone. The women played Mahjong while sipping sherry and pulled their cashmere capes around their bare arms and exposed necks, fending off the chill that permeated the car despite the train attendant's attempts to increase the heat that flowed into the compartment. With each sudden lurch of the train, the voices in the car were momentarily silenced as everyone turned their sights on the blizzard that swept across the prairie, the conversations resuming minutes later as if what was being said had been frozen in mid-speech, and then just as quickly thawed.

I thought myself to be very lucky to have been given the gift of this transcontinental train trip. My very wealthy Aunt Velda, my mother's older sister, who surprised me with the ticket to travel with her from Montreal to Vancouver had remained in her private car for most of the trip, preferring to be alone and read than to spend time among strangers. "Have fun and make friends, my boy," she said whenever I reluctantly left her to spend time in some other section of the train. She called me a boy, although I had reached my twenty-fourth birthday just a month prior to taking the trip. I lacked the sophistication for the crowd who congregated in the observation car, smoking car, bar, lounge and dining room designated for first class passengers. Unlike my aunt who married into a wealthy family, my mother had wed my father, a man of meager means who was satisfied with being a fireman and never aspired to anything higher. Aunt Velda, who had never had children, only took real interest in me after her husband died, leaving her in need of a traveling companion. In summer months while on break from university I traveled with her to Spain, England and France. She taught me as much as she could about how to blend in with the well-to-do, but while I managed some of the affectations of being rich, Aunt Velda frequently reminded me, "You're very rough around the edges, my boy."

It was while I was sitting in an overstuffed chair, a brandy snifter grasped in my hand, that the train came to a complete stop. Along with everyone else I peered out at the blinding white landscape and waited for someone else to say something.

"Is this usual for this train?" Mrs. Ballard, a widow with dark, heavy bags under her eyes asked as she pulled her cape tightly around her stocky body. Her daughter, Amanda, statuesque, brunette and gorgeous, sat across from her, swirling an ice cube around an empty glass that had been filled with a Long Island iced tea.

"It has finally stopped to let on that poor man who has been running after it since it left Winnipeg," Parker Upton, a high-priced lawyer from New York replied, resulting in a release of relieved laughter from everyone in the car.

Tom Skittle, the porter came into the car. "We apologize for the inconvenience," he said, "but the train is unable to make it any further through the snow drift piled on the tracks until morning. We can dig our way through it then."

"Everyone have your galoshes and shovels ready at sunrise," Parker said as he raised his half-filled snifter.

#

Dressed in the white dinner jacket Aunt Velda bought for me in Montreal, specifically to be worn for the evening meals on this trip, I stood looking through the window in the door of the last car in the first class section, and the last car on the train, I saw the purple and pink rays of twilight's sky reflected from the snow that blanketed the ground for as far as the eye could see. The snow continued to fall; thick flakes that drifted to the ground like feathers caught in wayward breezes. Earlier in the passageway I heard mention of sightings of arctic fox and snowshoe hares, but there was no life to be seen, not even the otherwise ubiquitous hawk or crow. Out of nervous habit and with no other use for it since I didn't smoke, I clicked up and down the lid of the silver lighter Aunt Velda had given me as one of the many college graduation gifts she had bestowed on me. At the time that I had taken it out of its black felt box I didn't know she intended on having me travel with her across Canada. There was talk of traveling by ship to Bermuda, but not to the north – during winter. The fragrance that crept up behind me was familiar; the expensive perfume worn by Amanda. I turned.

She stood less than a foot away, her footsteps having been muted by the plush burgundy carpet that extended down the four car-lengths of first class passageway. She was lit by the soft glow of the lights encased in etched glass that hung in exact-length intervals along the walls. She was dressed in a strapless, pale pink, satin, floor-length gown that clung to her shapely body. A matching silk jacket was draped over her right arm as if it was a fashion afterthought. She was a year younger than me and had just graduated from Vassar, but years ahead of me in class. She had been bred to live a privileged life.

"Isn't it exciting?" she said, nudging me aside enough to peer out the frost-covered window.

After several days of traveling, this was the first time when there weren't others around. I wasn't actually attracted to her in the romantic sense, but I found her fascinating; like observing an exotic fish through the glass of an aquarium.

"Why is it exciting?" I asked.

"Here we are, stuck on a train in a blizzard and mountains of snow out in the middle of nowhere," she replied breathlessly, "and Lobster Newberg is on the menu for tonight's dinner. It's all simply poetic."

"Is this your first cross-country train ride?" I asked.

"Yes, it is," she replied merrily. "We usually travel on my father's yacht, but one can't do that crossing Canada, can one?" She flicked her head, rearranging the way her hair cascaded over her shoulders. "Are you well-traveled?" she asked.

"Thanks to my aunt I've traveled a little."

She turned her head and glanced down the passageway at the doors leading into the private compartments. "I've seen but not had the pleasure of meeting your aunt," she said.
She doesn't seem to leave her compartment very often."

"She isn't a very social being," I said. "She'll be accompanying me to dinner tonight though. I'll introduce you to her."

"That would be simply poetic," she replied. She glanced at her watch. "Oh my, dinner will be served in twenty minutes. I like to find seats at the table before Mr. and Mrs. Rubadeu arrive so that I can get the chair by the window. The Rubadeu's are very kind, but very French, if you know what I mean." She flicked her head again. "Do stop by our table and introduce your aunt to us." She turned and rushed down the passageway, disappearing through the doors leading to the dining car.

#

Standing in Aunt Velda's private compartment I stared out the window and watched the shade of night spread across the snowscape, turning white to a monochromatic gray scale and the glistening falling snowflakes to the color of ash. The wind whistled beyond the glass as if being emitted by collapsing lungs expelling their last breath. From inside her private bath Aunt Velda hummed a tune I'd not heard from her before; in fact she rarely if ever hummed. Looking at my reflection in the window pane, I straightened my black bow tie and smoothed back my hair made slick and glossy with pomade scented with something similar to the faint aroma of cinnamon. On the pomade can the label said it was from India and had a picture of the Taj Mahal on the lid. Aunt Velda had bought it for me in a shop in London. It had remained unopened in my travel bag until this trip. I glanced at my watch and turned from the window.

"They're going to be serving dinner in a few minutes, Aunt Velda," I called out.

She opened the door, stood in the doorway, and held her arms out wide. "How do I look, my boy?"

She was dressed entirely in white satin covered with lace with a string of black pearls that hung from her neck; the only jewelry she wore. Her gown reached down to her shoes. Her white gloves stretched to her elbows. She was both stunning and slightly comic in appearance at the same time. There was nothing about how she looked that suggested everything she wore wasn't new, but she could easily have stepped out of the pages of a bridal magazine from another era. She was sixty-four, fourteen years older than my mother, and grew up during the 1950's and sixties, although none of that mattered at the moment. She looked timeless, ageless.

"What are you dressed up for?" I asked, careful to not sound as shocked as I felt.

"This is for Walter," she said. She pointed at the door leading from her compartment to the passageway. "Be the gentleman you've turned into and open the door."

"Who's Walter?" I asked as I walked across the room and opened the door.

"My first husband." She walked out as I stared at her, mouth agape.

Following behind her questions swirled about in my brain. This was the first time I had ever heard of my aunt having two husbands. My Uncle Leonard who she had been married to for as long as I could remember had died five years before from cancer. Her grief at his passing was real although he left behind a great deal of real estate, stocks, and a large savings which made her independently wealthy. I searched my memory for some recall of an Uncle Walter ever being mentioned by my parents or anyone else, and came up blank. We entered the dining room just as the wine stewards had begun to show the evening's wine lists to the seated passengers.

During evening meals, everyone sat at the same table – four to a table – they had been assigned to at the beginning of the trip. Breakfast, brunch and lunch you could set wherever you wanted. We shared a table with an older German couple who were amiable, but spoke very little English. They spoke in French to my aunt, who was fluent in that language, but she seldom dined in the dining car, preferring to eat alone, leaving me to sit quietly during dinner, concentrating on the expensive foods arranged on my plate. As we made our way down the aisle between the two rows of tables line up along the windows, my aunt politely nodded her head at the other passengers who stared at her and what she was wearing with a mixture of looks, from amusement to shock. At Amanda's table we stopped while I introduced my aunt to Amanda.

"Your dress is so poetic," Amanda said to Aunt Velda.

"What a lovely young thing you are," my aunt replied.

We took our seats at our table. Aunt Velda conversed in French with the German couple until we ordered wine and then our meals. It took several large gulps of a Riesling white wine and for the German couple to turn their attentions to one another before I was finally able to ask Aunt Velda the question that was burning a hole through my skull. "What do you mean this Walter guy was your first husband?" I asked her in a hushed voice as if I was asking about the secret location of buried treasure.

She glanced out the window and then looked into my eyes as if seeing them for the first time. "I had just turned eighteen and was on this very train on my way to university in Vancouver, when I met an American soldier, Walter Youngston, who was on leave and taking a leisure trip across Canada before he was due to be deployed to Vietnam. It may be considered romantic fantasy, but it was love at first sight for both of us."

The waiter placed our salads in front of us, turned and left.

She continued. "By the time the train pulled into the station in Vancouver we were engaged to marry. We got off the train, rented a car and drove to Seattle where we married. Two weeks later he went to Vietnam where he was killed in combat nine days later. We had told no one we knew that we had married and I never have, until now. I was a war widow before I had turned nineteen."

She took a sip of her wine. "What I'm wearing is a remake of the wedding dress I bought in Seattle and wore during the ceremony at the court house." She clutched the pearls. "These were the gift he gave me as a wedding present. Strange that being black was almost an omen of what was to come."

I was stunned into speechless for several moments before I said anything. "So you brought me along on this trip to celebrate some kind of anniversary?"

"Yes, but I didn't expect the train to stop near the very place where he and I first met."

I looked out the window, at the landscape shrouded by night. "You're not suggesting . . . ?"

"Who knows? There are mysterious forces at work in the world and maybe this is one of them, but that's neither here or there. His death has taken on yet another meaning for me seated here in this dining car after so many years when all I had was my memories of him, " she replied and then took another sip of wine.

#

In the afternoon sunlight the snow sparkled as if diamonds were scattered among the snowflakes. Amanda stood in a snowdrift holding a perfectly formed snowball in her gloved hands. The train whistle blew twice, indicating the tracks were cleared and it was prepared to continue on. The passengers who had disembarked to frolic in the snow began to board the train. Amanda's snowball hit me squarely on the side of the head just as I looked up to see Aunt Velda watching us from her compartment window, a huge smile on her face.

The End

28

MEISMA WRITES HER MEMOIR

Me.

Me, I, she, her, Meisma.

I write this before I forget to. This is what Meisma hear said is a memoir; it is your life story. Meisma writes her memoir.

Forgive Meisma for not being a good writer. I was taught how to read and write from two books, one about a girl name of Alice who falls into a hole and another about a man name of Gulliver. Meisma didn't understand meaning of either book. Then and now think there much nonsense in both. I was told neither true. Meisma's memoir is all true.

Meisma come here to this island to pick the coffee bean. I, then, a young girl of fourteen years, know nothing of the world. I not read or write when coming to here. I am stupid girl, I think. Having no talents I born with choices to pick fruit, have babies, or leave home to be a picker of the dark beans grown on the shrubs, I choose leaving home. I come here in a small, crowded boat with all men and boys. The waves that toss us around not make me sick like many of them. Meisma, smiling as they lean over edge of boat and throw up. Meisma think she should be sailor.

Leaving shore of my birthplace last time Meisma see her mother and father. They kiss Meisma and we all cry. Mother cry the most. They, and Meisma, not know we never see one another again. It part of Meisma's memoir. But it's a image in my head of Meisma's mother and father waving, crying, as boat goes to sea, that Meisma carries with her, like a photograph. I hear my parents were murdered by men who raid Meisma's village. This hurt Meisma to think about. Meisma's parents gentle people who never hurt anyone. Nothing to go back to if parents gone and village destroyed. Meisma could be dead if she had stayed home. Strange to think, coffee beans save Meisma's like.

When boat land here on beach, Meisma get out of boat and line up with men and boys. Mr. Hobson, coffee plantation manager, walk up and down in front of line looking at us. He stop in front of Meisma, look at Meisma from feet to head, and say, "You're a girl. Picking coffee beans is hard work. Why should I not send you back on the next boat?"

Meisma stick out her flat chest and hold out hands and show him." Then I say, "Meisma has strong back, strong hands."

He nod, say nothing more and walk away.

Meisma given cot to sleep on with only other female in room, Delores, who sleep on a big bed. Next day Meisma pick first beans.

#

Now Meisma write about the plantation because it is important in Meisma's memoir.

It sat high up on the island where once was a volcano. Tiered fields of coffee trees surround the top of the volcano, that is a volcano no more, replaced by a large flat field where stands the plantation owner's house, the barracks for the workers, and other small buildings. To get to the plantation is a long ride in a vehicle or by walking a far way up a winding dirt road. It is the soil and air up here that creates the color and taste of the coffee beans. First time Meisma see the owner's house she think it the biggest house in the world. Things get smaller as time passes. The grand house where Meisma was raised no more than a shack last time she saw it.

The owner of the plantation, Mr. Collins, was bachelor, but his woman when I first arrived, a Miss Huma lived in the house with him and slept in his bed like they were married. She was a tall woman with eyes like a panther, same color and shape. She never talk to anyone but Delores, and then just to tell Delores what not to serve her and Mr. Collins for their meals.

When first arrived I only see kitchen and main room. The kitchen, where Delores work, had what I think at the time was the biggest stove in the world. Delores only cook for Mr. Collins and Miss Huma. The cooking for the workers done by Teddy and Jute and done in big pots and on grills outdoors under a tin roof. Both those men sweat all the time from heat from cooking. The main room have zebra hides and heads of lions and bison on the walls though those animals nowhere around. Only animal on the island is small-sized monkeys.

Delores show me the kitchen and main room early in the morning when Mr. Collins and Miss Huma were still in bed. I hear them. What I hear, not two people sleeping!

On the front of the house was a large porch with lots of chairs where Mr. Collins, the plantation managers, and their favorite workers, sit at night, drink alcohol and smoke cigars.

#

The boys and men came and went from the plantation. The work was too hard for what little they earned, they said. There aren't any women except Delores who is too old and ugly and Miss Huma belongs to the boss, they said.

Delores acted like my mother. She taught me to learn letters and to read from the books about Alice and Gulliver. We sat in our room at night and with the lantern lit, Meisma learned about rabbit holes and giants. Delores also teach other things. "Boys are going to want to steal your softness," she told me, but she didn't explain what my "softness" was.

But by age 18 I knew what Delores meant, but I didn't give my softness away. I was as strong as any of the men and easily fought off any boy or man who tried to take it.

The thing about getting older is that everything else gets older too, usually at the same time. Miss Huma no longer looked like a fresh flower she looked like the first time I saw her. She had wilted into something that looked used. Doing nothing all the time does that to a person. Meisma looked in the mirror many times and said, "Meisma, you're prettier than Miss Huma."

I wanted to know how to become a Miss Huma but but not turn into a Miss Huma. These were questions I dare not ask Delores. It was hard enough asking her about a Mad Hatter or Houyhnhnms.

On Sundays Miss Huma would get into the back seat of a jeep and be driven from the house and down the road heading to the beach. She would take with her a large towel, a wicker basket, and a brightly colored umbrella. It was many months after being there that I said to Delores, "Where does Miss Huma go?"

"To spend the day lying on the beach," she replied.

Not until after months of being 18, Meisma woke before sunrise on a Sunday morning, and since we didn't work on Sundays, snuck out of the room, and walked down the long road to the beach. Hiding in the palm fronds, monkeys threw mangoes at me while I waited for the jeep to come, bringing Miss Huma to the beach.

All day after Miss Huma left alone on the beach, Meisma stay hidden, eat mangoes, and watch her lay on the towel under the umbrella, eat fruit and sweets from the basket, and sometimes wade into the ocean, but only far enough for water to reach her waist.

Returning to the plantation house late that day, Delores ask where I was all day.

"Watching Miss Huma."

#

"Meisma, what are you doing out so late?" Mr. Collins asks when I walk by the porch.

"Oh, you surprised me, Mr. Collins, I didn't know you were there," I say, though that not the truth. I knew he was there all the time.

"Come sit with me here on the porch, Meisma, so that we can get to know each other better," he says.

I can tell by the moonlight that shines in his face that he wants my softness. He is still a young man, age 30, and handsome. His age and that he inherit the plantation from his dead father; nobody knows what happened to his mother, is what I know of his memoir. I step up onto the porch and then sit in a chair near him. "Would you like to hear a story?" I ask.

He takes a cigar from his shirt pocket, lights it, and as curls of smoke spill from his mouth, he says to Meisma, "Anything you want to tell me is fine with me."

I don't tell him about Meisma's memoir that she has lived so far. I tell him the story of Alice.

"What a silly girl," he says when Meisma finish. "She should have stayed home to begin with and not chase after the rabbit. Then she would never have fallen into the hole to begin with."

I didn't want to tell him he didn't understand the meaning of the story, because Meisma didn't understand its meaning either. "Now Mr. Collins, your turn to tell a story," I say.

"Well, I . . . " he began.

This was interrupted by Miss Huma coming out of the house, and seeing Meisma sitting there with her man, made her green eyes shoot fire at me. I swear. "What are you doing here?" she said, which sounded like a vulture's warning while circling its prey.

"Just talking," I said. I stood up to go.

"Good night, Meisma. Thanks for telling me about Alice," Mr. Collins said.

"You're welcome," I said back to him. As I stepped down from the porch and began to walk away I hear Miss Huma screaming at Mr. Collins, "Who is this Alice? I'll kill her if she even gets near you."

#

I just turned 20 and though I never spoke to Mr. Collins again like I did that one night, we give each other looks and smiles whenever we see each other while I am picking coffee beans and he is seeing that his workers are doing what little he pays us to do.

We stop singing and telling stories when he comes around.

I tell the boys and men about Gulliver, but they just laugh. Some say, "How is it that this Gulliver is the only person to find those islands. It makes no sense."

I can't really argue about Gulliver's islands even if I wanted to. Secretly, I think they have a point.

Delores has been sick with a cough and complains about sore muscles and joints. During the nights she wakes up Meisma, saying, "Meisma, I need some water. Meisma, I need my legs massaged. Meisma, I think my end is near."

It is hard to imagine life without her.

Remember I told you about Mr. Hobson, the plantation manager who Meisma met when first arriving at this island? He and the other manager, Mr. Lawrence, have their own rooms in the barracks. Having your own room a big thing. The cooks, Teddy and Jute, have their own rooms too.

Gossip is that Miss Huma visit Mr. Hobson in his room. It very quiet gossip. Something like a secret, but not a secret. Talk about Miss Huma, quiet or not, always leads the boys and men to ask Meisma why she not find a man and get married.

I keep my mouth shut about that and never answer. When at night Meisma prays that Delores lives forever, prayers are asked for a husband suitable for a girl who has read the stories about Alice and Gulliver.

#

As present to self on her just passed birthday, Meisma goes to the beach on Sunday morning, getting there before Miss Huma get there. Instead of hiding in the ferns, Meisma finds a place further down the beach, where Miss Huma never goes. I have with me a sandwich that Delores made me the night before and a plastic jug filled with water. I have a regular-sized towel, but no umbrella. Cooled by the night, the sand is chilly.

When Huma arrive she sees me, and sees me seeing her. Her face twists into that of an angry turtle. She lays out her towel and puts up her umbrella in the same place as always.

As the day warms, so does the sand. It is just before the sun is at its mid-day place in the sky that Miss Huma stands to go into the water for the first time. She looks out at the water and I think she see the shark fins, but no. I say nothing to her as she walks in.

Meisma is a very strong swimmer and has been in and out of the ocean several times already despite seeing sharks swimming a bit further out.

To watch Miss Huma standing in the water, doing nothing but slapping the top of the water, is comical. I don't laugh out loud, but want to.

When she is suddenly pulled under the water, disappearing beneath the surface quicker than a bat of the eye, I try to feel alarmed. Try to. Meisma not accomplish everything she sets out to do.

I walk back up the road knowing with Miss Huma gone, Mr. Collins will want my softness. No one's heart is as soft as Meisma's can be. I will be a Mrs., though, not a Miss when I give Mr. Collins my other softness.

In twenty more years Meisma will write more of her memoir. Until then she will just live it.

The End

29

THE MISSOURI RIVER STORY

Jack awoke and opened his eyes to the sight and sound of box cars packed with cattle crossing the tracks over his head, showering dust and bits of hay down on him. He covered his face with his arm and lay still which protected his eyes but did nothing to stop the strong odor of cow manure from assaulting his nostrils. While the train passed he tried to remember where he was and what day of the week it was. After a couple of minutes of concentrating really hard he remembered it was Sunday but couldn't for the life of him recall where the railroad bridge was that he was now lying under. It was north of the Badlands in South Dakota, that much he knew, but even the memory of the ride he accepted to get to where he was, was hazy at best. What he did remember was that it had been night and much warmer. He also remembered a hand being placed on his leg, squeezing it, and that was all. As the last car of the train clacked off the far end of the tracks, Jack removed his arm from his face and looked around.

The bridge above him was no different then any other railroad bridge, a combination of steel and wood and cables, blackened with age, weather, use, or paint, he couldn't tell. Not far down the slope thick with prairie grass that he was lying on passed the gentle gray currents of a river. There were no trees on the bank he was on and none on the bank on the other side. The houses on this side of the river were about a half mile down river and along with those along the ridge on the other side revealed nothing special about their occupants, their history or their location. There were no boats of any size on the river or any piers jutting out into it and no landing docks. Other than the now faint sound of the train disappearing in the distance on its journey to wherever it was headed, and the slight splashing of the river currents against the bank, it was very quiet. At the side of the sleeping bag his clothes were laid out as if by a stranger who had just evaporated in them after lying down. His bladder suddenly made its presence known and need to be emptied.

Unzipping the bag, he shivered as the cool air washed over his naked skin. As he stood up and looked down the length of his lean body he wondered how he had gotten the bruises along his ribs on the left side. I'll try to remember that later he thought as he faced downwind and urinated. While watching his pee water a patch of brown prairie grass he heard the growl of a dog and looked up to see a skinny black mongrel a few yards away, its teeth barred and head tucked down but staring straight at him.

"Easy, boy," Jack said softly.

Despite the growling, the dog wasn't aggressive. It wasn't drooling so Jack slowly bent down and held his hand out, palm up. "I'm a nice guy pooch. I won't hurt you." It stopped growling but it's posture and distance didn't change.

"I guess I should find out where I am," Jack said standing slowly.

He got into his jeans and then picked up his t-shirt. Just before he slipped it over his head he stuck his fingers through a hole where a pocket had been. "Damn," he muttered, "this is my last one." He put it on. His small brown nipple showed through the hole.

#

With his backpack and sleeping bag hidden behind a piling under the bridge, Jack made his way to the main west-east road and highway going through the town. There were barely any vehicles traveling on it, but there were a couple of motels, small businesses and restaurants; a clear indication it was a main thoroughfare even if there wasn't much to it or anything to brag about. Jack walked eastward down the narrow sidewalk with the dog following behind but still maintaining a distance. At a small gas station and convenience store, Jack went in and bought a bottle of orange juice, a package of small chocolate frosted doughnuts, and a can of dog food. He placed the items on the counter and took several bills out of his jeans front pocket.

"Your shirt has a rip in it," the teenage girl behind the cash register said to him as she rang up his items.

"I know," Jack said, reaching up and feeling the hole and his nipple. "Do you have a can opener I can borrow to open the can of dog food?"

"You're not going to eat dog food are you?" she asked screwing her face into a look of disgust.

"No, it's for my dog. Well, he's not my dog, but I think he's pretty hungry."

She reached under the counter and pulled out a can opener and eyed him suspiciously as he removed the lid from the can. With his juice and doughnuts in a small bag in one hand and the opened can of dog food in the other, Jack left the store. The dog was sitting on the sidewalk but backed a few feet away as Jack scooped out some of the dog food onto the pavement. Jack sat on the curb a few yards from the pile of dog food and drank the juice and ate the doughnuts. Keeping his eyes on Jack, the dog slowly crept forward, sniffed at the food, quickly devoured it, and then sat down on the sidewalk, still watching Jack.

"Whatever made you so frightened of people I'm sorry pooch," Jack said as he stood and tossed the bag, empty doughnut package and empty bottle in a waste can outside the door of the store.

#

Led by nothing else other than curiosity, Jack turned off of the main street onto a tree-lined side street. Heading nowhere in particular he gazed thoughtfully at the modest sized houses and well-kept lawns.

It didn't look any different than many other small town streets he had seen since leaving wherever it was he had originally left. He assumed by the condition of his worn sneakers and what few dollars he had in his pocket that he had been traveling for some time and for quite a distance. Places he had seen recently along the way, like the Badlands, were still very clear in his memory. Usually he awoke in a new place, or found money in his pocket. He had had thumbed rides from one place to the next, that much he knew, but he had no clue where the money came from.

At the end of the street a narrow whitewashed bridge extended across a narrow tributary to a parking lot that bordered the banks of the river. Jack stopped and read the sign: Griffin Park. With the dog following, Jack walked across the bridge, passed by a car driving very slowly. On the edge of the parking lot, overlooking huge boulders on the bank of the river, Jack sat down and scooped another handful of dog food out of the can and put it on a rock. He remained perfectly still while the dog slowly inched forward and gulped down the food then backed away, once again sitting at a distance from his benefactor.

"They will give you a ticket if you don't have your dog on a leash."

Jack turned around and looked up at a young man about Jack's age with dark skin and long black hair tied in the back into a braided pony tail. "He's not my dog," Jack said. "He's hungry so I'm giving it some food, but he's not mine." Jack stood up and faced the young man and reached out his hand. "I'm Jack."

"I'm John Wind Feather," John said taking Jack's hand and shaking it. "Who gave you the black eye?" he asked pointing at Jack's left eye.

"My eye is black?" Jack asked, surprised, and putting his fingertips to it and wincing. "I didn't know it was black until you told me."

"Your shirt is torn also," John said pointing to Jack's exposed nipple.

"Yes, that I know about." Jack said suddenly feeling self-conscious and momentarily covering the hole with his hand.

"I haven't seen you around here before," John said. "Are you just visiting?"

"You could say that," Jack replied. "But I'm not exactly sure where here is."

John tilted his head and looked appraisingly at Jack. "It's Griffin Park."

"I know that," Jack said. "I meant what city is this?" he asked, sweeping his hand around like a malfunctioning compass arrow.

"You don't know what city you're in?" John said, somewhat amused. "It's Pierre. The capital of South Dakota. How could you not know what city you're in?"

Jack pulled at the hole around his nipple. "I wish I could explain that but I can't."

#

By the time Jack and John arrived at John's house on a nearby street, Jack explained what little he could, which wasn't much. At the door, Jack scooped the last of the dog food out of the can with his hand and put it in the grass for the dog that had followed the two, keeping a safe distance behind.

"Are you sure your family won't mind you bringing me home?" Jack said.

"It's just me and my grandfather," John said. "He's very old and doesn't know where he is most of the time either so you two will have that in common."

As Jack entered the house and directly into the living room he was greeted by two sights: on every wall and the ceiling was a painted mural of Native American themes, and John's grandfather was sitting naked in a rocking chair in the middle of the room in front of a large flat screen television watching "Leave it to Beaver." John closed the door and went to his grandfather.

"Thunkashila, where are your clothes? We have a guest," he leaned over and said loudly into his grandfather's ear.

"Hau cousin," John's grandfather said ignoring John and looking at Jack.

"Thunkashila, my grandfather, is saying hello in the Lakota Sioux way," John explained.

"It's a pleasure to meet you," Jack said, barely able to take his eyes off the brilliant colors of images of prairie landscapes, eagles, buffalo, and horses that adorned the walls. The ceiling was painted a brilliant baby blue with smatterings of snow-white clouds. "Who did the murals?" Jack asked John.

"My grandfather did most of it," he said. "All he does is paint and watch television. I did a little of it. He's teaching me how to paint." John turned to his grandfather, "Thunkashila I'm going to give my friend some food, okay?"

"Ohan, tokse ake," his grandfather said waving an arthritically gnarled hand at Jack while keeping his eyes on the television.

John led Jack into the kitchen and had him sit at a rickety wooden table while he pulled a plate of roasted chicken out pf the refrigerator and fry bread from an old tin bread box. Jack was staring at the colorful baskets and pottery painted on the walls as the food was placed in front of him.

"Who taught him how to paint like this?" Jack asked.

"He was taught by his grandfather. It is said by my family on Pine Ridge Reservation that my grandfather's grandfather fought at Little Bighorn and came back and put away his weapons and taught himself how to paint and never picked up his weapons again," John said.

After eating and in the bathroom Jack removed his shirt and looked in the mirror on the medicine cabinet and saw the black and blue bruising around his eye and the bruises on his side.

John opened the door. "You've been in here for an hour. I was getting worried about you. Can I come in?" John asked. "I have a t-shirt for you and some clean socks."

"Thanks," Jack said, trying to recall what he had been doing for an hour.

"Jack your back is covered in bruises," John said coming into the bathroom with the t-shirt and socks in his hands. "You don't remember what happened to you?"

"I wish I did," Jack said.

#

As a crescent moon glowed in the night sky, Jack sat on the slope beneath the bridge tossing pebbles into the Missouri River. John was stretched out on his back on the bank and chewing on the end of a long piece of yellow prairie grass. Above them a freight train rattled across the bridge.

"You could stay here," John said. "There is room with me and my grandfather."

Jack waited for a moment before answering. "Thank you, but I must go on."

"Go on to where?" John asked.

"Just on, wherever that is," Jack answered. He stood and said, "I'm tired and need to get some sleep."

"I understand," John said sitting up and spitting the blade of grass into the river.

Jack removed the t-shirt that John had given him and slid his shoes and socks and jeans off and now naked laid them all out beside his open sleeping bag as if they were still being worn by an invisible being. He laid down on his back and looked up at the dark bridge. He heard the dog lap some water from the river and then settle in the grass nearby. He said nothing as John removed all of his clothes and laid down beside him. Jack fell asleep.

When he awoke John was gone.

As he stood along the side of Highway 34 outside of Pierre going east he stuck his thumb out and quickly caught a ride with a middle-aged man wearing a white cowboy hat and cowboy boots driving a pick up truck. He put his backpack in the back seat and settled into the front passenger seat. He looked down and saw a ten dollar bill sticking out of his jeans pocket. As the man pulled the truck back onto the highway Jack could see the Missouri River in the distance. He turned his head hoping that he would remember this moment, this place. In the side mirror he saw the dog running down the highway after the truck, after him. As the truck sped up and the dog was lost in the distance, he told the man his name was Jack. The man put his hand on Jack's leg and squeezed.

The End

30

THE FLUTE

Lying in the spongy moss on the bank of the Amazon River, Cristiano stared up at the branches of the kapok trees and watched squirrel monkeys leaping from branch to branch beneath the thick canopy of leaves that blocked out a great deal of the late morning sunlight. From not far away howler monkeys shrieked, their cries reverberating through the rainforest. His legs hung over the bank with his feet in the cool water where minnows nibbled on the dry, calloused skin on the soles of his feet. He held his bamboo fishing pole in one hand and ignored the slight tugs on the string, awaiting something bigger to swallow the hook made from one of his baby brother's diaper pins. Gnats and mosquitoes buzzed around his head as he closed his eyes and drifted off to sleep. When he awoke, his fishing rod was gone and dark clouds filled what had been a bright blue sky. He sat up and stared out at the water, knowing that his fishing rod was gone forever, pulled from his hand by the strong river currents and carried away along with all the vegetation and debris scoured from the river banks. Replacing the rod would be easy – bamboo grew in abundance in the forest – but finding string and stealing another pin wouldn't be so simple. He pulled his feet out of the water and crossed his legs. On the other bank a large jaguar sat on its haunches, staring at him, too far away and separated by the river to pose a threat, but goosebumps raised on Cristiano's arms nevertheless. Jaguars were strong swimmers but it had to be something more tempting than a boy to make one cross the river.

He started to stand but as he placed his hand on the ground to push himself up, he felt something hard just beneath the surface of the moss. He reached in and pulled out a panflute, a siku, made with six lacquered tubes and bound together by reeds. Standing, he put the flute to his mouth and blew into two of the tubes at the same time. The notes emitted from the flute were clear and sonorous, a sound so satisfying to his ears, that he pulled the flute away from his mouth and stared at it in wonder. Many men in his village owned and played the siku, but none that he had heard, including the one his father possessed, produced such a deep and gratifying sound. He put his mouth back on the flute and moving his lips up and down the tubes, he played the instrument's scale. The beauty of the notes, from the lowest to highest, brought tears to his eyes. It then occurred to him that the flute belonged to someone. From the sheen on the tubes, and the tautness of the reed, it was obvious it had only been recently lost. He looked around, expecting the flute's owner to suddenly appear from the depths of the forest, drawn to the sound of the flute. When thunder rolled across the late afternoon sky, he knelt down and buried the flute in the spot where he found it. It started to rain just as he reached the dirt path that wound through the forest all the way to his village. The echo of his bare feet slapping the earth joined the myriad of bird calls and screeching of monkeys as he ran home.

#

The whir of the blades of the helicopter as it sat down in the mud on the outskirts of the village was accompanied by the shouts of the villagers calling out "*aquí está*" as they left their huts and climbed down the ladders to the ground ten feet below. In the purple haze of twilight, the lights from the helicopter shone brightly against the backdrop of the dark forest.

"May I come and see what the helicopter has brought with it?" Cristiano asked his parents from the straw mat he was sitting on, dangling a bird carved from wood in front of Luis, who grabbed at the object and giggled loudly when Cristiano quickly pulled it away.

"Stay here and take care of your brother," his father replied as he followed Cristiano's mother out the door. "I'll bring some candy back for you."

"Candy!" Cristiano grumbled aloud. "You think I'm still a child."

As soon as they were gone, he reached over and took three diaper pins from the small box his mother kept the infant's supplies in and shoved them into his britches pocket. He stood up, lifted Luis up to his shoulder and went to the door. As always, whenever a helicopter arrived bringing packages, supplies or medical personnel if needed, the rain forest was silent until the hum of he helicopter blades ceased. Children and mothers with babies stood on the narrow ledges of the row of huts across the unpaved, muddy street, all with their eyes turned to where the helicopter had landed. Except for a crying baby, they too were silent, like the forest, anxiously awaiting to see what the helicopter had brought with it.

From the base of the ladder to the hut where Cristiano lived, his friend Edmundo called up to him. "You catch any fish today?" he asked.

Cristiano leaned over and peered into the shadows near the stilts that held the hut up, keeping it from being flooded during rainy season and preventing the wild animals and snakes from getting in.

"Come out where I can see you, Edmundo," Cristiano said to his friend.

Moments later Edmundo stood a few feet in front of the hut. He looked up at Cristiano. In the ambient light of fading twilight the dark bruise around the boy's eye stood out like a circle on a target.

"Who hit you?" Cristiano asked.

"My father. He said I stole something of great value from Pedro Rega."

Pedro Rega was the wealthiest man in the village, the only villager with a real bank account in the city. His wife wore new dresses and high heeled shoes shipped from stores in Lima. He was a brutish man with a mean temper who frequently beat his wife.

"Was it a flute you took?"

"A flute?" Edmundo said. "I took nothing, but my father hit me before it was discovered that what Pedro had thought was taken had been misplaced. Why did you ask if it was a flute?"

"While fishing I found a flute buried in a bed of moss on the riverbank. It's the most beautiful flute I have ever seen or heard," he said. "It seems like it was hidden there for a reason."

"Can I see it?" Edmundo said as he lifted his foot and shook off a clump of mud.

"Yes, tomorrow. It's hidden in the moss where we always fish from. I'll show it to you, but you must say nothing to anyone about it."

"Okay."

"Do you promise?"

"I promise."

#

The next morning, a small stack of boxes sat against one wall of the hut. While his parents and Luis still slept, Cristiano climbed out of his hammock and tip-toed over to them. The evening before, his parents told him the long narrow, unmarked box contained his gift for his upcoming thirteenth birthday but that he couldn't open it until then. He put his ear against it and quietly shook it, trying to discern the box's contents. He had asked for nothing, and hadn't expected to get a gift brought from the city by the helicopter since his parents had no extra money to buy anything that wasn't essential. It was just past sunrise when he slipped on his pants and shirt, placed his straw hat on his head, and went out the door. He collected his remaining fishing rod from its place on the ledge beside the door, and climbed down the ladder. Humidity washed over him, wringing sweat from his body, soaking his shirt even before he placed his food on the damp earth. The rain that had fallen the night before had mostly been absorbed into the dry earth. During the rainy season the area around the base of the hut he lived in, around the base of every hut, and the entire street, would be like a pond. Hornbills in the nearby kapok trees emitted their raspy calls and brightly colored macaws perched on the branches squawked incessantly. A few minutes later he stood in front of Edmundo's hut and whistled three times.

Edmundo stuck his head out the door of his hut. "I can't come now," he said in a hushed tone.

"You didn't tell anyone about the flute, did you?" Cristiano said.

"No." From inside the hut, Edmundo's father shouted at him.

"I'll come later," Edmundo said and then went back inside.

Cristiano turned and with the fishing rod resting on his shoulder he entered the forest and followed the path to the mound of moss on the riverbank where he had fished from the day before, where he always fished from. He laid the rod down, reached into the moss and pulled out the flute. Tentatively, he placed his lips on three of the tubes and blew into them. The notes that arose from the flute took his breath away. It was how he imagined honey would sound like if it could make a noise. It was like listening to an orchid sing.

"What you got there?"

Startled, Cristiano turned to see the helicopter pilot, Dario, standing on the path at the entrance to the forest. He quickly shoved the flute under the moss. "Nothing," he said. "What are you doing here?"

Dario smiled, that smile that hinted at him hiding something. It was like a smile from a crocodile just before it struck.

"I just wanted to see one last time this place you fish from," Dario said.

"Last time?"

"I'm moving to Lima to be a pilot there," he said. "This is my last trip to this village."

Cristiano had known Dario for several years, when younger often following him around like a puppy, enthralled by being near a helicopter pilot. Dario once let him sit on his lap in the pilot's seat and explained how the helicopter was able to fly. It was the smell of Dario's leather jacket that Cristiano mostly remembered from that experience. But other than a rare display of kindness toward the kids, and allowing the boys and girls of the village to follow him around, Dario remained aloof. During the delivery layovers, he slept in the helicopter, drinking bottles of rum, instead of sleeping in one of the village huts with a family as the co-pilots did.

Cristiano cut his friendship off with Dario during the the pilot's last visit when he saw him and Pedro Rega's wife having sex in the back of the helicopter. Cristiano didn't like Pedro, but he knew what he had seen was a wrong thing for the pilot and a married woman to do. He told no one what he had seen, but Dario was no longer a man who made the air above the village come alive.

As Dario took a cigarette from a pack, put it in his mouth and lit it, Cristiano faced the river. On the other bank the jaguar had returned and stood watching him. He took a diaper pin from his pocket and bent it into the shape of a hook and tied it to the string on the fishing pole. He dug into the dirt with his fingers, found a grub, and put it on the hook. He cast the line into the water and jiggled the hook several times before turning to see that Dario was gone.

#

From the time that Dario left until Edmundo arrived a couple of hours later, Cristiano practiced on the flute, running scales and attempting rudimentary tunes. Several times there were hard tugs on the fishing line but he mostly ignored them, reluctant to set the flute aside. In the sweltering heat and humidity he removed his shirt and britches and wearing only his underwear and hat he played the flute and watched hatchet fish jump from beneath the surface of the water and fall back into the river making loud splashes. The jaguar came and went, laying on its stomach and watching Cristiano for brief periods of time before returning to the forest brush.

When Edmundo arrived, Cristiano held the flute up and showed it to his friend. "Is it not the most beautiful flute you have ever seen?"

Edmundo stripped off his outer clothing and lay down in the moss. "Play me something that will make me dream," he said as he closed his eyes.

#

"Tomorrow is your birthday. Are you excited?" Cristiano's father asked him as they stood in the doorway of their hut and watched sheets of rain fall.

"I already received a most wonderful birthday present," Cristiano said.

"You did? Who gave you such a gift?"

"Maybe God himself," Cristiano replied.

Cristiano glimpsed a small troop of capuchin monkeys huddled in the branches of the trees behind the huts across the street. They sat absolutely still, allowing the rain to drench them as if they knew it was useless to try to escape their fate.

Called to eat, the father and son turned from the door and went inside, sat on the mats around the small table and began to eat.

"I'm sorry I caught no fish today for our meal," Cristiano said. "The fish were not biting," he lied.

His mother scooped rice and beans onto his plate. "Tomorrow Dario leaves for the last time not to return," she said to him. "Are you going to miss your friend?"

"He's no longer my friend," Cristiano said as he shoveled a spoonful of beans into his mouth.

His parents glanced at each other. "What happened?" they said in unison.

"He's not to be trusted," Cristiano replied.

#

The next morning Cristiano left his hut just past sunrise, grabbed his fishing pole, and slogged through the muddy street to the path leading to where he fished. Water dripped from the forest canopy, soaking him before he arrived at the river bank. He took off his hat, shook water from it and then tossed it onto the carpet of moss. It was then that he noticed that there was a hole where he had hidden the flute and the moss around it strewn about. He fell to his knees and dug down, searching for the instrument, finding it gone. With tears streaming down his face he at last gave up and sat back. His stomach ached from the loss of the flute. His heart was broken. He thought, *but who would take what didn't belong to them?* "Dario!" he said with the same venom found in poison dart frogs.

He leapt to his feet, and leaving his fishing pole and hat behind, he ran through the forest back to the village. The mud caked around his ankles and legs as he made his way to the base of the ladder leading up to the hut of Pedro Rega and yelled. "Señior Rega, tengo algo que decirte."

Pedro came out of his hut and standing on the ledge around the hut, looked down at Cristiano. "What do you have to tell me so early in the morning?"

#

In the hours after the helicopter rose in the air and flew off, the entire village was abuzz with the retelling of how Pedro Rega dragged Dario from the helicopter and nearly beat him to death. It was only by the intervention by Pedro's wife who begged for mercy for both Dario and herself, that Dario escaped with his life.

It was that evening as a howler monkey filled the air with its loud cries, that Cristiano's father handed him the long box that had sat untouched against the wall. "This is from Dario who asked me to wish you a happy birthday," he said.

"I want nothing from Dario," Cristiano said.

"Open it, Cristiano, and be grateful to have such a good friend."

Cristiano opened the box and pulled out a brand new store-bought fishing rod with a packet of hooks and extra fishing line. "This doesn't make up for the theft of my flute," he muttered under his breath. He returned the fishing rod to the box, set it aside, and opened the few smaller gifts his parents gave him.

#

The next morning, Cristiano carried the box with the fishing rod in it to his fishing spot and tossed it in the river. From the opposite bank the jaguar joined Cristiano in watching the box float down the river atop swift and turbulent currents.

"Happy Birthday!"

Cristiano whirled about to see Edmundo standing at the pathway holding an object wrapped in bright blue tissue paper.

"My birthday was yesterday," Cristiano said.

"I know," Edmundo said, "but it took me all day to find this paper to wrap your gift in. I had to trade three of my comic books with that snake Carlos to get it. He stole it from his mother." He tossed it to Cristiano.

Cristiano slowly peeled away the paper, revealing the pan flute.

"Now it's a proper gift," Edmundo said, smiling from ear to ear.

Cristiano turned back to face the river and watched as the box disappeared in a cloud of mist and spray. He then looked across the river and saw the jaguar was gone, and then looked up at the sky, thinking he heard the whirling of helicopter blades.

The End

31

THE WELL WENT DRY

Ifeoma sat by Bunkechukwu's bed holding his hand, squeezing it tightly, as if to hold him tethered to her and to the Earth. She had the right eye open, keeping it on him, and the left in readiness to open when the right one grew tired. She had been winking her eyes at him since the last remaining rooster in the chicken enclosure had crowed at dawn. Silently her lips trembled non-stop as she mumbled one prayer after another, asking that her husband be healed, and soon, as the well had gone practically dry with only a few feet of water still at the bottom and only Bunkechukwu would know what to do about it.

He stared blankly, blindly at the ceiling, seldom blinking. His breathing was steady, but shallow. The feel of his hand, of his brow when she laid her hand on it, was clammy. The nearest hospital in Kano was nearly 99 kilometers away and they had already kicked him out when the money he had in the bank to pay for his care ran out. She had left the hospital with him wrapped in a blanket and lying in the back seat of the car, a few fresh wound bandages lying on his stomach.

Getting him to the hospital would have been a near impossibility anyway. Their car had been stolen and the local police claimed they were too busy fending off terrorists to look for it or for the thief who took it. She made matters worse when she angrily reminded them that the terrorists hadn't come this far north, and if they did, "They would be met by cowards wearing Nigerian Police uniforms." The police left her house swearing they wouldn't return under any circumstances.

Their neighbor, Azubuike Abara, who owned the oxen that gored her husband only laughed and said "better you try to sue my ox" when she demanded he pay her husband's medical expenses or she would take him to court.

Adamma kicked the front door open with her barefoot and came into the house holding a squirming monitor lizard that she had pierced through its tail with a sharpened stick. "Look Mama, can I put this in the soup?" the five year-old asked, her face beaming with excitement.

Ifeoma opened her left eye and at first wanted to yell at the child for breaking her connection with The Creator, and then quickly changed her mind. Lizard meat added to the miyan kuka would be tasty. "Kill it first so that I can cut it up."

"Yes, Mama," the girl replied. She raised the lizard in the air and then expertly, swiftly brought it down whip-like, striking its head on the floor, instantly killing it. With the lizard dangling on the stick, the girl gazed at it for a moment. "It's dead, Mama."

"That's a good girl," Ifeoma said, "go put it on the table."

"Yes, Mama."

As Adamma crossed the room to the table piled with okra, onions and chili peppers, removing the lizard from the stick, Ifeoma returned her attention to her husband. He was lying so still – no more than usual but in that moment it seemed so – that she panicked and quickly laid her head on his chest to listen for a heartbeat. Hearing a slow, rhythmic thumping from deep inside him, she raised her head and looked heavenward and uttered aloud, "Why must these things always happen to poor Ifeoma, me, your lowly servant?"

Holding a peeled onion, Adamma joined her mother at her father's bedside. "Is Baba going to be okay?" she asked and then took a large bite of the onion.

"He must get better, and soon, Adamma. The well is going dry." She looked at the onion. "Give your Mama that to take a bite from it."

#

Kwento leaned on the edge of the well and looked down at the dark, shallow pool of water at its bottom as Ifeoma looked on, nervously tapping her foot.

"Yep, appears your source of groundwater may be running dry," he said.

She had only known Kwento since marrying Bunkechukwu four years before and instantly took a dislike to him. He had smugly told her that she was lucky to find a man willing to marry a woman with a child born out of wedlock. His expression as he was asked to advise her about the well was no less smug.

"What does that mean?" She crossed and then uncrossed her arms and then crossed them again. Her foot was tapping an unintelligible Morse code.

"The spring that feeds it has stopped feeding it."

She briefly glanced down the well, then looked at him, befuddled. "How does that happen?"

"It just happens."

She bit into her lower lip. "What can be done?"

"A new well will need to be dug in a place where there's a source of groundwater."

She looked at the dusty, dry land on which the house, the gardens, and the chicken coups encircled by a mesh fence stood. A whirling gathering of dirt and dead vegetation blew across the dirt road that led to their property. Sunlight glinted from the corrugated tin roof of the house. "How do I find where to dig another well?"

"You don't," he said, turning and leaning back against the wall. "You'll need to hire someone to find another source of groundwater. That is where another well can be dug."

"How much will that cost?" She tried to ask it nonchalantly, having told no one how broke they were. She had shoved to the back of her mind her anger at Bunkechukwu for not planning ahead for the emergency she now found herself in. He had married her inflating the amount of money he had in the bank, something she didn't discover until he ended up in the hospital. He had always managed the finances in secret. Her job was to care for the garden, the chickens and his needs, and not ask questions. She knew Kwento had lots of money, but she would rather jump into the well and end her life than ask him for a loan.

"Finding a place to dig a well and having the well dug costs plenty," he answered. He fixed his eyes on hers. "Has Bunkechukwu enough money in the bank so that you can do such a thing?"

"Of course," she replied.

#

The dry dirt under Ifeoma's best shoes rose up in small clouds with every step she took. She counted the number of lizards she saw crossing the road as she hurried along, thinking about Adamma's skill at catching them with anything that had a sharp point. The child had been left home under the watchful eye of Chimoa, at eighty-two, the oldest woman in the church. Adamma was scared of the old woman, likening her to the witches in the stories that Bunkechukwu had read to her. Chimoa forbade Adamma from hunting lizards, or do anything other than draw pictures based on Bible stories.

It was a five mile walk to the home of Mr. Nwaokocha, the wealthiest man in the region, who Bunkechukwu was related to – distant cousins. To make the walk bearable, and survivable, Ifeoma carried with her a large glass bottle filled with water. She took small sips from it and at times dipped her fingers in and then splashed the water on her face.

She arrived at his front door, sweating, her shoes, dress and hair coated with a thin layer of dust. Before knocking she bent over and shook the dust from her hair, brushed off her dress, and took off her shoes and wiped them clean using the last of the water. She set the empty jar behind a potted plant, took a deep breath, and knocked lightly. The maid answered the door. She eyed Ifeoma head to toe and with her face scrunched disapprovingly, asked, "Are you the woman whose husband is dying?"

Ifeoma was momentarily taken aback that the reason for her visit had been discussed with the maid. "Yes, I am. My husband is a cousin of Mr. Nwaokocha."

"Here, everyone is someone's cousin. Mr. Nwaokocha is waiting. Come in." She stepped aside and waved Ifeoma in.

Ifeoma was immediately struck by the air conditioning aided in circulation by fans attached to the ceiling. Walking down the hallway, led by the maid, she stared, mouth agape, at the paintings of Chappal Waddi, the tallest mountain in Nigeria. Each one was the length and width of her front door and framed in ornate gold frames. She understood their meaning: she was entering the home of a man of great stature. At a closed door near the end of the hall, the maid stopped and tapped lightly. "Your cousin's wife is here," she said.

"Show her in," answered a gruff baritone voice.

The maid opened the door. Her knees shaking, Ifeoma walked in. Mr. Nwaokocha was seated behind a large mahogany desk. His hands were folded and resting on the desktop. She had seen him several times before since marrying Bunkechukwu, but never this up close and in an enclosed space. He was so large it was difficult to see anything but him.

He didn't invite her to sit down and didn't inquire into Bunkechukwu's condition. "I understood by your letter that you've come for a loan to have a new well dug."

"Yes, if you'd be so kind and God willing," she stuttered.

"If I make this loan you must pay it back within thirty days. Do you understand?"

"I understand," she replied. "Thank you and God bless you."

"I don't believe in God," he replied. "The universe will deal with you on its own terms should you not repay me. Your God can attend to other business."

"Yes, sir," she said with a giggle, not because she found what he said humorous, but because she had never heard anyone dismiss God in such a way.

Five minutes later she left Mr. Nwaokocha's home carrying a leather pouch filled with the money and a full jar of water. She floated on a cloud of happiness all the way home, reaching there only minutes after Bunkechukwu had died.

#

Ifeoma stood at the site where Bunkechukwu had been buried an hour before. According to Chimoa his death had come quickly, and with little suffering. His death didn't upset her as much as the thought that some of the money she had borrowed from Mr. Nwaokocha had to be spent burying him. It seemed like wasted money to pile dirt on a corpse. She then saw Adamma was poking at the mound of dirt that covered the grave with a pointed stick. She took the stick from her daughter's hand and tossed it aside, took her daughter by the arm and led her out of the cemetery and down the long road back home.

#

The money that Mr. Nwaokocha had loaned Ifeoma remained in the leather pouch, hidden under the mattress where Bunkechukwu had died, in the bed where Ifeoma still slept. Five weeks had passed since obtaining the loan during which time Ifeoma took small amounts of money from the pouch to buy new clothes and shoes for herself and Adamma. She also bought a used car from Kwento to stop him from continuing to badger her about her plans for a new well. She replaced the only electric appliance in the house, a run-down refrigerator that frequently stopped working, with a new one. At night she laid in bed and in the darkness she gave a great deal of thought to having a new well dug, feeling anger towards her husband for leaving the problem of the well for her to resolve. Each morning after waking from restless nights of sleep, she climbed out of bed and gave little thought to the matter of the well, despite the water in it decreasing daily. The last she looked there appeared to be a dwindling amount of water in it.

One morning, while sitting at the table where she and her daughter ate their meals, Ifeoma sipped on a steaming cup of Lipton Yellow Label Tea and pondered the matter of how to repay the money she borrowed from Mr. Nwaokocha. She couldn't understand how a man of such wealth believed that the universe was more powerful than God. She thought, *What kind of power over the matter of repaying the money can the universe have anyway?* It suddenly occurred to her that it had been several hours since she had seen or heard Adamma. The girl had left the house early that morning carrying an old broom handle that she had sharpened the end of with a kitchen knife.

She got up from the table, believing she would see the girl from the window, she carried her cup of tea with her taking sips from it. At the window Adamma couldn't be seen in the front yard. She then went to the front door, opened it, and took a step out and looked around. The little girl was nowhere in sight.

She walked to both sides of the house and not seeing Adamma there or in the chicken coup enclosure where a few scrawny chickens lazily pecked at the dirt, she walked completely around the small house, still not seeing her. From the front yard she called out her daughter's name several times and not getting a response, she walked back into the house, set the cup on the table, and grabbed her car keys.

Driving very slowly up the dirt road she looked out at the scrubland dotted with small groves of dogoyaro trees. The nearest house to hers at a little over .8 km away was that of Azubuike Abara. His oxen were in their enclosure. They barely moved, standing absolutely still in the hot sun, only their ears flapping and their tails batting the flies away. She wondered, *How did Bunkechukwu allow such a slow moving, stupid animal, to gore him in the side!* She stopped the car in front of his house, got out and not seeing any of the Abara family around, she knocked on their front door. Yetunde, Azubuike's wife, opened the door. The two women had never liked one another. Ifeoma considered Yetunde to be as dimwitted as the oxen they kept. "Have you seen my little girl?" she asked.

Yetunde glared at Ifeoma. "If she had come this far on her own you might give more thought to what kind of mother you are."

Ifeoma raised her hand, prepared to slap the other woman, but then the thought that maybe bandits or terrorists had abducted Adamma flashed through her brain. She ran to her car, got in and raced it to the police station a killometer away. She ran in. "My little girl has been taken," she exclaimed to the two policemen sitting behind the desk, their feet propped up on it. They both recognized her as the women who suggested they were cowards.

"By who?" one of them asked.

"Maybe bandits or terrorists."

They both laughed.

"I thought terrorists didn't come this far north," the other one said.

"Maybe not terrorists," she stuttered. "But surely maybe it was bandits who kidnapped her in hopes of ransoming her for money."

"You have money?" the first one asked.

She then remembered she had left her house, and the pouch with the money under the mattress, unguarded and vulnerable to anyone who might want to get to it. Maybe the *universe* was no more than thugs hired by Mr. Nwaokocha to get his money back. She couldn't think of a way to explain any of that to them, and Mr. Nwaokocha was highly respected by everyone, including the police, although no one knew how Mr. Nwaokocha had amassed his wealth. She turned and ran back to her car and sped home. She pulled to a sudden stop a few yards from the well and stared at the wall that surrounded it for a few moments.

It can't be, she thought.

She got out of the car and ran to the well and looked down into the shadowy darkness. At the bottom where only a small puddle of murky water remained, lay Adamma, her body contorted in the way only a broken body could lay. Nearby lay the broom handle, a motionless lizard skewered to the sharpened end.

"Adamma!" she cried out.

The child didn't respond.

"The universe!" Ifeoma screamed as she collapsed against the wall.

The End

32

THE MEMORY OF VISION

Fading in and out like poor reception on a television, Luke saw the waters of the Straits of Gibraltar glisten then darken several times before he looked away. Sitting on the small wall of white stone that surrounded the parking lot he ran his hands over the rough stone as he looked around for his partner, Mike. With Mike nowhere in sight, Luke could feel the panic rising in him, that sense of dread that started in his stomach and crept into his throat, at times almost choking him. He stood and walked carefully to the front of the red store with the sign that said The Last Shop in Europe and put his face to the glass and peered in. He could barely make out the images inside, but Mike was there, standing in front of shelves loaded with small objects, most likely souvenirs of Gibraltar. Mike bought souvenirs wherever they had traveled together.

Luke rested against the glass and squinted at the sunlit white Ibrahim-al-Ibrahim mosque and the white cliffs of Gibraltar behind it. It blurred into and out of shape as he stared at it, its minaret sometimes completely lost in the bright light of late afternoon. He rubbed his eyes and walked back to the wall and sat down again and faced Morocco, unseen but not so far away as not to be imagined. They planned to go there tomorrow by ferry. Above the waters of the strait Luke could make out a few seagulls dancing in the sky, their loud cries echoing much like bitter complaints.

It was in the Bahamas, on a white sand beach lined with tall palm trees, when the boats on the sparkling water faded from his vision that Luke had first became concerned. That was before the trips to see the missions in Arizona, or the Columbia Gorge, or the doll museum in Kansas City. Those places and all the others Luke remembered not so much for their own merits, but by the ever increasing inability to make out the smaller details and the feeling that his eyes were being closed without the involvement of his eyelids. It wasn't until they were standing in the National Gallery of Art looking at a white marble statue beneath a white light and it all disappeared from his sight for several moments that he admitted to himself and to Mike that something was terribly wrong with his eyes. The news that he was going blind and it could not be helped came soon after.

In Gibraltar the day before he and Mike had taken a road and then a path up the rock and fed peanuts and apple slices to the Barbary Apes. They then stood at the top of Gibraltar and looked down at the thousands of gulls swooping in and out of their nesting places on the cliff that shot straight up from the water. Luke had not told Mike how little of them, the gulls, he had been able to make out, how much they seemed no more than mists darting in and out of view. But he could feel their presence, that mass of feathered life he'd seen in other places, off the shores of Nova Scotia and Oregon. He didn't tell Mike about the dizziness either, something new and frightening. When he had grabbed Mike's arm to steady himself as they looked down from such heights, Mike thought it was an act of fear of the height or affection, and had gently patted Luke's hand. Mike rarely asked about how Luke was feeling or about the symptoms and Luke rarely volunteered any unsolicited information.

In the months that followed Luke did what he always did, he worked, read, went to the movies and spent time with friends, and he and Mike traveled, to San Francisco, to the civil war sites in Virginia, to Toronto. Knowing it did little good to complain, Luke never mentioned to Mike that the brighter the day the less in the distance he could see or that small objects often disappeared from his sight entirely. He bought post cards along the way, and when they returned home he would sit alone at his desk in the study and look at them through a magnifying glass and there embed into his memory those images he had not been able to see while at the actual sites. As his sight came and went unpredictably, he managed to fool even Mike who knew him better than anyone else, and traveled as if he were seeing everything. No one noticed that he talked little about what he saw, but said a great deal about what other qualities he recalled about a place.

There on the wall with Morocco not far away, Luke was suddenly overcome with grief. He had known for sometime the anxiety he felt about what lay ahead, but he had shoved his deeper feelings, his utter sadness, to some place deep within him. He closed his eyes and tried to imagine the straits of Gibraltar unseen, or going through the markets in Morocco and not seeing the faces of the merchants. His own tears surprised him as they ran down his cheeks. He wiped them away and opened his eyes and saw nothing, only blackness. He waited for things to come into focus, for the light to invade the darkness, but as he sat there alone and listening to the gulls and the world remaining shrouded in complete night, he knew that the time had arrived. He was now blind and there was nothing he or anyone else could do about it.

"You should have come in to the shop." It was Mike, sitting down on the wall next to Luke.

Luke heard the rustling of a plastic bag. "What did you buy?"

"A snow globe with the mosque inside," Mike said laughing. "Do you want to see it?"

"Not right now," Luke said. "I'm enjoying the view."

The End

33

NIGHTFALL AND THE CUBAN TANGO

In the Casa De La Danza, young women in hues of pink, orange, and green slinky satin dresses sit in a row of chairs along one wall. They look like different flavored shaved ices melting in the heat of the ballroom. The blades of the ceiling fans whirls slowly about, circulating the warm air that is heavily scented with the perfumes, colognes, and sweat of the dancers. The girls fan their rouged faces with bamboo fans. Impassionately, they watch the couples on the dance floor.

Mateo stands near the entrance, his hands in his pockets, a toothpick dangling from his lower lip. Surreptitiously he eyes Aymee who sits at the far end of the row of girls. While the other girls sit with their knees touching she has her legs crossed. Her foot wiggles, lazily keeping rhythm to the music. The bright green comb she has inserted into her dark brown hair piled high on her head like a mound of cascading chocolate is slightly askew. He has known her since they were children but hasn't seen her in long time. At that moment he wants her. He wants any woman. But not to dance with. These girls, the ones in the Casa De La Danza waiting to be asked to dance, do only that. Dance.

His patience with the slowness of the night is frayed. Despite his athletic good looks he is unable to compete with the men on the dance floor who move their bodies in ways he is unable to. He turns, spits out the toothpick, and leaves the building. The recent downpour has left the air even more humid than usual. The palm leaves on the tall trees droop as if oppressed by the rain, humidity, and their inconsequential existence. The asphalt that covers the parking lot is coated with rainwater that makes it shine like black glass. The cars in the lot are all older model Russian-made Ladas, all with excellent paint jobs in colors fit for an upscale whorehouse. His motorbike along with a dozen others stand side-by-side at a rack, chained there like animals awaiting slaughter. The boys who ride them are of the Cuban middle class, although technically a class system doesn't exist. His only consolation in owning a motorbike is that it gets him where he wants to go. He can't afford anything but what he has. He sweeps the water from the bike seat with his hand and unlocks the chain. He wraps the chain around the handlebars, and gets on. There's a moment of anxiety before he turns the key. Will it start or not? His motorbike is like the women he dates, ill tempered and unpredictable. It sputters momentarily and then he drives off.

The streets of Havana are busy. Old cars, junk-heap pickup trucks and aging buses move slowly along the crowded thoroughfares where pedestrians seem impervious to the headlights that catch them in their beams and the honking of the horns that implores them to get out of the way. The white light that shines from the moon that is peeking out from behind diminishing storm clouds illuminates the brightly painted facades of the buildings. Graffiti is scrawled on every available surface. Little of it is political, which could get the artist arrested. Most of it is intended to be poetic.

Mateo turns onto a side street with the intention of taking the less busy back streets. Only two blocks inside the meandering tangle of streets, his motorbike is stopped, surrounded by four men.

Standing in front of the motorbike, gripping the handlebars is Diego. "Hey man, word has it you know a way that could get an amigo off this goddamn island if he wanted to go to America."

Mateo looks around at the men surrounding him, and then back at Diego. He only knows Diego. He doesn't recognize the others. "Yeah, buy some oars and build a raft," he says. "Now, get outta my way. Abuelita can't soak her feet unless I'm there to help her and you know how cranky old women can get when they have sore feet."

Diego grabs Mateo by his shirtfront. "Listen *cabrón,* I'm gonna be keeping my eye on you and if I see you getting ready to depart Cuba without taking me along, I'm gonna cut your throat." He lets go of Mateo's shirt and shoves him back on the seat.

Diego and the other men hastily turn and are quickly lost in the throngs of Cubanos on the sidewalks.

Mateo puts his foot on the gas pedal and speeds on.

#

Mateo tears a piece of rind from the orange with his teeth and spits it on the floor. Around his chair there are several pieces of orange rind and a banana peel. He bites into the pulp, slowly swallows it, savoring the taste as juice dribbles down his chin. Doves perched on the wrought iron railing outside the kitchen window fill the air with their coos. In the next room his grandmother has the television turned up loud. A soap opera is on. The actors speak rapidly, in the heat of discussion about someone's unwanted child. Mateo tears another piece of orange peel from the fruit and spits it on the floor.

"*Cerdo,*" his sister, Adoncia, calls him as she walks into the room and sees the mess on the floor.

"Oink, oink," he replies as he bites into the pulp.

She goes to the regrigerator and takes out a plate on which sits six eggs. "Diego came here last night looking for you while you were out," she says. She places a frying pan on the stove and turns on the flame. "I told him you had gone dancing."

He wraps his hand around the orange, squeezing it. Choking it. "Why would you tell him that?"

"It's where you said you were going. You go dancing at the dance halls and clubs every Friday and Saturday night."

"I go to meet *jevas*, not to dance," he says.

She pours fat from a jar into the pan, waits for the fat to begin to sizzle, then cracks two eggs and drops them in the pan. "Anyway, Diego seemed in a rush to see you."

"He saw me. I saw him."

She pushes at the eggs with a spatula. "What did he want?"

"To see me," he says, rising from the chair. With his bare foot he brushes aside the debris he has left on the floor and leaves the kitchen. In the living room his *abuela* is rocking back and forth in the rocking chair Mateo made for her. Her favorite wool shawl is draped across her frail shoulders although the room is hot. Potted ferns and cactus are lined up on the windowsill that overlooks a noisy alleyway. He glances out the window to make sure his motorbike is still chained up just as he left it. He goes to his grandmother and kisses her lightly on the forehead.

"You're a good boy, Mateo," she says as she affectionately pats his hand without looking away from the television.

He kneels down by the chair and looks up at her wrinkled face. "I will be going away soon," he says.

"Where is there to go?" she says. "Where can anyone go?"

The actors in the soap opera are screaming at one another.

"There is a whole world beyond Cuba, Abuelita," he says. "I want to go to America."

"Be sure to wear a raincoat and make sure your sister wears hers." she says.

" Adoncia will stay here to take care of you," he says.

"Adoncia is such a good girl," she says.

Mateo stands, swats at a fly buzzing around his head, and goes into the bathroom. He strips off his boxers, steps into the shower, and turns on the cold water. Just like the water that comes out when the hot water knob is turned, it's tepid. Hot or cold knob, what comes out is always the same. While lost in thought, thinking about Aymee, and fully aroused, there is a sudden banging on the bathroom door.

It's Adoncia. "Mateo, something is wrong with Abuelita," she screams.

#

Mateo's grandmother lays in the hosptial bed blankly staring up at the ceiling. Mateo passes his hand in front of her face, but her eyes don't follow the movement. They follow nothing. There is no longer any life her eyes although her heart beats and she breathes. Tubes, monitors and IVs are connected to her body.

Adoncia is sitting at the bedside, holding her grandmother's hand, crying softly.

"How long will she live?" Mateo asks the doctor who stands at the foot of the bed making notes in a chart.

The doctor looks up, as if startled from a dream. "It's hard to say. She has had a severe stroke. If we keep her on life support she could remain alive for a long time. There's no way to really predict these things."

"My grandmother won't recover?" Adoncia says, not taking her eyes from her abuelita's face.

The doctor hesitates before saying, "At her age it's unlikely, but miracles do happen."

"And if she's taken off of life support?" Mateo says.

The doctor looks first at Mateo, and then at Adoncia who has her lips pressed against the back of her grandmother's hand. "Perhaps it's time you contact your priest."

#

The wet sand beneath Mateo's feet is cool and soggy. It oozes up between his toes but is washed away by the ebb and flow of the tide. In the early evening sky, seagulls perform a chaotic ballet accompanied by thier screeching cries. They have been drawn to crabs scampering beneath the cover of mounds of sea foam that washes in and out with every wave. Mateo has rolled up his pants legs revealing his muscular calf muscles. Whenever he looks at them he is reminded of his lack of coordination when dancing. He once took lessons on how to dance the

Cuban tango, but was told by the instructor, "You should just concentrate on walking."

The wind blowing in from the Gulf of Mexico is warm and filled with salt that is invisible but clings to his skin. On the horizon there are ships carrying large containers, heading for the open sea. Smaller vessels, many with white sails, ply the waters nearer to the coast. The sea craft of the Tropas Guardafronteras skim the waters, on constant lookout for anything that appears illegal. The bells of buoys mix with the blaring of horns from the boats, the crashing waves, and the ruckus of the gulls. Mateo came to the beach to think, but in the noise, he finds that hard to do. He turns to leave when he sees Aymee at a distance, walking up the beach, accompanied by two other young women. He hastily puts on his shirt and tucks it in. He stares out at the sea as if in deep contemplation, remembering that when they were children, Aymee was very smart. After several minutes of trying to appear intelligent, he turns his head and sees that Aymee and her companions have left the beach.

Returning to where he left his motorbike chained to a bike stand by the boardwalk, he finds the words "*no olvides*" spray painted on the bike seat in bright red. He wonders, *Don't forget what?*

He looks around for signs of Diego and his crew spying on him, waiting, but the boardwalk is mostly crowded with couples walking hand-in-hand or other loners like himself standing about, aimlessly search for something. Something real, but elusive.

The drive through the city is slowed by a sudden downpour. The large potholes in the streets quickly fill with rain water, forming small pools. The drainage system has quickly backed up, creating overflow from the sewers that carry garbage and vegetative debris in rapidly flowing streams along each sides of the streets. He is soaked by the time he reaches home. At the front door he removes his shoes, empties the sand from them, and along with his sopping wet shirt, leaves them on the ground next to the welcome mat. Inside it's quiet. He goes into the bathroom, removes his clothes and drys off. In his bedroom he puts on his best shirt, pants, and shoes. He goes into Adoncia's room, steals money she keeps in her jewelry box that she thinks she has hidden from him, and then calls for a taxi. Twenty minutes later he gets in the back seat. "*El Casa De La Danza,*" he tells the driver.

The ride to the dance hall is much faster than when he rides his motorbike. He feels slightly guilty for taking some of his sister's money, but his pay as a public servant mopping the floors of government buildings doesn't allow him the luxury of taking taxis and she'll only be angry for a short while when she discovers the theft. She can be mean, but forgiving. At the Casa De La Danza he pays the driver, who grumbles about not getting a tip, and dashes to the entrance attempting to keep from getting wet. The rain has diminished, but not by much.

Just inside the doors he stops at the ticket booth and hands money to Hernando.

"You going to dance tonight?" Hernando says. He hands Mateo the ticket to get in.

"I never dance," Mateo says, taking the ticket and stuffing it in his pocket.

"Why do you come here, then?"

"I dream of being able to dance."

In the ballroom, he stops and looks at posters propped up on easels. "*Concurso de tango cubano esta noche,*" is written in bold gold lettering accompanied by a photos of couples dancing the Cuban tango and one couple holding a large trophy.

He finds his usual place near a wall just inside the ballroom, near where the young women waiting to be asked to dance, sit. He sticks a toothpick in his mouth, leans back, and props one foot against the wall. The moist air from outside has given the ballroom the sensation of being in a hothouse. As he watches the girls fan themselves, he unbuttons his shirt to mid-chest, revealing the beads of sweat on the cleavage of his well-developed pectoral muscles. He has seen them all before, and they have seen him. There is a mutual, unspoken, bond of indifference between him and them.

The mirrored ball that hangs in the middle of the ballroom ceiling turns slowly, casting small squares of reflected light onto the dance floor and the dancers. The circle of fragmented light cast about the room is mesmerizing, hypnotic, despite Mateo's attempt to ignore it. Amidst the dancers caught in the glittering light Diego is dancing with Aymee. Mateo's rage boils up from the core of his being; rage towards Diego, Aymee and Cuba. He retrieves his ticket from his pocket, crumbles it in his hand, and throws it on the floor. Hastily departing the Casa De La Danza he runs into his best friend, Jose, who has just bought a ticket.

"Hey man, I just heard the news," Jose says.

"What news?"

"You don't know?" Jose says, surprised. "Your abuela has died."

#

"I think it was a sign," Mateo says. "I hadn't seen Aymee in a very long time and then I saw her three times in less than twenty-four hours. Three is a lucky number, no?"

Adoncia slowly shakes her head. "When will you return?"

Mateo shoves the last shirt into his duffel bag and closes it. "I must first get away," he says. "Diego has made it clear he intends to kill me if I try to leave without him."

"Like it or not, he is our older brother," she says.

"He never came around except to get money from Abuelita and then he doesn't show up at her funeral."

Adoncia presses a small wad of pesos in his hand. "When does the boat leave Havana?"

"At nightfall." He lifts the bag from his bed and places it on his shoulder. He looks at his sister who has tears welling in her eyes. "I will send for you when I'm settled." He leaves the apartment, glances at his motorbike set free of its chains, and waits for a taxi.

The End

34

THE VISITATION

See Sister Monica as she bends over the furrow in the ground, her knees in the dirt, grasping a trowel in one hand. In the heat of the morning, sweat pours from under her coif and wimple and streams down her face. Watch as she examines the bright green shoot of a tomato plant, tenderly taking its small leaves between her fingers and peering at them intently. A hot breeze blows across the convent garden carrying with it bits of dirt she recently tilled in the dry, crumbling earth. The cawing of a crow flying overhead catches her attention. She looks up at it and shields her eyes from the glare of the sun, dropping bits of soil from her gardening gloves onto the front of her habit, above the chest hemline of a denim apron that protects the rest of it from getting dirty.

"Damn," she mumbles.

See her look around to make sure she wasn't heard. Except for her, there are no other sisters in the garden that covers a small square of land behind the convent. There is a small grove of lemon trees on the border of the garden. The unpicked lemons that dangle from the drooping limbs are brown and withered, like oversized walnuts. In the center of the grove standing on a white marble base is a bronze statue of St. Fiacre, the patron saint of gardeners. The patina that covers most of his beard and robe is a mixture of brown and green hues. His face enclosed in a hood is shiny as if it has just been polished. His expression on his bearded face is benevolent. On the bronze plate fixed to the front of the marble base the inscription reads: I made gardens and parks and planted all kinds of fruit trees in them. Ecclesiatses 2:5.

Watch as Sister Monica bows her head and says a brief, silent prayer. She then places the trowel in the empty wicker basket sitting beside her and slowly stands. Her movements are slow, deliberate. She has learned to overcome her tendency to rush with anything she does. Prayer is sedation. She removes her gloves and puts them in the basket and then attempts to brush the dirt from her habit, causing the smudge to expand. Suppressing her frustration that wearing a white habit to do gardening in frequently causes such accidents, she steps across several rows of furrowed ground where dead sprouts from other recently planted tomato plants stick up from the earth. There is a pile of rotting wooden stakes sitting on the edge of the garden that were once used to hold up growing plants. See her walk around them, consciously avoiding glancing at the pile; they are a reminder that nothing no longer grows to maturity in the garden.

Hear the rusty hinges on the door to the garden shed squeak as she pulls it open. The heat inside the shed rushes out, escaping the entrapment of wood and corrugated tin, and washes over her, adding to her physical discomfort. She grew up in the southern United States, a daughter of an itinerant farm worker, but this weather – the unrelenting and unusual high temperatures – is almost more than she can bear. She hasn't told anyone in the convent that she suffers in the heat, but she has frequently told God. Holding the door open with her foot, she pushes her sleeve up her forearm, closes her eyes, and wipes the sweat from her face with the back of her arm. Watch as she opens her eyes and sees the naked young man lying on the floor of the shed. His physique resembles that of Michaelangelo's David. With her heart pounding, a gasp that escapes her lips is followed by her taking several staggered steps back. The door closes as she drops the basket and stares, dumbfounded, at the shed.

See her turn and stare at the convent as the bell is rung for the sisters to assemble in the chapel for pre-lunch prayers. Look at the small clouds of dust her shoes kick up as she runs across the garden and to the back door of the convent where she stops, hastily removes the apron and hangs it on a hook. Catching her breath, she says a quick prayer, crosses herself, and calmly opens the door and goes in.

At the doors to the chapel she inserts her hands into her sleeves, crosses her arms, and gets in line behind Sister Margret. She is bursting to tell someone, anyone, about the man in the shed, but entering the chapel she sees Mother Superior seated in her throne-like chair on the dais at the end of the aisle that separates two long rows of pews where the sisters sit. She knows to say anything at all would incur the Mother Superior's wrath, delivered with terrifying quietude.

Watch as Sister Monica sits on a pew on the left side of the aisle, crosses herself, bows her head, and begins to pray. "Hail Mary, full of grace, there's a man in the garden shed," she utters in a whisper so low that she alone knows she spoke.

#

After lunch, Sister Monica is at the sink and scrubbing a large pot. Mother Superior had passed by her before they had sat down to eat and glanced at the spot of dirt and frowned, but said nothing. Sister Monica uses suds from the dishwater to try to remove the smudge of dirt on her habit, spreading the dirt even more, turning a small part of her habit just beneath the neckline a dull gray, like a gathering storm cloud. See how she glances at what has happened to her habit, and her own dour expression, reflected in the shiny pot. During the meal the only words spoken by any of the sisters were related to scriptures. Still rattled by the morning's events and unable to think of a scripture that applied to finding a man in a garden shed, Sister Monica simply asked the other sisters to pray for her to be more accepting of God's mysteries.

Hear Sister Angeline as she comes into the kitchen, the soles of her shoes shuffling across the tiled floor. She stops in the middle of the kitchen and gently claps her hands. Sister Monica and the other sisters stop what they are doing and turn to face Sister Angeline. Sister Angeline is very old, older than any of the sisters in the convent. Her face is lined with wrinkles. Her voice is raspy, from age and disuse. "Mother Superior wishes to remind those of you who work in the gardens and grounds of the convent to make sure everything is in readiness for the visit from the Bishop, who is fond of gardens and such. He will be here first thing tomorrow morning."

Without looking directly at Sister Angeline's face, whose eyes and fixed stare reminded her of a bird of prey, Sister Monica asks, "Will the Mother Superior permit us extra time this afternoon to prepare for the Bishop's visit?"

"Yes," Sister Angeline replies and then turns and leaves the kitchen.

#

The intense heat of late afternoon envelopes Sister Monica as soon as she steps out the back door of the convent. She stops for a moment and glances up at the sun that fills the sky like a glaring white neon light and shakes her head, dismayed. The dry spell has lasted longer than the previous summer, which lasted longer than the summer before that. First, making certain there is no one who will see her, she grabs the apron and rushes across the garden to the shed. She stands in front of the door for several moments before opening it. She ducks down as a dove flies out and disappears beyond the brick wall that surrounds the convent. Inside the shed, the man is still there, in the same position he was in that morning.

She steps into the shed, letting the door close behind her. In the ambient light, the man's body emits a gentle glow of its own, as if he is lit from the inside. In the dim light, his nudity seems more pronounced; there is no escaping the sight of it. She lays the apron across his lower body and then kneels down beside his head and stares at his face. His complexion is smooth, without any imperfections. Light brown curls cascade over his forehead and encircle his ears. She places her hand on his forehead only because it is was the first thing her mother did whenever anyone was ill. His brow is damp; the slight perspiration that covers it feels like the cool spring water she swam in before leaving home seven years before. She then leans over him, placing her ear to his lips and listens to his slow, steady exhalations of air, and feels the warmth of his breath on her cheek, like the feel of a butterfly landing on cotton. There is an intimacy to the moment that embarrasses her and she sits back on her heels and watches the rise and fall of his chest.

"He doesn't seem harmed in any way," she mutters aloud and then says to him, "How did you get in here?"

See his eyelids flutter, and then open. His eyes as blue and clear as a cloudless sky gaze at her for several moments.

In his eyes she sees the world as she imagines it should be, as God meant it to be. She sees its purity and vastness. She also sees her own inadequacies as a nun; the impurities of her soul. She's certain that the man who lies in the dirt is a messenger sent by the almighty. An angel.

He speaks one word, "Thirst."

Startled by his voice, watch as she quickly rises from the floor, grabs the watering can, and leaves the shed.

Sister Francine is standing in the garden and turns to see Sister Monica.

"Is there any hope?" Sister Francine asks waving her hand around at the dead and dying vegetation. Sister Francine has cancer and has been on chemotherapy for several weeks. Despite being in constant pain, she has refused pain medication, preferring to pray instead. Her cheeks are sunken and her skin color sallow. Beneath her headdress her short red hair has fallen out, leaving her bald. Sister Francine and Sister Monica are friends even though friendships among the sisters is discouraged. "You're here to serve Jesus," Mother Superior often reminds the sisters.

Stammering, Sister Monica points at the shed and says, "In there, a man – an angel – sent by God."

Sister Francine smiles, weakly. "What are you talking about?"

"In the shed, an angel, perhaps the archangel Michael," Sister Monica responds breathlessly as she turns on the faucet attached to a garden hose. She puts the end of the hose in the watering can and begins filling it. "I looked into his eyes and saw my soul."

Look at the befuddled expression on Sister Francine's face. "Why would the archangel appear here, at this convent, in this garden?" she asks.

"Where better to begin to quench the earth?" Sister Monica replies. "The only word he has spoken is thirst. He speaks of his need and the earth's need at the same time."

"Does he?"

Sister Francine would like to go to the shed to humor the only other sister in the convent who she can talk to in the middle of the night when the pain that courses through her body is at its worse, but this is not how or where the archangel would appear, not in a garden shed, that she feels certain of. "You've spent too much time out in this heat," she says.

Sister Monica yanks the hose from the can and tosses it aside. As a stream of water runs from the hose into the garden and forms a small puddle on the hard ground, she stands, picks up the can, and goes to the door of the shed. "Come see for yourself," she says.

She opens the door and looks in. See her drop the can and fall to her knees. The man is gone.

#

At evening meal, during which time limited casual conversation is permitted, Sister Monica silently eats the salad made from wilted and colorless vegetables brought to the convent from the market in the nearby town. Sister Angeline, sitting to her right, tremulously holds her spoon as she slurps her soup. Eating at the head of the table, Mother Superior frequently glances up from her salad at Sister Monica, causing the young nun to squirm uncomfortably in her chair knowing that it can't be because of her habit; she was able to change into a clean one before supper.

See her try to surreptitiously try to get the attention of Sister Francine who is seated at another table by winking at her. Sister Francine has avoided her since the unfolding of events in the garden earlier in the day.

After the meal is finished and the dishes and silverware have been gathered up and taken into the kitchen, the sisters remain at the tables, their heads bowed, offering prayers of thanks for the meal while awaiting to be dismissed from the dining room by the Mother Superior. When she stands, a hush falls over the room and every sister looks at her, reverently and expectantly.

"In final preparation for the Bishop's visit, I ask that Sisters Beatrice and Monica join me for a walk around the convent grounds before the evening prayers."

See the stunned expression on Sister Monica's face. The Mother Superior has been out in the garden many times, but has never asked her to accompany her there. She glances at Sister Francine to see if she can detect in her friend's facial expression some sign that she had spoken to Mother Superior about the man in the garden shed. Or more precisely, and inexplicably, the man who wasn't in the shed. Sister Francine's face is a mask; a shield to block her from crying out from the intense pain.

As the other sisters rise and file out of the room to go to the chapel, Sisters Beatrice and Monica stand in place where they had eaten and do not move until Mother Superior waves her hand and leads them from the dining room. They walk down the long corridor of the convent in silence. Before Sister Beatrice opens the back door, Sister Monica raises her eyes heavenward and says a silent prayer that when the door is opened, a miracle performed by the archangel will have restored the garden to the days when what grew in it fed the sisters and the poor and needy in the surrounding towns with whom the bounty was shared.

The door is opened and where the garden stood is a large pool of muddy water fed by the garden hose that leads to it.

#

Watch as in the middle of the night Sister Monica gets out of her bed and quietly leaves her cell. The wing of the convent where the sisters sleep is quiet and full of shadows cast by the pale moonlight that streams in through the windows at both ends of the corridor. Barefoot, her footsteps on the tiles are no more than whispers as she treads lightly to the door of Sister Francine's cell. She taps lightly on the door – a tap that could easily be mistaken for the fluttering of a bird's wing from outside – and then enters her friend's cell. She sees Sister Francine on her bed, lying on her back, her cover pulled up to her neck.

Standing at the door, Sister Monica says, "There was a man in the garden shed, I swear it. Maybe it wasn't the archangel, but there was a man."

Sister Francine says nothing.

Awaiting her friend to say something, to absolve her of the guilt she feels for destroying what was left of the garden just before the Bishop's visit, Sister Monica sighs heavily. "Am I wrong to want to believe that the archangel would visit here, visit me?" she asks. Getting no response she turns and leaves Sister Francine's cell.

Hear the shrillness in Mother Superior's voice as she calls out from the end of the corridor. "What are you doing in Sister Francine's cell?" she demands to know.

Unable to find the words, an explanation of any kind that would be acceptable, Sister Monica is struck mute.

Listen to the thudding of Mother Superior's slippered feet on the tiles as she marches to Sister's Francine's cell, pushes Sister Monica aside, opens the door and goes in. A few moments later, Mother Superior calls out calmly, as if the words she says has no meaning, "Sister Francine is dead."

#

The Bishop is thin and frail and appears lost sitting in Mother Superior's chair behind her large mahogany desk. He has his hands folded and resting on the top of a small Bible that he brought with him. The bright red ribbon that divides the pages spills out of the Bible like streaming blood.

Sister Monica is unable to take her eyes off of it.

"Now, tell me again about this man who was in the shed," he says, his voice as high-pitched and light as that of a flute.

"I was certain he was the archangel come to restore the garden," Sister Monica replies.

"Why would the archangel Michael appear to you and no one else?"

Watch as Sister Monica slowly glances around the room, at the books on the shelves, the religious paintings on the walls, the iciness in Mother Superior's stare.

"Because I have such thirst," she says.

The End

35

GRAVEYARD OF THE PUFFINS

With her arm inserted through a wicker basket's handle, Kate carefully stepped over the shoreline's rocks as water sloshed inches from her feet. Tied by a blue hair ribbon, her sandals hung around her neck. A cool, salty breeze that blew in from the Atlantic Ocean made her calf-length tie-dyed skirt billow above her knees like an adrift parachute. Free from being bound, her silver hair that reached to the middle of her back floated in the air around her. Sunlight glinted from the dancing web-like strands. Her scrubbed cheeks were ruddy from the assault of wind, weather and exertion. She bent down and lifted a dead puffin from where it had become lodged between two rocks and placed its limp, battered body in the basket with another puffin. She stood and looked out at the water, holding her hand above her eyes, shielding them from the sun and water's blinding glare. She then spotted a puffin diving from the sky, and sighed audibly when it hit the water and then immediately rose back into the air, carrying in its bright orange beak a small fish.

She turned and climbed the few feet up to the carpet of grass, sat down and set the basket down beside her. She untied her sandals, and brushed wet dirt and sand from the soles of her feet before putting them on. As the wind whipped her hair about, she gathered it in her hands, shaped it into a bundle on the top of her head, and thread the ribbon through and around it. Within moments she had tamed it, having returned her hair to the way she always wore it, except for when gathering dead puffins from the shoreline's rocks. This act of releasing her hair and then rebinding it, and finding the puffins and saving their corpses from ignoble death, were mysteriously linked. It had been that way since the first time she found and found the first dead puffin when she was just a child. At that time it was her mother who loosed the ribbon and helped her walk on the slippery rocks.

The walk from the shore to her small bungalow wasn't long. With her own hands she had reshaped a path of freshly lain pebbles through the grass that led directly to the back door. Every summer, blue-bead lilies, coltsfoot, purple lilacs, and dandelions, grew in the tangle of weeds and thick grass that lined both sides of the path. At the start of summer, the first thing she did upon returning to the bungalow from her home in Halifax was to pull any sprouting weeds or wildflowers from the path and spread new pebbles where the winter storms or wild animals had created bald spots. Entering the kitchen of the bungalow she sat the basket on the kitchen sink and thoroughly washed the puffins, careful to avoid removing any more of their black feathers than had already been lost, under the circumstances. A dead puffin was a delicate thing that naturally shed its feathers quickly, but did so even faster when handled.

"Death quickly reclaims those things given a living thing," her mother had told her upon finding that first puffin. She had never forgotten it. Her mother said it with a sincerity she rarely said about anything. That was when both she and her mother were still young.

She toweled off the first one and turned it over in her hands several times prodding and poking every part of its body, then spreading its feathers and closely examining the its skin. Smiling, she laid it back in the basket and then turned her attention to the second bird. She repeated what she had done with the first bird, but almost imperceptibly, sadly, shook her head and laid it in the sink. More than half of the puffins she found on the shoreline ended up in the sink. It was long after her mother had passed away from Alzheimer's that she had begun separating the birds in such a manner, but her mother's words stuck with her.

"The unfairness of life lingers on beyond death," her mother once said.

She would later return the bird in the sink to the waves that washed it ashore to join most of its kind whose lives ended in the cold ocean water.

She walked away from the sink, carrying with her the basket with the other bird lying inside that she placed on a small antique table by the back door. She had bought the table many years before from a seller near the docks in Halifax who's store was cluttered with items obtained from ships. The table had been onboard a ship renowned for having circled the globe. She thought it perfect in looks, and by its history, for transporting the puffins from this world to the next.

When she was sixteen her father drowned at sea during a storm while sailing a lobster boat. Miraculously, among the six lobstermen aboard the boat, his body was the only one recovered. It was returned to the bungalow in a coffin the same color as the table. The sight of her dead father profoundly changed her life forever; it shook her already tenuous grasp on the nature of life and death. Through the years as a child of observing the dead puffins along the shore during her walks with her mother, death seemed a natural end to life. The sight of her dead father's corpse didn't strike her as being at all natural.

Her father was buried near the shoreline with a simple concrete marker that read: To the Sea, Evermore.

As her mother's Alzheimer's began to worsen, her husband, Kate's father, was the first prominent thing in her life she had no memory of.

Suddenly feeling weak – advancing age catching up with her – Kate covered the bird in the basket with a square of linen cut from a larger piece she kept hanging on a hook by the door, and went into the living room and sat in one of the two overstuffed chairs, the one with a pattern of sailboats on its upholstery. She laid her head back, closed her eyes, and tried to take a brief nap. Instead images of puffins falling from the skies filled her consciousness.

#

The day she heard that her father's boat was lost at sea, Kate left her mother sitting in the same chair, but with different upholstery, whales instead of sailboats, to walk to the shoreline. Her mother hadn't moved in the four hours since learning of her husband's disappearance. Going out the back door of the bungalow, the young Kate meandered along the dirt pathway, picking wildflowers as she made her way to the rocks. There she removed her shoes, tossed them in the grass, and climbed over the rocks to the water. Her parents didn't believe in God, and she had never been inside a church, but she closed her eyes and whispered a prayer:

Dear maker of puffins
send my father back to Earth
as soon as possible
we already miss him terribly.

She opened her eyes and tossed the bouquet of flowers she had collected into the water. In that instant, a puffin landed at her feet, flopped about for several seconds before dying. She looked heavenward. "Thank you," she whispered. She bent down, picked it up, and carried it to the small one room guest house her mother had always intended to turn into some kind of studio. She opened the door and carried the dead bird into the ambient dim light of twilight that shone through the one window.

#

It was the foghorn sounding from the recently installed warning system built on the rocks a bit north of the bungalow that roused her from her brief rest. She pushed herself up from the chair, brushed a few strands of hair back from her face, tucked them into her mass of hair, and walked back into the kitchen. The waning light of day shone through the window above the sink. The kitchen was filled with shadows. She flipped on the light, flooding the room with unnatural daylight. This had been her mother's favorite time of the day, when she would sit at the table and have a cup of tea while reading the latest edition of the Mariner's News. Up until she forgot her husband had ever existed, she had diligently read the Mariner's News page to page each week that it arrived in the mail just as her husband had done.

Kate went to the window and saw waves of fog rolling in from the sea, swallowing up the land around the bungalow beneath its blanket of gray clouds and mist. She left the window and took the flashlight from the drawer in the antique table, and flipped it on and off several times to make sure it worked. She had recently changed its batteries, but it was an old flashlight that, just like her own body, lost the will to work at inconvenient times. She then picked up the basket and went out the back door.

She knew the chill that fog rolling in from the North Atlantic brought with it, even in summer, and cursed under her breath for not wrapping around her shoulders the shawl her mother had knitted for her many years ago that hung on a hook by the door. The shawl had holes where she had caught it on nails that she always forgot to hammer all the way in, although they had stuck out in the same manner since the day they had been pounded in. Although still easily able to see through the thickening gray, she switched on the flashlight that required tapping several times against her leg before it came on.

"When anything can go wrong, expect it to every time," her mother often said about almost any accident or misfortune. Her husband's death was one of the rare times she didn't say it. About his death she said very little. Her years of mourning said it all.

Shining the flashlight on the path, Kate thought about the many times she had walked it from the bungalow to the guest house – hundreds of times, thousands, a million – that she had turned into a studio as her mother always talked of doing. The walk was shorter than that from the house to the shoreline, but traveled with the same excited, albeit respectful solemnity, when going to retrieve the bodies of dead puffins.

At the door to the studio she paused briefly before turning the doorknob. Although she knew what was inside, there were so few things she anticipated anymore that the moment before opening the door gave her a brief moment's pause. As she pushed the door open she was greeted with the scents of arsenic, borax, cedar dust, and glue. In the pale light that shone in through the window, the contents in the studio took on eerie or unearthly shapes, resembling anything from fierce dragons to angels. She reached over and flipped the light switch installed on the inside door frame.

Light flowed down from fluorescent lights hung from the middle of the ceiling casting a bright glow on the large oak table set up in the middle of the room where tools and bottles and boxes of chemicals were placed in orderly fashion at one end.

On wires hanging from the ceiling were hundreds of taxidermied puffins, their wings spread as if gliding through the air, or their heads pointing to the floor, in a diving posture. They lay tacked atop dowels standing on driftwood bases in the positions their bodies had been found in. They stood on paper mache rocks looking upward, four to five deep along the walls, and were stacked like cords of wood on the floor. Many were packed in lobster traps awaiting a final resting place, each with the words "To the Sea, Evermore" painted on placards attached to the netting, awaiting a final resting place.

The End

36

THE APPLE PICKERS

There's only one street and it has no name. Unpaved, the street is light brown dirt that hardens and cracks when the sun bakes it and turns to mud when it rains. Because the street rises at both ends, the middle of it is like a bowl that fills with dirty water during rainstorms. There are eighteen homes that line both sides of the street. The homes are built of plywood with tin roofs and there is a sheet of plywood lying on the ground in front of the homes which serve as porches. Only a couple of the porches have real chairs on them. All the rest have over-turned plastic buckets or baskets for carrying apples that we use to sit on. None of the homes have windows. The front doors are screen doors.

My name is Esteban and I pick apples.

#

In the morning as sunlight breaks through the dissipating hazy clouds I'm on the porch straining to hear the chirping birds in the trees beyond the street and beyond the field of dirt that surrounds us. Their music is discordant, but music nevertheless. The air is cool and still but filled with the odors that comes from the outhouses behind our homes. Miguel's mongrel dog is scrounging in the dirt in front of his house, in search of what I have no idea. Like the street, the dog has not been officially named. Everyone just calls it Dog. It's an old dog and practically blind. As I shift on the basket I am sitting on, Dog raises its nose and sniffs, unaware that I am nearby, then returns to scratching in the dirt.

My wife, Rita, comes out of our home carrying a cup of coffee. Steam is rising from it like a ghostly snake. She blows on the coffee's surface just before she hands it to me, momentarily chasing the snake away. "You tossed and turned all night," she says.

I hold the cup in both hands and sip slowly, savoring the taste. "I'm missing home," I say.

"We could go back now," she says.

I watch Dog chewing on something he found in the dirt. "It's too soon," I say. "At the end of the apple picking season will be better."

"There are beans, eggs and tortillas for breakfast," she says. "Come wake up Pedro and get him washed before we eat. We want to be ready when the trucks arrive." She goes back inside, letting the screen door slam behind her.

Miguel comes out of his home that is across from mine and waves. I lift my cup to him. He goes to the edge of his porch and whistles loudly. Dog turns, raises his nose, and bounds toward Miguel. Miguel stoops down and gathers Dog in his arms and accepts Dog's tongue bathing his face. Miguel takes something from his pocket and feeds it to Dog. As Dog devours it, his tail wagging feverishly, Miguel stands and says to me, "Do you think they'll ask you to be the new supervisor?"

"It's not what I want," I say. "It's too much work and no extra money."

"Maybe it would lead to something better," he says.

"An early grave isn't something better," I say.

#

I pump the tepid water into the metal sink basin and watch as Pedro cups his hands beneath the faucet and splashes the collected water on his face.

"Is that enough Papa?" he says as water drips from his ears and chin.

"That's enough," I say as I stop pumping and hand him a small threadbare towel. The drain makes a gurgling sound as the water goes down the pipe. It sounds as if it's swallowing.

Pedro wipes his face and ears with the towel then jumps off the empty suitcase he stands on when he's at the sink. He sits in one of the three folding chairs at the cardboard table. Rita is seated in another.

"Papa, can I take my slingshot today?" Pedro says.

I sit at the table and watch as Rita ladles black beans onto our plates from a pan. Using a spatula, she slides a fried egg from a plate onto each of our plates. "Yes, but don't shoot at anyone, just the rocks or dirt," I say.

"Esteban, he's only six years old. I don't like him shooting that thing," Rita says.

I put a forkful of beans into my mouth. "He's a boy. It's what boys do," I say.

The light bulb that is attached to a wire that hangs from the ceiling suddenly goes out. There is no use of electricity during most of the daylight hours. In the light that flows in through the screen door we eat our breakfast quietly, as if our electricity has been turned off also.

#

The dirt road to the orchards is bumpy and the truck bounces up and down. I hold Pedro in my lap and Rita is sitting next to me on a rickety bench. Everyone else who is in the truck are our neighbors and friends. It's only the driver, a white man, who I don't know. We are in the first truck of the three. There's an olive green canvas cover over the back of the truck, and sitting under it is like being in a large tent. I know the landscape we are driving through is mostly asparagus and cucumber fields and apple orchards, but I long to see them, not out of wonder, but to escape this feeling of being trapped. It's hot and I wipe sweat from Pedro's face with my bandanna. Inside the truck it smells of body odor and dust.

The truck has come to a stop and we sit for several moments before the tailgate is lowered. I carry Pedro as I step out of the truck. I place him on the ground and as he stands holding my hand I put my other hand over my eyes to shield them from the glare of the white sun. The baskets for the apples are stacked at the beginning of the aisles between the rows of trees. Wood ladders of various lengths are in the back of another truck. The supervisor, Ramon, tells us what trees are to be picked. We get the baskets and ladders.

As I step on the ladder leaning against a limb of a tree, Ramon says to me in almost a whisper, "The boss will make you the supervisor if I recommend it."

"Why are you going back home?" I say.

"Five years of picking apples every August to December is enough. And I miss home," he says.

I see the others climbing the ladders or picking apples from the lower branches and putting them in the baskets and am unexpectedly filled with sympathy. "I don't want to be the new supervisor," I say. "I may return home also. We've picked tomatoes, peaches, oranges and apples since Pedro was born. He knows nothing about life in Mexico."

Ramon pushes his white straw hat back on his head, turns and walks away. His worn boots kick up small clouds of dirt as he walks. There is a sweat stain down the middle of his back.

"Papa, may I play with my slingshot now?" Pedro asks as he tugs on my pants leg.

Rita is nearby and is holding a basket and putting apples in it. She looks at me with concern.

"Yes, but don't go far," I say.

#

Rita hands up the tin cup filled with cold water. The metal feels cool on my palms as I raise it to my parched lips. With my head tilted back I keep my eyes closed against the pulsating afternoon sun. It is unusually hot and visible waves of heat rise from the ground. The leaves are dry, as if they too need to have their thirst quenched. With my throat no longer feeling as if it is filled with dry dust I drop the cup into Rita's hands. She has pulled her long hair up to the top of her head into a bun. Her dark cheeks are pink from exposure to the sun. A basket filled with apples is at her feet.

A sudden cry comes from a nearby tree and then there is the sound of a ladder crashing to the ground. I rush down the ladder and with Rita and other apple pickers I go to Miguel who is lying on the ground, the ladder next to him. His leg is bent askew from the knee down.

"My leg is broken," he groans.

Ramon appears and kneels down next to Miguel. "How did this happen?" he says.

"Something small hit me in the face," Miguel says. He groans in pain.

"Help me carry him to a truck," Ramon says.

As Miguel is lifted from the ground by several of the men, Miguel grabs my hand and says, "Promise you will watch out for Dog."

"I promise," I say as he is carried away.

Pedro comes up behind me and pulls on my shirt. I turn and see tears streaming down his face. He has the slingshot firmly grasped in his hand. Bending down I put my lips to his ear and whisper, "Did you shoot Miguel?"

I turn my ear to his mouth and he says, "Yes, Papa. I didn't mean to."

#

Rain batters the tin roof sending gunshot like echoes inside our two room home. Rita has placed a metal wash basin on the floor beneath the constant drip of water coming through a small hole in the roof. The rain has cooled the air and damp wind blows through the screen in the door. Rita is sitting on one of the folding chairs sewing a button on one of my shirts. The glowing light bulb casts a harsh circle of light in the combined kitchen and living room.

Pedro comes from the bedroom and stands by me looking out the screen door at the mud and water sliding down the street. "Did I kill Miguel?" he says.

I put my arm around his thin shoulders. "Of course not son," I say. "He'll have a cast on his leg for a while then he'll be able to pick apples again."

He kisses me on the cheek then does the same thing with Rita, then returns to the bedroom.

Dog is sitting on Miguel's porch facing Miguel's screen door. He's drenched. I open the door and whistle and hold out a handful of pork scraps I saved for him from our dinner. He doesn't move. I toss the pork onto the porch and withdraw my hand and close the door. The last thing I see before I get up from where I'm seated at the door is how the street has been turned into a flowing creek.

#

Before breakfast and in the coolness of the storm aftermath I stand in the mud with many of the apple pickers staring at Dog's body floating in the pool that formed in the middle of the street. Some are mumbling prayers.

#

From the back of the bus I watch through the window the passing landscape. I've seen before these verdant hills, trees losing their leaves, and houses large enough for several families to make into their homes.

Rita is sound asleep in the seat next to me. Her long hair flows over her shoulders.

Pedro is in my lap and stretching the bands of his slingshot. "Will we pick apples in Mexico?' he says.

"I don't think so, son," I say.

The End

37

SONG OF THE MONSOON

Listen to Saraswati, the goddess of music, wisdom, and nature, as she sings songs for Brahma, Vishnu and Shiva while plucking the strings of the sarod. Her music enters Sajit's ears as softly as the sound of a butterfly landing on cotton. There's Sajit. See him standing in the courtyard, bathed in moonlight. Near him, the statue of Lord Indra, the god of the heavens, lightning, thunder, storms, and rains, sets atop a small fountain that sprays water from concrete elephant trunks. Large koi swim in the pool that surrounds the fountain, their bright orange and gold bodies glisten only inches beneath the water's surface. Pale purple lotus flowers in full bloom float on the water. The air is filled with the scent of marigolds that grow along the walls that enclose the courtyard. Watch as Sajit slowly pulls his purple kurta over his head and hangs it on the thick leaves of a plumeria alba that stands in a large turquoise blue porcelain planter. He then kneels on the green tiled wall that encloses the pool, bends down, and scoops up handfuls of cool water that he splashes on his face and chest. He rises up and water drips from his raven black hair, streams down his bare torso, and onto the front of his ankle-length lungi. See how he rests, facing the moon as he sits on the marble bench near the pool and lets the balmy night air dry his skin

Watch as Sajit looks up at the second floor of the bungalow and sees the lights in Jacob Swan's room are out. He puts the kurta back on and then walks the cobblestone path to the back door. He enters the kitchen, stops at the island in the middle of the room, and takes an orange from a bowl of fruit. Peeling it with his teeth he carries the orange into his room, which is connected to the kitchen, kept separate by a bamboo curtain. He leaves a trail of orange peels on the floor. He sits on his bed and slowly, with his eyes closed, swallows the segments of the orange, savoring the juice. It dribbles down his chin but he purposely doesn't wipe it away. It's like a cologne that adds fragrance to his caramel colored skin.

The oil lamp on the stand beside his bed glows brightly. It's placed next to an electric lamp that he doesn't use. There's a television in the room, but he never uses that either. Watch as he turns the knob on the oil lamp, lowering the wick, and extinguishing the light. With moonlight streaming through the slats of the white shutters on the window, he removes the necklace of black polished stones from around his neck and lays it on the dresser. He takes off his sandals and clothes, and lays on the bed. The clamor of the troop of macaques that lives in the banyan trees outside on the other side of the wall that encloses the bungalow spills into his room, adding to the sound of the fountain. See him roll on his side and face the wall next to his bed, and lie there for a long time, awake with his eyes wide open.

"The monsoon season will soon be upon us," Saraswati sings.

Sajit sighs. "And still I'm a penniless servant," he says. See him close his eyes and fall asleep shortly after.

#

Hear the peacocks in the gardens nearby as they greet the dawn with mournful screeching that echoes through the streets of the village. Sajit rolls onto his back and inhales the fragrances of cinnamon, cardamom, and curry carried by the soft, warm breeze that blows through the market, over the courtyard walls and into his bedroom. Stirred by the spices, his stomach rumbles. He glances at the shutters and sees the eyes of a macaque staring at him through the slats. He rolls onto his side to pick up a sandal and throw it at the macaque. See the startled expression on his face when he notices the translucent figure of a young man his age, an apparition, sitting cross legged on the floor not far from his bed. Sajit bolts upright. Trembling, he says to the young man, "Why am I being visited by a bhoot?"

The bhoot doesn't answer. A golden bowl suddenly appears in the palms of its hands. It holds the bowl out to Sajit.

"Sajit!" It's the voice of Jacob Swan calling from his room. The thumping of Sri Swan's cane on the floor of his bedroom resonates in Sajit's room.

The bhoot vanishes suddenly.

Sajit squeezes his eyes shut and then slowly opens them and seeing that the bhoot is gone, he shakes his head. He climbs out of bed, puts on a clean kurta and then his sandals, and goes into the kitchen. Hurriedly he prepares a pot of tea, slices two oranges and peels a banana, toasts and butters a piece of naan, and puts everything on a large wooden tray. Watch as he holds the tray above his head, barely shaking the teapot that sits on it, and runs up the steps. He pushes the door of Jacob Swan's room open with his foot.

"I hope you had a peaceful sleep," he says to Sri Swan as he enters the room. "How is your foot this morning, Sri Swan? "

"It hurts like hell. I'm getting too old to play cricket."

"It was an unfortunate stumble you took, Sri Swan," Sajit says.

Jacob Swan is a man of sixty-five with thick white hair and a beard to match. He's large, but in good shape for a man his age, with muscles that bulge beneath his silk pajamas. He's sitting on the edge of his bed with his foot propped up on a fringed ottoman. The cast on his foot is immaculately clean. Impatiently he taps his fingers on the cane lying across his lap. "You're late with my breakfast, again," he says with annoyance.

"I offer my apologies, once more," Sajit says as he places the tray on a bamboo table. "It's a wondrous morning." He opens the shutters to a doorway to a balcony that looks out over the courtyard. Sunlight streams in and the scent of marigolds fills the bedroom. A flock of green parrots chirp musically from the tree branches.

Jacob places his foot with the cast on it on the floor and slowly stands, steadying himself with the cane. He crosses the room and sits at the table. "Today I'm going to the tea plantation," he says as he picks up an orange slice and then stuffs it in his mouth. "Tony is growing restless with me not returning home. This will be my third monsoon season in India."

Sajit pours tea into a cup and sits it in front of Jacob. "Forgive me for my impudence in saying this Sri Swan, but measuring your life by the monsoons that come and go is not the way to live."

Jacob picks up the cup and takes a long slurping sip. With the steam from the tea curling in front of his face like a cobra preparing to strike, he says, "You're still very young, Sajit. What do you know about living?"

Sajit glances out at the balcony. Standing on it is the ghost that he saw earlier. There is a smile on its face and its eyes are fixed on Sajit. It holds out its hands and the golden bowl suddenly appears. See Sajit scratch his head, perplexed as he watches but doesn't understand the words the ghost is mouthing. "I am only nineteen and have a great deal to learn, about everything, Sri Swan," he says.

#

Sajit rides in the rickshaw that follows the one in which Jacob is riding. The rickshaws wind their way through a street crowded with cars, motorbikes, people on bicycles, and pedestrians. Stalls with vendors selling electronics, clothing and home appliances that line both sides of the street are busy. Vendors yell out what they have to sell and at what prices. Macaques cross above the street on electrical wires like tightrope walkers. The monkeys are ubiquitous, climbing the walls of the buildings and jumping from awning to awning above the stalls.

Watch as Sajit tilts his head, hearing Saraswati sing, her voice blocking out the cacophonous noise of the street. She sings of thunder that rolls across monsoon skies and of drenching rain that refreshes the earth. See Sajit close his eyes as daydreams of his village fill his heart and mind.

#

Sajit's mother and several other women walk barefoot along the un-paved road stirring up small clouds of dirt around their ankles. They carry bowls of mangoes and bags of rice on their heads. Their voices are like tiny bells that jingle musically.

Sajit is aged fourteen. He follows behind the women and kicks a football back and forth with his best friend, Aarav, who's left eye has been blind since his birth. Aarav kicks the ball with little enthusiasm, preferring to sit under a banyan tree and pretend he is serving tea and cakes. Aarav's hair hangs to his shoulders and, as he kicks the ball, he shakes his head as if to remind himself that his hair hasn't been cut off by his abusive father who slaps him for being effeminate. Aarav often tells Sajit that he wants to marry him when they have finished school.

"We're both boys and can't marry," Sajit always answers, wishing that Aarav cared more about soccer or cricket.

As they come upon the gate leading to Sajit's home, his mother says goodbye to her friends and enters the courtyard in front of Sajit's house. She kicks at the squawking chickens that run to her and peck at the dirt where she has left imprints from her feet.

Before going through the gate, Aarav grabs Sajit's hand. "I'll have your children," he says.

"Don't be silly," Sajit says. He looks up as thunder echoes across the dark sky. The monsoon rain begins to fall, quickly forming puddles, turning the dirt to mud.

#

Look at the way Sajit is startled out of his reverie. Sitting beside him, the bhoot holds the golden bowl in his lap. He gazes at Sajit, his eyes filled with light. Sajit looks at the back of the head of the rickshaw driver who seems unaware that there is a ghost sitting inside.

"Who are you?" Sajit stammers, mesmerized by the bhoot's gleam-ing smile.

The bhoot's first words are halting, whispered. "I've come to give you a gift," it says.

Sajit looks at the empty bowl. "That bowl will get me only a small amount if I sell it," he says.

"It's not the bowl I want to give you, but what's in it," the apparition says.

Sajit looks at the bowl closely and sees nothing in it. "It's empty," he says.

"Look closer."

#

The rickshaws leave the city behind as they continue on the road that bisects fields of tea plants. The floral fragrance of the tea fills the air. Women with baskets hanging on the back of their heads pluck tea leaves from the plants and put the leaves in their baskets. They turn their heads and watch the rickshaws suddenly stop. See how Sajit shakes his head as if awakened from a deep sleep, although his eyes are open.

"Sajit!" Jacob yells. "Come help me."

Sajit jumps from his rickshaw and runs up to Jacob's. "Sri Swan, your screaming will wither the leaves before they're picked," he says to Jacob who is trying to maneuver getting his foot out of the rickshaw.

"On the plants or in the warehouses, if I don't get my tea shipped before the monsoon begins, then the tea leaves might as well be withered anyway,"

"It helps to have faith, Sri Swan," Sajit says as he glances up at the darkening clouds.

"Faith will not get my tea from the warehouses to the ships," Jacob says as he hobbles his way to a row of tea plants and plucks a bright green leaf from a branch.

See Sajit turn his right ear to the sky as he hears Saraswati singing to the heavens.

#

In his room, sitting on his bed, Sajit gazes into the golden bowl being held by the bhoot that sits cross-legged on the floor. "Why do you show me these things?" he says.

"They are gifts sent by your ancestors," the bhoot says.

"How can the visions I see in the bowl be gifts when I don't understand what I see," Sajit says. "It is all a jumble of images that hypnotize me into stupidity."

The bhoot pulls the bowl to him and cradles it in his arms. "The future is much clearer when it turns into the present," he says.

The rumble of thunder shakes the open shutters. As if replying, the macaques sitting on the courtyard walls screech and holler.

"I fear that Sri Swan doesn't know that the monsoon has snuck up on us and is already on our doorstep," Sajit says.

"Even the aged have a great deal to learn," the bhoot says.

Sajit lays on his back and gazes out the window at the swaying branches of the banyan trees. See how he runs his fingers up and down the stones on his necklace. "Will I ever learn the meaning of what happened to Aarav?" he asks.

#

Hot wind carries soil from the fields and tosses it on the long line of men and women who stand near the train tracks. Aditi brushes soil from the shoulders of Sajit's snow-white kurta as she gazes affectionately into his eyes.

"Don't do that," Sajit hisses. "Others may see."

"What of it?" Aditi replies. "Isn't it proper that a young woman should tend to her husband?"

Sajit picks up his battered suitcase and holds it against his chest like a weight to keep him from being carried away by the breeze, and like armor, protecting him. "In my eyes you will always be Aarav, even in a saree and with rouge on your lips. You are not my wife," he whispers through clinched teeth.

"You say that now," Aditi says with a laugh, "but what about the kisses we shared during the monsoon?"

"Forget about those," Sajit says. "I was just happy to be leaving the village for good to make it on my own."

"You're just sixteen and you didn't finish school," Aditi says dismissively. "You will return here as soon as you begin to starve."

"But before that you will be stoned for dressing like a girl."

"I am a girl. If I die at the hands of others it doesn't change that."

The train appears far off down the tracks, blowing its whistle. A plume of white steam shoots from its chimney. Aditi takes a necklace of polished black stones from around her neck and presses them into Sajit's hand.

"So that you will come back to me," she says. She turns and runs, her long hair tousled by the wind.

#

In the middle of the night, Sajit awakens to the sound of distant sirens. He sits up, looks around the room, searching for the ghost, and then climbs out of bed. See the surprised expression on his face when he glances out the window and notices a fiery red and orange glow in the sky above the docks.

"The tea warehouses!" he exclaims. He runs from his room and up the stairs. When he opens the door to Jacob's room he sees him standing on the balcony facing the conflagration that consumes the warehouses and sends flames high into the air. Jacob is leaning on the balcony railing; he looks weak and feeble. Although Sajit can't see Jacob's face, he can hear him crying and sees the way Jacob's back shakes with every sob. Sajit goes and stands by Jacob's side and watches the sky above the docks explode into fireworks.

"Three years and all for nothing," Jacob says. "I'm ruined."

"You have your husband and a home back in America, Sri Swan," Sajit says.

Silently they stand there until sunrise, watching the fire, until streaks of lightning crosses the sky and rain begins to fall.

#

The images of crossing the sea and setting foot on another land that Sajit had seen in the bhoot's bowl became clear in his thoughts. He watches the throng of people on the dock waving to their friends and families standing with him at the railings aboard the cruise ship.

"Is it true I'll be welcomed in America?" he asks Jacob who stands next to him.

"That will remain to be seen," Jacob says, "but in good conscience I can't leave you behind. You have become like a son to me."

Sajit tilts his head and listens to the chords that Saraswati plays on her sarod.

He sees the bhoot standing in the crowd on the dock Next to the bhoot is another ghost. It's Aditi. Watch as Sajit blows her a kiss just as the ship's horn blares and the ship begins to pull away from the dock.

The End

38

THE PINEAPPLE DISILLUSIONMENT

Kelli Osawa stepped out of the skiff and onto the pier carrying a small suitcase. Her purse hung from her shoulder by a long silver chain. Mr. Koa, the owner of the skiff that had carried Kelli from Honolulu, had spoken only a few words to her from the start to the finish of the ride.

"Sorry, I was trying to figure out if you're Hawaiian," he said when she caught him staring at her face.

"I'm not from Hawaii. My grandparents were interracial. Japanese and French."

As she walked away from where the skiff sat, its motor idling, she could feel his eyes on her, or more precisely, on her white jersey skirt being flung about by the strong breeze blowing in from the open Pacific waters. With the one free hand she barely managed to keep the skirt from being lifted like a parachute above her thighs. Stepping from the pier onto the concrete pathway that led to the Four Seasons Resort, Kelli looked beyond the resort to the rocky, gently rolling hills that led north, toward the island's center. Somewhere in those hills was to be her new home. She had only seen pictures of it, and except for the two weeks spent in Honolulu and on Maui, this was the first time she had been to Hawaii. Coming from her birthplace and where she grew up, Cincinnati, Ohio, setting foot on Lanai felt like she had finally been set free from the prison of her unfulfilled past.

It was only when she was near the resort that she found a taxi parked at a curb, whose driver, Ben Mahelona, was leaning against the front of the taxi and vaping on an e-cig. He eyed her up and down, lowered the e-cig, and pursed his lips, about to whistle.

She grabbed the e-cig from his hand, and glared at him. "Don't even," she growled. "I need a ride to here." She uncrumpled a small piece of paper she had waded in her left hand and handed it to him.

"There's nothing there but old plantation houses and one of those tiny houses they brought in and set up a few days ago," he said.

"The tiny house is mine." She had received an email while at the hotel in Honolulu that her 8 x 20 ft house on wheels had arrived a few days before at the dock near where she had disembarked from Mr. Koa's skiff and was being hauled to its location on the distant outskirts of Lanai City.

His embarrassed gulp was audible. "It's real cute."

"Can you take me to it?"

"Sure, hop in."

He opened the back door of the taxi and took her elbow as she climbed in, holding onto it a bit too long, resulting in her jerking it from his tanned fingers. "Don't touch me," she snapped, threw his e-cig at him, and pulled her door shut.

Catching the e-cig, he hastily took several drags from it, and then got into his taxi. In the rearview mirror he watched her dab her eyes as tears ran down her cheeks. He started the taxi and headed north.

#

The narrow dirt road that cut through a large field of fountain grass led straight to Kelli's tiny house. She had gotten out of Ben's taxi after throwing his fare money at the back of his head as soon as he stopped at the beginning of the road she now walked on. She looked all around, not seeing a single pineapple growing anywhere. Back in Cincinnati it took some doing, and a bit of research, to dislodge her thinking that pineapples grew on trees, like coconuts. In the grass and scrubland that surrounded her on all sides, not a single wildflower lent color to the grass and earth colors. As she neared her tiny house, dozens of green anole lizards jumped from her boxes and trunks that had been stacked in the dirt in front of her house. She screamed in frustration and dropped her suitcase in the dirt as the lizards scurried away. She had been told that her things wouldn't arrive until after she did, not that they would be left exposed to the elements and blocking her ability to get into her house. What's more, the tiny house leaned a little to the right, the wheel on that side having sunk a few inches into the soft earth.

She glanced around, removed her skirt and pumps, and in her panties and blouse and barefoot, she first made a path through her things to the door of her house, and then slowly unpacked the boxes and trunks, and carried her things inside. It was midnight and in full moonlight that she sat on the stoop of the stairs leading to the front door and watched the shinning lights go out in the nearest house almost a quarter mile away. Until it had turned dark, and the lights shone through the windows, she hadn't noticed the house at all.

#

After a sound night of sleeping in the loft bed built above the back section of the main living area, Kelli was lying awake staring up at the ceiling that was an arm's length above her head. She was annoyed with herself for not asking more questions about pineapples on the property before buying the very expensive small plot of land. Then she heard a light but steady tapping on her front door. She slid out of bed, careful not to hit her head, climbed down the ladder and put on her robe that she had hung on a hook above the kitchen sink. When she opened the door, Rita Louise, was standing on the top stair holding a wicker basket containing a pineapple.

"Aloha, you poor thing," Rita said, her voice a mixture of cheerfulness and gloom that matched how she was dressed; in a calf-length black and white polka dot dress with a bright purple corsage pinned to the right shoulder, a black straw hat with a black veil that draped down over her eyes, and elbow-length black gloves with the fingertips cut off, exposing her bright yellow painted nails. "I'm Rita Louise. I live in the next house over. She pointed toward the house Kelli had seen the lights shinning from the night before. "Ben told me you were brokenhearted. Whoever hurt you, think of me as an adopted sister, on your side. Men can be such beasts!" She handed Kelli the basket and lifted her veil. She was much older than she sounded; her face was very tanned, as if she had once had fair skin but had spent too much time in the sun, unnaturally darkening it, and lined with deep wrinkles. Her thin lips were hidden by black lipstick, thickly applied.

"Who's Ben?" Kelli asked, staring at the pineapple that had a smiley face carved into it.

"That darling young man who drives the taxi. Quite a catch, that one. When your heart mends you two would make a lovely couple." She reached out and gently laid her hand on Kelli's arm. "I'm very empathic when it comes to matters of the heart and I can tell you're suffering."

Kelli looked up from the pineapple. "My heart's not broken, least of all by a man."

"Don't worry dear, I'm a very modern girl. It's not my thing, but liking other women is very natural for some gals."

"No, it's not that either, although at times . . ."

As if suddenly confused, lost in a myriad of questions, none that she could verbalize, Rita's fingers fluttered in mid-air for a moment before she lowered the veil over her face. "Well, you know where I live if you ever want to talk about it." She turned to go.

Kelli burst out in tears, and sobbing, said, "I'm just so lost. In the world, I mean."

Rita turned back. "Oh, sweetie, we all are in one way or another."

"Please come in," Kelli said, stepping aside and waving Rita the way into the house.

#

"By some miracle, I won the state lottery, which allowed me to finally get out of Cincinnati and to buy my tiny house and this property to put it on. I always wanted to live in Hawaii and grow my own pineapples." Kelli poured a little Scotch in the steaming tea in Rita's teacup. A wedge of pineapple hung over the lip of the cup.

Rita picked up her cup, took a sip, and licked her lips, savoring the taste. "Pineapples are very tempting things but Lanai is no longer the place for growing them. For the most part, that time has come and gone." She took another sip of the tea and then tilted her head one way and then the other. "Is it your Scotch that you put in the tea or does your house lean a bit to the right?"

"It's your Scotch," Kelli said. "You brought the bottle."

"Oh, that's right," Rita giggled as she patted the bottle in her skirt pocket.

Feeling another crying jag coming on, Kelli poked at a chunk of apple on the plate in front of her with a toothpick. "Is it easy to grow a pineapple plant?"

"Not too difficult. I grew a few when I first arrived here from New York, but buying them from the market or in a can is a lot easier." Rita finished her tea, stood, and on wobbly legs headed for the door. "The lure of the pineapple may just be a siren's call to those of us seeking some direction in life," she said over her shoulder.

"Or a cruel trick."

#

As the crew of four men righted Kelli's tiny house, she planted the top of a pineapple in the sandy soil not far from where the men were working. "What's she doing?" she heard one of the men say.

She poured water from a watering can on the planted pineapple top, sat back, shook her head, and then ripped the pineapple top from the mud and tossed it aside. She stood up and walked over to where the men were pouring concrete inside a wood frame where the right wheel would set upon.

"Would any of you guys be interested in helping me start a pineapple plantation?" The End

39

MAN ADRIFT

The metal cups and dishes in the cupboard clanked noisily against each other as the small yacht, the Brizo, bounced on the turbulent ocean waves. Lying on the bunk, Dave rolled onto his side and tried to focus his bleary eyesight on the canvas that swung from a hook screwed into the wall. The bright red, blue and green acrylic paints used to paint the tropical island scenery seemed to slosh back and forth as if the painting was no more than the hodgepodge of colors he had lifted from the palette, or like colorful currents on a windswept pond. He squinted, focusing on a palm tree until it took shape, and then began to see the painting for what it was: a lone bamboo lean-to with a palm thatched roof on a white sand beach with a tropical jungle for a backdrop. He moaned as his temples pounded with the headache brought on by being hung over. The whiskey in his stomach formed waves of their own. He leaned over the edge of the bunk and vomited on the mound of his clothing lying on the floor.

The yacht rolled violently on its port side, opening the cupboard doors and spilling the contents of the cupboard onto the counter. A stack of paintings leaning against a wall fell over and slid across the floor. The structure of the yacht groaned as if protesting being tossed about. When the Brizo righted itself, he slowly sat up and grabbed onto the edge of the bunk and waited until the surge of nausea that gripped his stomach passed. He kicked aside the clothes and stood up, holding his arms out to balance himself, and then he crossed the cabin to the communications radio attached to a small table. He toggled the on and off switch several times and momentarily heard static, but then it shut off, returning to its state of being dead, as it had been for a week. He turned and surveyed the condition of the cabin.

"I should be ashamed of myself," he said aloud as he looked at the floor cluttered with his canvases, empty tubes of paint, clothes, whiskey bottles, half-empty cans of food, plastic water bottles, banana peelings and coconut shells.

The yacht suddenly lurched forward, pushed from the stern by a large wave like a child pushing a toy boat in a bathtub. He flew across the cabin, landing with a resounding thud against the door leading to the stairs going to the helm. He slid to the floor, grasping his left forearm, certain he had broken it. Using his feet, he pulled a whiskey bottle to him. He raised it to his mouth with his right hand, put the metal cap in his teeth, and unscrewed it. He spit out the cap and drank the last of the whiskey in the bottle.

The Brizo rocked on its starboard side as a large wave washed over the ship, cracking into two the last mast that had still been standing, sending it and the sails tied to it crashing into the sea.

Dave glanced at the canvas that hung askew on the hook, wishing he had done a better job of painting it. He felt woozy and his arm burned with pain. He looked up at the porthole above the bunk and saw a man looking in at him.

Then he passed out.

#

Lying on the bunk, Dave awoke to the tapping of the waves against the hull of the yacht, like children knocking to be allowed aboard. A warm breeze scented with the fragrance of seawater blew in through the open porthole. Still half-asleep he gazed up at the ceiling of the cabin as if looking through fog, thinking it was strange that he was in the yacht instead of on the beach and inside the hut lying on a grass mat with Palila lying beside him. Then the realization of why he was aboard the Brizo and what was happening to him flooded his mind. He glanced at the open porthole and sat bolt upright and winced as pain shot through his arm. He grasped the bandage around his forearm, and then stared at it, thinking, *how did that get there?*

He swung his legs around and sat up on the edge of the bunk and looked around. The painting on the hook had been righted and his other paintings were arranged on the counters and against the walls as if on display. The colors used in the images of white capped ocean tides, moonlight on jungle pools, water cascading over boulders, and scenes of the beach and hut, seemed more luminescent than he remembered painting them. In the one painting of Palila it looked as if she was going to step out of the canvas and give him the mango she held in her hand. For a few moments he felt as if he was staring at paintings done by a stranger, except he remembered all too clearly the smile on Palila's face. He gazed at it for several minutes before rising from the bunk and in a moment of despair, swept the paintings from the counters and kicked aside the paintings on the floor. He then opened the door and climbed the stairs to the helm.

The glass in the windows of the wheelhouse had been blown out and the instrument panel and radio equipment was wrecked. He carefully stepped up to the helm, careful not to step on the shards of glass strewn on the floor. He placed his hands on the wheel and looked out beyond the bow of the yacht. The bright sunlight reflecting off the placid ocean momentarily blinded him. When the spots cleared from his vision he scanned the horizon, hopeful that there might be land within sight, but saw nothing but the endless green sea. He looked down at the compass. The Brizo was drifting southward.

He then stepped out of the wheelhouse and gazed at what remained of the broken masts. The sails and rigging were gone. A blue and white lifesaver ringed the stump of a mast, as if tossed there during a game.

"Your vessel has been destroyed."

Dave whirled about and saw standing a few feet behind him a naked man with green, scaly skin and gills that lined both sides of his torso.

He had a muscular physique and webbed fingers and toes. His was the face Dave had seen looking at him through the porthole.

"Who, what, are you?" Dave stammered.

"They call me Nereus. I'm from the sea, just as you are," he said. "Who are you?"

"I'm Dave. I'm not from the sea. I'm originally from Boston, that's a city on the coast of the United States."

Nereus cocked his head and gazed at Dave appraisingly. "You were born under the water sign, Aquarius, yes?"

"Yes, but that's meaningless."

"Is it?" Nereus looked into Dave's eyes, as if searching for something. "It's very easy to become disconnected from our origins."

"I was blown off course by a storm that raged for days," Dave said. "I've never seen anything like you before. Are you a fish or a human?"

Nereus chuckled. "I'm friends to both and sometimes enemies to both, but I am neither."

Dave pointed to his bandaged arm. "Did you do this?"

"Yes. I served as the surgeon on a pirate's ship. Your arm isn't broken, just badly bruised."

Dave gazed at Nereus thoughtfully. "How is it that you speak my language, or speak at all?"

"Long, long ago and far away, a man named Jonah taught me to speak while we both were inside the belly of a whale." Nereus answered. "Since then I've met many of your species."

David had a thousand questions he wanted to ask, but asked only one. "Can you tell me my location?"

Nereus looked out at the ocean. "You're here. This is your location. But if you wish to be somewhere else, since your sails are gone, doesn't this craft have one of those motor things I saw on when I was caught in the netting of some fishermen and then held captive in their fishing trawler?"

"It has an engine but the engine compartment was flooded and I can't get it to start."

A sudden loud thump against the side of the yacht turned Dave's attention away from Nereus. He turned and saw a large great white shark circling in the water.

"Is that a friend of yours?" he said, and then turned back and saw that Nereus was gone.

#

That night, Dave sat on the deck at the bow of the ship with the sextant to his eye. He had just found it while rummaging around in a storage locker and although he had received training in how to use it, that had been just before he left Boston, almost a year before. Frustrated with being able to figure it out, he tossed it into the ocean. He laid back and gazed up at the star cluttered sky. He tried to ignore the memories of laying on the beach and showing Palila the constellations, but he closed his eyes and imagined he could smell the fragrance of the orchids she always wore in her long black hair. A sudden loud thump against the side of the yacht startled him out of his reverie.

"I didn't intend for Lamia to follow me."

Dave sat up and looked behind him. Nereus was standing a few feet away.

"You're just an hallucination," Dave said.

"I am?"

"Jonah lived over two thousand years ago. That would mean you're that old, at least. Nothing lives that long."

"Regardless," Nereus responded, "Lamia poses a real threat to both of us."

Dave stood up. "Who is Lamia?"

"The shark that is trying to determine how strong this craft is. She plans on eating you soon, and me along with you if she can get her teeth into me."

Dave headed toward the wheelhouse. "I keep a speargun under my bunk," he said.

Just then Lamia rammed the side of the hull with all its might. The cracking of wood and fiberglass resounded in the otherwise still night. David ran into the wheelhouse and down the stairs. Water was rushing into the cabin through a crack that ran up the port side wall. The trash, clothes and canvases that had been on the floor floated in a rising pool of water. He splashed his way to the bunk and reached under it and pulled out a speargun and an emergency pack. He jammed a bottle of whiskey into the pack and then slung it over his shoulder, grabbed the painting of Palila and tucked it under his arm, and ran up the steps carrying the speargun in his right hand. He set the painting aside and tossed the pack and speargun out of a broken window onto the deck. He then pulled the inflatable raft from a compartment under the instrument panel and quickly dragged it out to the bow of the yacht.

"Here's the raft," he said to Nereus who stood by, watching.

"I was in the much colder waters far north of here years ago guiding a pod of whales home and watched a much larger ship as it sunk, the Titanic I think it was called, and they had much larger rafts," Nereus said.

"Those were lifeboats," Dave said. "This will be large enough for the two of us."

He pulled the cord on the raft and stood back. When it was fully inflated he tossed the pack into the floor of the round raft. Carrying the speargun, he walked to the edge of the deck and looked out at the dark water.

"Can you get the shark to come to the surface of the water?" he asked. "I'll shoot it with this as soon as I see it.

Nereus nodded. "I hope your aim is good. Lamia will waste no time." He then jumped into the water and began splashing.

"I didn't mean for you . . ." Dave started, and terrified, watched as Lamia surfaced a few feet away from Nereus. He aimed the gun and shot the spear, shooting it into Lamia's head. The shark grabbed Nereus by the foot, and as blood spurted out of its wound, the shark and Nereus submerged.

Dave stood on the deck for a long time watching for one of them to resurface.

#

Morning light spread across the ocean waves as the raft was swept from the deck of the Brizo. With the raft bobbing up and down on the choppy water, Dave felt the loss of three things as he watched his yacht sink: the Brizo, Nereus, and the painting of Palila that he had forgotten to go back and get. He reached into the pack, pulled out the bottle of whiskey, opened it, and took a swig. The liquor soothed his scratchy throat but landed in his stomach like an exploding grenade. It struck him that he hadn't eaten anything for almost twenty-four hours. He opened the pack and took out a protein bar. Just as he was about to unwrap it a large pod of dolphins surfaced, encircling the raft. They chirped and chattered like excited school children. He unwrapped the bar, broke it apart and tossed pieces to them, which they ignored, but it gave him a small amount of comfort to be interacting with another living thing, thinking it might be the last time he did so. A half hour later the dolphins moved on. Dave laid his head back on the rim of the raft, letting the hazy sunlight bathe his face, and thought about Palila.

#

He went to Tahiti hoping to trace some of the steps of his favorite artist, Paul Gauguin. He had sailed at a leisurely pace down the coast of the United States, stopping for a week in Miami, before sailing on to Panama and through the canal. In the approximate 4500 nautical miles from Panama to Tahiti was nothing but the vast Pacific Ocean. He spent the days manning the sails, sketching and drinking. Occasionally he passed other vessels, usually large container ships, but his communications with them via the radio was short. He left Boston with one intention, to reach Tahiti to paint, not to make friends along the way. He was lucky that in the more than a month that it took to reach the northern shore of Tahiti, near Tiare, he only encountered two severe storms that did no damage to the Brizo. By the time he reached land he had used all of his supplies, so he restocked his shelves, cabinets and larder in Tiare, and then sailed north along Tahiti's coast for a few days until he found the deserted beach he had spotted when first approaching the island. He dropped the anchor a short distance from the beach, pulled in the sails and tied them to the masts. Throughout the day he swam from the Brizo to land, carrying what he would need to live on along with his painting supplies and canvases.

He dragged bamboo and ferns from the jungle and built a lean-to, using palm leaves to reinforce the roof in the event of rain. He put everything in the lean-to, leaving enough space to lie down. For a week he spent the days painting scenes of sailboats on the turquoise water and parakeets perched in the trees and bushes that bordered the beach.

Then early one morning as he sat at the base of a coconut tree digging a hole into it with a penknife to get to the milk, he looked up to see Palila walk out of the jungle. She wore a bright red sarong and a gardenia pinned in her hair. In his forty-two years of life he had never seen such a beautiful woman. Awestruck, he stared at her, mouth agape, as she walked by him and walked to the edge of the water, removed the sarong, and then jumped into the waves and swam out a little ways. She then waved at him, beckoning him to join her. He dropped the coconut and then rushed to the water and dived in after her.

Every morning for the next three weeks, Palila would walk out of the jungle, and they would spend the the day together, swimming, having meals together, and he would work on a single painting of her, a work he hoped would be a masterpiece, something comparable to a painting by Gauguin. At twilight she would go back into the jungle.

When the painting of her was finished, she went into the jungle that evening and never returned.

Heartbroken, he took his things and some of the completed canvases, including the one of her, back to the Brizo. He restocked the yacht in Tiare and then set sail for the open ocean, with no destination in mind.

\#

Lying in the raft as a soft rain fell, Dave forgot how many days he had been adrift. Empty plastic water bottles and food wrappers floated in the puddle that had formed in the middle of the raft. He bent his head back and caught the rain in his mouth. He imagined hearing it sizzle as it hit his parched lips and sunburned skin. To fight off the feeling that he was being driven to madness by the endless sameness of the ocean, he pretended he had a canvas in front of him that he imagined painting on it Palila as she walked into the jungle. He had his eyes closed and was painting the gardenia in her hair when Nereus appeared at the edge of the raft.

"So, there you are." Nereus said.

Dave's eyes shot open. "Nereus! I thought Lamia had killed you."

Nereus smiled broadly. "She shook me about a bit, but that spear in her head put an end to her." He looked around the raft. "I see you're still rather messy. Do you mind if I join you?"

Dave grabbed the bottles as he moved aside. "Climb in. This is no Brizo, but its kept me alive."

Climbing into the raft, Nereus said, "Brizo the sea goddess has been looking out for you."

"Yes, she has."

Nereus sat across from Dave. "Did I tell you about the time I met a man who traveled the ocean in a boat that operated under water? A submarine he called it. His name was Captain Nemo."

Dave laughed. "That's impossible. He's a character in books written by Jules Verne. He's not real."

"Are you certain?"

Thunder rumbled across the clouded sky followed by streaks of lightning. As if responding to the storm quickly brewing in the sky, the waves began to leap from the water and roll across the surface in every direction. The raft started to bounce.

Dave took the almost empty whiskey bottle from the pack and unscrewed the top. "To a final goodbye to life," he said. He took a drink and then offered the bottle to Nereus.

"No thank you," Nereus said. "Your life isn't lost yet."

Dave drank the last of the whiskey and tossed the bottle into the water. "Life without Palila has no meaning anyway," he said.

# # #

The sailors who stood around Dave stared down at him with a look of astonishment on their faces. They mumbled to each other as the ship's acting medic thumped Dave on the back, forcing the water out of his lungs. The medic rolled Dave onto his back and stared into Dave's eyes.

"You're going to make it," he said.

Dave coughed, spitting out a small amount of water. "Where am I?"

"This is the merchant ship, the Palaimon," the medic answered. "How on earth did you survive swimming in the middle of the ocean?"

"I was on the raft, with Nereus," Dave answered.

"What raft?" the medic asked. "Who is Nereus?"

Dave closed his eyes and tried to recall what had happened, but other than the violent storm that tossed the raft about, his mind was blank. "My yacht, the Brizo, sunk . . ." he started, but his voice trailed off as he saw the disbelieving look on the medic's face.

"Look buddy," the medic said, "strange things happen on the sea and to those who travel on it, but I've been a sailor for over twenty years and I've never seen a man alive and floating on the kinds of waves you were pulled from as if you were just taking a nap."

"I can't explain it," Dave said resignedly.

The medic helped him stand and then led him into the ship, through several corridors, and into the infirmary. The medic gave him a cup of coffee.

"Where's this ship headed?" Dave asked as he looked around the cabin.

"Tahiti," the medic replied. "Have you been there? It's really beautiful."

Leaning against a corner was a canvas, its front facing toward the wall. He sat the cup on a table, walked over and turned the canvas around. It was the painting of Palila. "Where did this come from?" he asked.

"It was tossed onto the deck by a large wave just a few hours before we rescued you. Is it yours?"

Dave stared at it for several moments before he answered. "No."

The End

40

THE ALBINO
KANGAROO

Perhaps I should have known from the beginning how it was going to end. Perhaps.

My mouth was as dry as the arid scrublands that the highway cut through like a surgical incision. Dust devils of brown soil whirled across the barren landscape, skimming across the pavement as if purposely dashing from one side to the other. Even with all the windows rolled up, grit invaded the inside of the car, finding its way between my teeth where it settled; an irritant that I lacked the spittle to expel. The glaring sunlight that cooked the earth formed watery pond-like mirages on the highway that vanished just before they were reached. The only indication that there was life in the region, other than the infrequent truck stops, roadhouses and ramshackle motels or motor lodges was the images of kangaroos, wombats and camels painted on the yellow signs that stood along the roadside. Occasionally, a land train with several semi-trailers pulled by a prime mover sped by, heading east. They were like huge, terrifying, roaring metal beasts. Their tires stirred up clouds of dirt and tossed rocks like solid raindrops against my windshield.

My sister, June, had fallen asleep in the seat beside me soon after we departed Port Augusta. She curled up in the seat and remained motionless with her windbreaker pulled over her and slept silently and motionless, as inert as a pile of laundry that she resembled. I fought the urge to shake her awake and remind her that it was her idea that we drive the 1700 miles west, taking the Eyre Highway to see this stretch of the outback, the Nullarbor Plain and the Great Australian Bight. She had placed the cost for renting the car on her credit card, so there was that at least.

In the rear view mirror I watched the Volkswagen van that followed behind, keeping the same distance from my car from the moment it suddenly appeared out of nowhere fifty miles back. It was a 1980s model, blue, but in need of a paint job. Its front grill was dented and one of the headlights was missing. I tried to get a glimpse of the person driving it, but sunlight reflecting from the van's windshield hid his face; that it was a male was all I could tell. There was no one in the passenger seat.

For many miles, the scenery that I passed rarely changed. There weren't abandoned structures, or remnants of farms, silos, or ghost towns reminiscent of many highways in the American west. Unlike the plains of the United States, the vast space wasn't broken up by miles of fencing. There were no road turnoffs. It was apparent from the onset that the Eyre Highway would live up to its billing as the longest stretch of straight road on the planet. Looking ahead was mesmerizing, hypnotic, like staring into a never-ending tunnel filled with light. Miles of seeing nothing but the beige colored landscape sporadically dotted with a patches of saltbush and bluebush scrub produced the same effect I once experienced when becoming snow blind while trekking in the Alps; I lost my range of vision.

I might have missed the rest stop altogether had June not awoken in time to sit up in her seat and call out when she saw its entrance fifty yards ahead.

#

The heat was all-enveloping; so oppressive it made breathing difficult. It felt as if my lungs were being seared with every breath. Sitting
on a picnic table bench in the shade under a corrugated tin awning I
watched the visible waves of heat rise up from the pavement in the rest
stop. Unlike back home in Seattle where there was always the feel of
moisture in the air, on that stretch of the Eyre Highway, there wasn't
the slightest hint of it. The breeze that came from the north carried the
scent of baked earth. I had guzzled a full bottle of water and was halfway
through another one as sweat ran down my back in rivulets.

June was standing at a map of the area pinned on a corkboard under
a sheet of plastic near a row of soda and snack machines. She was slowly
tracing with her index finger the single black line that marked the highway as if unable to accept that the line never veered from its two-direc-
tional course. She had her hair pulled back into a ponytail held together
with a bright yellow scrunchie. As she tilted her head from side-to-
side, as if she was listening to music, her hair swept across her upper
back like the pendulum of a metronome. It was moments like that I forgot she was only a few years younger than me and we were no longer
children. At twenty-nine she had retained many of the same movements and gestures she had when she was a girl of six or seven. When
an orange-colored dingo wandered into the rest stop, she turned and
watched it, entranced, the entire time the wild canine sniffed about the
trash cans and around the doors of the restrooms. June had taken time
off from finishing her courses to become a veterinarian to take this trip,
so animals of any kind were of special interest to her. When it ran off,
returning to the open scrubland, she went into the women's restroom.
I shifted on the bench to get a better look at the Volkswagen van that
had sat parked in the driveway leading into the rest stop, arriving there
within minutes after we did. The driver of the van didn't get out. He sat
hidden in the shadows inside the vehicle.

I was considering talking to the driver of the van when June came
out of the restroom. She called out to me. "How far to go until we reach
The Bight?"

"Another hour or so," I replied. I looked to the west, uncertain even after looking at the map of Southern Australia a dozen times, where the Nullarbor Plain began and ended, and if we had entered it. The name alone conjured up in my imagination fantasies of places that seemed other-worldly, like the Sahara Desert and Machu Picchu.

June sat on the bench on the other side of the table. She rubbed her shoulder and winced.

"You shouldn't still be feeling pain there," I said.

"It's not actual pain," she replied. "It's psychological." She hesitated before asking, "Does anyone ever get over being shot?"

I looked to where the van had been sitting. It was gone. "I don't know," I answered her.

#

I stood on the edge of a sheer cliff holding binoculars to my eyes and looking out over the turquoise waters of The Great Australian Bight. A large pod of Southern Right whales breached the surface, shooting fountains from their blowholes. At the base of the cliffs, small waves washed up onto the narrow strip of beach that extended along the coastline. Seagulls circled and swooped above the white-capped currents. Far out, the white sails of a large yacht gleamed in the late afternoon sunlight.

June sat on the ground near me, her legs dangling over the edge of the cliff. Bits of grass she tossed into the air fluttered above her head like wounded butterflies before being blown inland or sucked into the ocean breeze and pulled seaward.

After a long silence between us, she said flatly, "I miss Patty and Mom."

The suddenness of the statement took me out of the moment and hurled me back to Seattle the year before. I had just returned from a trip to Iceland and was sitting at the kitchen table in our mother's condominium drinking a glass of iced tea. She was leaning back against the sink and stirring a cup of coffee that she held in her hand. The sliding glass doors that led out to the balcony that looked out on the Puget Sound were open and a fish-scented breeze blew in. She gave birth to

June and I when she was young and as she gazed at me it struck me that she could have passed for a woman in her early thirties. There wasn't a single wrinkle on her face. "Even when you were a toddler, I couldn't hold on to you. You always wanted to run off and explore," she said.

June came into the kitchen at that moment, her arm draped around the shoulders of her girlfriend, Patty. They were giggling like adolescent schoolgirls which suited June's bubbly personality at that time but was unusual for Patty who was usually sober and restrained. They had flown in from Chicago the evening before to join me at Mom's to celebrate our mother earning her masters in social work.

"What are the two of you so happy about?" Mom asked them.

June kissed Patty on the cheek and with a huge smile on her face, said, "Patty and I have decided to get married."

Just as quickly I was brought back from Seattle to that cliff when I realized June was sobbing. I let the binoculars drop against my chest and hang there by its strap and sat on the ground next to her. I put my arm around her and pulled her against me. She rested her head on my shoulder as we sat there staring out at the whales until they disappeared from sight.

When we stood up I turned and saw that the Volkswagen van was parked not far from where I had left our car. It pulled away and returned to the highway as we began walking toward our car.

#

Twilight saw the spread of bands of purple and gold across the darkening sky. The Nullarbor Plain stretched out beyond the opposite side of the highway like an endless dirt carpet, looking as if it had been bulldozed. I stopped the car a few times so that we could watch troops of kangaroos crossing the plain, the first large number of them we had seen, which was surprising given that their images were on every sign and their remains littered the highway. The landscape didn't seem to offer much in the way of vegetation for them to eat. June got out of the car each time we spotted a troop and took dozens of pictures of them and then got back in, breathless with excitement as she chattered on about them. When we were children it was she who had pet dogs, cats, rabbits, hamsters, canaries and fish. I was still inside the car when I heard her shout, "An albino kangaroo!"

I got out of the car and standing by her side saw an entirely white kangaroo hopping along with the troop. To me it resembled a large white mouse.

"Do you have any idea how rare an albino kangaroo is?" June asked as she took pictures of it.

"I think an albino anything is kinda rare," I replied.

Minutes later I realized she was holding her camera up to her eye, with the lens pointed at the albino kangaroo, without snapping anymore pictures. "As rare as I used to think it was to be shot by a mass murderer's bullet," she said at last, and then put the camera back in its case and got back into the car.

I watched the albino kangaroo for a few more minutes before getting back into the car and opened the map, spreading it across the steering wheel. I had the town of Cocklebiddy circled in red ink. It was about a half hour away.

June had rolled up her window and had her head resting against the glass. Her eyes were closed.

"Are you okay?" I asked her.

She sighed, expelling breath like a punctured tire. "Now that I think about, maybe coming on this trip wasn't such a good idea after all."

"You got to see an albino kangaroo and you said they're rare."

"Yes, they're rare."

In the ambient light of night I could see the Volkswagen van following us, maintaining the same distance and always at the same speed.

#

Countless stars glittered in the night sky, distracting me from what would have been an otherwise very boring trip from the time we saw the albino kangaroo until we reached Cocklebiddy. June said only a few words during the long stretch of darkness, keeping her eyes closed during most of it, although I could tell from her breathing that she was awake. I tried to entertain her with anecdotes from my travels, but after twenty minutes of not getting a response from her, I drove the rest of the way to Cocklebiddy in silence. Upon approaching and entering the small town I had the uncharacteristic response of feeling happy to see lights; my preference being to travel where there was less civilization. There was a roadhouse in the town for those just passing through and a small motel where I had pre-booked two rooms for us before leaving Port Augustus. When I pulled up to the curb in front of the motel June opened her eyes and gently placed her hand on my arm.

"What happened will be with us for the rest of our lives," she said, despondently.

"I know."

#

The Italian restaurant in the Capitol Hill area of Seattle catered to a gay clientele which is why June and Patty chose it to celebrate Mom's achievement and their plans to get married. Although it was Mom's car we used to go to the restaurant, June drove and Patty sat in the front passenger seat. Mom and I sat in the back seat. Along the way, Mom pointed out everything that had changed en route to the restaurant since it had been three years since I had last been in Seattle, which was to attend my father's funeral. The trees that lined the curb in front of the restaurant were strung with white lights and two large rainbow flags hung from its facade. We parked a block away and walked to the restaurant, merrily chatting and laughing the entire way. The restaurant wasn't as crowded as we thought it would be, so we managed to get a table by the front window. Before I sat down I looked out and saw a blue Volkswagen van park across the street from the restaurant. I sat next to June. Patty and Mom sat across from us. We were almost done eating when I saw a man get out of the van and cross the street, but gave it little thought and didn't see what he was carrying, until he walked into the restaurant, raised an AK-47 assault rifle and began shooting.

In a moment of disconnect, I thought it was firecrackers I was hearing and not gunshots, and then I saw Mom get hit in the back and Patty shot in the head. June was struck in the shoulder before I had the presence of mind to react. I shoved her from her chair and threw my body on top of hers. The shooting, the killing, seemed to last forever. It was only later that I learned the shooter had been tackled and pinned down by an off-duty policeman until help arrived. The killer owned the Volkswagen van.

#

The motel in Cocklebiddy had a sign in front of it with an image of a young kangaroo peeking out from its mother's pouch. The name of the motel was Joey's Motel. The woman at the check-in counter was gregarious and talked non-stop while I checked us in. When she paused long enough for me to answer her numerous questions, I explained that it was June who had decided on the trip across Southern Australia. I didn't explain anything further. June had remained at the motel office door, staring out at the street as if lost in thought. When we got to the doors of our rooms that were next to one another, June opened her door and went in without saying anything, and shut the door.

My room was nondescript with hardly a suggestion that it was Australian. I threw my backpack on the bed, laid down next to it, and without intending to, I quickly fell asleep. I awoke with a start a few hours later overcome with a sense of dread. I bolted from my room, ran to June's and pounded on the door. When June didn't answer back, I turned the doorknob and it opened.

Moments later I found June lying in a pool of blood on the bathroom floor, dead. She had slashed her wrists.

I've not seen the blue Volkswagen van since then.

The End

41

TO CATCH A GOPHER

I grew up on a farm where my father grew maize in the northern region of central Mexico, on the edge of the Sonoran desert, just a few miles from the U.S. border. It wasn't a good place for growing much of anything and the water that fell there barely watered a houseplant. It never occurred to me that we could have lived anywhere else until I began to question everything, including, "Why here?"

That applied to many things.

Many young unwed girls of the village have babies. "Why here?"

TB is prevalent among the older villagers. "Why here?"

Very few children attend school. "Why here?"

The only fun thing to do is try to kill the gophers. "Why here?"

From the age of six I worked in my father's fields. Not really worked. Sitting near the edge of a gopher hole holding a shovel and waiting for one to stick its head up and smashing it wasn't work. It was hours of sitting in the blazing sun, stripped down to my shorts, faint from hunger and thirst, but it wasn't work. The fun came when a gopher made the stupid decision to make a run for it, emerging from its tunnel only to have its brains splattered by my shovel or the shovel held by my friend Luis who sat at the other opening of the gopher's tunnel.

By age ten I was a gopher expert. I understood how they thought, what drew them out of their tunnel, and what made them stay hidden.

#

Many of the locals who dug the tunnels under the border of the Mexico and U.S. border ended up in shallow ditches with a gunshot to the backs of their heads for their labor. It was the way the cartel thanked them for all their sweat. Those of us who carried the drugs through the tunnel rarely picked up a shovel or pickaxe.

The tunnel I found myself sitting in mid-way through was a little under 1400 yards or about 4200 feet. It was five feet in height and a very narrow two feet wide. All together that's a fair amount of dirt dug out and carried away so that the tunnel couldn't be easily discovered by the authorities on either side of the border.

But inevitably most tunnels were found out, including the one I and my two companions squatted down in, frozen in place. We talked in whispers.

"Why aren't they coming in after us?" That was Jorge, at seventeen, the youngest of us three.

"They're waiting us out," Mendocino, the oldest of us, at twenty-six, replied.

"But why?"

"They know we carry guns," I said. "The US and Mexican border agents aren't in a hurry and don't want to risk getting shot in the process."

"It's a standstill and we're caught in the middle," Mendocino said.

"Right on – or under – the Mexican and U.S. border," I added.

Six hours after being stopped by the sounds of voices at the US end of the tunnel, only Jorge had taken off his shirt because of the heat. He had the body of an old man; scarred from knife fights carried out in the back streets of Mexico city, wrinkled by years of poor nutrition and drug abuse. He had lived mostly on cerveza and fried tortillas since running away from home at thirteen. He thought becoming a gang member would be easier than his years of living on the streets and sleeping under the bridges and doing whatever he needed to do to earn the pesos he needed to feed his addiction to heroin. It wasn't.

He sat on one of the burlap sacks filled with the millions in cash that we stole from the cartel. The scent of his sweat filled the air; it smelled like sour milk. He sweated like a fat man, although he must not have weighed more than fifty-four kilograms. He was short and very slender, but surprisingly strong. He had the face of a pretty girl, with thick lips and long, dark eyelashes. He pulled his knife on any guy who even hinted at his effeminate looks. Carlos Mendoza brought him into the cartel to guard over the stacks of bags filled with cash that was kept in an underground tunnel near Tijuana.

Sitting in the glow of one of the oil lamps that hung from the ceiling above him he scratched at the needle marks and scabs that lined his vein on his left arm. His AK-47 laid across his lap. "I'd give my left nut for an ice cold Corona," he said, "or even a warm one."

Sweat dripped from his long black hair.

"They don't give you beer in American prisons," Mendocino said.

"And you can't drink it if you're buried in the Mexican ground," I added, thinking about the cartel.

#

In the village near our farm, the Le Sombrero Negro Saloon served beer to boys at any age as long as you had the money. On Saturdays my father would go there, taking me with him after I reached the age of twelve, with the promise that I said nothing to my mother about what went on there. It was a nine mile walk to the saloon. Along the way he told me tales of the many times he had visited Tijuana. He bragged of his sexual prowess with the prostitutes who "lusted after him." He talked of mutilated bodies found in the streets and hanging from the bridges, but never explained how the bodies ended up there or mentioned the cartels. I was born a devout Catholic, and being young, thought that Tijuana was where you went to wait to go to heaven if you had died in a horrific way. I thought of Tijuana as a special kind of purgatory. During his trips to Tijuana he learned how to speak and write

English from the prostitutes. On our walks to the saloon, he taught it to me. Needless to say, my vocabulary included a lot of vulgar terms.

In the saloon I sat on a stool at the bar surrounded by friends who's fathers brought them along as a kind of rite of passage just as my father did. While I swilled down the two bottles of beer my father allowed me, he went into the backroom with Rita. She always wore the same thing, a black slip and red high heels. She was plump but very pretty. She hugged me every time I came into the saloon. She smelled like honey and vanilla. I knew what she and my father were doing behind the curtains that divided the back room from the bar area of the saloon. I never told my mother about my father and Rita, but I think she knew anyway. Where he got the money to pay for the beer, and for Rita, I never found out, but it may explain why I went barefoot.

#

I think the border agents found the tunnel by accident, or someone within the cartel tipped them off. Who knows? It was past midnight when we arrived there, hauling the stolen loot on our backs, our guns hanging from our shoulders. We climbed down the ladder at the Mexican end of the tunnel. Me first, followed by Jorge, then Mendocino. We made our way through the pitch dark hitting our heads on the hanging unlit oil lamps. Half way in, border agents at both ends of the tunnels using bullhorns, told us to come out with our arms raised. Jorge and I froze, but Mendocino dropped his bags, rushed to the Mexican end of the tunnel, and began firing his AK-47 up through the hole in the ground. It was a stupid move. It told the agents at both ends we were heavily armed and not afraid to use our guns against them. They could play a waiting game out in the fresh air. We were trapped in the tunnel like gophers. I lit a lamp and we sat on the bags of cash. Mendocino pulled a cheap cigar from his pocket, and began nervously rolling it between his thumb and forefinger.

"Someone had to have tipped-off the agents we were coming," he said.

That made sense.

"How could they have been tipped off?" Jorge said. "No one but us three knew we were going to take the money tonight and try to escape through the tunnel."

That made sense too.

We sat in silence for a while, each of us trying to sort it out in our own head. *Which of us was the snitch, and why?* Drug smugglers were never given leniency by either government and the cartel promptly executed anyone caught stealing from them.

It was Mendocino who spoke first. "Did either of you think to bring along some water?"

I took a half full bottle from inside my shirt and handed it to him. "Just a sip," I said.

He held the bottle to his ear and shook it. A grin spread across his face as the water sloshed around.

#

The child of migrant farm workers, Mendocino was the only one us who had ever been inside the United States beyond the city of Nogales, where the tunnel led to. He was nine and his parents were picking pears in Mendocino County, California, when he acquired the nickname, Mendocino, which stuck with him from then on. On Sundays the workers were given the day off and his parents would hitch a ride to the town of Mendocino, located on the coast, and swim in the ocean and walk the streets of Mendocino, allowing themselves the cost of and treat of one ice cream cone a piece. They'd return to the migrant camp late at night, hungry, but happy.

"It was the only happy time in my childhood," he once told me soon after we both joined the cartel. "From then on my life has been shit."

Mendocino was angry; angry at the world and angry at anyone who was better off than he was. He wore his anger on his sleeves, in his fists, and in the dark bags under his eyes. He never slept, fearing that if he closed his eyes for very long that he'd see the images forever imprinted on the insides of his eyelids of his father being beaten to death and his mother strangled to death by the men who burst into their home to steal the 7982 pesos his father kept in a shoe box under the bed. He was sixteen at the time and would have been killed also hadn't he fought off the man that held a knife to his throat, forcing him to watch what was happening to his parents, and run out the open back door of their house.

I met him in Tijuana during a cookout hosted by Carlos Mendoza a year after I arrived there. He, Jorge, and I became an unlikely trio of friends who did drug runs between Mexico and the U.S. long before the tunnel we found ourselves trapped in had been dug.

He leaned back against the tunnel wall, and looked at the tip of his unlit cigar. "How come they're not smoking us out with tear gas or something?" he asked.

"Whose to say we don't have gas masks just like they do?" I said.

"We don't have gas masks," Jorge said.

Sometimes Jorge wasn't so bright. "They don't know that. The last thing they want is to walk into a smoke filled tunnel with bullets from our AK 47s flying every direction. They can do this the easy way. The easy way for them."

Mendocino put the cigar in his mouth. "What's the easy way?"

"They wait us out. We can't stay down here forever." I looked over at Jorge who had a vacant look in his eyes and he was hugging himself as if cold. He was showing signs of needing a fix which he planned on getting once we were in Nogales. "Or even for another few hours."

\#

I don't recall whose idea it was that we steal the money from Carlos and the cartel. It all seemed to fall into place. Jorge knew how and when to get to the money, I knew the area where the tunnel was being dug since it was close to the village where I grew up and how to make a quick getaway in Mexico if it came to that, and Mendocino knew how to get us to Northern California where he had connections to help us unload the money and hide out. We stole a car off a street in Tijuana and from there it was easy-peasy, although we took more money than we had intended. Instead of taking one large canvas bag filled with dough each, we each took two. Taking the additional cash slowed us down.

We ditched the car a mile from the tunnel and burdened down with the bags of cash we trotted across scrubland on a moonless night. As we expected, the tunnel wasn't being guarded when we got there. At least that was what we thought. And it was our second mistake.

The first mistake was that stealing from Carlos Mendoza.

Carlos wasn't the top man in the cartel we were members of, but he was close enough to the top to easily smell the farts of the drug lord who commanded an entire army of thugs, thieves and murderers who dealt in drugs, prostitution and revenge killings throughout most of Northern Mexico. I had never met him, but I had seen him on many occasions as he rode through the streets of Tijuana in the back seat of a bulletproof limousine.

Carlos was a squat, mean little man who had a penchant for torturing anyone who betrayed him in any way before having one of his henchmen put a bullet in the victim's head. I know this because I was one of those henchmen. If any one of the three of us who took millions of dollars from him had only taken a few hundred, the result would have been the same if he had ever caught us.

It was easy to see how he could figure out that theft was carried out by Jorge, and by extension to Mendocino and I because of our friendship with Jorge, but sitting in the tunnel we didn't know if Carlos or any of his henchmen had followed us. But we felt it, in the same way it feels to have a toothache, knowing the tooth needed being pulled. We didn't talk about it, but we were afraid of being caught by Carlos a lot more than we feared being captured by the border agents.

#

Nine hours after finding ourselves trapped in the tunnel, it began to stink of our piss and shit, despite our attempts to bury any excrement. Occasionally an agent from either end of the tunnel would call to us through a bullhorn telling us to give ourselves up, and then it would return to silence. They thought they had caught drug traffickers. As Jorge was bent over puking his guts out a little ways down the tunnel I looked around at the bags of cash and then it struck me. There was a simple solution to the first problem. Or so I thought.

"We gotta burn the money," I said to Mendocino.

"Burn it?" he said, his bloodshot eyes widened to the size of silver pieces.

"Yeah, every bit of it, including the bags."

"Why?"

"If they catch us with nothing, no drugs or cash, the only thing they can arrest us for is trying to enter the U.S. illegally.

I must have been talking louder than I intended. From down the tunnel I heard the clicking of the safety on Jorge's gun and turned to see him pointing it as us. Even from a distance I could see it shaking in his trembling hands. "You ain't burning the money," he said. "You guys are my friends, but I didn't risk having a bullet being put in my head by Carlos just to watch it go up in smoke. I'll kill you before I let that happen."

"Jorge, listen, this is our only . . ."

Mendocino raised his gun and filled Jorge full of bullets. The youngster flew backward, landing on the floor on his back, blood streaming down his body. Aghast I turned as Mendocino lowered his gun and asked, already knowing the answer, "Why?"

"He was willing to kill us. It was him or us," Mendocino said. "The agents probably heard the gun fire. We better burn the money, fast."

What quickly came to my mind was there was now a new problem: murder.

"Pile the bags of money at under the entrance on the Mexican end of the tunnel," I stammered, picking up two bags and running that direction. Mendocino slung his gun over his shoulder and followed on my heels, also carrying two bags. We threw them down, ran back and got the two that had belonged to Jorge, along with a lit oil lamp. With the bags in a pile I doused them with oil and then set them afire. Mid-way back where I had left my gun, I stopped, picked it up, and aimed it at Mendocino. He was near Jorge's body when he stopped and turned.

"What are you doing?" he said.

"Sorry my friend. You killed Jorge and all I have to tell anyone for either of us to get away scot-free is that you were going to kill me. It's self defense," I said. My gunfire drove him almost all the way back to the U.S. entrance to the tunnel before he fell to the ground.

The agents waited until the smoke stopped streaming out of the Mexican end of the tunnel, and not hearing any more gun fire for a while, before they clamored down the holes at both ends, taking aim at me. I was standing on the American side of the border with my gun on the ground and my arms raised.

Getting away free, wasn't as easy as that. There was still the matter of the other problem: Carlos and the cartel. For the next year I was housed in a maximum security prison, kept in seclusion so that no one could get to me, during which time I brushed up on my writing skills, and told the U.S. authorities everything I knew about Carlos and the cartel in exchange for U.S. citizenship, a new identity, and a house in Northern California, near the town of Mendocino.

As it turned out, neither Carlos or anyone in the cartel knew we had taken the money that night. For the three of us, fear was a powerful force behind our paranoia.

Some days I feel bad about what happened to Jorge and Mendocino, but I learned very young, that when it comes down to it, gophers are solitary animals.

The End

42

THE BUS

Carl awoke gasping for breath. He clutched his chest but quickly realized the pain that had radiated from his heart to down his left arm was gone. He slowed his breathing, purposely inhaling and exhaling at a normal rate until he was doing it without thinking about it. Then he became aware of the large fans with bamboo blades whirring softly and rhythmically on the ceiling above him. At that moment he felt the coolness of the cement floor under his body. Carl sat up and looked around. He was in a busy bus station. The signs on the walls were all printed in Vietnamese. He glanced down at his naked body to his feet and saw Bao standing there.

"Am I dead?" Carl said.

Bao gave an enigmatic smile and adjusted the chin strap on his conical hat.

"Your wife sent you a birthday cake," Bao said, and Carl reached into a brown paper bag that suddenly appeared sitting on the floor at his side and pulled out a cake smothered in chocolate frosting with twenty-two burning candles. "Make a wish."

Carl closed his eyes but before he made a wish he opened his eyes and saw that he was standing in a rice paddy. The water was up to the top of his Army boots. In the heat and humidity, rivulets of sweat ran down his spine and his uniform stuck to his skin. The M-16 in his arms was so heavy he had a hard time holding it up.

In formation, the men of Company D who he had gone through boot camp with were marching by, sloshing through the bright green rice grass.

"Ain't no sense in going home," they sang in cadence.

Perkins, Mott, Lawson and Adams turned their heads and looked at Carl.

"Jody's got your girl and gone," they sang.

They faced forward and marched on, singing, "Your left, your right, now pick up your step."

Watching Company D disappear into the jungle, Carl dropped his rifle in the water and took off his helmet. He took a fork from his shirt pocket and dipped it into the helmet and lifted out a forkful of chocolate cake. He closed his eyes as he put the cake in his mouth.

He opened his eyes to find himself standing beside a hospital bed that Bao was lying in. Bao was asleep. There was a large bandage on his upper right chest.

On the other side of the bed, a young Vietnamese nurse in a crisp, white nurse's uniform and wearing a white nurse's cap was taking Bao's blood pressure. When she removed the cuff from his arm, she looked up at Carl and said, "Are you the American soldier who saved his life?"

Avoiding the nurse's admiring gaze, Carl said, "Is he going to be okay?"

She nodded. "He'll recover from the bullet wound and should live to an old age," She brushed Bao's hair back from his forehead. "We'll always be grateful for what you did but visiting hours are over."

"I didn't get your name," he said to the nurse.

"Duyen."

Carl turned and stepped into the dark jungle. Ahead he heard Company D singing, "And it won't be long 'til I get back home."

#

Carrying a chocolate cake sitting on a glass platter with thirty candles stuck in the frosting, Chloe waded through the meadow of waving, sunburnt, yellow prairie grass. In the distance the light pink and purple layers of the rock formations of the Badlands glowed in the intense sunlight.

Surrounded by prairie grass and sitting in a beach chair in dark blue swim trunks and holding a mai tai, Carl watched Chloe coming toward him. With his index finger he pushed at the maraschino cherry that floated on the top of the drink beneath a small, red, paper umbrella. The cherry sunk to the bottom of the glass and exploded, sending fragments of cherry and pieces of umbrella into the air as the mai tai vanished.

"Get down!" a voice yelled from somewhere behind where Carl sat.

Carl turned to see Perkins, Mott, Lawson and Adams running out of a grove of quaking aspens with M-16s in their arms. Their uniforms were torn and splattered with mud and blood. They vanished as they ran into a cloud of smoke.

Carl turned back to see Chloe was now seated at the other end of an oak dining room table in front of him and smiling at him in a beguiling way. Her long blonde hair was being tousled by the breeze.

On the table in front of him was the cake and a small, square, gift wrapped package with a red ribbon tied around it. He picked it up and turned it over several times.

"Open it, darling," Chloe said.

He untied the ribbon and then tied it around his left wrist. He then removed the wrapping. The gift was a framed photograph of Bao and Duyen sitting on a white wicker sofa. Bao had his arm around Duyen. Both were smiling.

"Thank you for the gift, sweetheart," he said.

"You're welcome. Now close your eyes and make a wish before you blow out the candles."

He closed his eyes.

Instantly a voice said, "The bus is ready for boarding."

He opened his eyes. The bus station boarding platform was bustling with travelers. Four buses were lined up in a row, their doors open. Drivers stood in the doorway on the bottom step of each bus. The bus driver on the step in front of him had a handlebar mustache and ruddy cheeks.

"That's a nasty scar on your cheek," the driver said. "Where'd you get it?"

"A bar fight," Carl said.

The driver shook his head sympathetically. "You getting on the bus or not?"

"Where's the bus going?" Carl said. He shifted the duffel bag he held on his shoulder.

"Hard to say."

Carl sat the duffel bag down at his feet. He saw he was wearing brown leather cowboy boots.

"This is all a dream, right?" Carl said.

The driver twisted the end of one side of his mustache. "That depends on how you look at it, but you're going to miss this bus if you don't get on now."

"What do I do with my duffel bag?" Carl said.

"Just leave it there. It'll get sent along." The driver went up the bus steps and got behind the wheel.

Carl stepped over the bag and onto the bus steps. He was enveloped in darkness as the door closed behind him.

#

Riding atop a chestnut horse as it leapt out of a wall of dense smoke into a small, circular patch of muddy ground encircled by dipterocarp trees, Carl held onto the horse's reins with one hand and held his white Stetson from falling off his head with his other hand. When the horse's front hooves landed in the mud it splashed onto Carl's cowboy boots and brown leather chaps. Carl pulled back on the reins, stopping the horse in the middle of the mud patch. He patted the horse's neck.

"Good boy, Thunder," he said.

Echoing from the surrounding jungle was Company D singing, "They say that in the Army, the chow is mighty fine. A biscuit fell off a table and killed a friend of mine. Oh Lord, I wanna go home."

Carl looped the reins around the saddle's horn and climbed down, stepping ankle deep in the soup-like mud.

Perkins, Mott, Lawson and Adams ran out of the jungle. They stopped in a semi-circle around Carl.

Adams, the youngest of them, freckled with bright red hair hidden beneath his helmet, said, "You shouldn't be here."

"I had no choice. I was drafted," Carl said.

"Incoming!" Mott, a sergeant and the highest ranking among them, yelled.

Carl remained standing as the other men laid face down in the mud. A hand grenade landed at his feet and sunk in the mud. Expecting the grenade to explode, he closed his eyes.

"Dad?"

Carl opened his eyes. Standing in front of him on a porch that overlooked an open stretch of prairie was his teenage daughter. She was holding a cake with the number 40 written in white icing across the chocolate icing. There was a red ribbon tied around her wrist.

"Lisa, where's Thunder?" Carl said.

Lisa looked at him with confusion and concern. "Thunder died years ago, Dad, before I was born, while you were in Vietnam. Don't you remember?"

He felt a lump in his throat. "I loved that horse," he said.

The screen door squeaked as it opened. Carl turned and watched Bao walk out. There was a large, wet blood stain on his upper right chest. Bao took a couple of steps, then collapsed on what was now bare dirt.

Carl looked around at the burning huts that surrounded him. The men of Company D had gathered together the remaining villagers and were ushering them away from the fire.

"Tôi là một nông dân," Bao said.

"Medic, this man's just a farmer," Carl yelled as he bent down by Bao's side.

A cloud of smoke blinded him as he put his hands on Bao's wound to stop the bleeding.

#

Sitting in a beach chair, Carl wiped his eyes, and then opened them. In front of him the vastness of the ocean stretched out beneath bright sunlight. He lifted the sunglasses from his lap and put them on. Tides washed up onto the beach, pushing clumps of foam towards where Carl sat. He picked up his Army boots from the sand and placed them between his legs, and then brushed sand from his blue swim trunks.

In a chair next to him, Chloe sipped on a mai tai through a red plastic straw. A maraschino cherry floated on the top of the drink beneath a red paper umbrella.

Screeching seagulls circled and swooped in the sky above the beach.

Looking up at the gulls, Chloe said, "I saw an eagle flying over the Badlands yesterday."

Carl glanced at the red, white and blue eagle tattoo on his forearm. His skin glistened with beads of sweat. "Am I dead?" .

She took a sip of the mai tai. "Not to me, you aren't. Why do you ask?"

"I can't seem to wake up." He looked over and saw that Chloe and her chair were gone. The mai tai was sitting in the sand. Next to the drink was a cake covered with chocolate frosting. A wax candle in the shape of the number 50 stood on the top of the cake.

He turned back to the ocean. A white bus drove out of the water and onto the beach. It came to stop a few feet away from him. Its door opened. The driver with the handlebar mustache walked down the bus steps and stopped on the bottom step.

After twisting the ends of his mustache, he said, "So, this is where you went to."

"I had to get off the bus. I didn't know where it was going."

"Few people ever do with any certainty," the driver said. "Are you ready now?"

Carl looked down the beach and saw two people in the distance walking toward him. He put his hand over his eyes to block the glare from the sunlight. "That's Bao and Duyen."

He turned and saw that the bus was gone. He put on the glasses and his boots, and then ran to the couple. "Have you seen Chloe?"

"She was sitting at the bar at the hotel having mai tais," Bao said. "Are you enjoying your return to my country?"

"It's changed since the last time I was here." He looked toward a tall hotel that suddenly appeared at the end of the beach. Blinding sunlight reflected from its white paint and blue tinted windows. The sunglasses did nothing to block the intense light. He closed his eyes.

#

With Lisa leaning against him, Carl opened his eyes and saw that he stood at the head of the long picnic table. Seated around it were Lisa's husband, Frank, his twin cousins and their wives, Tom, the bartender from the saloon in Scenic, the mailman, Earl, his two ranch hands, Glenn and Sean, Bao and Duyen, Perkins, Mott, Lawson and Adams and their wives, and at the other end of the table, Chloe.

He raised his mai tai and said, "Cheers."

Everyone else did the same thing. Each person had a red ribbon tied around their wrist. Following Carl's lead, they pushed aside their red paper umbrellas and took a sip.

Carl lowered his mai tai and looked out at the prairie that surrounded the rock formation that they were on the top of. A small herd of buffalo was moving slowly through a dry stream bed. An eagle soared in the sky above the formation.

"We made you fifty-five chocolate birthday cupcakes, Dad," Lisa said.

Carl glanced at the cupcakes, each one with a burning candle stuck in it, following the lined rows of cupcakes on the picnic table to where Chloe was sitting. Ben Mason, his best friend from high school, was standing behind her, his arms around her and kissing her neck. She was laughing.

Instantly, Carl found himself in an open field and carrying Bao on his back. His uniform was stained with Bao's blood. A chopper was ahead, its blades whirling noisily.

Bloodied and muddied, Company D was marching at a double step around the chopper singing, "Jody's got your girl and gone. One, two, three, four."

The chopper and Company D disappeared, replaced by Thunder who had wings, like Pegasus.

Carl placed Bao on Thunder's back, put his cowboy boot in a stirrup, and then climbed on behind him. Thunder lifted from the ground and flew through the sky. Carl looked down at the prairie bathed in sunlight. His ranch sat amidst a sea of grass. A herd of buffalo were crossing the northern border of the ranch, headed toward the Badlands.

"That land is heaven on Earth," he said. As the gentle wind bathed his face, he closed his eyes.

#

He opened them.

The bamboo blades of the ceiling fans churned the cigarette smoke-filled air. The bar was crowded with Vietnamese locals, American expats, tourists, and American military veterans. Their combined voices created a cacophonous din.

Carl, Bao, Perkins, Mott, Lawson and Adams sat around a square, rickety table. In the middle of the table was a chocolate sheet cake with "Happy Sixtieth" written on it with blue icing.

"You would have been left to die if it weren't for Carl," Perkins, gray bearded with a large stomach, said as he raised a mai tai to his lips.

"I know," Bao said.

Lawson, bald and thin, said, "Carl, do you remember the first time we were here? It was right after we returned from the jungle and you just found out that Chloe had cheated on you. You drank so many mai tais we had to carry you out of here."

Carl turned to see Thunder coming through the door. The horse stopped, whinnied, and then turned and walked out. Carl ached with longing.

"That was the greatest horse I ever had," he said. He closed his eyes as they filled with tears.

#

He felt the burning, white sand sink beneath the weight of his Army boots and opened his eyes.

Company D was marching down the beach, singing, "Tiny bubbles in my wine, make me feel happy, make feel fine. Your left, your right, your left, right, left."

Carl stopped and laid his M-16 in the sand, and then stripped off his clothes. He looked up as an eagle crossed the sky, casting its shadow on the beach. He walked to the entrance of the hotel bar, stepped over his duffel bag that lay in the threshold, and then looked around.

Chloe was in a pale blue house dress with her hair in curlers and sitting at the bar. She had a mai tai in her hand. A naked man with greasy blonde hair was sitting on a bar stool very close to her and also holding a mai tai.

Carl rushed over and yanked the man from the stool. "Leave my wife alone," he snarled at the man who laid on the floor with a broken mai tai glass in his hand.

"Carl, have you lost your mind?" Chloe said.

"You're not going to cheat on me again," he said.

"That was years ago, Carl. Aren't you ever going to forgive me?"

The man leapt up from the floor and slashed Carl down his left cheek with a jagged piece of glass. Carl fell backwards and hit his head on a corner of the bar.

Before he opened his eyes the scents of the prairie, earth and grass, filled his nostrils. His eyes open, he stared up at large cotton-like balls of clouds slowly drifting across the baby blue sky. On all sides of him, prairie dogs dodged in and out of their burrows, chirping and barking excitedly. A meadowlark perched on a nearby post warbled its brief aria.

He felt the warmth of the sun warming his cheeks. He raised his forearm and wiped sweat from the eagle tattoo. He untied the red ribbon from around his wrist and held it out to let the breeze catch it, and watched as it floated away.

#

The chopper blades slashed the hot late afternoon air as Company D climbed into the choppers, carrying their wounded and dead with them. Smoke formed a dark cloud above the burning village.

Bao and Duyen sat on a white wicker chair in the rice paddy, his arm around her shoulders. His hair was nearly white. Her hair was streaked with gray and arranged in a bun on the top of her head.

"My husband has something he wants to tell you," Duyen said.

Standing in front of them, his cowboy boots ankle deep in water, Carl looked at Bao, who had his head bowed. "What is it?"

Bao looked up. "I was a Vietcong. I was hiding in that village."

"If I had even suspected it, I would have killed you," Carl said.

"Instead, we have been friends all these years." He took Duyen's hand in his. "Thanks to you I met my wife who I love more than anything else on Earth."

Smoke blew into Carl's face. He closed his eyes.

"Happy birthday to you. Happy birthday to you," was being sung as he slowly opened them.

Chloe was standing in front of him on the front porch. She had a chocolate cake on a silver platter in her hands. There was one large candle in the middle of the thick frosting; its wick was burning. The blonde in her hair had faded to the color of dull yellow and it was cut short. There were small wrinkles around the corners of her lips and at the sides of her eyes. "Happy sixty-fifth birthday," she said.

"Why did you cheat on me?" he said.

"Are you going to go to your grave not forgiving me for that?" She threw the cake over the porch railing. An eagle swooped down and caught it in its talons and carried it away.

The movement of a small herd of buffalo walking through short, brown, dead prairie grass near the Badlands formations caught his eye.

"I forgive you," he said, still watching the buffalo. "I love you."

He turned his head to see that Chloe was gone.

#

A sudden pain shot from his chest down his left arm. He clutched his chest and closed his eyes.

When he opened his eyes he was naked and lying on a cold, cement floor. Hearing many voices around him he raised his head and looked around. There were buses lined up at a boarding platform. Lines of people of all ages, races and nationalities were standing at the open doors of the buses. His duffel bag was lying at his side. He looked down at his feet.

The bus driver with the handlebar mustache stood there rubbing the ends of his mustache.

"I'm dead, aren't I?" Carl said.

"Dead seems like such a final way of saying it," the bus driver said.

Carl sat up. "Can you tell me what has been happening to me since I got here?"

"You've been jumping around in the dreams of those who remember you and having some final memories of your own while you wait to catch the bus to take the trip to the great beyond."

"Why a bus?"

"Everyone catches a bus in the end," the driver said. "This is just the station where you wait until you're ready to get on one. If you are, we'd prefer you stay on. Getting on and off a bus is frowned upon."

"What do I do with my duffle bag?" Carl said.

"It'll get sent along," the driver said.

Carl stood up. "Will I still be in other people's dreams?"

"For as long as the memory of you lives on."

"I wish I could do it all over again," Carl said.

The driver twisted the ends of his mustache. "In your memories, you always will."

"I'm ready to get on the bus."

The End

43

ALL THE LOVELY NIGHTMARES

Abigail Keaton awoke with a start. She looked around the sunlit room to catch her bearings. Yes, she was in her bedroom in her new house, that wasn't new at all, having been built nearly 150 years before in the verdant and hilly Cotswolds district of England, in the rural and historic village of Coln Saint Dennis. Yes, her unpacked boxes and steamer trunks brought from her seaside home in Halifax, Nova Scotia, were still stacked in the corners of the room. Yes, her joints ached as they always did first thing in the morning. Being seventy wasn't easy.

The sound of creaking wood, footsteps on the stairs, and the tinkling of china alerted her that Marta was on her way, bringing breakfast for Abigail's first morning in her new abode, just as Marta promised the night before that she would do.

Abigail sat up in the bed and propped her pillow behind her back. She folded her hands on top of the goose down-filled comforter and smiled brightly, trying to hide the subtle pain that coursed through her arthritic hands. "How lovely of you, dear Marta," she said warmly as Marta pushed the door open with her foot and walked into the room. The also elderly Marta carried a tray with a porcelain coffee pot, coffee cup, a saucer with blue images of Chinese dragons, a plate piled with slices of melon, pears and apples, and another plate ladled with a large mound of scrambled eggs, sausages and two slices of buttered toast. A large dollop of blackberry jam sat near the rim of the plate.

"This should restore you to health after such a long trip," Marta said. She placed the tray across Abigail's lap and stood back and looked on with anticipation as if she had just presented Abigail with a work of art and was awaiting the review of an art critic.

"I'll never be able to eat all of this,"Abigail said with good humor as she stared at the tray. She poured coffee into the cup she poured a bit of cream into it. She lifted the steaming liquid to her lips and slowly took several small sips.

Mildly crestfallen that Abigail hadn't been more effusive with praise or showing more eagerness to eat, Marta brushed crumbs from her apron turned to the window. "Looks to be a perfect spring day," she said in a sing-song manner. "The primroses and violets are in full bloom already."

Abigail placed the cup on the tray and picked up a slice of toast and lathered jam onto it. "I'm so eager to see Coln Saint Dennis in its entirety," she said. "Do you think your Harvey could drive me around later today?"

Marta turned from the window. "Are you sure you'll feel up to it? The village will still be here tomorrow if you would rather wait."

Abigail bit into the toast and while chewing, said, "I've heard of this village, of this entire part of your country ever since I was a little girl, and now that I've inherited this estate I'm busting at the seams to see everything there is to see." Jam dribbled down her chin.

"Why didn't you come here before this?" Marta asked, trying to keep her eyes averted from the sight of Abigail eating with her mouth open.

"I had my teaching duties to tend to during most of the year for forty-three years and during the summer months there was always my mother and father who needed me to be around."

"You must be very proud of your career teaching so many children."

"It was what my mother wanted me to do."

Marta turned back to the window. "Your Aunt Helen talked of your mother quite often. The bond between twins is quite strong, isn't it?"

Abigail took another bite of toast. "Yes, quite strong. They are together again now just as they were before they both married and Aunt Helen moved here from Edinburgh and my mother and father moved to Halifax." She took another sip of coffee, washing down the toast. "About Harvey?" she asked, wiping the jam from her chin with the back of her hand.

Watching a kestrel cross the sky, Marta replied. "I'm certain it won't be a problem."

#

The road leading into the heart of Coln Saint Dennis wound its way through the countryside, weaving its way between farms and rural residences where honey-colored homes built of Cotswold stone sat back from the road, many partly hidden by stone walls with vines that draped over them like decorative art. Tall oak, wylch elm and maple trees, thick with leaves for so early in the year, stood like solitary sentinels in the fields and meadows, where meandering small flocks of sheep grazed amidst patches of bluebells and dog's mercury.

With her window rolled down just enough to let the moist, warm air blow in and tousle her snow-white hair, Abigail sat with her purse in her lap and stared out at the passing scenery, repressing the deep sadness she felt over not seeing this landscape before old age had crept into her bones. Despite Harvey's protests, she had opened the door to the front passenger side and had settled in, refusing to allow him to treat her as his chauffeur. "We ride together as old friends or not at all," she had demanded.

He had been quiet from the moment they pulled out of the driveway. The aromas of pipe smoke and stale ale wafted from his sweater. When she oohed or awwed at a scene of particular beauty, he slowed down and didn't speed up again until the scenery was no longer within sight. "Misses tells me you were a teacher," he said at last during a long stretch of road lined with walls.

She turned her head, studied him for a moment, and brushed her hair back from her face before answering. "Yes. I taught in a private school for girls and boys under the age of thirteen in Halifax."

He nodded approvingly. "It's a fine profession, that," he said. "I wasn't much of a student when I was school age. The teachers had to beat reading and writing into me. The seat of my britches were shiny from being swatted so often." He chuckled, to himself, as if he had instantly forgotten he had said that out loud. "Maybe it's easier teaching now that there is so much importance placed on education."

"Not as easy as you might think," she replied. "Children always resist learning. They can be lovely in their own right, but . . ." Her voice trailed off and she turned her head and looked out the window again. During a brief break between the end of one wall and the start of the next one she watched a woman lead a white horse out of a stable by its reins. A saddle on a red and blue tartan blanket sat on the horse's back. "I should have liked to ride horses," she said, wistfully.

"They don't have horses in Nova Scotia?" he asked.

With the wall once again obscuring her view she turned her gaze to the front window. "Certainly they do," she replied. "Many of my students rode them but when I was a young girl my mother didn't consider it ladylike to ride a horse."

"That's a funny attitude for your mother to have, seeing as how she and your mother were born in Scotland," he said. "Horse racing has been a popular sport there for hundreds of years."

"My mother gave up her Scottish Kerr heritage when she married my father and became a Keaton," she replied. She opened her purse and sorted through the tissues, bottles of medication, brush, comb and compact until she found a small opened bag of candy. She pulled it out held it out to him. "I bought this in the airport in Halifax before getting on the plane. It's not very good candy though."

"No, thank you," he answered. "I'm not one much for sweets."

She took a piece of candy from the bag, unwrapped the red cellophane from around it and plopped it in her mouth. She stuffed the wrapper and the bag into her purse and snapped it shut. For the next several miles she made loud sucking noises as she pushed the candy around with her tongue.

In the village, Harvey pulled the car to the curb outside of the Old Abbey Bookstore. "I thought this might be of interest to you," he said. "It was once part of an abbey, but that was long, long ago."

Behind a large plate glass window, rows of books on shelves lined the display case. The building looked as if it were being held together by spit and glue. The yellowish Cotswold stone that the walls were built from was cracked with veins that ran from the ground to the ornately carved oak eaves. She rolled down her window and while inhaling the fragrance of orchids that were in bloom in a row of window boxes, she gazed at the building and the books. "Except for what was required so that I could teach the subjects, to my mother's dismay, I never read for leisure. She could recite lines by memory from the works of Robert Burns, Walter Scott and many other Scottish authors until the day she died at age ninety-two. I never had that interest in literature of any kind."

"Your Aunt Helen was the same way as your mother," he said. "Despite that bit of difference, there is much about you that reminds me of your aunt."

In silence, Abigail rolled up the window. "We both never married," she said at last.

He turned the key in the ignition. "Shall we see the rest of the village?" he asked.

"I saw a sign for the River Coln," she said. "I'd like to go there if we could."

"Certainly," he replied. He pulled away from the curb and slowly drove down the street, passing the few shops in the village before they left the town and entered a stretch of road lined with groves of tall beechwood trees. The ground around them was thick with blossoming wood anemone. Their white petals gleamed in the sunlight that streamed through the beechwood canopy.

Abigail burst out crying.

Harvey quickly pulled the car to the side of the road and turned off the engine. As she sobbed, her body shaking, he gently patted her shoulder. "Now, now, nothing is worth all that, is it?"

With tears streaming down her face, she looked out at the woodland scene. "I've missed seeing so much of the beauty that the world offers," she said. She opened her purse, took out several tissues, and dabbed her eyes. "My parents were very strict when I was young, you see, and when I obtained my degree to teach and then began teaching at the school, my duties to it and to tending to my parents, both who suffered from poor health, consumed my life."

He withdrew his hand, wiggled his fingers, and stared at them, as if trying to understand how they worked. "Just imagine all the learning you put into the head of all of those young ones," he said cheerfully.

"Yes, imagine," she replied almost inaudibly. She opened her purse and thrust the damp tissues in and then closed it. "You and Marta worked for many years for my aunt. You're not obliged to stay around now that I'm here."

"We have no other place to go."

"Oh," she replied with solemnity. "I hope you don't mind me saying how glad that makes me."

"Not at all," he replied enthusiastically. "Would you like to see the river, now?"

"Yes, that would be quite lovely."

#

Bands of gold, purple and red fanned out across the twilight sky. With a cup of tea in her hand, Abigail stood in the driveway looking up. Blue tits nesting in the nearby trees chirped melodically in the otherwise silence as the sun slowly set. When Marta came out of the house, Abigail turned and watched her walk toward her on legs as thin as twigs.

"Did I hear Harvey drive off after supper?" Abigail asked.

Marta came up next to her and she too glanced up at the sky and then looked at Abigail. "Yes. He's gone to have a pint with his pals at the pub. It's a nightly habit of his. You know how men can be."

Abigail took a sip of tea. "Except for my what were my father's, I know nothing of men's habits."

"Did you never fancy men?" Marta asked, and then felt her cheeks burn with the brazenness of the question.

"When I was young I fancied a few, but I never had the face or figure that men fancied in return," she replied. "My parents discouraged me from seeking a husband." She ran her fingers self-consciously through her hair and let out a short self-deprecating laugh. "It's too late to do anything about it now, isn't it?"

Marta looked up at the sky again. "This was your aunt's favorite time of the day. She too would come out with a cup of tea just as you have and stare up at the sky." She then took a small diary from her apron pocket and handed it to Abigail. "Your aunt wrote a line or two in this whenever anything new happened in her life. I found it when I was unpacking your things away while you were out with Harvey and thought you might want to see it."

Abigail took the diary and held it open in the palm of one hand. The breeze slowly flipped the pages. Most of them were empty. She closed the diary and took a sip of tea. "I've often wondered why my mother and Aunt Helen wrote to each other so often, but never made the effort to see one another."

"So many secrets we all take to our graves with us."

"I hated teaching," Abigail blurted out with a laugh. "That's one of my secrets."

"I've always been a cook but I hate cooking," Marta said, also laughing.

"I hate children."

"What?" Marta responded, her facial expression registering her dismay.

"Children are monsters," Abigail said icily, her demeanor as changed as day to night. "There wasn't a school day that went by that I didn't hate the sight and sound of them. I should never have been a teacher, but I had no skills to do anything else. I've wasted my entire life on the ungrateful little heathen. They're living nightmares, every last one of them."

Marta was silent for several moments before saying, hesitantly, "Surely they never knew how you felt about them?"

"No, I never let on." Abigail replied coolly, and then a smile slowly crossed her face. "If I had had a gun I would have shot each and every one of them."

The End

44

A DEATH IN TELANGANA

The first thing Lt. Clark Emerson saw as he disembarked from the plane was a mural on the Airport terminal wall of the Bay of Bengal with letters in gold that said: Vizag. The City of Destiny. He hadn't come to Vizag for something as lofty as finding his destiny. It was to be a stopover to see the Submarine Museum and maybe tour the Eastern Naval Command headquarters if they would permit it, but even more importantly experience the beaches of Vizag, before heading home after a leave in which he vacationed in various spots across India. He had booked a room at one of the best hotels in Vizag that promised a beach and bay view. A driver with a vehicle was supposed to meet him as soon as he arrived. He looked around, hoping to see someone holding a card with his name on it. Instead he was greeted by a small crowd awaiting a local celebrity to deplane. He hoped that if the driver from the hotel was in the crowd he wasn't looking for a U.S. Naval officer in a Navy uniform. He wore something much more casual: shorts, a hooded sweatshirt and sandals.

He made his way through the crowd, looked around for a few minutes, then went to claim his luggage, which comprised of a suitcase and a backpack too stuffed to be carried on. He carried with him his uniform and two of his nicer shirts and dress pants in a garment bag. Retrieving them turned out to be easier than he thought it would be, after which he walked out of the terminal to the outside sidewalk where Uber vehicles, taxis, and motorized rickshaws lined the curb. He searched again for someone who appeared to be awaiting an arriving passenger, or a vehicle that had the hotel's name on it, but saw neither one. He had come to enjoy riding in rickshaws despite the near-death experience he had while riding in one in Kolkata, so he walked up to the one nearest to him.

"Can I get a ride to the Novotel Visakhapatnam?" he asked the driver who was busy texting.

The driver looked up from his phone. "The Novotel Visakhapatnam? I know of better hotels, Sir, if you want a better time for less money."

"No thanks. The Novotel Visakhapatnam is supposed to be the best in the area and I already have a room with a view booked there."

The driver shrugged. "Whatever Sir wishes is Abeer's command," he said.

Clark tossed his things onto the seat and then climbed in and sat down. Abeer had returned to texting someone, only stopping once again when Clark said, "Okay, I'm ready."

Abeer started the rickshaw and pulled away from the curb nearly colliding with a van with Novotel Visakhapatnam's name and logo on its side. The driver of the van hung out his window and shouted a curse word at Abeer, which Abeer ignored as he continued on, weaving in out of the heavy traffic in front of him. When they cleared the area around the airport, Abeer turned his head and looked at Clark completely for the first time. "You're American, yes?"

"Yes," Clark answered gripping onto the back of the seat in front of him to be kept from being jerked about by Abeer's driving. "Will you please watch how you drive?"

"Yes, Sir. Sorry, Sir," he replied turning his head facing forward. "Would Sir mind if I made a quick stop en route to your hotel?"

"Yes, if it's on the way."

"Is in part of city known as Old Town, Sir." Abeer said turning off onto to another road. "Sir will find it very interesting. Much to do and see there."

"I'll take your word for it, " Clark replied, "but I didn't have it on my list of things to see in Vizag."

"Things Sir should see won't be found on most lists. If Sir will pardon me saying so, but the destiny of Hinduism is to lead a life according to your Dharma. Your Dharma is your purpose of life."

"Great, just what I wanted, a rickshaw driver who is also a philosopher."

Abeer chuckled. "Pardon me, Sir, I don't mean to be argumentative, but Hinduism is not a philosophy."

#

Twenty minutes later Clark sat in Abeer's rickshaw which had been parked alongside the curb of a back street lined with old buildings, mostly warehouses. A steady stream of men flowed by in both directions, some carrying roosters, going in and out of a warehouse door. Those going in knocked three times, paused and then knocked four times before the door opened. Clark was a smart guy and was well-traveled and well-read, so it didn't take him long to figure out what was going on. He abhorred animal cruelty in any form and had walked out of a bullfight in Cancun, Mexico after only a few minutes, sickened by what he witnessed, having gone in only to have his worst suspicions confirmed. Bloodsports, even including birds that were responsible for the chicken and eggs he ate, angered him to the core of his being. Stuck where he was, awaiting Abeer's return, he wondered how cockfighting persisted in a country he knew it to be illegal.

It was a half hour before Abeer did return, to a rebuke from Clark.

"How dare you leave me here to go watch a cockfight!" Clark said in a forceful manner, refraining from yelling at the rickshaw driver.

Abeer held up a fistful of rupees. "But Sir, Abeer makes a month's wages by making a smart bet on a rooster that I bet on only because of having seen the rooster fight a few days ago and learning it would fight again today."

"Um. . .Abeer. . .cockfighting is morally wrong as well as illegal."

"Sir, I have a large family to feed," Abeer said quietly.

Clark absorbed what the driver had said, and the manner in which it was said, before saying anything. "Can we go now?"

"Of course, Sir," Abeer answered. He stuffed the money into his pocket and climbed into his rickshaw and quickly started it, did a u-turn in the street, and drove off.

Thirty minutes later, after cruising with abandon through heavy traffic, Abeer stopped the rickshaw near the entrance of the Novotel Visakhapatnam.

Clark stuck his head out and glanced up at the beautiful but imposing hotel facade. He turned and looked the other direction, at the water of the Bay of Bengal, and had second thoughts about this being the adventure he was seeking. "You say you know of another hotel?" he said to Abeer.

"Yes, Sir," Abeer replied, beaming.

"My name is Clark," the lieutenant replied.

#

On the way to the Dynasty Hotel, Clark couldn't find it listed anywhere in his Vizag tourist guidebook. When Abeer pulled up in front of a shabby three-story apartment building where a hand-painted sign with Dynasty Hotel in uneven lettering on it, he knew why. He climbed out of the rickshaw prepared to yell at Abeer, but was immediately greeted by a beautiful young woman in a pale blue sari.

She reached out her hand. In Telugu she welcomed him to the hotel and then seeing the blank expression on the lieutenant's face she repeated the same greeting in Hindi, again receiving the same look from him."Welcome to our hotel, Sir," she said, finally in sing-song English. "Our friend Abeer let us know you were on your way."

His full lips broke into a huge smile. "Thank you. Please call me, Clark," he said. "Who do I have the honor of speaking to?"

She brushed her long black hair back from her shoulder. "I'm Dairka," she said, returning his smile. "We have an apartment with a view of the water awaiting you."

He turned and looked out toward the barely visible beach and the water beyond, doubting that being up a few floors would make seeing anything any easier. As Abeer pulled Clark's things from the back seat, Clark patted him on the back. "Great . . .hotel," he said, sarcastically.

He took his garment bag from Abeer and followed Darika into the building, with Abeer following behind carrying the suitcase and back-pack. They walked up three flights of stairs where on the third floor Darika unlocked and opened a door. A warm, ocean-like breeze rushed out.

"I opened the sliding door to your apartment so that it is a welcomed greeting that you would find your liking," Darika said as she stood at the door and waved him in.

He walked into the living room, which was minimally furnished with only a sofa and two chairs, but it wasn't as bad in appearance and cleanliness as he was expecting. The opened glass sliding door allowed a view of the bay water and the beach that also surprised him. He strode across the room, laying the garment bag on the sofa along the way, going through the open door and walking out onto the small balcony where he leaned on the iron railing and gazed out. Behind him Dakira said, "I hope it meets with your approval."

He turned about, and mesmerized by her dark eyes, said, "Another lesson to never judge a book by its cover."

"A wise saying," she said.

"At the restaurant down the street where Dairka has arranged a special meal to be prepared for you, you will meet a Mr. Samar Tiwari, who I invited to join you for dinner," Abeer said from where he was seated on the sofa, texting.

"Who is he?" Clark asked.

"A very learned man, very knowledgeable in the field of cockfighting."

Clark scowled, and then turned to Dairka. "I hope you'll join me for dinner," he said, his tone dripping with honey.

"I most kindly accept your invitation," she said, her cheeks blushed.

#

Across plates ladled with chicken biryani with matan kyma on mounds of rice and side dishes of kamat fry pieces biryani and alpha dum biryani, Clark gazed into Dairka's eyes. At 29, and considered very handsome, he hadn't yet fallen in love but was certain he could with her. He had nothing but her looks to go by, as yet, but in the small and rundown restaurant he was in, seated across from the talkative, Mr. Tiwari, it was enough.

"There is better profit selling Kaaki Dega, Dega, Kaaki Nemali breeds as the demand for them is very high," the dark-skinned Mr. Tiwari said as sauce from the chicken biryani dribbled down his chin.

"In Telagu, cockfighting is called Kodi Pandem," Darika added.

"Do you know a lot about cockfighting?" Clark asked her, concealing his disgust of it.

"Oh, a great deal," she answered. "My father brings home news from everyone he enters a rooster in."

Clark's eyes widened to the size of silver coins. "He enters . . .?"

"Buyers spend thousands of dollars on buying a good rooster, especially during the Makar Sankranti festival in January," Mr. Tawari interjected.

Seeing Clark's discomfort with the conversation, Abeer tried to shift it elsewhere. "The Submarine Museum is one of Vizag's major attractions," he said. "I'm sure the Lieutenant is anxious to see it."

"Oh yes, it's very interesting," Dairka replied. "But I've only been there once."

"There is an entire manual in the ancient Hindu texts about cockfighting. It's called kukudshastra," garbled Mr. Tiwari as he shoveled a forkful of alpha dum biryani into his already stuffed mouth.

When the small group finished their syrupy gulab jaman, and Mr. Tiwari patted his rotund stomach, offering a belch of satisfaction afterward, it was Dairka who suggested they gather together the day after next to take Clark to a cockfight. "Wouldn't that be the perfect thing to do while you're in Vizag?" she asked him, excitedly.

"I beg your apologies, but I will be unable to accompany you to that cockfight," Mr. Tiwari said. "I am preparing a paper for a the Indian Alliance of Veterinarians and am already behind in meeting my own deadline."

"You're a veterinarian?" Clark said, astonished.

"I am many things, my friend," Mr. Tiwari replied.

"My father is entering his prized rooster in a cockfight that day," Dairka said. "He will enjoy us going along with him."

Clark was handed the bill that included what everyone at the table ate and drank just as he was about to decline the cockfight offer, but seeing the amount of the bill, his voice got caught in his throat before he could answer.

That evening, as Darika affectionately, and boldly, squeezed Clark's hand just before leaving his apartment, where she had named off in very slow order a list of the best fighting breeds of roosters, "Kaaki, Setu, Nallamachala Setu, Parla, Savala, Nalla Savala, Kokkirayi, Kowju, Myla, Poola, Telupu Gowdu, Yerupu Gowdu, Pingali, Nallabora and Yerrapoda, Kaaki Dega, Dega, Kaaki Nemali" Clark felt his heart would beat right through his chest over his love for her.

The lieutenant was left alone with the rickshaw driver. "Shall I strangle you with my bare hands now or at the cockfight?" he said to Abeer.

"My dear friend, imagine how many rupees I have lost by seeing that you get a glimpse of Vizag that few foreigners see that also included a glimpse of the lovely Dairka," Abeer replied.

"How do I tell her I detest cockfighting?

"Telling a young woman like her, that you detest anything, is a very difficult thing to do. Pretty women prefer pretty words."

#

The next day, at twilight, on the beach, Dairka's father, Krishna walked a few steps behind his daughter and Clark, making certain that the lieutenant didn't breech good manors and maintained proper decorum with his daughter. The romantically-inclined pair had little time to talk. Krishna let loose a steady stream of information about cockfighting, having heard from his daughter that it was a subject that interested Clark,

"It is believed that Kaaki Dega and Dega roosters are more ferocious during the morning while others would fight better in the evenings, but I find a rooster with the will to fight is a good fighter regardless of breed," Krishna saud.

Gazing at the gold and purple colors of the gently fading twilight sky shining on Dairka's face, Clark said to her, "Are you interested in visiting the U.S. sometime?"

"Oh yes. Is cockfighting allowed there?"

Before he could answer, Krishna said, "The food costs for the man who rears fighter birds for sale pays a lot of money for the care and feeding of his roosters. The birds live on a nutritious and balanced diet of millets, cereals, dry fruits, mutton kheema and receive training that sharpens their natural instincts on when to attack and when to back off from another rooster. It is the man who first owns the bird who trains it how to fight with a blade attached to its legs."

Clark turned his head and glared at Krishna. "Putting blades on a bird's legs is . . ."

Darika laid her hand gently on his arm. "Do you think of marrying someday?" she asked, her tone as sweet and melodic as a canary's.

Clark looked into her adoring eyes and quickly forgot what he was about to say to Krishna. "I didn't think of marrying until I met you," he answered.

#

Seated in the back seat of Abeer's rickshaw, squeezed in between Darika and her father who was holding in his lap his rooster Galaxy Blue, Clark found himself alternating between swooning from the light and floral fragrance of Darika's perfume and the irritating noise that Krishna was making citing everything he knew about cockfighting and that of the clucking rooster. But it was the rooster that he couldn't keep his eyes off. Its body feathers were a shimmering blue-black and it tail feathers were brilliant shades of purple and gold, with a few snow-white feathers mixed in. "The white feathers are a sign of good luck," Krishna had explained. "And Galaxy Blue has been very lucky for me every time I put him in the ring."

"The colors of his tail feathers is why he wins fights?" Clark asked, derisively.

"He has been blessed with the destiny of a hero," stated Krishna.

"Harrumph," was Clark's reply.

Moments later Krishna caught Clark staring at his noisy rooster. "A good rooster cackles in odd numbers."

His side pressed tightly against Krishna's he tried to listen to what Darika was saying while trying to ignore the number of cackles Galaxy Blue was making. By the time they reached the warehouse in Old Town where the cockfights were held, he had heard enough about the rooster's long list of wins to be feel impressed by the rooster's fighting skill and also feeling sickened.

Abeer pulled his rickshaw up to a curb near the entrance to the warehouse and everyone got out. It was the first time Clark had worn his uniform since arriving in Vizag. It drew looks of admiration as well as mistrusting glares from those entering and exiting the warehouse. Krishna did the required knocks on the door, and when it opened, he and those he was with were waved in.

The small but spacious warehouse was filled with the persistent cackling of more than a hundred roosters, most of them being sold and tied to posts as potential buyers walked slowly by, eyeing each one, examining more closely those they were interested in.

"May the planets be aligned in Blue Galaxy's favor," Krishna said as he handed the rooster to the kaiker responsible for tying the blades to the rooster's legs.

"Planets? What does that have to do with the bird's destiny?" Clark asked, snidely.

As if suddenly tired of and a bit annoyed by Clark's inability to understand destiny, Krishna pointed to an open space around the ring where Clark, his daughter, and Abeer could stand to watch the fight.

"From there you will see what a good fighter Blue Galaxy is," he said, and then turned to watch the kaiker wind a long piece of kait around a blade, securing it to the rooster's left leg.

At the fence erected around the circle of dirt floor that served as the ring, Abeer sidled up to Clark's side. "Something I have failed to tell you are two Hindi words you should know, my friend, which I have overlooked because it is of such simplicity that anyone interested in cockfighting would already know it, no matter where they are from."

"I'm not interested in it," Clark said adamantly.

Abeer ignored him. "A rooster is called a murga in Hindi. Cockfighting is called murge ki ladaai in Hindi."

"And what is animal cruelty called in Hindi?" Clark replied just as Darika drew his attention to what was happening in the ring. Krishna had entered carrying Blue Galaxy in his arms followed by another man, also carrying a rooster. They were directed to the middle of the ring by a third man, a kind of referee, and instructed to place their roosters on the ground.

Those standing at the fencing began to shout, clap and whistle.

The other rooster attacked first and fast. In less than a minute the fight was over. Blue Galaxy lay on his side, a huge gash in his neck where the other rooster's blade had sliced it.

Krishna dropped to his knees, picked up the rooster and cradled it lovingly in his arms.

Clark dashed out of the warehouse and standing on the curb only a few feet from the warehouse door, threw up.

#

The next morning, Clark and Abeer said very little to one another on the way to the airport until as if unable to hold it in any longer, Abeer said without looking at Clark in the backseat, "It is a pity you did not see our Submarine Museum, go to the Naval Command, or visit so many of the other things Vizag has to offer."

"I saw a cockfight," Clark answered acidly.

Abeer was quiet for a few moments. "What of the beguiling Darika?" he asked.

"We parted ways amicably, as friends," Clark replied.

"Perhaps that was your destinies, that you should meet for such a short time and then go your separate ways."

"Destiny had nothing to do with it," Clark said, "it was that damned cockfighting."

Abeer steered his rickshaw to the curb near the airport entrance. He helped Clark with getting his things from the backseat and handed them to the lieutenant, watching as he put the backpack on his back, slung the garment bag over his shoulder and grasped the suitcase by its handle. "Remember me as your friend," Abeer said.

"I think I'll never forget meeting you," Clark said, avoiding Abeer's kind gaze.

Clark entered the airport, checked in his backpack and suitcase, and carrying his garment bag he went to the check-in counter. The last thing he saw of Vizag before boarding the plane was the mural with the wording: Vizag. The City of Destiny.

The End

45

THE LAST MATADOR

The hotel was small and stood between two large apartment buildings as if it had been squeezed in as an afterthought. Its facade was painted a bright yellow that drew attention to it but the absence of a sign lured very few to enter through the glass door on the street level to inquire what the building was. The hotel had three floors. One of the rooms on every floor had a sliding glass door that faced the street. There was a small balcony outside each of those doors that was enclosed by an intricately designed black wrought iron railing. The hotel had set up a small cafe table, a chair with a yellow cushion, and a potted cactus on each balcony. The balconies still gave no clue that the building was a hotel, but not many looked up at them anyway, as the street was busy and crowded mostly with tourists going to and from their more elaborate hotels who had little time for seeing what was above their heads.

On the third floor balcony, Adelaide Hurque sat at the table and turned the page of a novel that she had purchased at a used book store just before leaving her hometown of San Francisco. The pages of the novel were yellow from age and many were dogeared, and a few were torn, but she considered she was meant to read it, having kept her eyes closed when she reached into the overflowing bargain bin located on the sidewalk in front of the bookstore and pulled it out. The hotel didn't have room service, but she had made an arrangement with Jorge, the day desk clerk, for him to bring her a coffee and a lemon flavored pan dulce each morning at nine in exchange for her spending fifteen minutes every day helping him improve his English. As she turned the pages of the novel she held the cup of coffee to her lips, inhaled the aroma of cinnamon that had been added to the coffee, and took small sips. She savored in equal measures the flavor of the coffee, the words in the book, and the lemony sweetness of the pan dulce that she bit into at the end of every five pages.

It was on her third day after arriving at the hotel, which had been recommended to her by a friend with similar tastes in travel and accommodations, that she finished her cup of coffee, ate the final crumbs of the pan dulce, and had read forty pages of the novel, when she arose from the chair, carried the book, cup and plate into her room and picked up the phone. "Hello, Jorge," she said into it, "what do you recommend I do today?"

#

Adelaide generally preferred traveling to countries where the climate was more moderate. Her fair skin burned easily and she feared adding more freckles to those that already speckled her face, a condition she likened to an affliction from an early age. Her sole reason for traveling to Cancun was that it was at the opposite end of the Yucatan peninsula across from the more historically interesting Merida, where she spent the first week of her vacation while also visiting Chichen Itza. Cancun was near to Tulum, which her friend had advised her to see, but didn't really interest her.

With a light blue parasol lined with white fringe raised above her head to shield her exposed skin from the glaring sunlight she garnered amused looks and a few snickers as she sat on a bench at the Gran Puerto Cancun ferry dock. The breeze blowing inland from the warm, turquoise water of the Bahio de Mujeres played with her floral patterned cotton skirt that extended down to her calves. She kept her knees pressed tightly together and the skirt tucked between them to keep the skirt from filling with air and ballooning out. As the ferry returning from Isla Mujeres pulled into its berth alongside the pier, a man with a green ball cap with the word Matador stitched on its bill sat down next to her.

"*Discúlpeme, señora,*" he said to her. "*¿Habla usted español?*"

She was uncertain she was being spoken to because strangers seldom spoke to her without her speaking to them first. Even though he was looking directly at her, she hesitated before replying. "*Sí señor,*" she replied in perfectly enunciated Spanish. Before the trip she took to Spain a few years before she had learned to speak fluent Spanish. Since that trip, in San Francisco she attended a weekly Bible study group where only Spanish was spoken, which kept her abreast of the modern moral applications of the scriptures as well as being able to practice speaking the language. The man appeared to be near her age of forty, with black hair and dark brown eyes. His naturally dark complexion showed the signs of a lifetime of exposure to the sun, with lines that formed deep crevices in his cheeks.

"Are you and your husband traveling to Isla Mujeres for the first time?" he asked her.

"Yes, this will be my first time visiting the island," she replied, wary of telling him that she wasn't married and that she was traveling alone.

"I was born and grew up there," he said. "Be sure to see the entire island and not just the markets. Isla Mujeres is magical but the magic isn't found in the shops that sell trinkets. "

When the last of the passengers coming from Isla Mujeres stepped off of the ferry, it sounded a horn. The small crowd that had been waiting on the pier, began to board it. She stood up and smoothed the wrinkles from her skirt while also holding it down as the breeze whipped the folds of the material.

"Thank you for your courteous advice," she said to him as she walked toward the boarding plank.

"But where is your husband?" he asked.

"I'm not married," she answered.

Following close behind her, he said, "Neither am I. I'm going to have lunch with my parents who still live on the island. Perhaps you will allow me to show you the place of my birth?"

She stepped onto the ferry. "Perhaps," she answered.

"My name is Juan-Miguel Estrada," he said, stepping behind her onto the ferry.

#

Juan-Miguel's elderly parents were polite, but mostly quietly, looking from him to Adelaide as he asked Adelaide questions one after the other about her travels and San Francisco. The four of them had a lunch, that while normal in size for typical Mexicans, proved to be too much for Adelaide. By the time the main entree of roasted chicken was served, she was already satiated by the large bowl of lime soup that she had been given. She poked at the chicken, beans and rice on her plate with her fork while answering his questions and gazed about the dining room at the numerous pictures of the Madonna that hung on the walls. Adelaide approved of how Catholics revered the mother of Jesus, but felt it should be done in moderation. The young woman who was the cook and served the meal lifted Adelaide's mostly uneaten plate of food from the table just as Juan-Miguel asked Adelaide about the bullfights she had seen during her travels in Spain.

"I never went to a bullfight," she said, happy to have the food taken away and out of sight.

A noticeable silence settled over the table as if a blanket had been thrown onto the proceedings.

"You didn't go to the Las Ventas in Madrid, or the Plaza de Toros de Ronda, or La Maestranza in Seville?" he asked with incredulity.

She took a sip of her iced tea. "No. I believe killing animals for fun is wrong."

He removed his ball cap and held it up, displaying the word Matador. "I do not kill bulls for fun," he said. "Bullfighting is a tradition, an honor, a profession that has been passed down many generations in my family. My father was a Matador and I am a Matador."

Up to that moment Adelaide had been so charmed by the attention Juan-Miguel had paid to her, and by the sparkle in his eyes when he smiled, and the whiteness of his teeth, that she had forgotten to ask what he did, or even who he was beyond being a very desireable man. She thought the word Matador on his cap had the same significance as a fast food worker wearing a Yale t-shirt.

"I had no idea," she stuttered, in English.

#

That evening while sitting on the balcony outside her bedroom window, Adelaide flipped through the brochure for the Plaza de Toros Cancun that Juan-Miguel had given to her as he walked her to the front door of the hotel. They had left his parents home after lunch and walked and took taxis from one end of the island to the other, which given that the Isla Mujeres was only about five miles long and not very wide, didn't take that long. At the south end of the island where a statue of Xchel, the Mexican fertility goddess, stood alongside a paved trail, he took her hand in his and gently kissed the back of it.

"Do me the honor of coming to the bullring to see me fight a bull tomorrow," he said.

With the shaft of her parasol resting on her shoulder, she twirled it, just like she had always imagined she would do when being flirted with by a man like Juan-Miguel. "Is it important to you?" she asked, certain from the look of yearning on his face what his answer would be.

"Yes, tomorrow is my last bullfight," he said. "I'm the last Matador of my family and my parents are too frail to come see me in my last fight. I will be fighting El Rey, a very mighty bull. It would bring me great pleasure to see you sitting in the stadium."

#

At nine the following morning Jorge delivered a cup of coffee and a pan dulce to Adelaide.

"Have you heard of Juan-Miguel Estrada?" she asked him as he placed the things on the table. She felt haggard and worn after having an awful night's sleep with thoughts of Juan-Miguel being gored by a bull named The King.

His face lit up. "Oh yes, he is a very famous Matador."

She sat in the chair and put a sugar cube in the coffee. "I'll be seeing him in his last bullfight this afternoon," she said.

"I haven't been to a bullfight since I was a young boy," he said. "It terrified me and I've never wanted to see another one although that makes me feel like I'm not a true Mexican." He turned and left.

Adelaide bit into the pan dulce and grimmaced. It was coconut flavored. She didn't like coconut in any form, especially in a breakfast pastry, and definitley not on the morning she awoke after little sleep fully convinced she had fallen in love with a man she had just met. She had another fifteen years of employment as a dentist to look forward to before retiring, after which she planned to do nothing but take ocean cruises, but that morning she had the one repeated thought recycle through her brain. *What does a Matador do after he retires?*

#

A gust of hot wind hurled dirt into Adelaide's face as she stepped out of the taxi and onto the pavement in front of the entrance to the Plaza de Toros Cancun. Spitting grit from her mouth she looked up at the lackluster stadium as the taxi pulled away, carrying away her parasol laying in its back seat with it. Following the crowd, she purchased a ticket, was handed a flier, its message printed on white paper, and found a seat in the first row that overlooked the bullring. With the glare of the bright sunlight penetrating her expensive sun glasses – the ones she bought before her trip to see the glaciers in Alaska – she stared at the print on the flier. There would be a show honoring Juan-Miguel's retirement before he engaged in the fight with El Rey, the final bullfight of the day. Not wanting to risk diminishing the thrill of seeing her newfound love in the only bullfight she had ever seen, and feeling the sun burning into her skin, she dreaded the thought of adding another freckle to her face and rose from her seat and went into the concessions area of the stadium where it was darker and somewhat cooler. The action happening in the arena could be heard broadcast through the speakers mounted on the walls. She bought a bottled water and while standing in a corner for the next hour and a half she listened to the details of the bullfights, the cheers of the crowd, took sips of water, and anxiously waited to hear the announcement of Juan-Miguel's entrance into the bullring.

At last hearing his name, she re-entered the seating area in time to see Juan-Miguel enter the arena carrying a small red cape and a long sword. With his head held high, he entered walking with a strut, displaying the graceful masculinity of his physique in his silver and black costume. She quickly scanned the arena and saw El Rey standing to one side. She had heard over the speakers that the banderilleros had weakened it with their darts, but the sight of the blood dripping down El Rey's sides horrified her – for a moment. And then as Juan-Miguel taunted El Rey with the cape, waving it in dance-like fashion in front of the bull, she felt her cheeks grow hot and felt breathless exhilliration. When the bull charged and Juan-Miguel evaded El Rey's horns she jumped to her feet with the rest of the crowd and shouted Juan-Miguel's name. She waved her handkerchief and blew him kisses. This happened several times and finally when Juan-Miguel thrust his sword into El Rey's neck and the bull fell to the ground, dead, Adelaide fainted from orgasmic fervor.

#

On the flight back to San Francisco, Adelaide sat next to a pretty young woman with unblemished skin that glowed with a healthy new tan. She said she had gotten it by spending all of her time on the beach in the Hotel Zoneria. "What did you do in Cancun?" the girl asked.

Adelaide hesitated before answering. "I fell in love and saw a bullfight."

The girl gasped. "How could you watch an animal be killed in such an inhumane way?" she asked, her voice full of righteous indignation.

Adelaide raised the wilted rose to her nose that Juan-Miguel had given her and inhaled what remained of its fragrance. "Yes, that part of it was horrific, but to tell you the truth, I mostly had my eyes on the matador."

The End

46

THE HILLS HAVE EARS

Tacitus awoke, startled by the silence from his wife's side of the bed, rolled over onto his side and was relieved to see Alicia, his wife, was breathing. She usually snored as she slept, not a loud snore, but noticeable and constant. In the dream he had been awoken from, feeling alarmed even before he left dreamworld, she had been smothered by the hand of God. The hand was invisible, but in the dream he was certain it was God's. He wasn't religious and sometimes doubted that God existed, despite being raised a Catholic. Everyone in his village was Catholic, though, so not wanting to stir up any resentment among his neighbors, friends, and family, he kept his lack of interest in religion and his occasional doubt of God's existence to himself. An obedient and dutiful husband, he attended mass and took communion every Sunday as Alicia wanted. Just to make certain that the steady rise and fall of her chest was her actually breathing and not some trick of his imagination, he placed his hand on her breast.

She awoke instantly, not liking to be touched while she slept. Sleepy-eyed, she glared at Tacitus. "What are you doing?"

He quickly pulled his hand away. "I thought you had died."

"Feeling my breast won't bring me back from the dead," she replied. I know, but I had a dr. . ."

She cut him off. "Why are you starting an argument so early in the morning?"

"*Mi amor . . .*"

"This isn't the time to try to sweet talk me," she said, tossing aside her sheet and sitting up. "You start your new job today and Carina will want to be fed soon."

Unintentionally and unconsciously he glanced at her swollen breast.

She immediately caught where his eyes had wandered to, if only for that brief moment. "You're as bad as Fabian. He never gives poor Jazmin rest," she said. "He will sex her to death one day." She got out of bed, put on her robe, and left the bedroom.

He slowly got out of bed and put on his new miner's clothes, which were actually no more than an old pair of jeans and a shirt with a torn pocket, but new in that this would be his first day wearing them for his new job, going into the mines to dig out coal. He almost didn't get the job when he repeatedly pressed the man doing the hiring for an answer to why machines weren't digging it out. Tacitus spent enough time at the saloon, El Jaguar Sediento, in the nearby larger town, talking to other men better informed than he was to know that machines were taking over many jobs once done by manual labor.

"Do you want the job, or not?" the man – who had a name tag clipped to his shirt pocket that had been accidentally turned around – asked, acting as if he were about to toss Tacitus's application in the trash basket next to his desk.

"*Si, si,*" Tacitus replied quickly. "I need to work."

From the other room, Tacitus heard Carina crying. "Now her breasts will get some use," he mumbled. He put on his socks and boots and went to the window. The sun hadn't yet risen but the air that came in carried with it, night and day, the moist, warm air, generated by the breeze blowing across the surrounding rain soaked hill that rose high above the village a few hundred yards back, and through the dense rain forest on other three sides of the village. He closed his eyes and inhaled through his nostrils the faint fragrance of orchids. The myna birds and cockatiels were having a busy, noisy, and song-filled morning. He turned from the window and steeled himself for one of Alicia's breakfasts. Admittedly he married her because she was beautiful, not because she could cook, but he wondered *how difficult can it be to fix scrambled eggs properly?*

#

The truck that took the mine workers from the village to the coal mine was parked at the start of the road that cut through the forest to the major road leading to the mines in one direction and to the nearest town in the other direction. Carrying the new tin lunchbox Alicia had sold her deceased mother's silver broach to buy for him, Tacitus walked to the truck, his boots clotted with mud gathered from the streets in the village. He climbed onto the truck, followed by Fabian, who looked haggard, as always since marrying Jazmin. Fabian was nineteen and had worked at the mines since age sixteen. He and Jazmin had been married for only eight months.

The two men sat down next to one another on the wood benches that lined the cargo bed. Each man who climbed into the truck afterward sat down, greeting Tacitus with *"Bienvenido a los raspadores del túnel."* Tacitus hadn't given much thought to going into the mines as scraping it out of the tunnels, but he heard one of the men at the saloon say, "Coal is scraped out like the inside of a decayed tooth." The last of the fourteen men from the village climbed into the truck just as the sun began to rise. Its light shone first across the top of the hill.

On the ride to the mine the men joked around about their bulging stomachs and argued about politics and football. Marriage was spoken of in crude and sometimes vulgar terms that Tacitus didn't engage in. At El Jaguar Sediento he had a lot of things to say – funny, sexually graphic and insulting about the local prostitutes – but he never talked about Alicia in that way. If it weren't for the wedding band on his finger, most of the men at the saloon who didn't know him already would have had no idea he was married. At the road between large, rocky hills, the truck he was in pulled into a line of trucks carrying men from other villages. It slowly made its way on the muddy road, coming to a stop about twenty yards from one of the gaping holes leading into the tunnels. He and the others climbed out of the truck as the men who had worked the night shift came walking out of the mine, covered in dirt and coal dust, so blackened by the dust they looked as if they had been been burned to a crisp.

As Tacitus entered the tunnel he was handed a pick axe by the supervisor, Quique, a surly looking man with a crooked nose and skin permanently stained by coal. Tacitus walked on, following close behind Fabian who had a shovel resting on his shoulder, like a soldier carrying a rifle. Tacitus held his breath as entered the dimly lit passageway leading to a world of darkness hidden beneath a world filled with light.

#

At the end of his shift, Tacitus walked out of the tunnel, dirty and drenched in sweat. He deliberately gasped, trying to swallow as much fresh air as quickly as his lungs could take it in. He felt as if he had been holding his breath the entire day. Squinting from the sunlight he made his way to the awaiting truck where Fabian was already seated. Tacitus climbed into the cargo bed and sat down next to him. They said nothing to one another, silenced by the exhaustion of working in the mine. As the truck filled with the rest of the men, none of them said anything. They sat with their backs bowed and their heads hung. Once back at the village they waved weakly to one another as they went their separate ways home. Before going into house, Tacitus looked at the hill behind the village. "Be careful or one day that God that is supposed to be up there (he pointed to the sky) will scrape out your insides too."

As soon as he walked through the door, Alicia yelled at him. "You're filthy. Stay outside and I'll bring you a bucket of water, soap, and fresh clothes."

"You want me to wash my body where everyone can see me?" he asked, embarrassed at the thought of it, even though he saw the men who lived around him who worked in the mine do the same thing.

"*No seas un bebe,*" she said, repressing the urge to laugh.

"I'm not being a baby," he said as he backed out the door, sulking.

While standing outside, leaning against the doorframe, he watched as his neigbor, Rodrigo, stripped off his clothes and stepped into a tub of water and washed off as his wife poured water over his head. Rodrigo was middle-aged and had a bulging stomach like the men had joked about, but he didn't display any hesitancy in exposing his naked body. Rodrigo and his wife talked and laughed as she helped him bathe. When Alicia appeared at the door and handed him the bucket of water, he said, "Aren't you going to help me wash?"

"*Estas loco?*" she replied. She then tossed him a bar of soap, his clothes, and slammed the door.

Minutes later, hiding his private parts with one of his dirty socks, he poured the bucket water over his head and watched as rivulets of black coal and mud ran down his body. He was almost finished when Fabian appeared at the corner of Tacitus's house. Fabian whistled in the way a man whistles at a woman. "If I leave Jazmin, will you marry me?" he said, followed by an outburst of laughter.

Tacitus flashed him the raised arm 'up yours' gesture. "*Estúpido*," he said. "What do you want?"

"Jazmin and I just had our first fight. I'm going to El Jaguar Sediento for a couple of cervazas. Do you want to come along?"

"What was the fight about?"

"She wants to have a baby right away. I don't."

Tacitus began to dress. "We waited ten years before having Carina. Waiting that long was a mistake. Give your wife what she wants."

Fabian scowled at him.

"How are we going to get there?"

"For a very small fee one of the men from the mine will take anyone from the villages there. I just called him. You coming?"

"Yeah." He finished dressing and placed the empty bucket and dirty clothes at the door. As if the cloudy sky had suddenly sprung a watermain break, rain poured down. He glanced worriedly at the hill behind the village and left with Fabian.

\#

Inside El Jaguar Sediento most of the men there who worked at the mine hadn't gone home yet and sat huddled together at the tables, still covered in coal dust, looking like piles of dirty laundry. They seemed to be competing for who could be the noisiest. Rowdiest of them all was Quique, who Tacitus thought looked as ugly then as he did at the beginning of the day's shift, but at least now he was laughing, uproarously, as if laughter was his way of expelling the grime that had collected in his lungs. He had known Quique by sight for many years. Before being permanently laid off, Tacitus worked six years for an NGO on projects related to rainforest animal conservation and protection, and during that time he had no interest in getting to know Quique. He still didn't.

Tacitus sat at the bar with Fabian, Rodrigo and two other men from their village. The mood was sedated and grew more introspective with each cervaza the men quickly guzzled down.

"Once you get *enfermedad del pulmón negro* it's only a matter of time before they lay you in the ground forever," Rodrigo said. As if to prove his point he began involuntarily coughing and didn't stop until he took a large swig of cervaza.

"I don't plan to work in the mine long enough to have my lungs turn black like that," Fabian said. "Jazmin and I plan to move to the coast, work in a fancy hotel, and grow old together, happy and always as in love as we are now."

The other men nodded approvingly although they knew such dreams rarely happened.

"I pray God hears you," Rodrigo said. "My wife and I once had those kinds of ambitions."

"God!" Tacitus uttered derisively. "If there is a God why does he not improve our lives without us having to work so hard to do it?"

The others looked at him, astonished, slightly fearful.

"Tacitus, my friend, don't say such things, God will hear you," Fabian said in a near-whisper.

"It's just as likely that eyesore of a hill will hear me," he said, and then gulped down the last drops of his cervaza. He slammed the bottle on the bar. "I must be drunk. I'm suddenly missing Alicia nagging at me. I'm ready to go home."

#

The last piece of furniture that Alicia hadn't sold after Tacitus lost his job was the armoire that her grandmother had given her as a wedding present. She had sold most of the dresses that once filled it, leaving only a few still hanging on the rod. She kept them to one side and used the mirror she had Tacitus install on the inside back panel to check her hair. Some days she mourned the loss of her vanity dresser as much as she grieved the passing of a loved one. Holding Carina cradled in the crook of her arm as she breastfed the infant, she looked into the mirror and ran her fingers through her thick, lustrous hair, grateful that while some parts of her body were showing signs of aging, her hair was no different than it had been when she was a teenager. It was then that she heard the front door being opened. Tacitus was home.

He picked up the bucket that Alicia had set there as if it was now a permanent fixture since he now worked in the mine. He never mentioned it to anyone but he found having a two-year college degree and being unable to find a job and reduced to becoming a coal miner, humiliating. His clothes were thoroughly drenched from the ten minutes it took to walk from the main road where the impromptu taxi had let him and the others out, through the village, to the front door of his house. The downpour hadn't let up during the two hours he was at the saloon. Forgetting for a few moments that he was hugging the bucket tight against his chest, he watched as Fabian and Jazmin walked past him, snuggled against one another, both dripping wet. She had been waiting for him at the main road, unable to restrain her joy of him returning as soon as he stepped out of the vehicle.

"*Mi ángel*," he cooed to her all the way back.

It was at that moment that there was a cracking noise, as if a giant egg had just been cracked open, followed by an earth tremor that strongly shook the ground under Tacitus's feet.

The hill split apart, spilling hundreds of tons of rocks and liquified earth onto the village, washing over homes and streets so quickly that no one inside or outside had time to react.

#

In the days that followed, the men from the nearby villages and the nearest town dug through the mud searching for survivors.

Fabian and Jazmin were pulled from the mud, in a loving embrace, dead.

Alicia was discovered alive inside her crushed armoire, still holding onto her perfectly healthy baby.

Tacitus clawed his way out on his own, wearing the bucket on his head.

The End

47

NIGHT TRAIN TO PORTO

After boarding the train at the station in Lisbon, Kirk was happy to find an empty seat facing forward that was next to a window. The seats around him were empty also, so he placed his backpack on the seat he faced. He sat down, rested his feet on his backpack, and turned his head to watch as the train began to pull out of the station. The final wisps of purplish twilight sky faded to the dull blackness of early night and the lights of Lisbon began to twinkle and glow in the darkness.

Within minutes the train began to chug along, the sound of its wheels on the track emitting a combination of steady clacking and a low-pitched hum. Kirk folded his arms across his chest and closed his eyes, prepared to sleep for the entirety of the approximate two and half hours it would take to reach Porto, where he had a room reserved in a small hotel located near the Porto train station. Fully relaxed, but not yet asleep, he was startled by the sudden thump on the seat next to him. He opened his eyes. A leather suitcase had been placed in the seat next to him.

A man wearing a crumpled button down shirt, with one of the buttons missing, and wrinkled khaki slacks, stood in the aisle. He peered at

Kirk over the top of wire rimmed glasses. "I almost missed this train," he said, breathlessly. "You're an American also, aren't you?"

Kirk hesitated before answering. "Yes, I am."

"Funny how you can always spot us Americans. We men always look like we just climbed out of bed and the women look like they're just about to crawl in." He reached out his hand. "I'm Trevor Lauder."

Kirk smoothed out the front of his rumpled t-shirt and shook Trevor's hand. "I'm Kirk Newberry." Trevor's hand was hot and clammy.

Trevor glanced around the train car and then back at Kirk. "These seem to be the only seats available. Would you mind if I sit where you're sitting? If I ride anywhere but facing forward and by the window I throw up."

Reluctantly, Kirk lowered his feet. "Maybe you should carry some kind of medication for that when you travel."

"I was so busy getting ready for my wedding that I didn't give it any thought," Trevor said.

Kirk stood up, pushed his backpack aside, and then sat down in that seat. "You came all the way to Portugal to get married?" he asked.

Trevor sat down in the seat that Kirk had been sitting in. "My fiancé is from Portugal. Her family demanded that the wedding be held here." He wiped beads of sweat from his forehead with the back of his hand. "Why are you on the Lisbon to Porto train?"

"I'm touring the Iberian Peninsula during summer break," Kirk said.

Trevor pushed his glasses up to the bridge of his nose and peered owl-like at Kirk. "Do you know if there is a mafia in Portugal?"

"I have no idea. Why?"

"I'm certain her father is a boss, or a don, or whatever you call the guy who leads the mob. I met him in New York a year ago and he was dressed like a mobster from an old movie. He told me he would break my kneecaps if I hurt his daughter."

Kirk squirmed uncomfortably in his seat. "It sounds like he means business. How long have you been engaged?"

Trevor looked down at his shirt and noticing the missing button, he stuck his finger through the button hole. "Six years," he said. "I was never certain Pilar was the right one for me."

Kirk pulled his legs up, crossed them, rested his elbows on his legs, and placed his chin on his fists. He stared into Trevor's bloodshot eyes. "A six year engagement is a long time. What's wrong with her?"

Trevor removed his glasses, breathed onto the lens, then wiped off the lenses on his shirtsleeve. "That's the problem. There's absolutely nothing wrong with her. She's perfect. Too perfect. She's smart, funny, kind and very sensual. Plus she comes from a very wealthy family." He let out a long, exaggerated sigh. "Did I mention she's gorgeous?"

"I don't see the problem," Kirk said.

Trevor spread his arms. "Look at me. Do I look or seem like the kind of guy that deserves a woman like that?" He put his glasses back on.

Kirk tried to look beyond Trevor's messy clothes, balding head, rotund build, and pale pallor, to see what kind of person Trevor might be inside. His mind went blank. "I don't know you, but if she has stuck around for six years then you must offer her more than meets the eye."

Trevor opened his suitcase, pushed aside a crumpled tuxedo, reached under clothes, underwear, and socks, and pulled out a framed picture of Pilar. He held it up, showing it to Kirk.

Unintentionally, Kirk let out a sharp whistle of admiration. Pilar was wearing a bikini that showed off her curvacious, tanned body. Her black, wavy hair cascaded over her shapely shoulders. Her smile was warm, her teeth perfect. Her face invoked thoughts of super models. "I see what you mean," Kirk said. "She's amazing."

"And she wants to marry me," Trevor said in disbelief. "There has to be something wrong with her that I haven't seen yet. It could come out when I would be least expecting it. How can any man live under that kind of pressure?"

Kirk chuckled. "It seems too late to question it now. Her father wouldn't take kindly to you implying that his daughter has some hidden defect that will come out after she's married you."

Trevor put the picture back in the suitcase, covered it with the tuxedo, and then zipped up the suitcase. "I've given lots of thought to how to go off the grid in the event her father has any reason to come looking for me."

Kirk glanced outside, seeing nothing but the countryside mostly hidden in the darkness, and then looked at his watch. "We still have about two hours until we get to Porto. I spent last night in a very noisy hostel and I spent the day seeing the sites in Lisbon, so I'm really tired. I'm enjoying our talk but I need to get a little shuteye."

"Go right ahead," Trevor said. He took his cellphone out of his shirt pocket. "I have lots of emails I need to send."

Kirk leaned his shoulder against the window, crossed his arms across his chest, and closed his eyes. Within minutes he fell sound asleep.

#

Kirk awoke with a start. Trevor was returning to his seat. He had changed clothes and now wore a neatly pressed shirt and bluejeans. "Are you going to meet your fiancé and her family at the station?" Kirk asked.

"Not exactly," Trevor answered. "I had slept on a park bench in those other clothes last night and they were beginning to reek."

Kirk sat up. "Why did you sleep on a bench?" he asked, unable to hide his puzzlement.

"The wedding. Getting married. The thought of it scares me to death. I wandered around Lisbon half out of my mind and by the time I calmed down, it was too late to find a hotel room. I spent most of the day sitting in the grass and staring at the Belém Tower."

The whistle from the train sounded.

Kirk looked out the window. The lights of Porto lit up the night sky. He looked at his watch. "Looks like we're pulling into Porto right on schedule."

The wheels of the train screeched as the train slowed and pulled into the station.

Trevor stood up and grabbed the handle of his suitcase. "I hope you enjoy the rest of your trip."

Kirk pulled his backpack into his lap. "Thank you. Despite your worries, good luck with your wedding." He stood up. "Where is the wedding going to be held?"

"Pilar's father pulled some strings so that the ceremony could be held tomorrow morning on the grounds of the Castelo de São Jorge," Trevor answered.

Kirk stared at Trevor, mouth agape. "The Castelo de São Jorge is in Lisbon," he said.

"Yes, I know," Trevor said. He picked up his suitcase and started down the aisle toward the exit. Over his shoulder he said, "If anyone should ask, you never met me."

The End

48

FROZEN EARTH SONATA

This place, *this place,* where tall oak trees that border the fields shed the last rust-colored leaves of Autumn that blanket the earth shorn of hay, where the dry, dead leaves crackles under Gracie's footsteps, is soon to be the burial place of her beloved cat, Ginger. It is here, in *this place* where Gracie feels most detached from her home back in Ohio, disconnected from what defines her, as a member of a small community, as a school teacher just retired at age 67, that she wanders alone across a field, carrying the wooden pine box, built by her husband, Walt, that contains the body of Ginger.

Hanging tied to her belt is a small shovel. She hugs the box, the object she stubbornly refuses to think of as a coffin, close to her body. Though it's just imagined, and Gracie is well aware of it, she's giving warmth, her body heat, through the wood to her ginger-haired dead cat. Hours before, holding Ginger while allowing the vet to euthanize Ginger, was the hardest thing she ever had to do. Despite being told otherwise, and even after Ginger had become so ill from kidney disease in her last days that she could no longer stand, Gracie is convinced she murdered the one creature she vowed to never harm.

The air is crisp, full of moisture. It has brought a shiny, reddish blush to Gracie's cheeks, like buffed Red Delicious apples. She has stopped crying, sobbing, and wiped the tears from her face before leaving the cabin, but her tears, and her handkerchief, left her skin vulnerable to the elements. The leaves shaken from their tenuous grasp on the tree branches by the damp, steady breeze, flutter to the earth around her like wounded butterflies. Other than sounds she makes walking, it's silent. This is a place of quietude, only invaded intermittently by the barking of a dog from the nearest farm. The town in Ohio where Gracie spends most of her time – where she lives – with Walt, is also quiet, but not like this. There, in the town in Ohio, cars can be heard passing on the road in front of the house, and the shouts of children playing in the neighbor's yard frequently echo through the open windows. Gracie has often complained to Walt that it's too quiet here on this small farm where only hay is grown, that *this place* is like living in a cemetery. And now, in a bit of unintentional prophecy, she's looking for a place to bury Ginger.

Ahead, a single, small oak tree standing near the shallow manmade pond, replenished every spring with a small quantity of trout when its frozen water thaw, Walt lures the trout to their deaths with worms he digs from the ground and skewers on the hooks of his fishing pole. There beneath the tree's strong bows and beside its thick trunk is the place where Gracie decides Ginger should be laid to rest.

She sets the pine box on a pillow of leaves, unties the shovel from her belt, and uses it to brush aside leaves and twigs, revealing a nearly bald area of earth large enough in which to bury the box. She then begins to dig. In this place, *this place* that makes Gracie wish she were back home in Ohio with her friends and former students at her side, sharing this moment in laying Ginger to rest in a place there, perhaps in a spot where Ginger warmed her fur in the summer sun. She jabs the shovel in the ground, surprised that the ground is so hard even before winter has been officially declared. She thought it impossible that the ground would be frozen before the first frost of late Autumn had arrived, but the ground is so hard that it breaks her heart even more to think it was the place where she would place Ginger, an animal who had never experienced hardness or hardship during its sixteen years of life.

After some time, and sweating profusely, with the hole in the ground large enough for the box, she lifts it up and held in a tight embrace, kisses the lid, places it in the hole, and covers it with the dirt.

Carrying the shovel, with the breeze chillier, and the leaves on the ground and those that remained in the trees more agitated by the wind, and with her head bowed, she slowly walks back to the cabin and places the shovel against the door frame for Walt to clean. Inside, she throws two logs into the wood burning stove, stirs the bright red embers and ashes, and closes the door as flames ignite and swirl around the logs like multiple arms of a fiery creature. She removes her beige wool sweater, the one she knitted while attending Ladies knitting Club meetings in Ohio and hangs it on the coat rack, and then looks around the living room and over at the kitchen floor dreading collecting those things that belonged to Ginger.

Bereft, drained of emotion, as empty as the fish aquarium that still sits on a table in front of the window, its different colored pebbles still on the bottom like dull and faded jewels. Abandoned there by Walt who tired of transferring the fish back and forth between the cabin and their home in Ohio during their vacation jaunts to the farm. She takes her place on the sofa. Immediately the space beside her where Ginger always curled up beside her, or stretched out, his front paws kneading the air, feels empty. So does her lap, where the cat's purrs would gently tremble through her skirt.

Then, Walt walks in, his heavy boots sending tremors throughout the room. He's a heavy man; everything about him his noisy, he carries loudness in his body. He fills every space he's in with that noise. Before retiring he worked in a concrete plant for forty years, running machinery and equipment that invaded Earth with its constant rumblings. He rumbles like a whirling concrete mixing drum.

He brings with him inside the cabin, the odors of the woods: tree bark, streams teeming with fish, wet earth. A dead beaver dangles from his meaty left hand.

"What did you do today?" he asks, his voice like sandpaper applied to the inner ear.

"I buried Ginger," she replies.

#

Snow flurries dance in the moonlit sky. It's beautiful to see, to witness, like watching a crime of wonderment being committed in front of her eyes, but Gracie only feels the cold that has filled the cabin, the space, *this space*, that is a prison from which she wishes to escape. She pulls tight around her shoulders the blue and pink knitted shawl the other ladies in the Ladies Knitting Club gave to her as a gift on the day she retired. The summer and fall since retiring sped by like a train heading through a dark tunnel. Nearby the burning logs put in the wood stove by Walt just before he lumbered off to bed crackles and snaps. She places her hand on the window and allows the condensation streak down from her palm print before removing it, staring at the wet lines that crisscross her palm, imagining they are tiny rivers that flow on in never-ending bad fortune.

Startled by a thump on the front door, she turns from the window, wipes her hand on her pale green nightgown, and stares at the door for several minutes, expecting it to open and seeing Ginger stride in, his fur and paws covered in dirt and frost. Turning to the closed bedroom door, the thought of waking Walt to see what made the thump sparks images of his confused, angry reactions when he's awoken from a deep sleep. Judging by his loud snoring, he was as buried in sleep as Ginger was buried in the hard ground. Tentatively approaching the door, the leather soles of her furry slippers sliding across the hardwood floor, she grabs Walt's industrial-sized long handled flashlight from the stand next to the door, and raising it as a weapon in readiness to hit an intruder on the head, she opens the door.

On the stoop just on the other side of the door, a large icicle that had broken free of the roof is stuck upright in the stoop, its pointed end buried deep into the wood, like an arrow shot into a target. She thinks, *Had anyone been under it they would most certainly have been killed.* A blast of cold air makes her look up, then she sees it, the thin layer of snow that carpets the landscape caught in the moonlight, sparkling like frozen teardrops that have fallen from the heavens. Her gasp is audible as she clutches her throat as if being strangled by the beauty of the scene. She steps back and grabs Walt's hunting jacket from the coat rack, puts it on, and swallowed by the large volume of heavy material that smells of hickory smoke, fish and dried deer blood, she pulls the door closed and walks away from the cabin, away from the safety of the space she never leaves after nightfall. There is light in this darkness. She slowly walks into it.

Quickly caught in a swirl of snowflakes, some attach to her face and instantly melt there, extinguished like candle flames snuffed out between two fingers. Gracie stands still, allowing the snow to bathe her in the damp cold and the moonlight to wash over her in iridescent warmth. Her breath forms small clouds with every exhalation as she surveys the surrounding landscape that is glazed with crystalline snow. Icicle earrings hang suspended from the branches of the trees that surround the farm, standing bare of leaves and seeming more rooted to the frozen earth than in warmer weather where they appear prepared to walk away in search of more fertile ground. Drawn to the tree where Ginger is buried, she walks on, the icy snow splintering beneath her slippers. There, she circles the tree trunk several times, kicking aside the drifting snow, unable to find the cat's last resting place. She thinks, *maybe the next thaw*, and walks away and heads toward the pond. Walt's large bootprints are still barely discernible just beneath the glistening coating of ice that marks his path to the pond. She knows he hadn't gone fishing that day and wonders aloud, muttering, "What reason did he have to go to the pond?"

Even before she gets to it, she can smell it. To her the pond has always had the scent of algae and the trout that live in it during warmer climates. By winter, Walt has fished most of them out. Those few left are trapped in the in the ice, frozen there like ice sculptures. She approaches it slowly and carefully; it's coated with snow, blurring the bank and the edge of the pond. There she sees Walt's bootprints go both directions, coming and going. *He was circling the pond,* she thinks. *But why? He knows there are no live fish left in it.* She turns and walks back to the cabin.

Inside she takes his coat off and hangs it on the coat rack. The fire inside the stove is still going strong. She opens the stove door and with her hands held near the burning logs, she rubs them, warming them. Walt's snoring rumbles through the cabin reminding her that she's not alone. This time, while he's asleep, is when he is the least silent; he tells her so little, giving little verbal indication of where he goes or what he does while they stay at the cabin. In *this space* she is mostly invisible to him. They don't talk about his fishing, or hunting, about his feelings, or about his thoughts about her, or her feelings, about anything. It's this last thing, her feelings, that she becomes most uncertain of. She wishes she had her friends from Ohio around to talk to them about her feelings, to validate them, to validate her.

#

The dirt road to the town nearest to the farm is muddy. Spring thaw has turned most of the earth to varying stages of liquification, from puddles to mud. Each time the tires get stuck, the mud acting like an adhesive that results in them spinning and bringing the movement forward to a halt, Walt slams his fist down on the steering wheel, cursing loudly. He gets out of the car, and in his boots he slogs through the mud to the back of the car and pushes the vehicle as Gracie gets behind the wheel and takes control of the pedals, stick shift and steering wheel. It's one of the few times during the time they've been away from Ohio he's allowed her to manage anything other than cooking and keeping the cabin clean. The last time after the car gets stuck just before reaching the paved road leading to town, he kicks off the mud that clung to his boots and returns to his place behind the wheel, and shoves Gracie back into her place in the passenger seat. She says nothing about the pain – physical and emotional – being manhandled by him causes her. It's the kind of abuse that takes place nowhere else, only here, in *this here,* the here that wasn't Ohio. In Ohio she always feels safe.

The remainder of the ride into town she sits in stony silence and stares out the passenger-side window, musing how nothing ever changes here; houses never receive fresh coats of paint and the same clothes hang from the same clotheslines. She thought clotheslines were a thing of the past. Even everyone in her small town in Ohio had clothes dryers. Seeing so few people in their yards or on their front porch, makes her wonder, *What are they all hiding from?*

Entering the business area of town, Gracie turns her head to watch out the front window, aware that she and Walt haven't spoken to one another since he pushed her. Both sides of the street are lined with booths and stalls where pedestrians are walking from one to the next. Brightly colored ribbon is wrapped around the telephone wires and poles. The store awnings have all been withdrawn allowing the spring sunlight to shine on the sidewalks.

"Looks like there's some kind of street festival going on," she says.

"Yep."

"I'd like to get out and take a look at what they're selling at a few of the booths."

"Why?"

"Because I want to," she screams. *She screamed it.* Her voice filled the car, taking up the space previously filled by molecules. "Stop this car, now!" she screams. *Another scream.*

He slams on the brake, bringing the car to a screeching stop.

She opens her door and gets out, taking the air, and molecules, from the inside of the car with her and slams the door closed. If he immediately drove away or watched her walk away, she couldn't have said. She had disconnected from him in a way she rarely did.

The first thing she notices as she begins to walk along the line of booths and stalls isn't what is being sold, but the faces of the vendors or the other pedestrians. Their expressions are dour. There is no festivity in this festival. She doesn't recognize a single one of them. It's a market devoid of familiarity. She feels lost, adrift as a stranger in a small river of strangers, afloat amidst a gently flowing current of unfamiliarity. There's nothing to latch onto, nothing that defines her, or defines the location she is walking through. There is no here, here. She suddenly wants Walt to be nearby. She needs him to keep from drifting toward total obscurity.

When a Styrofoam cup is blown down the street by a moist breeze, she turns and watches it, thinking how much its color is that of snow. The thought sends a chill down her spine. Before she walks on, a female vendor with snow-white hair and lifeless blue eyes holds out a handmade apron patterned with toddlers chasing butterflies that is exactly like the other dozen stacked on the counter. "Something every grandmother should have," the female vendor says. Gracie gives fleeting thought to explaining why she and Walt never had children, but recalls it's something she has only shared with the women in the Ladies Knitting Club because they knew her and understood that Walt didn't want children. They knew Walt. They also *knew about Walt.* Sharing it anywhere else, especially here, *this here*, with women not in the knitting club diminished the importance of those women, and they were very important, especially when they seemed so very far away. "No, thank you," she replies and walks on.

At the end of the street a man selling snow cones holds one up and asks, "Want one? Only seventy-five cents."

She looks at the shaved ice in the white paper cone and wants to laugh at the absurdity of the moment, the absurdity of winter being offered in a cup. She wants to laugh, but doesn't.

Walt pulls up in the car and rolls down the window. "Time to go home," he says. "Back to Ohio."

The End

49

THE INCIDENTAL
AMERICAN

Miranda adjusted her white sun hat that rested precariously on her expensively coiffed pile of bright red hair before picking up her suitcase and makeup case that she had set down on each side of her. She then slowly descended the winding marble staircase, testing the fit of her new white stiletto heels that she had ordered online from her favorite frequent shoe supplier, but had just taken out of the box just before leaving her bedroom. She had stopped going to shoe stores while still a teenager having decided that no one should touch her feet but the Korean woman who gave her pedicures. At thirty-two she had stuck with that thinking all through her ten years of marriage, not allowing her husband, now ex-husband, to touch them. As the heels of her shoes clicked on the marble steps, one step at a time, like the slow and deliberate tapping of a hammer on a nail, she listened for any sign of the heels being inferior. She knew stilettos weren't the right style of shoe for the summery flock she was wearing, but she had purchased them for other reasons. They allowed her to imagine the heels of the stilettos being driven into the skull of her ex-husband.

At the bottom of the stairs she crossed the foyer where large oil paintings of Greek gods and ancient, crumbling structures, inside gold, ornately designed frames lined the walls. The foyer led two directions, to the double doors leading to the outside, and past the staircase to the interior of the first floor. She placed her suitcase and makeup case by the door, turned about and walked to the closed doors of the drawing room. She had been told by the upstairs maid that her parents were in the room waiting on her. She knew from the conversation at the dinner table the night before they were actually waiting on her father's business attorney. They didn't expect her to actually follow through on her plans to leave and humored her each time she made threats of going to South America.

"But dear, what do you know about picking coffee beans?" her mother said. "You know how much you detest the outdoors."

"I drink only the very best coffee. What more is there I need to know?" she replied.

She smoothed her tailored jersey purple and white print dress with a flouncy skirt, cinched at the waist with a white leather belt, tapped on the door before opening it, and then entered the room.

Her mother looked up from her freshly filed fingernails. "Miranda, dear, we missed you at breakfast," she said. "You don't function well on an empty stomach."

"I'm waiting on James to bring the car around to take me to the airport," stated Miranda.

"Stuff and nonsense," her father said, his face hidden behind an opened, spread newspaper.

"It's not nonsense, Father," Miranda replied. "My flight to Brazil leaves in a little over an hour."

Her mother chewed off a small piece of cuticle and politely spat it into a half empty glass of bourbon. "Cook is preparing roast lamb for dinner, dear. You know how much you love Cook's lamb and that mint jelly she makes to go with it."

"You two are impossible! I said I'm going to Brazil to work on a coffee plantation and that's exactly what I'm doing."

Her father turned a page of the newspaper, and with only the top of his balding head showing, uttered mockingly, "Send us a postcard when you get there."

"Really Father! No one sends postcards anymore," she snarled and then in a huff spun about on her heels and left the room. At the front door she picked up her things and went out.

#

Miranda stepped off the plane in Rio de Janeiro and was immediately blasted with a hot, humid swirl of air. Her skirt blew up around her waist resulting in her dropping her makeup case as she struggled to right her skirt., spilling its contents on the tarmac. She looked around, waiting for someone to come rushing to assist her with gathering up her lipsticks, compacts, makeup and hair brushes, and a dozen other items that lay strewn about. But, as other passengers walked by, barely glancing at her, she bent down and put things back in the case, leaving many of the things on the ground, closed it, and then stood, tightly grasping the handle of the case. Sweat poured down her face causing her eye makeup to run in black streaks. *So-much for expensive no-run eye liner,* she thought.

It suddenly occurred to her that she was thousands of miles from home. She had purposely left her cellphone on her bed back home, vowing to disconnect herself from her country of birth. There was no one she would have called anyway, even if she could have. "They're all wanting me to fail," she muttered as she stood proudly, unwavering, on her spiked heels, and then strode into the airport terminal with her back stiffened and her facial expression set in a mask of stone.

She collected her suitcase from baggage claim and then walked out of the terminal. The curb was lined with Taxis and Uber vehicles. Going to the nearest one she cleared her throat to get the attention of the man texting on his phone while leaning against his taxi. He looked up.

"Puedo conseguir un paseo?" she enunciated, sounding out each word slowly.

He cocked his head. "You an American?"

"Incidentally, yes," she said. "Why?"

"Here, Portuguese is spoken," he answered.

Her eyes widened in surprise. "But this is South America. Spanish is spoken everywhere."

"Here, Portuguese is spoken," he repeated.

"I learned Spanish anticpating coming here," she said. "Can you take me to the nearest coffee plantation?"

He eyed her up and down and chuckled. "The nearest coffee plantations are about 73 kilometers, about two hours away. I can take you but it will soon be night and travel is not always safe at this hour."

She stomped her stilleto like a child about to throw a tantrum. "Take me to the nearest four star hotel then. I'll go in the morning."

"Si senorita," he replied accompanied by a mischevious grin.

She got into the back seat of the taxi as he put her suitcase and makeup case in the trunk. When he got in behind the wheel he turned his head and looking at her, said, "If I may be nosey, why do you wish to go to a coffee plantation?"

"I want to pick coffee beans."

"Pardon me again. Why?"

"Working on a coffee plantation would give me something to do."

He looked down at her stilletos "You will need different shoes," he said before turning back to the wheel and turning the key in the ignition."

#

As the rising sun of dawn spread its luminescent light on Sugarloaf Mountain, Miranda stood on the balcony of her hotel room looking out at the mountain's majestic point while sipping on a cup of Brazilian Arabica coffee. She sighed contentedly, thinking, *Beans for this coffee would be delightful to pick.* She then closed her eyes and let the warm ocean breeze caress her freshly made-up face. The suggestion by Francisco, the taxi driver, that she allow the concierge of the hotel buy the makeup items she needed to replace, along with a pair of locally made sandals that would be stylish as well as comfortable, had been an excellent suggestion. The makeup supplies and sandals were delivered at the same time as breakfast was wheeled into her room on a cart and set up on a table on the balcony. She opened her eyes, took a last look at the mountain and turned and set the empty cup on the table. She called for a bellhop to come pick up her suitcase and makeup case, put on her sunglasses, and picked up her sun hat and placed it on her head. She slung her purse slung over her shoulder, and left the room, then took the elevator to the lobby. She then went to the desk and checked out of the hotel.

Before going out she gave the concierge standing at her station near the doors a hefty tip. She then walked out into the sunlight where Francisco was waiting for her at the curb with the back door of his taxi opened, awaiting her, as they had planned the day before for him to do.

Once settled in her seat, and Francisco behind the wheel, she lowered her sunglasses, leaned forward and tapped him on the back. "I saw your famous mountains this morning," she said, "is there anything else you recommend I see before we leave Rio?"

"Christ the Redeemer," he answered.

"I thought he was dead," she replied.

He pulled away from the curb resisting the urge to laugh out loud. "I think it best if you're looking for a coffee plantation to pick coffee beans that I take you directly to the Arabica Plantations near Sau Paulo," he said.

She settled back in her seat and raised the sunglasses to her eyes. "Excellent choice, Francisco," she said. "I like the idea of picking beans for a coffee that I've tasted and like."

\#

Traveling west on BR 101, Miranda filed her nails as she watched the passing scenery through the open window. Fearful of using the air conditioning the enitire way because of the stress it would put on the vehicle's engine, Francisco had turned it off in spite of Miranda's complaints. As the warm, moist hair blew in, she found she was enjoying the feel of it on her face. She didn't want him to know that. *Clearly he doesn't understand that I'm the paying customer.* The light fragrance of the Camelia Rose resembled that of her mother's perfume. She didn't regret leaving her mother, but the flower's scent made her slightly homesick.

The pink flowers grew along the sides of the highway. "What is that flower?" she asked Francisco.

"It's the Camelia Rose," he said. "Many years ago, it was common practice for abolitionists to plant camellias in a show of solidarity."

"Were abolitionists gardeners?" she asked.

"You might say that," he replied.

After ten more miles during which the two returned to silence, thinking of the one time in her marriage that her ex-husband had given her roses, Miranda stared at the back of Francisco's head for several minutes before asking, "Francisco, are you married?"

"I'm divorced."

"Divorced? Getting divorced is allowed in Brazil?"

Bemused, he glanced at her in the rearview mirror. Judging by the expression on her face she was genuinely surprised and interested. "Divorce is allowed in most countries," he said.

"I haven't traveled much," she said, her voice tinged with regret. "I thought divorce was mainly an American thing."

A few miles further down the road he steered the taxi into a gravel lot in front of what looked like a normal two story house. A sign above the door read: Restaurante Para Viajantes.

"Perfect! Restaurant for travelers," she said with a laugh.

She understood the sign, Francisco thought, a bit perplexed.

"The owners are friends of mine," he said. "They serve the best home cooking in all of Brazil. We're early for lunch, but I'm sure Adriana will gladly serve us brunch." He opened his door and started to get out, looked back at Miranda, and saw her looking into a compact mirror and applying fresh lipstick. "There is no need to that. Adriana and her husband Lucas are simple people. They're also old-world Brazillians who only speak Portuguese."

"They're your friends," she said. "I want to look presentable."

A few minutes later, inside the restaurant, where small tables were covered with red checkered plastic tablecloths and bamboo ceiling fans whirled above their heads, Miranda and Francisco were seated at a table by Lucas, a middle-aged man with skin the color of burned caramel.

Francisco introduced her to Lucas, who kissed the back of her hand before handing them menus anyway after apologetically saying the only things that Adriana could serve before lunchtime was scrambled eggs and Pão de Queijo.

"Obrigada, isso é perfeito," Miranda said in perfect Portuguese.

When Lucas went into the kitchen, Francisco leaned across the table. "How did you know to say that in Portuguese and do it without any hint of an American accent?"

"I watched a little television and read the room service menu before going to sleep last night," she answered.

Mouth agape, he watched as she opened the menu and read aloud the listed items, all written in Portuguese, as if she had spoken the language her entire life.

#

"How did you learn the Portuguese language in such short time?" Francisco asked as soon as they pulled out of the restaurant's lot to continue their journey to the Arabica plantations.

"I learn and understand languages with very little effort by listening to foreign cooking shows on television," she said. "It's the way I learn most things that interest me. I hate reading. Sad to say, but I didn't finish college because I wasn't good at studying."

"How many languages have you learned that way?"

"Fourteen, I think."

Francisco let out a long whistle. "That's incredible! You're some kind of genius."

She turned her head and looked out the window. "My ex-husband didn't think so. He admired me for being pretty and throwing elaborate dinner parties, but otherwise thought anything else I did was silly and useless."

"You should forget what he thought and do something with your ability to speak so many languages."

"I'd rather just pick coffee beans," she said.

For the remainder of the ride, the two talked, in Portuguese, about their upbringings. She had always been rich. He came from near-poverty. She did poorly in school. He got top grades, and learned the English language, but with great difficulty. He always had lots of friends. She never had any.

"Even now the people who I thought were my friends stopped accepting me into their homes as soon as I got a divorce. As much as I tried to please them all the time I was married, it was my husband who they were, and are, friends with," she said icily.

At the Arabica Plantations administrative office building, Francisco took her suitcase and makeup case out of the trunk and set them at her feet. "Are you certain you don't want me to wait, just in case they don't hire you?" he asked.

"What can it take to pick coffee beans?" she said.

He handed her his card and kissed her on both cheeks. "Call me if you ever need a drive somewhere."

"Obrigado meu amigo," she said and then adjusted her sun hat, picked up her things, and went into the building.

#

Two and a half hours later the Uber taxi pulled into the lot of the Arabica Plantations administrative offices. Miranda came out of the building and handed the driver, Joao, who was young and said only a few words to her in broken English as he tossed her things in the trunk of his car.

What had happened in the Arabica adminstrative office was this:

The man who did the hiring came out of his office, looked her up and down, his eyes lingering on her manicured, polished nails and her sun hat. "You're not from Brazil, are you?" he said in English.

"No, I'm an American," she said, "but my friend Franciso tells me I speak your language perfectly."

"Who is your friend?"

She handed him Francisco's card.

He stared at it for a minute and then looked at her. "He's just a taxi driver," he said, and gave her a look that she recognized. It was the same one her ex-husband used to give her. "You're not made to pick coffee. I recommend you look for work elsewhere, possibly in your own country where jobs are plentiful. Good luck." He then turned, went back into his office, carrying Francisco's card with him, and closed the door.

Miranda and Joao got into the vehicle and as they pulled out of the lot she told him she would like to stop at the Restaurante Para Viajantes for lunch on the way back.

"I hear the food and service there is terrible," he said. "You're an American, yes?"

"Incidentally," she answered.

"I'll take you to McDonalds when we get back to the city."

"Just take me straight to the airport," she said. "My Swahili is excellent and they grow coffee in Kenya where Swahilli is spoken, according to the television show *Kenya Cooks.*"

The End

50

ENCOUNTER WITH A SHOEBILL

I sat in the front of the motorboat manned by Mukisa, who held onto the tiller, guiding it slowly through the narrow alleyways between the islands and peninsulas of dense papyrus grass. A steady hot and humid gentle breeze blew across the Mabama Bay Wetlands, carrying with it the scents of vegetation, alive and dead, and that indescribable smell of fresh water teeming with aquatic wildlife. I inhaled it until it filled my lungs; until they ached. I tried to see everything all at once, as if the watery landscape alive with birds, mammals and lizards was a photograph capable of being viewed with a single panoramic glance. I knew there was nothing that could quell my enthusiasm, my excitement, as an observer of this world so far away from the streets, pollution and noise of my neighborhood in inner-city Chicago. It was the death of – or more precisely, a small inheritance left for me by – my grandfather on my mother's side that allowed me to take this trip back to his birthplace of Entebbe, Uganda. My otherwise state of poverty be-damned.

Birds were everywhere I looked. All kinds of birds; warblers, king-fishers, herons, storks, ducks, cuckoos, on and on, then there it was, standing in the reeds near the bank, a shoebill. It was the shoebill stork I wanted to see. An endangered species, prehistoric in appearance and thought to have roots in the last days of the dinosaurs, it was estimated there were only a few thousand remaining in the wild. It stood there on long spindly legs, about 4 foot tall, its feathers a blend of powder blue and dusky gray. There was a tuft of feathers sticking out of the back, top of its head. Its bill looked like a shoe for an extremely large foot. On the tip of its bill was a reddish mark, like a birthmark, shaped like a hammer. It stared at the boat, at me, with unnerving intensity. "Stop the boat," I called out to Mukisa, "I want to have a closer look at the shoebill."

He turned off the engine, and picked up an oar. As he guided us closer to where the bird stood, I thought it would fly away, or at the least walk further back from the bank, but it remained where it was, immovable, fearless, walking only a few feet, only to stand motionless again. A couple yards away from it, Mukisa, stuck the oar into the mud in the water, bringing the boat to a halt. "Against law to interfere with natural habitat or wildlife," he said.

The shoebill stared at me, its dark yellow eyes fixed on me with such unwavering focus that I felt embarrassed, as if I had been caught outdoors, naked. It then shook its head as if dislodging ear wax, and then began to do what Mukisa had earlier told me about shoebills, was bill-clattering. Its quivering bill sounded like a machine gun, the only form of vocalization it made. I lifted my cellphone and took several pictures of it as Mukisa busied himself keeping the boat from drifting deeper into the weeds.

The first "pssst" that I heard the shoebill make, as if made by someone wanting to secretively catch my attention, I thought was some kind of physiologically emitted noise, like a bird form of a hiccup or a sneeze. I lowered my cellphone and met the bird's gaze.

"Hey, fella," it said in a barely inaudible whisper.

Uncertain what I had heard, from a bird that was said to make only one noise, I dismissed as the rustling of the reeds at best, my imagination at worse. I raised my cellphone, prepared to take another picture, and then heard it again.

"Pssst." It was the Shoebill.

I lowered the phone and stared at the bird. "What?" I said tentatively, with astonishment, also in a whisper.

"What's your problem?"

It then spread its wings to a full 5 foot wingspan, flapped them a few times, lifted into the air, and flew off.

#

I had booked a room at a small, modest hotel located in downtown Entebbe. When I returned to it after my foray into the wetlands with Mukisa I expected more than a typical "welcome back" greeting from the clerk at the check-in desk. I wanted to be asked if I had seen a shoebill, which I had, or if I had figured out an answer to the stork's question, which I hadn't. To be honest, I didn't even think I had a problem, but when a bird asks you that question, it requires some reflection. I went to my room, showered, and took a short nap before leaving the hotel to wander around the local area on foot and find the restaurant the desk clerk suggested I might like. Many of the shops and stores had open fronts with a lot of merchandise on display in front of them, something rarely seen in Chicago. It made me wonder about shoplifting in Entebbe. Then I thought, *I'm too negative. Maybe that's my problem.* I found the restaurant, The Bird's Nest. On their menu, to my surprise, was Chicago-style pizza. That's what I ordered. I thought, *I'm not into experimenting with different foods. Maybe that's my problem.*

Before returning to the hotel I took a taxi around the city and to see Lake Victoria. I felt I had seen enough of Entebbe to satisfy the ghost of my benevolent grandfather. I tried to hide my feelings that other than Mabama and Lake Victoria, I wasn't thrilled with Entebbe. It was a new place, a new city, I should have been thrilled. *Maybe that's my problem.*

I returned to the hotel at sundown, went straight to my room instead of sitting in the lobby to talk with the other tourists who had congregated there, and went straight to bed. I spent a sleepless night thinking about the shoebill. Even before I received my requested wake-up call from the front desk I was wide awake, although blurry-eyed. I never get enough sleep. *Maybe that's my problem.*

#

The flight to Pakuba, Uganda, located within the Murchison Falls National Park, took a little over an hour. Before booking the trip to my grandfather's birthplace, I had searched online things to see and experience in Uganda, and the Murchison Falls park was at the top of every list. My plan was to stay in a lodge there for three days, and then return to Entebbe to make contact with the side of my grandfather's family who lived there. At no time growing up do I recall him ever mentioning any of them and I drew blank stares when I asked my parents about them. I thought it was something I *should* do. At the Pakuba airport I was met by Ochieng the guy who drove one of the lodge's jeeps.

"You have come to see the many wildlife in the park, yes?" he said to me as he tossed my backpack and small suitcase in the back of the jeep.

I didn't want to tell him that originally it was seeing a shoebill that I was interested in, but having seen one in Mabama, and not fully enjoying actually – meeting – one, my interest by default now lay in seeing the elephants, hippos, giraffe and the antelope-like Ugandan kob in their natural habitats. I was never really a wildlife kind of guy, seen either in their natural habit or otherwise. It had been years since I had been to the Lincoln Park Zoo in Chicago.

"Yes, to see the wildlife," I replied with faux enthusiasm.

"The park has many, many bird species also," he said as he got behind the wheel.

I climbed into the seat next to him. "I saw many birds in Mabama," I said.

"Did you see one of our famous shoebill storks?" He started the engine.

I hesitated before answering. "No."

"Anyone who comes to Uganda must try to see a shoebill," he said as he drove the jeep away from the curb.

On the way to the lodge I saw the animals I told Ochieng I wanted to see, with the exception of hippos. I felt I had already used up at least two days of exploring the park in a single drive. He assured me I would see the hippos the next day when out on a boat to see birds and to look for a shoebill. After arriving at the lodge, I spent the rest of the day and evening sitting on the front porch sipping ice tea and listening to the bird watchers chatter excitedly about the different birds they had seen. None of them had seen a shoebill, but they all remained hopeful.

#

The motorboat I had hired for the tour through the part of the Nile River that flows through part of the park and feeds the Murchison waterfalls left the dock a little past dawn. Manned by two men, Damba and Irumba, one at one end guiding the boat and the other on lookout at the front, I sat alone in the center, having paid extra to reserve a boat for myself. We slowly glided on morning sunlit water through the tributaries that meandered through the park as Irumba pointed out many birds, alligators, koba and even a troop of chimpanzees before a shoebill was spotted standing in a thick carpet of grass. It remained in place, only slowly turning its head to watch as Damba guided the boat closer to the shore. I should have been thrilled to see a second shoebill, but instead I felt as if hundreds of the parks' butterflies had taken up residence in my stomach. The shoebill looked exactly like the one I had seen in Mabama. *But don't most shoebills look identical?* I thought, suddenly feeling feverish. As we watched, it walked closer to the bank and stared right at me. On its bill was the hammer-shaped marking.

I gasped.

When three alligators approached the boat from the other side, Damba and Irumba turned to gently prod them away from the boat with the boats' oars.

"Pssst." It was the shoebill, its eyes fixed on me.

"What?" I whispered back.

It raised its head, clattered, and then lowered its head, shook it a few times, and then locked its eyes on mine. "What's your problem?" it said.

"Who said I had a problem?"

"Don't you ever think about your life, examine it? To quote, Socrates . . ."

"You can quote Socrates?" I said, astonished.

"I can still quote the last tyrannosaurus rex I met before the great extinction," it said. "Socrates said the **unexamined life** is not worth living."

"What's that have to do with me?"

"Look around you," it said. "Really look."

With the alligators turned away, Damba and Irumba, returned to their places.

The shoebill rose into the air on gently flapping wings and flew away.

#

I did see hippos that day. I returned to Entebbe and met several of my grandfather's relatives, none who remembered him. I returned to Chicago and took up my life where I had left off. I repeatedly ask the question of myself and others that the shoebill asked me. "What's your problem?"

The End

51

GIRL ON ICE

Her name is Sarah. She knows that because it's on her driver's license. Sarah Brighton. It's the same name that's on her library card. The two pieces of identification she found in her handbag that is blue cloth, beaded, with a drawstring top. She knows her name, and the purpose of a driver's license and a library card. She knows the names of everything she sees: clouds, sky, snow, glacier walls, and the large slab of ice on which she floats. She recalls nothing about Shoreline, the town listed on her pieces of identification. She remembers no one else, although she's certain there are others because the signatures on her identification are different than hers, and the labels on her handbag, on the inner cuff of her right glove, and on the pocket of her down-filled coat have names different than her own. But she can't recall other faces, what other people look like, what other people do that is different than what she does: sit on a floating chunk of ice while seals follow alongside. Oh, and there are the seals. She knows what they are called. Each night one of them climbs onto the ice and snuggles against her, giving her the warmth of its body as she sleeps.

But she wonders, *why is no one searching for me?*

She also knows what a polar bear is. There is one that has followed her, trailing along from the bank of the icy river for as many days as she can remember, although she has no real idea how long she has been floating on the ice. Each night she carves a notch in the ice with a pair of fingernail clippers she keeps in her handbag to count the passing day, but in the morning the notch is gone. Time is meaningless. Her birth date is on her license but she has no idea what year it is, or even what month. The photograph on her license is of a young woman, pretty, but her age is indeterminate. When she looks at the reflection in the mirror in her compact she stares at in wonder, not seeing her face, only seeing a blank slate where all the things she doesn't know about herself should be evident. She tries to fill in all the missing details of who she was or is, but other than what her identification tells her, she has no idea what other details there could be.

The days are filled with shielding her eyes from the bright glare of the sunlight reflected on the glacier walls and the glinting of twinkling light on the snow and ice. She travels through a glacial canyon with only enough bank on the right wall for the bear to walk along. She bends her neck back to stare up at the sky or lies on her back, her hands behind her head as pillows, and follows the ascent and descent of the sun and moon and the slow passing of the clouds.

At night, with a seal lying beside her, she looks up at the stars imaging the shapes of things she remembers but have no real meaning: animals, flowers, human contours. She has looked for an outline of her own body in the stars, but her body remains unseen and unknown, in the stars and on the ice.

The bob of seals that glide alongside the ice on which Sarah floats, take turns going beneath the water's surface, reappearing a short time later, and toss salmon into her lap. Sarah understands death, without knowing why, but as the fish utter their last gasps of breath, she is filled with sadness. She scrapes their scales from their skin with an emery board and removes their fins with cuticle scissors. The raw meat of the fish is slightly sweet and satisfying. Water is plentiful, of course. She dips her hands into the freezing water, filling her palms, and pours it into her mouth. Afterward she blows her breath on her hands, rubs them together, and puts her gloves back on. It's only her face that she has difficulty keeping warm. At times it feels as if her face is a frozen mask.

She is surrounded by sound. Wind whistles in a constant hum through the canyon. The seals splash the water with their tail fins, and bark, as if talking to one another, as if talking to her. The flowing current of the water sounds like the rustling of silk. Chunks of ice crash into one another sending off thudding echoes that resonate between the glacier walls. When a portion of a glacier wall falls into the river, it's like the noise made by rumbling thunder, only more amplified.

When she dreams, she hears music, but the dreams are filled only with images of things she has seen while on the ice.

She wakes every sunrise thinking, *why is no one searching for me?*

#

When the polar bear plunges into the river, snatches one of the seals, and returns to the icy bank with the seal in its teeth, Sarah is at first shocked by the violence of the act, by the brutality of the killing. But other than a momentary excited frenzy, the other seals don't react and don't leave the sides of the ice on which she sits. However, now the bear seems closer, more threatening. After feeding on the seal the bear returns to its parallel position to where she is floating, following along as before, its huge body now seeming monstrous.

Sarah spreads the contents of her handbag onto the ice and counts them, as she has done several times before. There are twelve items, some that she has used since being on the ice, some that she hasn't. She has a cellphone, but it's dead and has no use. Of the items in her handbag, it's the only one that's of no use at all, but she has no memory of what it is anyway. It's a slab of plastic, similar in shape to the ice she floats on. She knows what it's called, but not what it's used for. She holds it in her hands for several minutes, staring at its black screen, and then returns it to the other items, keeping it instead of throwing it into the water only because having possessions, even useless ones, feels like it adds importance to her existence on the ice.

In the night, a seal snuggled against her suddenly pulls away and slides into the water. Sarah sits up and sees lights on the river, growing larger and brighter as they draw nearer. The lights are mounted on a small boat that takes form and shape in the glow of its light and the ambient illumination of the moon and stars. She grabs her handbag and holds it close to her chest as the boat approaches. In the beam of one of the boat's lights, she feels exposed, as if her clothes had been ripped from her body.

"Sarah Brighton?" a voice blares from a loud speaker aboard a boat.

The End

52

THE CHILDREN'S CHILDREN

I could see the square structure on the top of the Pyramid of KuKulkan no more than three miles away, marking the way to Chichen Itza. The humidity was oppressive, making it hard to breathe and wringing rivulets of sweat from my body. The jeep bounced up and down as the wheels hit the numerous potholes in the dirt road that wound through what felt like endless jungle. The kapok trees formed a canopy that allowed little direct sunlight to reach the jungle floor creating twilight in the late afternoon. The moisture in the air carried the aromas of wet earth and decaying vegetation. The screams of black howler monkeys, their vocalizations unnerving and haunting, reverberated through the dense foliage.

I paid close to 2,000 pesos to a complete stranger who I met at the bus station in Cancun for the hand drawn map that lay on the seat next to me, weighed down by a Chichen Itza guidebook and a bottle of water to keep it from being blown away. My Spanish wasn't very good, but adequate enough to have a conversation with the man who stood outside of the station offering travel and tourism advice which he advertised by means of hand written words on a poster board that sat at his feet. He drew me the map without asking questions, only warning me that what I was doing could get me arrested.

I glanced in the rear view mirror at the back seat and saw Aapo's brown eyes opened wide as saucers as he searched the passing jungle for remembered landmarks.

#

Earlier that morning in the city of Valladolid I sat on a bench in the plaza in front of the San Gervasio Cathedral and watched the Mexican flags that hung from the bell towers flapping in the hot breeze. Two men in beige city uniforms walked side by side chattering in Spanish as they pushed their brooms across the concrete, sweeping up the trash left behind by a festival held the night before. A large flight of pigeons alighted on the pavement where the men had just swept and began pecking at the ground, picking up the bits and kernels of popcorn that the brooms had missed. A helium filled red balloon tied to a street light and caught in the shifting breezes danced on the end of a long piece of twine.

Walking alongside the low wall built in front of the cathedral, Aapo followed a bright green iguana that scampered along its top. He carried a twig that he scratched on the dusty surface of the wall, marking the lizard's trail. The wind tousled his black hair forming different shapes; a bird's crest, writhing snakes, a crown. When the iguana climbed down the side of the wall and ran off toward the direction of the cathedral, he sat on the wall and used the twig to poke at a small scab on his left forearm. The flat expression on his face was inscrutable.

An old woman wearing a lemon yellow scarf sat down on the opposite end of the bench. She held a woven hemp basket filled with oranges in the lap of her floral print skirt. Her sun-darkened brown face was perfectly oval shaped and lined with deep wrinkles. For a moment I imagined I smelled the scent of the oranges wafting from those in the basket, but I was just remembering the fresh oranges in the large ceramic blue bowl that sat in the middle of the table at my mother's house during Christmas that added their fragrance to the dining room. The old woman picked a large one from the basket and held it out to me in her tremulous hand.

"*¿No quiere comprar una naranja, señor?* " she asked, smiling, displaying a gold tooth.

Caught in the sunlight, the peeling on the orange glowed. I looked at Aapo who had his arms out, waving them like the wings of a bird. "*Sí, dos por favor,*" I answered holding up two fingers.

She handed me two oranges and said, "*Cincuenta pesos.*"

I took the money from my pocket and gave it to her. She put it in a brown leather change purse, got up and walked away. I held the oranges to my nose, inhaling their sweet, pungent aroma as I watched the pigeons create a pathway for her as she sauntered through them. The way she walked reminded me of my grandmother working in her garden as she manuevered her way around lush lilac bushes a few months before she died. I put the oranges in the pockets of my windbreaker and headed for the jeep that was parked in front of the hotel where I had stayed the night before. I heard following me the slapping of Aapo's bare feet on the hot concrete.

#

I slammed on the brakes and sharply turned the steering wheel. The jeep skidded in the dirt, coming to a stop in a patch of ferns alongside the road. The guidebook, bottled water and map slid from the seat and fell onto the floor. I caught my breath and wiped sweat from my eyes with my fist. The buzz and hum of flying insects filled my ears. I turned in time to see Aapo leap out of the jeep and run up to the statue that lay in the road a few feet ahead of where the jeep had come to a stop. I picked up the bottle, unscrewed the cap, and took a long drink of the warm water. I looked up to see a crested flycatcher with bright blue and yellow plumage sitting on an overhanging kapok tree branch looking down at me as if studying me. I placed the cap back on the bottle, returned it to the seat, and then climbed out of the jeep.

The statue was a chacmool, a reclining figure with its head turned at ninety degrees. There were a few pictures of it in the guidebook. This one was mansize. Its facial features had been worn away by time and weather which did nothing to dimish the mesmerizing stare in its hollowed out eyes. Vines were coiled around it, almost hiding the sculpted bowl that sat upon its stomach. Aapo had brushed aside some of the leaves in the bowl and placed in it one of the oranges he had carried with him all the way from Valladolid. I scanned the area around the statue, wondering how or why it had been left there undisturbed for so long. It marked an abrupt end of the road, something the man who drew the map failed to include or mention.

I walked around the chacmool while Aapo used a small tree branch to poke at a black-tailed indigo snake that lay curled on the top of the statue's head. Although harmless, the snake held its head up as if ready to strike.

#

The week before, I left the Legion of Honor museum in San Francisco after wandering through an exhibit of Mayan art and stood on the steps and watched a mother and her child sitting in the grass nearby sharing an orange. She peeled the orange carefully, stripping away the bright orange peeling with her long painted green fingernails, then fed the little boy segments of the orange, placing them on his tongue and laughing with him as he bit into them causing juice to squirt out and dribble down his chin. Not far away, water that sprang up from the middle of a pool created the sound of heavy rainfall. I walked to the edge of the museum grounds, looked out over the Pacific Ocean, and watched a ship making its way south. Restlessly I slapped the museum brochure that I held in my hand against my leg. The statue of the Mayan boy on its cover resembled me – or to be more accurate, how I looked as a young boy – in a way that had left me feeling both uncomfortable and slightly lost.

It was there that I met Aapo. He walked out of the museum, came to where I was standing, and silently gazed out at the water. I turned and started to leave when he grasped my hand.

"*Yaan wa'a a paalal?*" he asked.

#

We waited in the jeep or sat on the chacmool until the purple and golds of twilight filtered through the canopy. The trek from the statue to the outer edge of the Chichen Itza grounds took less than a half an hour. Along the way, Aapo collected colorful stones and plucked clusters of huayas fruit and stuffed them in his pockets. We hid behind a large kapok tree with above-ground roots that spread out across the ground like octopus tentacles, listening for the sounds of those who guarded the site after the tourists had left. Roused by the coming nightfall chachalaca birds filled the air with their grating calls that sounded like the grinding of rusty gears. Mosquitoes swarmed around our heads. It was dark – in those minutes before the stars and moon begin to shine – when we made our way from the tree to around the base of the Pyramid of KuKulkan. At the bottom of the long, steep flight of stairs that lead to the top of the pyramid, I stopped and surveyed what else I could see of Chichen Itza. From every direction it seemed the vacant eyes of other chacmools and the withering gazes of sculpted serpent heads were fixed on me. Aapo ran up the stairs, losing some of the stones and fruit that fell out of his pockets.

#

Two days before, visible waves of heat rose from the tarmac as I stepped from the plane stairs after landing in Cancun. It smelled as if the earth had been cooked. It reminded me of the aftermath of the fire that burned entire neighborhoods in the Oakland firestorm in 1991 when I was a boy. My mother and grandmother took baskets of canned goods, freshly baked loaves of banana bread, and bags of oranges to people displaced by the fires and living in motels. The hot wind blowing across the runway carried the smell of jet fuel mixed with the scent of the Caribbean waters. I had stashed a bottle of water I had gotten while on the plane inside my wind breaker and walking to the airport terminal I could hear the water sloshing around inside the bottle. Aapo bent down and scooped a gecko from the ground and carried it in his hands as he walked beside me. He put it in his pocket as we walked through the glass doors.

During the ride in the taxi from the airport to the small hotel in downtown Cancun, Aapo kept his face against the window glass, staring wide-eyed at the passing sandy and windswept landscape. A recent hurricane had stripped the fronds from the top of palm trees and filled the lagoons with debris. I leaned forward, my arms resting on the back of the front seat and talked to the driver, who spoke perfect English.

"What is the easiest way to get to Chichen Itza?" I asked him.

"There are tour buses that you can catch at most of the hotels early in the morning," he said. "Just ask your hotel concierge or a clerk."

"What if I want to go there on my own and not with a group, and through the jungle?" I said.

He looked at me in his rear view mirror, his eyebrows raised. "You can rent a jeep but it's expensive and you will need a good map to get you there. I should warn you, it's illegal to enter Chichen Itza other than through the front entrance. "

"Where can I get a map?"

"Talk to the guy standing outside of the bus station who always has a sign advertising his services to tourists," he said.

#

"The physical traits of our ancestors pop up time and again after skipping a few generations," I remembered my mother telling me as she fed me orange segments when I asked why I looked different than my own brothers. My hair was black, while theirs was light brown. I was short in stature, they were tall. The color of my skin was like coffee diluted by milk. Their's was white. "It's rumored we are descended from the Mayans," she said. "Our ancestry never leaves us entirely."

#

The pinpoints of glittering stars were scattered across the sky. From the west a quarter moon cast pale moonlight across Chichen Itza. Breathless, Aapo returned at a run from a chacmool across the compound where he had emptied his pockets of the last of the stones and fruit into their bowls. When he sat down by me on the steps at the bottom of the pyramid I took the orange from my pocket and slowly began to peel it.

"I have no children of my own, yet," I said, at last answering the question he had asked when we first met, neither knowing how I finally came to understand what he had asked, or if he understood my reply. I handed him a segment of the orange and laughed when he bit into it, squirting juice that dribbled down his chin.

I don't know when I fell asleep, but I awoke just before sunrise on the ground, curled into a ball. I sat up and looked through the mist that had formed a few feet from the ground. Aapo was gone, but that was how it was meant to be from the beginning.

The End

ABOUT THE AUTHOR

ABOUT THE AUTHOR

Steve Carr is a native of Cincinnati but has traveled extensively in the United States and abroad. He began his writing career as a military journalist during his three years in the Army. He was also in the Navy, for four years. Possibly fearing he would accidentally hurt someone or ignite an international incident, neither branch of the military gave him a weapon after their respective boot camps. His claim to military fame is that during his four years in the Navy he never once spent any time on a ship, which defeated his initial reason for enlisting in a second branch of the military. He had joined to see the world as the Navy advertised, but spent almost the entire time, after specialized training in the care of patients with psychiatric disorders, teaching at the Psychiatric Technician School at the Portsmouth, Virginia, Naval Hospital.

With double majors in college in English and Theater, he has turned to playwriting several times in his long on-again, off-again, writing career. His plays have been staged in several states, including Ohio, South Dakota, Virginia and Missouri. In 2001 he started a theatrical production company south of Tucson where he produced a few of his own plays and considers his musical *Nantucket* to be his crowning achievement. However, staged in an abandoned winery with no air conditioning, the audiences nearly fell out of their chairs from heat exhaustion from ninety-degree weather during the shows, adding to the near-mayhem, they bought too much wine served at a bar set up in the back of the renovated space.

After giving up his dream of becoming a Broadway sensation, he moved to Richmond, Virginia in 2002 and gave up writing until 2016. While mentoring a college student in fiction writing, thinking he should practice what he was preaching, he took up the art of writing short stories, with immediate success. Since then he has had over 570 short stories – new and reprints - published internationally in print and online magazines, literary journals and anthologies. He has over 150 print publications that include one or more of his short stories listed in his Amazon bibliography. He has been nominated for the Pushcart Prize twice. Collections of his short stories, *Sand, Rain, The Tales of Talker Knock*, and the hardback edition *The Very Best of Steve Carr: 52 Stories* were published by Clarendon House Publications. His collection of short stories, *Heat*, was published by Czykmate Productions. These collections are no longer available. His self-published debut novel, Redbird, was released in November, 2019. Hating the process of writing a novel, he swore he'd never write another one and has stuck to that declaration. He independently published *LGBTQ: 33 Stories*, which was released in January, 2020. It was discontinued for sale in late 2021 due to poor sales performance. His collection of 50 short stories, *The Theory of Existence*, was published in May, 2020. He considers it his next best collection second to *A Map of Humanity*.

He is the founder of Sweetycat Press which was initially launched as a Facebook group in February, 2020, to support emerging writers through providing tools for self-promotion. Toward that goal, five high-quality books (*Who's Who of Emerging Writers 2020, The Book of Books, I, The Writer, The Wordsmith Chronicles*, and *To Be Or Not To Be A Writer*) were published within a year. The books remain for sale on Amazon.com with any money from their sales after April 1, 2021 to go toward continued support of emerging writers through book publishing. The Sweetycat Press Facebook group began at the same time that the COVID-19 pandemic sprung up, leading to the site being shut down due to the pandemic's impact on the Facebook group's mission. Continuing Sweetycat Press as an independent publishing imprint, the books published under that imprint include so far, *A Love Letter (or Poem) To . . .*, that includes letters and poems from 202 writers worldwide. *The Whole Wide World*, an episodic crime novel co-written by 80 authors from around the globe, Visions and Memories: A Collection of Poems by Mike Turner, Who's Who of Emerging Writers 2021, and *Beyond Wishes*, a YA novel by author, Joan Herr. All Sweetycat Press books are available on Amazon.com. Sweetycat Press is currently focusing on anthologies which give emerging writers the opportunity to see their works in print and helps build their writing resume and further establish their brand and name recognition. Any profits made from sales of an anthology go toward the publication and advertising costs for the next anthology. Steve believes in recycling, including recycling of the profits.

Lightning Source UK Ltd.
Milton Keynes UK
UKHW010712100122
396903UK00001B/4